DIABLO MESA

A Nora Kelly Novel

DOUGLAS PRESTON & LINCOLN CHILD

GRAND CENTRAL
PUBLISHING

LARGE PRINT

Copyright © 2022 by Splendide Mendax, Inc. and Lincoln Child

Cover design by Flag. Cover images of skull, landscape, and silhouetted figure by Getty Images. Cover copyright © 2022 by Hachette Book Group, Inc.

Grand Central Publishing
Hachette Book Group
1290 Avenue of the Americas, New York, NY 10104
grandcentralpublishing.com
twitter.com/grandcentralpub

First Edition: February 2022

Grand Central Publishing is a division of Hachette Book Group, Inc. The Grand Central Publishing name and logo is a trademark of Hachette Book Group, Inc.

The publisher is not responsible for websites (or their content) that are not owned by the publisher.

The Hachette Speakers Bureau provides a wide range of authors for speaking events. To find out more, go to www.hachettespeakersbureau.com or call (866) 376-6591.

Library of Congress Cataloging-in-Publication Data has been applied for.

ISBNs: 9781538736753 (hardcover), 9781538736739 (ebook), 9781538723340 (int'l edition), 9781538724033 (Canadian edition), 9781538710142 (large print), 9781538722114 (B&N signed edition), 9781538722107 (signed edition)

Printed in the United States of America

LSC-C

Printing 1, 2021

To Montague Rhodes James, O.M.,
in appreciation
QUIS EST ISTE QUI VENIT?

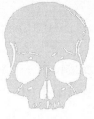

I

Dr. Marcelle Weingrau, president of the Santa Fe Archaeological Institute, slowly unfolded her hands on the glossy expanse of desk in front of her. Then, equally slowly, she reached for a slim manila folder, which she pulled close with exquisitely manicured nails. Even Weingrau's simplest movements, Nora Kelly noted, had the appearance of being premeditated. But she'd grown used to this since Weingrau had accepted the presidency and knew it was neither a signal of encouragement nor one of alarm—necessarily.

Now Weingrau gave Nora a broad, warm smile. "The reason I asked you here this morning," she said, "is because of an opportunity that has come our way. A wonderful new project—extraordinary, really. Connor and I would like you to direct it."

Nora felt a flood of relief. She wasn't sure why she had been summoned to the president's office that morning. Ever since she'd been passed over for a promised promotion in October in favor of Connor Digby—who was seated nearby—she and Weingrau had maintained a formal, carefully calibrated relationship. Nora and Digby shared adjacent offices, and while he was a good archaeologist as well as a friendly if unremarkable fellow, her relationship with this unexpected new boss had been awkward. In the six months since his promotion, she'd kept her head down and focused on her work, trying, and failing, to get over a sense of betrayal and resentment.

"Not to bring up an uncomfortable subject," Weingrau went on, "but I know you were disappointed not to get the chief of archaeology position. You've done excellent work for the Institute and brought us some welcome publicity. In fact, this new project is a direct result of that." She tapped the folder three times with a red fingernail.

"Thank you," said Nora.

"This project is a little different, perhaps, than

what we normally undertake—although well within our archaeological mission."

Nora waited to hear more. Weingrau's mix of words—complimentary and chipper—was uncharacteristic.

"Your work in locating and recovering the Victorio Peak treasure attracted the attention of a well-known businessman—and potential donor, I might add—who is the motivating force behind this exciting project."

At this, Nora felt a faint stirring of unease. Why was Weingrau laying it on so thick?

"His name is Tappan. Lucas Tappan. Perhaps you've heard of him?"

Nora paused. "The private space company guy—Icarus? That person?"

"Exactly. Tappan is best known as founder of Icarus Space Systems, but his major interests lie in wind power. The space thing is a bit of a side effort. All worthy businesses, I might add. And he's a man of means." Another broad smile.

Nora nodded. He wasn't just a "man of means"—he was a billionaire.

"Mr. Tappan has brought us not only a very intriguing proposal, but a grant to go with it. Connor and I have discussed it, and we've gotten approval from the Executive Committee of the board."

Nora found herself growing more uneasy. Normally, the board of the Institute did not get involved in project approvals. And why hadn't she heard anything about this before?

"I'm going to let Connor fill you in on the details," the president said.

"Right." Digby turned toward Nora. He was considerably more nervous than the cool Weingrau. "Um, are you familiar with the Roswell site?"

Nora wasn't sure she'd heard correctly. She stared at Digby.

"The Roswell site," he repeated. "It's located in the remote desert, north of—"

"Do you mean the place where the supposed UFO crashed?" Nora interrupted.

"Yes, exactly," said Digby, charging ahead before Nora could respond. "To recap: In 1947, the foreman of a ranch northeast of Roswell, New Mexico, found the wreckage of something unusual on a section of BLM land leased by the ranch. The military went out to investigate and, on July 8, issued a press release stating the 509th Composite Group had found the wreckage of a flying disk. Two hours later, the announcement was quickly emended to say it was a weather balloon that had crashed. It was only years later that investigators began to uncover the truth: that a UFO, apparently monitoring U.S. nuclear tests, had been struck by lightning and crashed. The government had recovered the remains of the spacecraft and possibly the remains of several aliens. All this was followed by a massive government cover-up."

He said all this in a rush, then stopped.

Nora continued to stare at Digby. Why would he call this wacko theory "the truth"?

"Mr. Tappan has brought us a proposal, well prepared and fully funded, to excavate the Roswell site. A professional archaeological dig, done by the book."

"And this is the wonderful new project you want me to direct?"

He gave her a nervous smile. "Exactly. With all the staff, equipment, and money you require to do an excavation to the highest professional standards."

When Nora continued to stare at him, he fell into a nervous silence, taking a pencil from his shirt pocket and starting to fiddle with it.

Nora finally turned to Weingrau. "Is this some kind of joke?"

"Not at all," she said. "The project's been thoroughly vetted and board approved. Something crashed there. What, we don't really know."

"You've got to be kidding."

"Please don't jump to conclusions, Nora. We're not endorsing any UFO theory. What we've agreed to is a professional excavation of the crash site. That's it."

"With all due respect, Dr. Weingrau, by even *agreeing* to this, you're endorsing it. I mean, that UFO incident was debunked years ago."

"Reasonable people disagree. Nobody knows for sure. As Connor mentioned, there's evidence of a government cover-up. Mr. Tappan has done considerable research into the incident, and he's come upon new information confirming that alien technology was recovered from the area, possibly even remains."

"As in, alien bodies? I'm sorry, but do you really mean to involve the Institute in something as...*tacky* as this?"

"We already have," said Weingrau, her voice taking on an edge. "This is a done deal. And I take exception to your characterization. I've been patient with you, Nora. Very patient... even as you continue to work on the Tsankawi project long past the expected deadline, with no end in sight."

Nora could hardly believe what she was hearing. "I imagine that, in addition to funding the dig, Tappan has promised the Institute a wad of cash—right?"

"While a generous donation is involved, that's not why we're doing it. This is a genuine unsolved mystery. If we can shed light on it with archaeological science, there's nothing wrong with that. I'm giving you a wonderful opportunity to polish your CV and raise your profile."

"Forget it," said Nora before she could stop herself.

"Denying the existence of things beyond our knowledge is as dangerous as promoting them."

Nora tried for a moment to think about it from the president's perspective, but she couldn't quite get there. "I'm sorry, but I won't do it. I *couldn't* do it."

Weingrau stared at her. "Perhaps I gave you the wrong impression. We're not asking for your approval. The project has been accepted and you're going to direct it. Period."

"This isn't right," said Nora, getting control

of her anger and lowering her voice. "I wasn't consulted while all this was being decided, and by rights I should have been. I'm in the middle of an important project right now, delayed through no fault of my own by that business with Victorio Peak. You can't dump something like this on me with no notice. The fact is, you haven't been treating me with the professionalism I deserve since you came here—and this is just another example. It'll make the Institute the laughingstock of the archaeological community. It won't raise my profile; it'll endanger my career. I decline to participate."

"You heard Dr. Weingrau," Digby piped up shrilly. "It's already been decided."

She fixed a cool eye on him before looking back at Weingrau. This demand, on top of everything else, was the last straw. "Here's an idea. Get your toady to direct it."

"That's not only uncalled for, it's offensive."

"You're probably right. So let Digby speak for himself." She turned to him. "Why don't *you* direct the excavation, Connor?"

"Because..." he stammered, "Mr. Tappan mentioned you specifically."

"Is that right?" Nora said coolly. "Well, please tell Tappan I'm not available."

A tense silence developed in the office. Finally, Weingrau said: "Is that your final word, Nora?"

"Yes, it is."

"Then I suggest you go back to your office, gather your personal effects, put your files in order, and take your leave of the Institute."

Nora took a deep breath. This abrupt airing of her grievances, tumbling as it had from her lips, was almost as unexpected to her as it must have been to Weingrau. But it was now said—and, maybe, for the better. The fact was, being honest with herself, for some time now she'd been practically looking for an excuse to leave. And here it was, gift-wrapped. If the Institute wanted to ruin its reputation, at least she wouldn't be around to catch the blowback.

"In other words, you're firing me," she said.

"If you drop off a letter of resignation on your way out, we won't have to term it a dismissal. We'll call it a resignation."

"No."

"No what?"

"If you're going to fire me, *fire* me." She turned to Digby. "Good luck. You're going to need it."

And with that, she stood up and left the office.

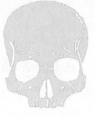

2

Ninety minutes later, Nora exited the main door of the Institute into the bright April sunlight, carrying a box and a backpack toward her car. Her rage was starting to cool, replaced by bitter regret and second-guessing. If she'd handled the situation differently; if she hadn't pushed back so hard; if she'd only said she needed to give it some thought; if she hadn't called the project tacky or Digby a toady...maybe she could have talked her way out of it and sloughed the excavation off on him. Beyond that was the sheer stubbornness that kept her from taking the resignation offer. It was going to be hard enough to find another position in the current academic job market, but with a dismissal on her record...What was she thinking? And yet the thought of submitting a resignation letter now, after all she'd said, was just too much humiliation for her to bear.

And she couldn't help but worry about her brother, Skip, who also worked at the Institute. He was likely to quit in a huff as soon as he heard she was fired. He was in a tougher position than she: he hadn't exactly put his Stanford physics degree to good use. How many collections manager positions were there in Santa Fe? But even if he didn't quit, Weingrau might fire him just to spite her. Nora didn't want to see him spiraling back down to the dark place he'd been in a few years before.

A vehicle was idling in the parking lot, blocking the way to her car. As she walked around it, wrestling with her stuff, a man got out.

"Dr. Kelly?"

She stopped. "Yes?"

"Could we have a moment to chat?"

"I'm sorry," she said. "I'm really busy and I've got to go." Whatever he wanted, whatever he was doing here at the Institute, was no longer of interest to her. She resumed her walk.

"Here, let me help you with the box," he said, hurrying over.

"No thanks," she said sharply. She arrived at

her car, fumbled out the key, unlocked the doors, and threw the box in the back seat, tossing the backpack in after it. She slammed the door and realized the man had come up and was standing behind her.

She ignored him, opening the driver's door and getting in. He placed a hand on it, preventing her from shutting it in his face.

"I take it you quit?" he said.

She stared, momentarily flummoxed. Had word gotten around already? Nobody knew that, not even Skip.

"Who the hell are you?" she asked.

He smiled. "Lucas Tappan." He held out his hand.

She stared at him, really seeing him for the first time. He was around her age, mid- to late thirties, in a linen jacket, black lambskin cowboy shirt, jeans, suede Lanvin sneakers, with curly black hair, gray eyes, white teeth, cleft chin, dimples. She immediately disliked him and his smug *I've got unlimited money but it hasn't really changed me* look.

"Get your hand off my door or I'll call the police."

He complied, and she slammed it and shoved

the key into the ignition. The engine started and she twisted around to back up, pressing the accelerator harder than she intended and spinning the wheels in the gravel.

"I'm glad you quit," he said, raising his voice to be heard through the window. "Now we can work free of encumbrance."

She jammed on the brakes, rolled down the window. "What?"

"I was hoping this might happen. Frankly, I wasn't looking forward to working with that Weingrau lady."

"You were *hoping*? This is ridiculous—"

"Look, can we talk? Just for a moment?"

Nora stared at him. "I really don't have time for this."

"You have all the time in the world. You don't have a job."

"Thanks for that. You're an asshole, you know? And you're crazy. UFOs. Roswell. What a crock." All her anger spilled out.

"Okay, fine. I've been told all that before and worse. Five minutes? Please?"

She was about to drive off, but then stopped. All of a sudden, she felt herself deflate, as if her energy had escaped along with her anger. Had the last two hours really happened? Earlier that morning, she'd been in her office, working on one of the final Tsankawi write-ups...and now she had no office, no job, only a couple of burned bridges still smoking in her rearview mirror.

"Oh, for Christ's sake. Five minutes, then." She waited behind the wheel, crossing her arms.

"Do you think maybe we could *not* have this conversation through a car window? I want to show you something."

Against her better judgment, Nora eased the car back into the parking space and got out, then followed Tappan to what was obviously his vehicle. An ice-blue Tesla. Of course.

"Would you mind getting into the passenger seat?"

She did as he requested, sliding onto the buttery white leather. The dashboard gleamed with burl wood, satin nickel, and a large computer screen.

She shut the door; the man pushed a button, and the windows magically darkened. He reached under the dash and removed a large rolled-up document, which he proceeded to unfurl.

"Take a look." He held it open so she could see.

Nora immediately recognized it.

"It's a ground-penetrating radar survey—" he began.

"I know what it is," said Nora impatiently.

"Good. Now, do you see this area here? This is our target area—where the UFO is said to have crashed. What do you see?"

Nora looked closer at the grayscale image. It was clear, right off the bat, that something had happened there.

"You tell me: Is that disturbance consistent with the crash of a weather balloon?"

She looked still more closely. She could see, just barely, a blurry but deep-looking furrow or groove in the sand, along with other evidence of extensive and widespread disturbance.

"Not really," she replied.

"That's right. And look how it's surrounded by old traces of earthmoving equipment and vehicles. The GPR also revealed two faint roads leading from the area, and another one circling around it. At one time this was a heavily traf-ficked place. Suggestive, don't you think?"

"Isn't this kind of small for a UFO? I mean, that groove isn't very wide. And it could be anything—a missile, small plane, even a mete-orite. I don't see evidence it was a UFO."

"The point is," said Tappan, "that something happened here totally inconsistent with a balloon or nuclear monitoring device crash. And then you can see where topsoil, here and here, was moved to bury the target area and cover up all these tracks—and smoothed over. Why would they have gone to so much trouble to cover up a balloon crash? That's a lot of earth-moving."

She scrutinized the survey more closely in the confines of the car. There were signs of a lot of old activity extending from the target area.

Tappan smiled. He took out another chart and unrolled it. This was obviously a magnetometer survey, a tool archaeologists used to record the magnetic properties of soil for mapping subsurface terrain. There were various anomalies and dark spots in and around the target area. The disturbed area with its faint furrow was also vaguely delineated.

"All those dark spots and smudges are what we laymen would call 'buried stuff,'" said Tappan. "Stuff that your excavation will unearth."

"It could be anything," Nora said. "Rocks, tin cans, trash."

Tappan tapped the charts with a finger. "Maybe

so, but this proves one thing: The government lied. There was no weather balloon or secret nuclear surveillance device. Why would they lie?"

He stared at her with gray, searching eyes. It was a fair question.

"And the lying goes on," Tappan said. "A few years ago, the government allegedly declassified its files on UFOs. There was some startling stuff in there, as you probably know—videos of objects taken by fighter pilots and so forth. But even earlier they had released documents indicating the Roswell crash was not a weather balloon, but a classified government device, developed at Los Alamos for detecting aboveground nuclear blasts. It was being tested but got away in high winds and crashed at the Roswell site. The 'disk' that witnesses described was actually a radar reflector, used for tracking purposes."

"Sounds reasonable," she said. "That might explain the furrow—the thing getting dragged along the ground, perhaps."

"The furrow is at least fifteen feet deep. No—the nuclear device with a radar detector attached was also misinformation: a second layer of it. First a weather balloon, then a secret surveillance device. All disinformation. Nothing to see here, folks! The *real* Roswell files—and the artifacts and debris they found at the site—remain secret."

She shook her head. "And the alien bodies?" she asked sarcastically.

He smiled. "Look, the point is, there's more to be found at the crash site. You can see it in these two surveys. A professional archaeological excavation would reveal what, exactly: not only a ground disturbance, but something more... perhaps *much* more." He rolled up the maps. "What do you say, Nora?"

"Um, are these charts all you've got?"

"All? I think it's quite a lot. Look, I didn't want the Institute. I wanted *you*. I thought you'd probably quit when you heard the proposal, and I was right."

"You were wrong. I was fired."

He chuckled. "Now that I've met you, I can see how that might have happened. Digby, that poor homunculus..." He shook his head sadly. "Have you really been reporting to him these last six months?"

Nora deflected the question. "Why me?" she asked. "There's plenty of archaeologists out there."

"I followed the Victorio Peak treasure story with great interest. And then I acquainted myself with the work you did at Donner Pass and, before that, the Quivira site. I don't want some slope-shouldered academic. You've got all the qualities I need: courage, ability, perseverance, judgment. I built my business by finding the right people."

She watched almost with regret as he snapped rubber bands back on the charts and put them away.

"I'm sorry," she said. "I can't do this. I just can't."

"I'm not asking you to make a decision now. All I'm asking is that you come and see the site for yourself. Meet the team, look at the evidence. The site is on Bureau of Land Management property. I've got all the federal permits, equipment, engineers, a couple of semidomesticated postdocs—everything necessary for a first-class excavation. All I need is a credentialed archaeologist. I'm offering a good salary."

She shook her head.

"My chopper is waiting at Sunport Aviation. We can be at the site in just over an hour, and you'll be home by six. Or if you decide to stay, you'll have a custom Airstream to yourself for the night."

She sighed. The "good salary" part, at least, was tempting. She and Skip shared a house, and they were always scrambling to pay the mortgage. Santa Fe was an expensive town, and the Institute was not exactly generous.

"I'm very sorry," she said, opening the door and getting out. She turned to see Tappan looking back at her with surprise and dismay. He clearly wasn't used to having people turn him down. "Thank you for the offer, but I'm afraid I have to decline."

She closed the door and went back to her car, wondering as she did so if she'd just made the worst mistake of her life.

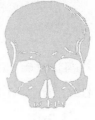

3

NORA ARRIVED HOME at their small house on the south side of town. She dropped her box of stuff on the kitchen counter, tossed the backpack in the corner, put the pot on for coffee, and flopped down in a chair. Mitty, their golden retriever rescue, came rushing over, wagging his tail so hard his entire back end was swaying. He pushed his nose into her hand. She petted him absentmindedly, wondering what the hell she was going to do now. It was one o'clock and the day stretched ahead endlessly. Maybe she should start sending out CVs.

"Nora! You're home!"

She just about jumped up as Skip came rushing in.

"So are you," she said. "Why aren't you at the

Institute?" She had a sudden fear that Weingrau had fired him, too.

"I quit!"

Oh God, no. She tried to keep the dismay out of her voice. "You quit? Why?"

"I got a new job!"

The kettle started whistling.

"I'll make the coffee for us," Skip said, "and tell you all about it." He busied himself with the grinding and filter while Nora absorbed this new information. Skip? What better job could he possibly have gotten?

"So what are *you* doing home?" Skip asked, spooning grounds and then pouring water into the French press.

"Um, I was fired."

Skip halted. "*What?*"

"Fired."

"What do you mean, *fired*? You're their star archaeologist!"

Nora sighed. "They asked me to dig up a UFO. I said no."

That was followed by a sudden silence. Skip went back to pouring the water. "A UFO?" he repeated feebly.

"You know that crazy Roswell conspiracy

theory about a UFO crash and dead aliens? They actually wanted me to direct an excavation of the site. I told them I didn't want to become the laughingstock of the archaeological world. One thing led to another—and Weingrau fired me."

Skip fussed with the French press. The silence stretched on. Nora began to feel a creeping sense of unease. "Skip?"

"Yes?"

"Tell me about your new job."

Another long silence. "Why do you think the Roswell story is so crazy? I mean, there's a lot of evidence supporting it. A *lot*. There are witnesses. There are documents. Retired military officers have come forward and said they were there, that they saw the wreckage, even saw the alien remains."

"Um, Skip? By any chance is your new job working for a guy named Tappan?"

He came over with two coffees, set them down defiantly on the table, and took a seat. "As a matter of fact, yes."

She shook her head. This day was just getting worse and worse.

"Nora, will you listen to me for a moment? First of all, Tappan's done a huge amount of research. This is a serious effort. Nothing flaky about it. He's already done magnetometer, lidar, and ground-penetrating radar surveys. He's got all the permits, everything."

"How much is he paying you?"

"Sixteen hundred a week."

"Is that all?"

"Hey, cut the sarcasm. This is a fantastic project—and a great opportunity. It's going to blow the lid off the biggest government cover-up of all time. Look, I've been interested in the Roswell Incident and UFOs for years. You know that." He paused. "I can't believe you turned down the opportunity. And got yourself fired! What the *hell*?"

Nora took a sip of coffee and tried to organize her thoughts. "When did he hire you?"

"At noon today. He just walked into my office at the Institute, introduced himself, told me what he was doing, and asked me to join the team. He already had a letter of employment printed; I signed it, wrote my resignation, and dropped it off on my way out."

That must have been right before she ran into Tappan in the parking lot. At least the man hadn't gone to Skip *after* she said no...She sighed. It was just like Skip to rush headlong into something, get in over his head, and then go down in flames. Before he'd gotten the job at the Institute, she couldn't even count the number of jobs he'd been fired from. How were they going to pay the mortgage?

"The guy's a billionaire, Nora! He owns that space company, Icarus. He's a green-energy guy, too, building giant wind turbines and solar power plants. He's the real deal."

"I ran into him in the parking lot after I was fired. He offered me the job again. I said no."

Skip seized his hair with both hands in horror and rocked back and forth in his chair. "You said no *twice*?"

Mitty began barking.

"I can't put digging up UFOs on my résumé. It's too weird."

"There's nothing weird about a serious, professional excavation of that site," said Skip. "We could've been working together. It would have been so much fun!" He pulled out his cell phone. "I'm calling Tappan right now and telling him you've changed your mind."

He started punching in a number, but Nora stayed his hand. "No. Please."

At that moment, her own cell phone rang. Relieved to get out of the conversation with Skip, she answered it—only to find Tappan on the other end.

"Nora? Am I disturbing you?"

She almost answered in the affirmative, then thought of Skip. "Can you hold the line a moment while I go somewhere private?" she asked.

Skip, immediately guessing who was on the phone, leapt up and started dancing around her, gesturing. She quickly walked into her bedroom and shut the door in his face.

"Okay," she said.

"I wanted to apologize for ambushing you in the parking lot. I fear I didn't give you enough breathing room to really consider my proposal."

"You hired my brother."

"His primary job will be working with our astronomer and artifact curator, Noam Bitan, taking care of his library and the collection. He majored in physics, seems to know a great deal about the Roswell Incident already, and has the requisite collections management background. Apparently, he also has a lot of experience assisting at a dig site—thanks to time spent with you, no doubt."

"You hired him to get to me."

"Not at all! We're very glad to have him. Nora, here's the reason for my call. I'll be flying Skip out to the site tomorrow morning to introduce him around, show him his new quarters. Why don't you come? No obligation. You can meet the team, see what we're doing, and get a sense of how Skip will fit in."

"It feels a little like blackmail, you hiring Skip."

"Nora, I know how close you are to your brother, and I know…" He hesitated. "I know you experienced a great loss. I just wanted to create as welcoming and comfortable an environment for you as I could. I'll be sending someone to your house to pick up Skip tomorrow at nine. Would you care to join him?"

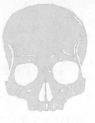

4

Nora hadn't spent much time in helicopters, but she could tell that Tappan's was more like a private jet, or maybe even a luxury yacht, with its plush carpeting, leather, and gleaming mahogany trim. Two rows of seats faced each other, with Skip and Nora on one side and Tappan opposite.

Skip was enthused that she'd agreed to come along and almost beside himself with excitement. During the ride, Tappan was curiously quiet, spending most of the time reading a novel. Skip, on the other hand, talked almost nonstop about the Roswell Incident, UFOs, aliens, SETI, and the Drake equation. Nora was surprised at how much he knew. As he'd said, he'd always been interested in UFOs, but she hadn't realized to what extent.

Tappan closed his book. "We're approaching the site," he said. "A look out the window will give you a good overview."

Nora turned, grateful for the interruption in Skip's enthused outpouring. The helicopter was flying over a landscape of broad desert mesas and high plains, cut by sinuous threads of arroyos and canyons, with sprinklings of piñon and juniper. In the distance she could see a large, dry lake bed, all white, with dust devils crossing it. Coming into view on a low tableland, she saw what looked at first like a small town, but as they grew closer it resolved itself into a camp, with trailers, motor homes, a row of Quonset huts, two large prefab sheds, a dirt parking area full of cars and heavy equipment, and a brand-new cement helipad, all serviced by an equally new dirt road winding off toward a line of distant hills.

"Quite a setup," Nora said.

"I think—if you choose to take the assignment— you'll find it comfortable. We're too far out in the middle of nowhere to commute, so staff will be living on-site."

The chopper came in for a landing, circling as a flight-line worker motioned them in with Day-Glo batons. A moment later, they had eased onto the helipad and were powering down, and soon the doors opened. Nora followed Tappan out with Skip, and they scooted away from the rotors toward a waiting jeep.

Tappan turned to Nora. "Tour first, or a review of the project plan?"

"Project plan, please," said Nora. If she didn't like the plan—and she wouldn't—there was no point in a tour.

"I figured as much." He turned to the driver. "Quonset One." He turned back to Nora. "I'm going to introduce you to the Three Engineers."

The jeep drove through a neighborhood of Airstreams and class-A RVs to a row of Quonset huts, each one labeled with a number. They halted in front of number 1 and Nora and Skip followed Tappan inside. Passing several cubicles, they emerged into a large open space with a long worktable. Three people in white lab coats, two men and a woman, were standing behind it. Evidently, they'd been awaiting their arrival. On the table before them were some large, rolled-up documents.

"Ladies and gentlemen," said Tappan, "I'd like to introduce you to Dr. Nora Kelly and Mr. Elwyn Kelly—"

"God, no," Nora's brother interrupted. "Call me Skip, please."

She suppressed a smile; Skip loathed his given name.

"Skip it is, then. We're all on a first-name basis here, anyway. Skip is Noam's new research assistant and Nora is, I hope, going to be our chief archaeologist." Tappan paused, then said: "Perhaps you'd introduce yourselves and your specialties? Nora, by the way, has a doctorate from Stanford and has worked at both the New York Museum of Natural History and the Santa Fe Archaeological Institute. A very impressive résumé."

The three glanced at one another and greeted her with nervous smiles. Nora had a feeling the trio had been pulled together very recently and were still unsure of their roles. The Three Engineers, indeed: they did look sort of goofy and mismatched, with a short, dark fireplug guy; a tall, skinny pale woman; and a Black man of in-between height with a bald head, full beard, and thick glasses—all three gloriously and reassuringly nerdy.

"Vitaly, you first," Tappan said. "Tell us about your background."

"Vitaly Kuznetsov," the short young man said with a hesitant nod. "Lidar mapping engineer. MS from the University of Houston, National Center for Airborne Laser Mapping."

"Cecilia?"

"Cecilia Toth," said the young woman, brushing back a mass of curly red hair with her hand. "Geophysics engineer, specializing in ground-penetrating and synthetic aperture radar and magnetometer analysis, PhD from Texas A&M."

"Greg Banks," said the man with the beard and shaved head. "PhD from Imperial College London, postdoc in planetary geology and exobiology." He had a British accent.

"Good to meet you," said Nora. Tappan had obviously managed to assemble a high-powered group. But then, he had billions to spend—nothing like the usual academic penuriousness she was so familiar with. She couldn't help but wonder what it would be like to work with an unlimited budget for a change.

"Thank you," said Tappan. "Nora, you've already seen some of this, but these charts are at much higher resolution. Vitaly?"

Kuznetsov unrolled a large sheet. Peering at it,

Nora saw it was a grayscale 3-D view of the site, mapped using lidar.

"You're familiar with lidar?" Kuznetsov asked. "Ground mapping with infrared lasers?"

Nora nodded. The chart was of the entire mesa top and surrounding areas, beautifully done, showing almost unbelievable topographical detail, down to the bunches of grass and cacti.

Skip gave a low whistle.

"Resolution is less than a centimeter," said Kuznetsov. "We mapped to a radius of a mile out, just to make sure we didn't miss anything." He pointed at the center of the survey. "As you can clearly see, the target area shows historic disturbance of an undetermined nature, surrounded by old tracks of earthmoving equipment and vehicles. A whole lot of activity, a long time ago. A great deal of topsoil was moved around to bury the target area. You can see it's higher than the surrounding terrain."

Nora nodded. It was weak evidence for a UFO crash, but she said nothing.

"Thank you, Vitaly," said Tappan. "Cecilia?"

The tall woman with the tumble of red hair gave Nora a smile, then unrolled a vividly colored display. "What we have here," she said, "is a ground-penetrating radar map of the site and environs. We're lucky it's mostly dry sand, because radar penetrates such material very well—up to three meters."

Nora stared at the image. This was one Tappan had showed her yesterday, but larger and higher resolution. The V-shaped furrow in the ground was clearly visible, and Nora had to admit it looked like a crash signature.

"When was this survey done?" Nora asked.

"About two weeks ago," said Toth. "This is the combined data from an overflight of a helicopter carrying SAR, digitally merged with a GPR system deployed at ground level."

Tappan spoke. "Whatever made that long gouge came in fast at an oblique angle. This was no balloon payload. It was *moving*."

"I see that," said Nora, "but it's still not proof it was a UFO."

"UAP," said Toth. "Unidentified aerial phenomena: that's what the DoD is calling them these days. Less stigma. Anyway, take a look at this." Toth unrolled another chart. Nora immediately recognized it as a magnetometer survey, recording the magnetic properties of the soil. Once again, she could see that the ground was peppered with various anomalies and dark spots, indicating the presence of objects or possible artifacts. The groove was, again, vaguely outlined.

"Alien artifacts, possibly," murmured Skip with ill-suppressed excitement.

Nora stared at the image. There were indeed things down there. She found herself intrigued, despite all her misgivings.

"Greg is our team exobiologist, a specialist in what alien biochemistry might look like and what exotic materials they might have used to build their spacecraft." Tappan sounded like a proud father.

Banks nodded.

"So that's where we are," Tappan concluded. "All we need now is to break ground and see what's down there. How about it, Nora?"

Nora refrained from answering. She was still looking at the large magnetometer chart. "What's this?" She pointed to a small, very faint rectangle visible near the edge.

"That's five hundred yards from the target site," said Tappan. "We haven't analyzed or processed it at hi-res. Do you think it might be important?"

A magnifying glass was at hand, and Nora

picked it up to examine the images and the magnetometer survey. "Are there any prehistoric Indian ruins in the vicinity?"

The three engineers looked at each other, then shrugged.

"There's nothing around except the old Pershing Proving Range, fifteen miles north in the Los Fuertes Mountains and mothballed decades ago," Tappan said. "Why do you ask?"

"Because that image looks like it might be a burial."

"An Indian burial?"

"Yes. It should be investigated. If it is a prehistoric burial, or in fact any kind of burial, there are laws against disturbing it in any way, and we'd have to rope it off."

"We'll have to look into that," Tappan said. "But now, I want to introduce you to our in-house astronomer and extraterrestrial specialist, Noam Bitan. He's in Quonset Two." He thanked the three engineers, who said an effusive good-bye to Nora.

They think I'm going to be their boss, Nora mused as they departed, Skip following. She had to admit she was intrigued—this was more, in every sense, than she had expected. On the other hand, she couldn't imagine any way this project could positively impact her overall career. Noam Bitan—the name seemed vaguely familiar.

Tappan led them into the adjoining hut and down the narrow central hallway to a door on the right. He tried the handle, but it was locked.

"Noam?" he called out, knocking.

"I'm tied up," came an irritated voice.

"I'm showing Dr. Nora Kelly around—the archaeologist I'm hoping will direct the excavation. And her brother, who will be our librarian and your collections manager."

"Fine and dandy," the voice replied, with a marked Hebrew accent. "Bring them back in an hour."

Tappan rolled his eyes at Nora and said, sotto voce, "Noam's a bit eccentric." Then, in a normal tone: "Noam, we're on a tight schedule. If you don't mind...?"

With a grumbling sound, the door opened. A man stood inside with a scruffy beard and unkempt brown hair, an irritated look on his face. Nora would have guessed him close to fifty years of age.

"May we come in?" Tappan asked, a slight ironic edge to his voice.

"Sure." The man glanced at Nora with a quick smile. "Hi." Then he cast a critical eye on Skip and merely grunted.

He led them into a capacious office, surprisingly neat given his disheveled appearance. He sat down at his desk without offering anyone a chair. Tappan guided Nora and Skip to seats opposite the desk, then sat down himself.

"Noam was formerly chairman of the science advisory board of SETI," said Tappan, "and a professor of astronomy at the Weizmann Institute of Science in Israel."

Nora suddenly realized who he was. She'd occasionally seen him on talk shows: an eccentric and often excited presence, gesturing and talking about aliens.

"Noam, first I'd like to introduce you to Skip Kelly. Skip worked at the Santa Fe Archaeological Institute as a curator of their artifact collections."

Bitan looked at Skip with narrowed eyes, but before he could say anything, Skip burst out: "I'm so pleased to meet you, Dr. Bitan! I loved your book on SETI. Really loved it. I thought you laid out a most impressive body of evidence that the Earth is currently under alien surveillance."

This was exactly the right thing to say, and Bitan's critical gaze vanished as his face lit up with delight. "Thank you, Skip."

Tappan introduced Nora to Bitan, and asked her if she had any questions.

"I'm sorry I haven't read your book myself," Nora began.

Bitan held up his hand, rose from his chair, and removed a book from a shelf. He placed it on his desk, flipped it open, scribbled a note, closed it, and handed it to her. "Now that's taken care of," he said.

"Thank you," Nora said. It was entitled *The Second Revelation*, with a cover depicting the Cat's Eye Nebula. "I have a few questions, if I may?" She was going to be as nice as possible to the man who'd be Skip's boss—but she still needed some answers.

"Of course."

"Where do you think the UFO—that is, the UAP—came from?"

"Something that large would be hard to accelerate to close to light speed, so it was probably from a nearby star system. But in a larger sense, that's not important."

"Why not?"

"Because I believe that a *galaxy-wide* civilization has already been established and is keeping tabs on us. The government, of course, has thoroughly covered it up."

"Why haven't these aliens revealed themselves to us?" she asked.

"They know how disruptive it would be to human culture. We've seen this in our own world: when an indigenous people come in contact with technologically advanced Western society, their own culture is almost inevitably destroyed."

"So you're saying we're sort of like a primitive tribe, living in a nature preserve, protected from contact with the outside world," said Skip.

"Exactly," said Bitan.

"My next question," Nora said, "is why did the government give you a permit to excavate? It's federal land, and you got a federal permit. If the government was trying to cover it up, why let you dig? It doesn't make sense."

At this, Bitan turned to Tappan. "That's in your court."

"This is BLM land, which is under the Department of the Interior. I got the permit directly from the Secretary of the Interior, who happens to be an old friend of mine. Years ago, between high school and college, we met as rafting guides in the Grand Canyon. He was my sternman. That's like being war buddies—you really get to know your fellow boatmen. Anyway, when I first applied for the permit, there was some push-back out of left field—and then it was suddenly dropped. Interior went ahead with the permit with, I might add, the backing of the president. I'm also in the wind-power business, and we're involved with Interior on some of our larger projects. So, yes, I got the permit through the help of some very powerful connections." Tappan shook his head. "We never could figure out where those objections came from, but I'd guess there are some people deep in the Pentagon unhappy about what we're doing. They withdrew their pressure before drawing attention to themselves."

"Yes," said Bitan. "And that's why I showed Lucas how to check his car for explosive devices!" He laughed loudly at his joke. "Do you have any other questions?"

"Just one more. If these aliens had the advanced technological capability of interstellar travel, how is it that they stupidly crashed their spaceship?"

Bitan looked at her a long time. "I've asked myself that, too."

There was a long silence.

"Well?" Nora asked.

He gave a little smile. "The only answer I can come up with is that even aliens make mistakes."

Nora had the sudden, distinct feeling that Bitan was not being straight in his answer; that he had another theory, one he didn't wish to share.

"I know why," Skip said out of the blue.

All eyes turned to him.

"Those alien pilots just can't hold their liquor."

There was a moment in which nobody spoke. And then, suddenly, the room erupted in laughter. Skip grinned, obviously pleased with himself. Already, Nora thought, he looked at home here.

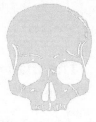

5

THE MAN WITH chestnut-colored hair locked the door carefully behind him, trotted down the front steps, then—as was his habit—paused to gaze around and breathe in the morning air. It was a crisp spring day, the kind Virginia rewarded its inhabitants with after a cold, wet winter. The residential street was quiet, the tidy houses still asleep in dappled shade.

As he stood there, steeling himself for the morning commute, he saw his neighbor, Bill Fossert, descend his front steps. This was unusual: it was quarter to eight, and Bill, an investment banker, usually left for work around nine. Maybe he had an early meeting.

Fossert saw him as well and paused. "Hey, Lime."

The man with chestnut hair nodded in return. "Fossert."

"Looks like another nice day," the man said, glancing up as if to divine the weather through the labyrinth of tree branches.

"Looks like," Lime replied.

"Last cold front of the winter coming in this weekend, though."

"So I heard."

"Well," the neighbor said, "I've got to run. Nice seeing you."

"Likewise."

Bill Fossert stopped at the front door of his car. "We'll have you over for dinner," he called out. "It's been too long."

Lime, who by now had reached his own Subaru, smiled in return. "Sounds good."

He got into the car and waited while Fossert started up his BMW 5 Series, backed it down the driveway, and headed off. There was a time when he'd been pretty chummy with the Fosserts. Lime had shown Fossert how to change the spark plug in his snowblower, and how to remove the ground loop causing 60-cycle hum in his expensive sound system. Fossert's wife had been close to Caitlyn, especially once Cait got pregnant. But time had passed, and now Lime only met Fossert by accident—like today—to exchange pleasantries and invitations that were never followed up on.

He pulled the zipper of his windbreaker halfway down, started the car, and caught a reflection of himself in the rearview mirror. He was thirty-seven, but Cait had said that, with his features, he could have been any age between twenty and fifty. "You've got the face of a spy," she'd said, laughing. "Handsome, but hard to remember."

He drove away from the trim Colonial—smaller than most of the houses on the block, but neatly landscaped. When they'd first bought the house three years ago, Cait—on track to be the youngest partner in her law firm—had pronounced it a good starter house, considering the baby that would inevitably come along. But now, given just his income, it was becoming increasingly difficult to keep up with the Joneses—or the Fosserts—in a pricey suburb like East Falls Church.

He made his way through the pleasant streets until he reached I-66, better known to locals as the Custis. Traffic was heavy, as usual, and given his car's poor acceleration he had to wait nearly thirty seconds before he could merge. One victim of his budgeting was the Subaru, which he probably should have sold a year or two ago. But it had held out for 170,000 miles; chances were good it would last 30,000 more.

The laboring sound of the engine, and the aggressive traffic, kept him company until he turned off the Custis onto Highway 120 south, half an hour later. Maybe he should downsize, he thought for the hundredth time—but downsize to where? Most of northeastern Virginia was one overpriced suburb, save for tiny pockets here and there where the crime rate stubbornly refused to drop. He could move farther out, of course, to Fairfax or Springfield, or maybe someplace in Maryland. But he hated commuting, and the idea of spending more time each day on the road was like a lead weight on his soul. Besides, he was sure that—

Now the Subaru intruded into his thoughts again. In addition to its usual hum of complaint, it had started to make a regular ticking sound that—given all the Humvees he'd repaired in a previous life—he recognized with dismay as a failing timing belt.

He continued down 120 for a few miles, hoping he was wrong. He wasn't: a few misfires confirmed the diagnosis. Now he was left with a choice. He could gamble, wait to get home and repair it himself. But the risk—a damaged piston, bent valve, maybe even a cracked cylinder block—didn't seem worth it, especially if he wanted to trade it in once it rolled over 200K.

That meant leaving the highway, pulling into a gas station, and seeing what the damage to his wallet would be.

With a muttered curse, he took the next exit. Here, at least, fortune smiled on him: the off-ramp emptied onto the kind of anonymous commercial strip replete with fast food joints, cheap motels...and service stations. If he lived here, he mused, his commute would be much easier. Affordable, too. But of course it was one of those spots where nobody wanted to live and real estate would be a lousy investment.

He drove a few blocks, looking for a gas station with a promising-looking auto shop attached. He chose one on the opposite side of the four-lane road, with a convenience store grafted to one side, set close beside a forlorn-looking creek. He pulled in next to the shop—cars on the lifts, but no mechanics in sight—and, zipping up his windbreaker, walked into the store.

It was then he realized that fortune wasn't smiling on him after all—and that this might be the start of a very bad day.

Even before the glass-fronted door closed behind him, he understood a robbery was in progress. A skinny man, hair askew and clothes wrinkled, was standing just behind the sales counter, gun trained alternately on a cashier and the small group of people—two mechanics, an elderly patron, and what looked like another shop employee—standing close together on the far side of the lotto rack.

As the door chime sounded, the man turned, gun swinging wildly. Lime froze, then raised his arms slowly, fingers apart, careful not to further antagonize the gunman.

"Get over there," the man said in a reedy voice, directing Lime to join the hostages on the far side of the counter.

Lime did as he was told, and the gunman turned back to the clerk, resuming a conversation that had been interrupted. "You're full of shit," he said. "You gotta have more than that."

"Swear to God," the cashier said, voice

trembling nervously. "It's still early. There's only a hundred, a hundred and twenty maybe, in the till." He took a step back. "Look for yourself."

The gunman didn't move. "What about the safe?"

"Only management has access to that, man," the clerk replied. He was sweating and obviously—at least to Lime—telling the truth.

The armed robber was sweating, too. "That's bullshit. You're just told to say that." Suddenly, he swung his gun back toward the small group. "You move again," he shouted at one of the mechanics, "and I'll splash your brains all over this place!"

The customer behind Lime—an overweight man of about seventy—let out a faint, high whimper of fear.

"Now open the goddamned safe!" the gunman yelled at the clerk. "And the rest of you, take out your wallets and toss them over!"

Lime reached into a back pocket for his wallet, taking the opportunity to step forward as he did so. He was good at reading people. Although the man's clothes were creased, they were clean. He was sweating, but that was from agitation; his pupils weren't dilated, and Lime couldn't make out any needle tracks. This wasn't a career criminal or a junkie. The gun looked old, but it wasn't a crappy Saturday Night Special.

"What do you need the money for?" Lime asked calmly.

The man was still menacing the clerk, and it took a moment for the question to sink in. "What?" he asked, eyes still on the clerk.

"I said, what do you need the money for?"

This time, the man turned his attention, and the barrel of his gun, to Lime. "Shut the fuck up." He took a moment to glance over the others, eyes bright with hostility and suspicion. "I *said*, empty your wallets."

As he spoke, Lime took another step—not toward the gunman, but flanking him, arms still raised. As he did so, the knot of hostages loosened slightly, instinctively edging away from each other.

"Don't move!" the gunman said, the muzzle of the gun bobbing from person to person.

"What do you need the money for?" Lime asked a third time, making sure to get the man's attention focused back on him. He held his wallet in one hand. "I mean, this is probably going to get that poor guy fired. And if I'm going to hand over all my money, I'd kind of like to know where it's headed." He paused. "Drugs, I suppose?"

The man looked at Lime as if he were an idiot. "Fuck you," he said.

Lime shrugged, as if confirming his own suspicion.

"I look like an addict to you?"

"I wouldn't know."

"Well, I *would* know. The system's fucked me up the ass. I been fired from three jobs. If I don't pay my rent today, I get evicted."

"Evicted," Lime repeated, lowering his hands in order to open his wallet invitingly.

"That's what I said. Evicted. The state gets custody of my kid. Not that it's any of your fucking business!"

This last was said in a louder, more threatening tone, accompanied by a fresh aiming of the gun. The man was wavering a little now, unsure of himself, but Lime sensed this only made him more dangerous. The other hostages were forming a loose semicircle behind him.

"*Stay* the fuck *back!*" the man yelled, threatening them.

Silently, Lime nodded at them to obey.

"So now you're desperate," he told the man. "I get that. But think about what you're doing. You're no thief. Okay, so you lost three jobs. You feel the system has let you down. Maybe it has. But if you go to prison, you'll become part of a different system. An ugly system. A brutal system that only leads in one direction." He paused. "You haven't stolen any money yet. You haven't used that gun. It's not too late."

"Shut *up!*" the man said, enraged. "What do you know about anything? You got a wife? A kid? *Huh?*"

Lime nodded.

"And are they about to be kicked out, no roof over their head?"

"No."

"See?" The man laughed in bitter triumph. "You don't know shit about it—sucker."

"My wife is dead," Lime told him. "My baby died with her."

The man's laughter died, and Lime took the opportunity. "How much do you need?"

The gunman frowned, not comprehending.

"How much money do you need? To put that gun down, walk out of here, and go pay your rent?"

The man seemed taken aback by the question. This wasn't going according to plan, and Lime stayed silent as the guy thought it through.

"Three hundred dollars," he said after a silence.

Lime glanced out the window. They'd been lucky, in a perverse way—no other customers had shown up to complicate things. Now he opened his wallet wider.

"I've got about two hundred." He turned to the group. "How about any of you? Can I get a little help here?"

There was a muttering, a shuffling of feet. Eventually, the mechanics each ponied up a fifty.

Lime collected the money from them, keeping his movements slow, and then added the contents of his own wallet. "Okay," he told the man. "Now: put down the gun, take the money...and find some other way to pay your bills. Because I guarantee: if you care about your family, getting yourself locked up or killed isn't going to help them."

The desperate man was silent as this sank in. Lime held out the money. The man stared at it hungrily, then began to reach out. As he did, Lime withdrew slightly, nodding at the gun.

Slowly, hesitantly, the man knelt, placing the weapon on the dirty linoleum—and then, with remarkable speed, he rose, grabbed the money, and darted out the door, disappearing in the dirty glaze of the window.

For a moment, everyone remained frozen— stunned not only by what had just transpired, but by how abruptly it ended. One of the mechanics finally cursed under his breath. The clerk wiped the sweat from his forehead with a sleeve, then closed the till.

One of the mechanics stepped forward, picked up the gun, tried to rack the slide. "Hey," he said. "This is a fake."

Lime reached out and caught the gun as the auto worker tossed it over. Sure enough: it was a fake, a replica actually, of a World War II–era 1911. Pretty good one, too: even the weight felt right. Idly, Lime wondered where the man had found it. Or if, perhaps, his grandfather had been a vet.

"What did you do that for?" the elderly customer demanded. "You threw away your money...*and* you let him go!"

Lime turned toward him. Strangely, he felt angrier at this aggrieved Joe Citizen than he had at the would-be criminal.

"Did you get hurt?" he asked. "Lose any money?"

The man shook his bald head.

"Then you've got nothing to cry about. Maybe that guy deserved a second chance. If he'd gone to jail, his life would be ruined—and costing taxpayers a hell of a lot more than three hundred dollars."

He went back outside, tossed the replica into the muddy creek, then walked over to his car and opened the hood. Sure enough: the timing belt was about to go.

When he walked back in, nobody had moved.

"Aren't you going to call the police?" the fat old man asked, voice full of righteous indignation.

"About what?"

"Armed robbery, of course."

"Nobody got robbed," Lime said. "And nobody was armed. But you can do what you want...now that it's over." And with that, he walked the mechanics into the body shop and asked if they could fix his timing belt while he was at work.

One of them walked with him to the Subaru, glanced at the engine, then nodded. As he did, Lime noticed a small tattoo of crossed sabers on the webbing between the mechanic's thumb and forefinger.

"First Cav?" he asked.

The man nodded again. "You?"

Without responding, Lime pulled out his phone. He was close enough to work now to order a taxi without it costing him an arm and a leg.

A few minutes later, his ride arrived—a yellow Subaru, not unlike his except five years and a hundred thousand miles younger. Lime said goodbye to the mechanics and got into the back of the cab.

"Where to?" the driver asked.

"Pentagon, please," Lime replied. "River entrance."

As the driver pulled out into traffic, Lime sat back in the seat—but not before removing his Glock 19 from his waistband and slipping it into a more comfortable location, farther away from his spine.

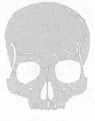

6

TAPPAN LED NORA out of the Quonset hut into the afternoon light. The entrepreneur had spent much of the day showing her around the site, ending up here, near where they'd begun. Skip had stayed behind to help unpack Bitan's library and organize the books on the shelves. The sun was lowering in the sky, casting long shadows over the desert grasslands. A scattering of April flowers dotted the mesa with spots of color. In the distance, white dust rose from the dry lake bed, and beyond that stood some hills and canyons leading into a range of purple mountains.

"At night out here," Tappan said, sweeping his arm, "there isn't a single light. This has got to be one of the most remote areas in the lower forty-eight."

The landscape had a Zen-like emptiness that Nora, too, found enchanting.

"They call this Diablo Mesa; nobody knows why. In Spanish days there was a watchtower on this mesa, where they kept a lookout for Comanches heading west to raid along the Rio Grande. That vast area beyond is called the Plains of Atalaya, and the white area in the middle is Dead Lake. Those distant peaks are called the Horse Heaven Hills. The buttes beyond are Los Gigantes, the giants, and the mountains on the horizon are Los Fuertos: the stronghold."

"Horse Heaven Hills—what a picturesque name."

"I looked into the history—in Spanish times, those hills were El Cielo de Caballos. I've always been intrigued by place-names. Someday I'm going to explore them and see just what horse heaven looks like. Lots of grass, I imagine." Tappan guided her toward a particularly long, gleaming RV. "Nora, may I invite you to my trailer for a few minutes? So we can talk?"

She nodded.

It was a huge Prevost conversion coach with its sides extended. He opened the door and led the way into an elegant but understated living room, with leather sofas and wing chairs arranged around an antique coffee table. Against the back wall were a wet bar and a media center. The floor was covered with Persian rugs and the walls were paneled in cherrywood, decorated with prints by Piranesi. A spectacular arrangement of star lilies and other fresh flowers dominated the table.

"Welcome to my dorm room," he said. "Please, have a seat."

Nora did so, trying not to be impressed. It looked more like the salon of a manor house than an RV. She had a sense he was now going to press her again about accepting the job. She wondered what to do. If it were just her, she'd probably still decline…but the truth was, she worried about Skip. The night before, she had Googled Lucas Tappan and was not fully reassured by what she'd found. To his credit, Icarus was involved in a number of green-energy projects—wind and solar—but there had also been NIMBY disputes, and Tappan tended to roll over the opposition. He was currently embroiled in a controversial wind-turbine project in the ocean off the coast of Maine. Despite his relaxed façade, he didn't suffer fools gladly and demanded a lot from his subordinates. He also had a history of abruptly firing people. How long would Skip survive in that kind of environment?

"Can I offer you a drink?" he asked, bringing her thoughts back. "I note the sun is below the yardarm, which means it's time for my martini." He went over to the bar. "I allow myself just one in the evening. What can I get you? We have everything from beer and wine to liquor, or kombucha, Pellegrino—whatever's your pleasure."

"A Pellegrino would be fine." Nora felt awkward; it was almost like a date. She had never met a billionaire before, let alone one her own age, and the novelty was still sinking in.

Tappan came back with a straight-up martini in one hand and mineral water in the other, and took a seat in the wing chair adjacent to her. "Nora, do you have any questions—I mean, before we return to the heart of the matter?"

"Can I speak freely?"

"Nothing's stopped you so far."

"Okay." She paused to glance around again. "I just wonder: Why this? There are so many things you could be doing with your money. Why UFOs?"

"Meaning, it seems eccentric to you?"

"Frankly, yes."

"Fair enough." He took a sip of his drink. "Tell me: What's the greatest discovery we human beings could make? Even greater, say, than finding a lost civilization? Greater than the discovery of fire, or the wheel?" He paused dramatically. "It would be to learn that *we're not alone*. To learn there are other intelligent species out there."

"But... it's so far-fetched."

"I respectfully disagree. In the past decade, astronomers have learned there are at least fifty billion Earth-like planets orbiting the habitable star zones in just *our* galaxy. You don't have to be a mathematician to realize that the odds of other intelligent species being out there are incredibly high. And here's another thing to consider: Our star is young. It's only five billion years old. Meanwhile, there are countless stars in our galaxy twice as old. There may be civilizations that are millions or even billions of years older than ours. Just think what technological heights they have achieved!"

"If they didn't destroy themselves first."

"You mean the so-called Great Filter? That's

a common argument, but I don't buy it. We've had the means to destroy ourselves for seventy-five years and we haven't done it. Nobody else came along to blow us up, either." He paused. "Imagine: fifty billion planets. And there are a trillion other galaxies beyond. That makes sextillion planets where intelligent life could have developed. The fact is, mathematics *requires* that our universe be teeming with intelligent life. So, no: it's not far-fetched at all."

All this tumbled out of Tappan in a rush of enthusiastic words. Nora couldn't help but find his eagerness charming and boyish—and genuine. Tappan was like the kid who never grew up and now had the money to make his childhood dreams come true.

Tappan paused and chuckled, abruptly self-conscious. "I do get on my hobbyhorse from time to time. Sorry. But here's the crux of the matter: If there are thousands, if not millions, of alien civilizations in our galaxy—are any of them aware of us? Have they ever stopped to take a look? I think they have. The proof of it is right here. And we're going to find it."

Nora took a deep breath. "Look: If I do this, I'll be known forever as the UFO archaeologist.

I'll never be taken seriously again. How do I reconcile that?"

"*Only* if nothing is found. And that's not going to happen. I promise, you *will* find something of significance. You've seen the crash pattern on the ground. You've seen artifacts scattered like raisins beneath the surface. Something crashed here. This is a legitimate archaeological investigation. You won't be known as the 'UFO archaeologist,' but as the archaeologist who finally revealed to the world that we've been visited by extraterrestrials. What's more, I'll have your back, Nora. I'll make sure your work is taken with the seriousness it deserves." He paused. "As far as the specifics of your employment go, the salary I'm offering is two hundred and twenty-five thousand dollars per annum. We expect the active phase to last five weeks, but to be followed up by an indefinite analysis phase. In other words, permanent employment. I'm setting up a nonprofit organization, of which you'll be the director."

Nora swallowed. That was a pretty astonishing salary—and an amazing offer. "But I have to ask again: Why me?"

"It's like I told you back in the parking lot of the Institute. I attribute my success not just to my own brilliance, but to the fact that I find the best people." He smiled deprecatingly. "That's the key. There are plenty of archaeologists out there, but I want someone with not only the brains, experience, and skills—but also the capacity to think outside the box. Just like you did at Quivira, and Victorio Peak, and probably a dozen other digs I haven't heard of. Consider this: in our lifetime, we'll never get the chance to visit aliens on their home planets. The only chance we'll get to examine them is if *they* come *here*. Now—will it be yes or no?"

"I have to think about it."

"Another thing about me: I'm an impatient person. You have all the information you need to make a decision right now. Certainly, feel free to think about it—for the next five minutes."

Nora stared at him. "Five minutes?"

"After that, I'll be going to the second name on my list." He paused. "I find the best decisions are made quickly and intuitively."

She could see he was serious. *Five minutes. Well, what the hell.* It was a lot of money, she'd just been fired, and she had no immediate prospects. Besides, the more primitive part of her brain loved the idea of Weingrau's fury when she found out Nora had accepted the directorship of a nonprofit—and the Institute not getting Tappan's big donation or the project, after all. And, perhaps most important, she could keep an eye on Skip.

"All right," she said. "I'm on board."

"Fabulous!" he cried.

"There's a catch."

"What's that?" His smile vanished.

"Skip and I have a dog, Mitty. We need to bring him. He needs to be welcome here."

He seized her hand. "Is that all? Christ, of course! I love dogs. This is the best news I could have—dog included. Welcome to the team!"

He clinked his martini glass with her Pellegrino, then drained it and placed it on the table. "Let's get you and Skip back to Santa Fe to pack up your things and fetch the dog. You'll be back in time for a late supper."

"You don't waste any time."

"No."

Nora paused. "If I'd said no, who was the next name on your list?"

He laughed. "There was no next name. That was just a negotiating ploy." A pause. "I hope you'll forgive me."

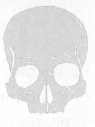

7

TAPPAN WAS AS good as his word: that evening, Nora and Skip were flown back to Santa Fe, where they packed up their stuff and Mitty, then returned by helicopter to find dinner waiting for them in the galley of a custom two-bedroom Airstream trailer assigned to them. It had a fully stocked kitchen and larder. Skip, the cook of the family, went through the freezer and found it filled with gourmet meats, poultry, and fish. Similarly, the vegetable drawers were packed with fresh greens, and the pantry cupboard brimmed with all kinds of delicacies.

Nora unpacked as Skip looked through it all, *ooh*ing and *aah*ing and talking about the fine dishes he was going to prepare—even though Tappan had told them the camp was equipped with a two-star Michelin chef named Antonetti.

They were up before dawn the next morning. While Nora worked on her laptop in the small office area, answering introductory emails and getting up to speed, Skip took Mitty around the camp, making friends with everyone. On his return he whipped up a celebratory breakfast of scrambled eggs, bacon, and avocado toast—despite the lobster eggs Benedict being served in the canteen—and now, at nine sharp, Nora was seated at the head of a conference table in Quonset 1, before an audience of the Three Engineers, Noam Bitan, Skip, two postdocs, and Tappan. That morning, Nora had prepared a preliminary timetable and excavation plan for the first week, and she now distributed it to the team. Tappan had made it clear to everyone that she was in charge, but she wondered if he'd honor that dictum himself if push came to shove. For now, he seemed perfectly content to let her run the meeting.

"As you can see," she said, "we've got quite a lot to do. After gridding off the site in one-meter squares, we'll open ground in the northwestern quad and then work east and south, meter by meter. We'll keep going down layer by layer, until we reach the 1947 horizon. This is a delicate excavation, because the site is really just sand on sand, with a scattering of artifacts."

She went on to describe the plan for that first week in some detail. "But," she added, "there's a small issue we have to deal with immediately. If you look at the excavation plan, you'll see that five hundred yards due west of the target area is a small archaeological feature, a seven-by-four-and-a-half-foot rectangle containing what appear to be human remains."

Papers were shuffled as everyone located the feature.

"When I first saw this yesterday, I speculated that it might be a prehistoric Pueblo burial. I say this because the archaeological survey map of New Mexico indicates a thousand-year-old Pueblo seasonal campsite at the edge of Diablo Mesa, two miles west. There's also a Spanish watchtower, apparently, so these might be historic burials. By law, we have to determine if there's a grave, and if so, take steps to protect it. And we have to do that right away—before anything else."

"Can't we just rope it off and stay clear?" Tappan asked.

Nora shook her head. "It's the law. But it won't take long: we only have to open it enough to identify it as a burial, and then we can fill in the hole and leave it alone. It won't take more than a few hours."

"Good!" Tappan said. "Let's get it out of the way, then."

An hour later, Nora stood observing while the two postdocs, Scott and Emilio, hammered pins into the ground and gridded out the possible grave with Day-Glo string. To her dismay, everyone had come to watch this first breaking of ground. But she wasn't surprised: the discovery of a grave on a dig, it seemed, always aroused a level of morbid curiosity.

"We'll open grid one-A first," said Nora. "I think that's where the heads would be oriented."

It was often easy to determine if a cranium was ancient Pueblo Indian or not, because most prehistoric Southwestern skulls had flattened backs, deliberately deformed in infancy by binding the baby's head to a cradleboard. If so, all she had to do was uncover one cranium, establish it as prehistoric because of the deformation, and then they could bury it again and get on with the real work of excavating the target site. If it were Spanish, that might require a more extensive excavation, but they would undoubtedly find Spanish artifacts. Carbon dating would quickly establish the age.

She had decided to do the actual excavation herself, as there was only room for one in the meter square, and she wanted to show everyone she was going to be a hands-on director. In addition, since this was almost certainly a prehistoric site, she wanted to make sure it was done properly. Scott and Emilio seemed competent enough, but they were young and she suspected they might need guidance.

Laying out strips of canvas around the area to be opened, she donned knee pads and knelt, using a trowel to remove the bunchgrass and a scattering of purple locoweed and set them aside, to replace when the hole was refilled. According to the GPR, the bodies—if indeed they were bodies—lay roughly three feet deep. As she troweled off the sandy topsoil, inch by inch, she filled a bucket placed in one corner, which Skip periodically picked up and dumped on a screen, while the two assistants searched it for artifacts. This went on for close to an hour, as Nora went down inch by inch. Nothing was showing up on the screen but pebbles—until Skip abruptly cried out and held something up.

"Hey, take a look at this rare and ancient artifact!"

There was an initial stir of excitement until people saw he was laughing, an old brass bullet casing between his fingers.

Nora took it from him. It was a deeply tarnished Remington .45 ACP that had been fired. Odd, she thought, to find it in a layer a foot down. But then she considered there was a lot of wind and sand in the area: stuff could get buried pretty quickly.

She handed it back to Skip.

"What should I do with it?" he asked.

"Trash."

She continued digging until she reached the three-foot marker. She paused and, taking a slender bamboo probe, poked it into the sand. Sure enough, there was something a few inches deeper, the right size and shape to be a cranium.

She proceeded now with palette knife and paintbrush. She could feel everyone above her, hovering, looking down. It was irritating—she didn't like being watched while she worked—but she knew from prior experience they eventually lost interest and went away. Archaeology was deadly boring 95 percent of the time, an endless moving of small piles of dirt from one place to another. Rarely was anything of note found.

She slowly deepened the layer, brushing the sand to one side and scooping it into the bucket, whisked away by Skip with less frequency now.

She paused again and probed with the bamboo. The object was now just below the surface.

A few more swipes of the brush revealed a wrinkled surface the color and texture of a morel mushroom. This was odd—prehistoric burials were normally fully skeletonized, but this looked desiccated, mummified. More brushing revealed what appeared to be a dome-like forehead. The color turned out to be from dried skin, partially covering the skull. And where there was no skin, the skull itself looked oddly smooth, with what appeared to be faintly etched, regular grooves...as if it had been polished on a grindstone with a burr on it. This was strange, like nothing she'd ever seen before—not even the desiccated body she'd found six months ago in the Jornada del Muerto. She could feel the pressure of the eyes above as she worked.

More brushing revealed the edge of an eye socket. She uncovered it, whisking away the sand with short, quick strokes. She could hear a murmur rising in the peanut gallery as the head came into view.

Just get it over with, she told herself, working the brush around the sides and uncovering more bizarre brown skin, pitted and scaly like some ancient reptile's. At least, she thought—hoped—it was skin. One more sweep of the brush brought both eye sockets into full view, yawning, unexpectedly huge—and Nora stopped, rearing back in surprise at the sight.

"What the *hell?*" somebody cried out in a choked voice.

Nothing else was said. A silence of pure astonishment fell over the group, and only the wind could be heard, rustling through the prairie grass.

8

Nora stared at what the last few brushstrokes had uncovered: a large, domed head covered in lizard-like skin; two eye sockets that gaped like hollow caves; two holes for a nose; wrinkled stubs for ears; and thin, dry lips drawn back in a snarl from white teeth. A murmur of incomprehension drifted down into the shallow hole from the crowd above.

As alien as the head had looked at first glance, Nora began to realize it was simply too human in aggregate to be anything but a person. What was throwing her and everyone else off was the scaly skin texture; the smoothed-out—almost dissolved—facial features; and the eye cavities, whose shadowy depths made them look much larger than they actually were.

It was human—but it was certainly no Native American burial. Spanish, perhaps?

Ignoring the buzz of talk from above, she resumed brushing away the sand in larger strokes and quickly uncovered the neck area—along with the rotting collar of a modern checked shirt and a thin gold necklace with a Catholic medallion of Saint Christopher. Another hush fell as she cleared more sand away from the posterior part of the head, revealing the cause of death: an obvious bullet hole in the left temple, behind the ear, which had exited the right, taking much of the rear section of the skull with it.

She stopped and stood up, brushing sand from her clothes, then climbed out of the hole. Tappan's face had gone white. She spoke to him in a calm voice. "It's not, obviously, a prehistoric burial," she said. "I think what we have here is a murder victim." Taking a deep breath, she turned toward her brother. "Skip, I guess you'd better retrieve that shell casing from the trash. Don't touch it with your fingers this time—it's evidence. Use tweezers and place it in one of my artifact bags. It seems we're dealing with a burial *and* a crime scene."

Finally, Tappan spoke. "A crime scene?"

"You can see as well as I the execution-style shot to the head, the clean entrance hole, the gaping exit wound. This is not a suicide: dead people can't bury themselves. And obviously this is not an alien—right? Not with a Saint Christopher medal and a checked shirt collar."

After a moment, Tappan nodded. The color had returned to his features. "Of course. I see that. But what about the strange-looking skin, and the lack of features? It may be human, but it's no ordinary corpse."

"I haven't a clue about that," said Nora. "All I know is, we need to report this."

"To whom?"

"Since we're on federal land, to the FBI. And as it turns out, I know the right person to contact in the Albuquerque Field Office."

"Really?" Tappan looked at her speculatively. "And who might that be?"

"Special Agent Corinne Swanson."

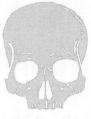

9

This is some desolate country out here," said Special Agent Morwood, behind the wheel of his candy-apple-red pickup truck as they headed south of Vaughn, New Mexico, on Route 285. The road stretched ahead of them like a gray slash through a landscape of grass and chamisa, with a few splotches of April flowers visible here and there. "I've been back with the Albuquerque FO for half a dozen years, and rarely do we have a case out in these parts."

"Why is that?" Special Agent Corrie Swanson asked.

He chuckled. "Nobody lives here. There's nobody to get into trouble."

The truck hummed on the highway, going ninety, but the land was so empty it almost felt to Corrie like they weren't moving. They were being followed by the Evidence Response Team van, with two ERT technicians. Theirs were the only vehicles on the road, as far as Corrie could tell.

"Be sure to give me plenty of advance notice of our turnoff," Morwood said.

He had asked Corrie to navigate, and she was doing so with her iPhone. They had gone out of cellular range a while ago, but the GPS still seemed to be working. She hoped to God she wouldn't get them lost.

"It's another forty miles, sir."

"Christ." He drove for a while in silence. "So, Corrie, I've been thinking: How would you feel if I put you in charge of this case? I'll be your junior partner, so to speak. All the decisions are going to be yours. Of course, I'll step in if I think there's a problem, but for the most part I'm going to let you take the lead."

"Thank you, sir. I appreciate that very much." She knew, as an FBI agent with just over a year's field experience under her belt, that this was the next step in the "ghosting" process: to run her own case, with her mentor acting as a junior partner. She tried to tamp down her nervousness and excitement. After all, it couldn't be as dangerous, or as complicated, as the two major cases she'd already worked on since joining the Albuquerque FO.

"When we get there, I want you to take charge and establish your authority in a nice, easy way. I'll remain in the background."

"Yes, sir." Her nervousness increased.

Like all rookie agents, Corrie had been assigned a mentor for her first two years, someone to supervise her cases and make sure she didn't screw up. When she first met Morwood, she had not been impressed. The supervisory special agent was approaching fifty, a plain man in a blue suit, balding, with a stock of forgettable ties and a dry manner. The only surprising thing about him was the confiscated Nissan pickup truck he used as his G-ride, with its racing stripes and giant decal of a Chinese dragon emblazoned across the side and hood. He joked that it allowed him to go around incognito.

Early on, his cool manner and devotion to the rule book had put her off. But over time, she'd realized he genuinely had her best interests at heart and was, in fact, a very fine agent—even while the reason he'd given up a stellar field career to supervise new hires remained an endless source of conjecture among the junior agents. While the two would never have anything approaching a friendship, it was, at least, a relationship of mutual respect and even regard.

Another brief silence, and then Morwood asked: "So. What do you know about the Roswell Incident?"

"Not much beyond what I read on the internet last night. It didn't make a lot of sense." Corrie had spent hours reading and taking notes, astonished by the mass of contradictory and bizarre information. Apparently it was one of those things, like the Kennedy assassination, that drew conspiracy theorists like moths to a flame.

Morwood chuckled. "More like nonsense. How did your friend Nora Kelly get involved in this?"

"I've no idea. And I wouldn't actually call her a friend. More like a colleague."

"The Roswell Incident," Morwood said after a moment, "is actually pretty banal—once you strip away the layers of conspiracies. What's known for sure is that something crashed in a remote section of J. B. Foster's ranch in July 1947. The land had been leased by the rancher from the BLM, Department of the Interior—making it federal land. The ranch foreman was said to have found a bunch of silvery material, along with a disk and other strange stuff. The foreman called the sheriff, who called the Roswell Army Air Field and spoke to one Major Jesse Marcell. The RAAF command went out to the site, allegedly collected everything, and issued a hasty and poorly written press release that spoke of a crashed 'disk.' That generated a front-page story in the Roswell Daily Record with the headline: RAAF CAPTURES FLYING SAUCER ON RANCH IN ROSWELL REGION. A day later the RAAF quickly issued another press release contradicting the first and insisting it was nothing more than the wreckage of a weather balloon. And then the story simply sank from sight."

"But it somehow got revived?"

"Yes. In the late seventies, interest in UFOs went through the roof and people began to focus once again on the Roswell Incident. The two contradictory press releases gave the impression of a government cover-up, and that, of course, fired up everyone's imagination. By this time, the recollections of those involved had faded— or become exaggerated. There were also plenty

of opportunists who leapt onto the story looking to make a buck. In 1980, a book called *The
Roswell Incident* came out, and that really set the
story on fire. It claimed there had been a massive conspiracy to cover up the fact that a UFO
had crashed and that alien bodies and technology had been recovered. More books followed,
including one by a retired lieutenant colonel
named Philip Corso. In his book, Corso actually
claimed to have been in charge of a storehouse
of alien artifacts and bodies recovered from the
crash. He said that some of the key inventions of
the modern age—lasers, computer chips, fiber
optics—had come from reverse engineering the
alien technology." He shook his head. "People
just ate it up. The thing is, they were right
on one level: there *was* a government cover-up.
Only it wasn't of a UFO crash."

"What was it?"

"In 1994, the government produced an official
report on the Roswell Incident that finally explained what really happened. It wasn't a weather
balloon, after all, but a classified nuclear-test
monitoring device sent aloft that crashed. Part
of a secret program called Project Mogul. The
device had a large dish that acted as a radar

reflector, for tracking purposes. To cover up the true nature of the device, the government insisted it was a weather balloon and did nothing to tamp down stories of a UFO. But by that point, the conspiracy theorists had already put such a huge investment into the UFO theory that this report seemed like just another effort at covering up. And then, there was the crazy theory promoted in a book published a few years ago, *Area 51*."

"I've heard of that one."

"It rejected the alien theory entirely. It said the crash was a Soviet disinformation effort, in which deformed children who looked like aliens were put in a bizarre aircraft and sent over the North Pole to crash in North America. The idea was to trigger hysteria over fears of an alien invasion. Taking a page from the Orson Welles playbook, with his *War of the Worlds* broadcast."

"That's nuts."

"Even crazier than a UFO, if such a thing is possible."

"If you don't mind me asking, sir: How did you learn so much about Roswell?"

Morwood was silent for a moment, then shook his head in a rueful way. "Back in the late nineties, when I was a rookie agent just like you, I was ghosted by a man named Mickey Starr. He was an upstanding guy, a real brick agent."

Corrie nodded. She knew that, on the job, a "brick agent" was someone who'd spent their entire career in the FBI until it almost became part of their DNA. Such agents didn't care about politics, especially Washington politics; they saw their role as fighting crime and prosecuting criminals—sometimes to the exclusion of everything else in their lives.

Morwood raised a hand from the wheel, coughed behind it. "My first case involved the murder of a scientist from Los Alamos. It was a pretty strange business—kind of a closed-room mystery."

"What was the outcome?"

"You mean, how did we resolve the case? We didn't. It's still open, in fact—to this day."

There was a sour edge in his voice she had not heard before. Obviously the failure to close the case as a rookie agent still rankled him. That was something Corrie could understand.

"That happened around the time the Roswell conspiracies were firing up again, and everyone was talking about UFOs. So of course people assumed the scientist had been abducted or murdered by aliens, and we had a deluge of tips involving Roswell and UFOs, which we had to follow up one at a time. Or rather *I* had to follow up, since Agent Starr left the stepping and fetching to me. Believe me: I've had enough contact with Roswell nutjobs to last a lifetime."

He fell silent, and then asked, "How many more miles to the turnoff?"

Corrie checked her phone. "Thirty, sir."

"Son of a bitch."

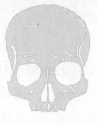

10

AFTER THE TURNOFF, the landscape began to change, breaking up into mesas, hills, canyons, and dry lake beds with occasional dust devils twisting across them. At a certain point, Corrie made out, on a long, low mesa, what soon resolved itself into the excavation's temporary encampment, with RVs, Quonset huts, and various work vehicles. Even as they approached, she heard a throbbing sound and a helicopter settled down into a billowing cloud of dust.

"Quite a setup," said Morwood as they slowed before a ranch gate set into a new barbed wire fence, staffed by a young man. They stopped and Morwood rolled down his window and held up his badge, dangling around his neck on a lanyard.

"We're expecting you, sir," the guard said, opening the gate to let both vehicles through.

As they drove into the compound, Morwood looked around and said, "Nice to be so rich you can devote a few million to looking for little green men."

"I recall reading aliens were silvery, not green."

Morwood laughed as he turned into a freshly bladed dirt parking area, where they pulled up next to a couple of Hummers. Just beyond the motor pool was a small group of people that, Corrie could see, included Nora Kelly.

As they stepped out into the cool air, Corrie caught a faint whiff of Morwood's aftershave—unusual in scent, sparingly applied, its brand the source of much curiosity back in Albuquerque. She looked around. It was a pleasant April day, not too hot, the great dome of the sky above them like a gigantic blue egg, while a gentle breeze stirred the grasses.

Nora approached, accompanied by a tall fellow with curly black hair wearing a lambskin cowboy shirt with mother-of-pearl buttons, jeans, and sneakers.

"Lucas Tappan," the man said, extending his hand with a brilliant smile. Corrie took it, a bit dazzled. So this was the famous billionaire funding the whole thing. Surprisingly young—and good-looking, too. Of course. She remembered Morwood's advice: display confidence and take charge.

"Special Agent Corrie Swanson," she said. "I'm in charge of the case. This is my, ah, partner, Supervisory Special Agent Morwood."

This announcement raised a few eyebrows. Tappan said: "Nice to meet you, Agent Swanson. And you, too, Agent Morwood."

Nora then introduced them to everyone else. Corrie noticed there weren't any uniforms or other insignia distinguishing scientists from support staff.

"Well, shall we have a look at the, ah, corpse?" Tappan asked. Corrie already sensed he was someone who hated to waste time.

"Lead the way," Corrie said.

A brief walk along the mesa top brought them to an area that had been gridded off with stakes and Day-Glo string. One square of it had been excavated, exposing the face of a buried corpse—or rather, Corrie realized as she stared in horror, a quasi-face.

"As soon as I realized the deceased was of

relatively recent vintage," Nora said, "I stopped working. I've never seen a skull like that."

Corrie had never seen anything like it, either. "For now, we'll be treating this area as a crime scene," she said. "You can see what looks like the entry and exit wound of a projectile. I would guess that we're looking at an execution-style homicide."

"We recovered a casing," said Nora. "Bagged it as evidence. You'll find my brother's prints on it." She paused. "The ground-penetrating radar indicates there might be a second body beside this one."

"Thank you." Corrie looked around. Tappan, Morwood, Nora, and Nora's brother—Skip was his name, she remembered—had accompanied them to the site, but now they were all looking to her for direction. "I'm afraid we'll have to borrow Dr. Kelly for a few days to excavate the site."

Tappan frowned. "We've just engaged her to work on our project. Can we perhaps divide her time between the two duties?"

Corrie hesitated. Morwood, who seemed out of breath, wasn't jumping in, and Nora remained silent as well. It was up to her to respond.

"I'm sorry, I'm afraid not. We need to give this priority."

Tappan quickly covered up his annoyance. "Of course. We're glad to cooperate with the FBI."

"That's much appreciated, Mr. Tappan. Dr. Kelly, how long do you think it will take?"

"If nothing more unusual surfaces, I'd estimate two days."

"How soon can you begin work?"

"Right away," Nora said. "I can have my team on it in half an hour."

"Very good." Corrie looked around. "We're going to set up a perimeter here, out to a radius of a hundred feet. I'll have to ask everyone except the archaeologist and her assistants to keep clear of the area. The Evidence Response Team will be performing a sweep with metal detectors."

"I wonder," Tappan said, "if I might be allowed to observe more closely than from behind the tape."

Corrie considered this. Take one, give one. "Okay," she said. "I don't see a problem with that. But the rest will have to remain behind the barriers."

"Thank you."

Skip and the others drifted back.

"I'll have to get some tools and roust up my assistants," said Nora. "I assume you'll be staying while we work?"

"Yes. We'll remain until the bodies are out of the ground and in evidence coffins."

"Where are you planning to spend the night?"

"Roswell." The drive to Roswell was at least two hours over bad roads, but there was no place closer. Corrie had made reservations at a local motel.

"Nonsense," Tappan said. "I've got a couple of trailers here for visitors and guests. Why don't you stay? I would consider it a favor, since it would allow your work to proceed more efficiently."

Corrie glanced at Morwood, who seemed curiously impassive, awaiting her decision. "Thank you," she said. "We'll take you up on that. Very kind of you."

Now Morwood spoke up. "Perhaps Mr. Tappan could show me to our quarters while Dr. Kelly and Agent Swanson get to work."

The two men walked off, leaving Nora and Corrie alone for the first time.

Nora said, "You're getting better at this, you know that?"

"I'm trying. There's a lot of stuff they don't teach at the Academy."

"So you'd better tell me now," said Nora. "Is it going to be 'Dr. Kelly' this and 'Special Agent Swanson' that—all over again? Or will it be Nora and Corrie?"

Corrie thought for a moment. The titles bolstered her authority, kept everything on a professional level. But they were also tiresome and stiff—and, after all, the two women had saved each other's lives. "Hell with it," she said. "Let's go back to Nora and Corrie."

Nora smiled, obviously pleased with the dispensing of formality.

"But I've got to ask you—how is it you're involved in this? I mean, it doesn't seem the kind of thing the Institute normally does."

Nora's smile faded. "I'm no longer with the Institute. It's a long story. We have to go to the field office to collect my gear and assistant—I'll explain on the way."

As they walked, Nora told her the story of how she had been fired and then persuaded by Tappan to join the team.

"Do you think a UAP really crashed here?" Corrie said.

"Of course not. Something impacted here, though, and it wasn't a balloon carrying a monitoring device or a weather station. The GPR survey indicates that whatever it was came down at high speed and gouged out a furrow. The disturbance was later covered up by bulldozers."

"Weird. Do you think all that has anything to do with the body?"

"Bodies—like I said, I'm pretty sure there are two." She paused. "It's a little hard to believe that a murderer would bury bodies way out here, by coincidence, hard up against the Roswell site."

They stopped at one of a line of Quonset huts. Nora led the way in and introduced Corrie to two young men who were working on Macs.

"These are my assistants," Nora said. "Emilio Vigil is a postdoc in archaeology at UNM. And Scott Riordan, also a postdoc, from Colorado State."

Vigil and Riordan shook Corrie's hand gravely, one after the other. "Pleased to meet you."

Nora said, "Let's get to work."

Vigil, Riordan, and Nora, loaded down with equipment, left the Quonset hut. As they headed back to the site, Nora explained the situation to Vigil and Riordan while Corrie brought up the rear. The FBI team had finished stringing up caution tape and was starting to sweep the area with metal detectors, pausing every now and then to flag something. Morwood returned with Tappan, followed by several workers who set up a temporary shade, some chairs, and a cooler full of soft drinks.

All we need is a hot dog vendor and the ball game can commence, Corrie thought. She turned to watch as Nora, with Vigil's and Riordan's assistance, laid out a piece of canvas and arrayed her tools on it. They donned knee pads, got into the shallow gridded square, knelt, and then began gently whisking sand away from the corpse.

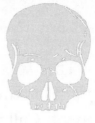

11

THE GROUND WAS soft and dry, and to Morwood's unpracticed eye the work appeared to go rapidly. After a while, Tappan left their shady oasis and went over to stand at the edge of the dig, watching the archaeologists work. There was a time when Morwood would have gone with him, but now he stayed put, watching from afar as they painstakingly brushed sand from the corpse, collected the dirt, and ran it through a screen, looking for things of possible interest.

Morwood felt unusually fatigued that day, but out of long practice he kept it well concealed. Only he and his personal physician knew the full extent of his condition. And he intended to keep it that way for another eighteen months, when he'd retire after a full twenty-five on the job.

That was especially important to him: *on the job*. He would never agree to a medical retirement. Call it truculence or stubbornness—with him, it was a point of honor. From the time he was ten, when he devoured reruns of *The F.B.I.*, he'd wanted to be an agent. These days, of course, when he mentioned the show's star, Efrem Zimbalist Jr., younger agents just gave him blank looks. But unlike many childish dreams, that ambition had persisted into adulthood, particularly as the asthma that plagued his youth slowly went away. He'd charted a careful path, and by twenty-six he was a full-fledged special agent, with ambitions having matured away from Efrem Zimbalist and more toward Eliot Ness. And he wasn't planning to put in just the requisite twenty, either: with another year and a half, he would hit twenty-five with the extra years of service and pay grade increases...and still retire before the mandatory age of fifty-seven.

The ERT guys had finished their sweep. Morwood rose from his chair, went over to their van for a brief update, then returned to his spot in the shade.

Those early years with the Bureau had been the most exciting of his life. He had a knack for breaking cases, and a degree of recklessness that put him in the middle of dangerous fire-fights during raids or arrests. The FBI rewarded hard work with regular promotions, and his starting pay grade was behind him almost before he knew it. Lady Luck, he'd thought, had definitely been smiling down on him.

Until the day she suddenly made a one-eighty.

A dozen years into his career, after his re-assignment from Albuquerque to Chicago, he knew nothing about autoimmune disorders. He started getting winded after a hard workout or chasing a suspect, which he attributed to being out of shape. When he hit the gym harder and it became obvious this was not the case, he told himself it was his asthma, acting up again after being dormant so long. Instead of visiting a doctor, he bought nebulizers and over-the-counter inhalers, and steadfastly ignored it for several more years.

Eventually, when he could overlook it no longer, it turned out he'd waited too long. The pulmonologist he consulted told him he should have been on anti-inflammatories. Now the dam-age to his lungs, the scarring, was permanent. The best things he could do for interstitial lung disease—quit working, eliminate occupational exposure—were unthinkable. So he took other steps, some of them mortifying. He removed himself from the task forces, focusing more on investigative background. And he hid his shortness of breath from his colleagues, keeping the severity of his condition a secret. But finally, after an age-required FBI physical, an internist with the Bureau copped to his condition and told him the "chronic dyspnea" mandated a change of venue. And it was not optional.

He was disturbed from his reverie by a rising murmur of voices over by the dig—apparently, something of interest had been uncovered. Morwood knew it was time to join them. He took a few lungfuls of the desert air in preparation, then stood up.

They'd sent him back to New Mexico precisely because of the "clean desert air." What a joke—the air might have been clean, but half the time it was so full of dust from the wind that it seemed half the town was hacking from dust pneumonia. The locality pay here sucked. What bothered him more than anything was the altitude: almost a mile above sea level. But he knew speaking up would only make things worse, so he kept quiet and tried to lose himself in mentoring new agents. He'd been able to leverage his exemplary field experience into a supervisory instructor position and was now on track to retire as a GS-14 step 8, or maybe even step 9.

He wasn't able to hide his condition completely, of course, but he could keep people guessing. Rumors began to circulate about his past: how he'd been exposed to poisonous gas during an arrest or sucked in a lungful of battery acid during a shootout in an auto warehouse. He did nothing to quell such rumors, because they were more colorful than the truth. Now he just toughed it out from one day to the next, controlling the condition as best he could with albuterol scrips.

Reaching the dig site, he found that Nora Kelly had almost completely exposed the body. It lay on its back, one arm thrown over its chest and the other resting by its side. Morwood noticed it was male, even though all the hair seemed to be gone except for a fringe on the back of the head. A few tatters of a shirt clung to the rib cage, with the pants in better condition. One leg was slightly crooked. Given its position, the body appeared to have been unceremoniously rolled or tossed into the grave. As Morwood watched, Nora's whisk uncovered first one foot, then the other, exposing a pair of oxford wing tips, much shriveled.

"Inappropriate footwear for out here," said Tappan.

"Quite," said Nora. She rose and called for a break.

Morwood found her sense of timing excellent. They relaxed in the chairs, drinking sodas and looking at the body, now almost entirely exposed within the trench.

"It's funny," said Corrie, "that the weird skin texture is confined to the facial area. Everything else looks normal—under the circumstances."

"I noticed that, too," said Tappan. "Agent Swanson, your partner said you're a forensic anthropologist. Do you have any idea what might cause those peculiar scales on the face?"

"Offhand," said Corrie, "it looks like acid. Or perhaps the features were burned off with a flamethrower."

"I vote for acid," said Nora. "I don't see any evidence of charring."

"We'll do some histopathology in the lab," said Corrie. "What we do is infuse the tissue with paraffin, then slice very thin sections for microscopic examination. And we'll do toxicology tests as well. I'm pretty sure we can solve the mystery."

Morwood noticed she glanced at him for approval. He remained impassive. Corrie was one of the best agents he'd mentored, but she had a weakness: she was tentative, and others could sense it. She hadn't mastered how to project a sense of confidence. It was a tricky thing to do, but a good FBI agent had to learn how to convey self-assurance and control to those around her, even if she didn't feel it inside.

Break over, Nora and her assistants went back to work in the grid. They began opening additional quadrants. Morwood watched as they removed the surface plants, setting them aside in flats, evidently for later replanting, and then began scraping off thin layers of crusty sand. The work proceeded apace until they reached a depth of three feet—the same depth as the other body. A discoloration now appeared in the soil. Nora and the assistants exchanged trowels for palette knives, loosening the dirt and then sweeping it off.

At this point, Morwood rose and joined them.

The first thing to appear was skin of the same scaly texture. This soon revealed itself to belong to the forehead of another corpse.

There is a second body, Morwood thought. He felt an uncharacteristic excitement, almost as if—subconsciously—he'd been expecting this would happen.

"Same execution-style shot to the head," he said.

"Yes," said Corrie.

As Nora brushed, an object suddenly gleamed in the sunlight.

"And there's another .45 casing," said Morwood. He glanced at Corrie. "Doesn't it seem these two bodies could date to the late forties? Those oxfords, those gabardine slacks...?" He glanced over at her, arching his eyebrows.

"It could be," Corrie said.

"What would you think if, as soon as both bodies are fully uncovered, we transfer them onto tarps and search them for ID?"

"I would say that's a good idea, sir."

They continued to watch Nora work. This body looked much like the other one, the face partially obliterated by some as-yet-unknown agent. Once again, it was lying on its back in a loose and careless position, but as Nora moved down to the torso, Morwood realized with surprise that it was not a man but a woman.

He quickly covered up his disappointment. "Well, well," he said, "Look what we've got here."

Tappan breathed out in surprise. "This just gets weirder and weirder."

Nora, Emilio, and Scott continued working, uncovering the rest of the body. The sun was now an hour from the horizon.

The dirt winked with another sudden glint. Rapidly Nora's brush uncovered a smooth, gleaming metal surface resting next to the hip bone of the second corpse. With every sweep, the exposed object looked stranger and stranger: two gleaming ovoids of a silvery metal, one six inches in diameter, the other perhaps eighteen inches, connected by a complicated maze of tiny metal pipes, tubes, and valves. At one end was a dial.

Nobody said anything, but the surprise and consternation deepened. Nora finally paused in her work and she and Emilio climbed out of the hole while Scott put away the tools. The six of them stared at the object in utter silence. It was so peculiar, so perfectly made, so...*alien*, that Morwood was taken aback.

"Well," said Nora after a long moment. "Anyone got a guess as to what that is?"

Given all the rumors about Area 51 and UFO abductions, Morwood could surmise what people were thinking. But nobody voiced their thoughts.

"Finish clearing away the dirt and let's remove it," said Tappan, his voice gravelly with suppressed excitement.

Nora took a series of photos of the object in situ and then continued digging around it with a palette knife, flicking and sweeping away the dirt. Emilio and Scott had paused working on the lower extremity of the corpse and were now spectators as well.

After ten minutes, she had completely exposed the object. She inserted a wooden chopstick underneath and, ever so carefully, pried it from the grip of the earth. With gloved hands, she turned it over.

Stamped on the bottom, in clear script, was:

HICHEM INDUSTRIES
EDISON, NEW JERSEY
^{3}H Bleed 1X-20X

This was followed by some stamped numbers.

There was a silence. Then Tappan began to chuckle, which became a laugh. "And who said God doesn't have a sense of humor? For a moment there I was convinced that was an alien object!" He shook his head ruefully. "Sure got my heart rate up. Although I should note it *is* from New Jersey."

"Well," Nora said, "if it isn't an alien artifact, what the hell *is* it?"

"Tomorrow," Corrie said, "we'll lift those bodies. In the meantime, let's put that device into an evidence box. We'll get all this back to the FBI lab and I promise you, we'll have answers soon."

Morwood felt an inner glow of satisfaction at Corrie's authoritative tone. That was more like it. But when she threw him a glance to check for his approval, he frowned and looked away.

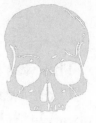

12

Lime, driving his Subaru west on Dolley Madison Boulevard, took the back exit into CIA headquarters, then drove slowly through one parking lot after another until he found a spot he liked near the Memorial Garden. He'd spent much of his free time after work giving his vehicle some TLC, and it was once again paying him back the love.

Exiting the car, he followed the sidewalk that looped around to the main entrance. It was a longer walk than necessary, but the weather in Langley was fine and—since he'd spent many recent working hours in a cubicle—he wanted to enjoy it. He entered the chilly lobby with its long rows of tall, narrow columns; went through the usual ID checks; then headed for the elevators. People were walking, as usual, back and forth over the large CIA seal set into the floor, engrossed in their business and paying it no mind. Lime, as always, was careful to step around the image of the eagle, shield, and compass rose.

He made the familiar trip up to the third floor, down a maze of narrow corridors, and past another ID checkpoint before he reached his destination: a closed door of dark wood, with a nameplate beside it that read RUSH, J. He smoothed his shirt front, then knocked on the door.

"Enter," came the voice from inside.

Lime opened the door and stepped in, shutting it behind him. The office looked straight out of a Hollywood set dresser's manual: large desk, laptop, three phones, drawn shades, photo of the president on the wall, bookshelves holding shadow boxes full of military medals. Colonel Jack Rush fit the image, too, with his carefully clipped hair, wiry frame, high, gaunt cheekbones, and immaculate uniform.

"Lime," he said. "At ease. Take a seat." And he indicated the lone chair directly in front of the desk.

"Thank you, sir."

"How are things at the Pentagon these days?" Rush asked.

"About the same, sir."

"I'm sorry you had to pull that duty. I know you prefer spending more time in the field. But as they say, eternal vigilance is the price of liberty."

The full-bird colonel had an impressive fund of aphorisms, maxims, and clichés that he drew on frequently. Lime answered in kind. "In our business, sir, a quiet day is a good day."

"Amen. Well, as you might have guessed, I wouldn't have asked you to report if today were a quiet day." Other than the phones, his desktop held only one folder, liberally stamped and sealed. Now he opened it. "It appears," he said, turning pages, "that we might have a breach in the levee."

These words were spoken almost casually, but upon hearing them, Lime instinctually stiffened.

"Intel is still being assembled," Rush said, "but as you know, with this kind of situation we can't wait. We have to mobilize."

"Of course, sir."

Rush closed the folder and pushed it across the desk. "You'll get further orders via normal channels. But this should give you the background you need to begin an initial reconnaissance."

As Lime reached for the folder, the colonel placed his own palm on it. "Looks like you'll be getting a break from desk duty."

"Yes, sir. Thank you, sir." Rush lifted his palm and allowed Lime to take the folder from the desk and place it in his own lap.

"The missile operations officers in old nuclear silos liked to say their job was ninety-nine-point-nine percent boredom, and point-one percent panic," Rush said. "What we do here for our country is never quite that boring, and with vigilance we're able to keep it panic-free. But the principle is the same. We maintain watch against those who would do us harm. The worst kind of harm: the kind that comes, intentionally or not, from inside. And when necessary, we act. The only difference is those missile officers were given credit for their loyalty. The sacrifices we make for our country—the purpose we've dedicated, and sometimes lost, our lives to— must remain secret."

"It's the most difficult kind of patriotism—and the most important."

This statement came not from Rush, but from

someone behind Lime. Immediately, the colonel stood, and Lime followed his example, turning as he did. To his immense surprise, standing just within the office was Major General Zephyr, in overall command of their unit. Zephyr—his actual name was unknown—was a figure of legend, and Lime had seen him in person only twice before: on his squad's induction day, following advanced training school, and again two years ago, at the end of a particularly puzzling and frustrating hunt.

Lime had not heard him come in or close the door. He realized his presence here could only be to underscore the importance of this mission.

"We're guardians of a sacred trust, Mr. Lime," he said. "Always remember that."

"Yes, sir," Lime replied.

"And there is no more dangerous enemy than the one who appears to be an ally and friend—but whose actions threaten our safety and, indeed, undermine our very existence."

"Yes, sir."

"This time, the stakes are particularly high. Discretion and patience will be of utmost importance, because those who threaten us with their ignorance are very close to home. But you must not let that cloud your judgment . . . or your mission."

"Understood." Yet Lime felt puzzled: everyone in his unit would die to protect America in an instant—no questions asked. How close to home did the general mean? He told himself to wait until he'd read over the material in the folder.

"Very good. You'll be taking your orders—and mission authorizations—directly from Colonel Rush. I wish you good luck."

They saluted, then the general turned and stepped out of the office. Lime blinked once, twice, still mildly shocked. Then he turned back to Rush.

"As I said—no more desk duty for a while." And the colonel offered the ghost of a smile. "Dismissed."

13

THE FOLLOWING AFTERNOON, Nora watched the corkscrew of dust drift off the horizon into blue nothingness, signaling the departure of Corrie, Morwood, and the FBI team with their van carrying the corpses, the bizarre device, and other evidence. Tappan stood next to her—he always seemed to be around, an interested but quiet presence—and he said: "Strange, don't you think?"

"Very."

"Those bodies weren't buried here by accident. There are a million acres around us perfectly suited for that purpose. So why five hundred yards from the Roswell site? There's got to be a connection."

Nora shook her head. "I guess we'll know more when they identify them."

"You think they will?" Tappan asked.

"I *know* they will. Corrie—that is, Agent Swanson—is specially trained. In the last case I worked on with her, she reconstructed the face of a dead man that was so accurate, it was immediately recognized."

"I'd like to hear that story sometime."

Nora turned her attention back to the grid that Emilio and Scott were laying out over the area to be excavated, hammering in the last of the wooden stakes and stringing Day-Glo twine.

"You'll be breaking ground tomorrow," Tappan said, not quite phrasing it as a question.

"I expect to. If we don't stumble over any more dead bodies."

Tappan chuckled.

The sun was low on the horizon and the day's work coming to an end. Corrie and her team had taken longer to finish up than she expected, sifting dirt, screening it, and searching the area. Off to one side, she could see Skip chatting with Bitan. She couldn't hear what they were saying, but Bitan was one of those people who gestured dramatically as he talked, and now he was quite animated indeed. She was relieved Skip had made a good first impression on the famous astronomer—more than good. They were both enthusiasts of the same stripe, and Bitan obviously liked having an acolyte around.

"If you don't mind," Tappan said, nodding at the iPad she was holding, "can you give me a lesson in how that archaeological software works?"

"It's pretty simple," she said. "As we dig, everything we find, every layer removed, every soil sample taken, is photographed in situ and then input to re-create the physical dig in 3D, showing how it has evolved over time. You can rotate it, look at it sideways or even from below—not to mention do all kinds of analysis. As stuff is uncovered, we drop the photos right in. The CPU does the rest."

"Excellent. And what is your plan for these quads? Do you open one at a time, or what?"

"We're going to start with quad one and go across, left to right like a lawn mower, taking a layer of dirt off each time as we go down."

"How far down?"

"Through the 1947 horizon, as deep as the disturbance goes, and then a little deeper to make sure we're in prehorizon strata. SOP."

Vigil pounded in the last stake, tightening and

tying the string around it. He then closed up the survey tripod, slung it over his shoulder, and walked over to them. "Done!" he said with a dusty grin below a pair of round sunglasses. "Piece of cake."

"Glad to hear it," Tappan said. "What are your thoughts about the site, Emilio?"

"It's ideal," Vigil said. "Flat ground, almost no vegetation, soft sand but with enough moisture underneath that it's held in place. Couldn't ask for better."

Now Bitan came drifting over, with Skip in tow. Soon everyone seemed to be gathering, including the Three Engineers. "Very impressive," Bitan said, looking out over the expanse of gridded ground.

Greg Banks turned to Nora. "I was hoping to get soil samples as you proceed."

"Of course. We can take as many as you like, where you like."

"Great. Could we get a hundred-gram sample from each square meter at, say, each twenty-centimeter depth?"

"Done. Are you looking for anything in particular?"

"I want to do mass spectrometer analyses, just

to see what compounds might be present. And I'll be examining the samples microscopically for anything unusual."

"No problem—we archaeologists do sampling like that all the time. Who's doing your mass spec?"

"UT Austin, Applied Research Labs. I plan to FedEx them samples on a daily basis."

Nora nodded. That would cost a fortune, but why not? Nothing but the best for this project.

"Hoping to find alien compounds?" Skip asked.

"Always," Banks said, to a general laugh.

Tappan looked around. "We're done for the day, folks. And I've planned a special celebratory dinner. Cocktails in the dining car at six, dinner at seven."

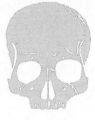

14

Nora entered the Airstream she shared with Skip. It was cozy, two tiny bedrooms on either end with a shared living and dining area in the middle, along with a bathroom with a tiny shower. Skip had set up a nook for Mitty in a corner of the sitting area, with a dog bed and his food and water bowls. While the trailer was small, it wasn't all that much smaller than the house they shared—and was substantially more modern.

Nora went into her bedroom to shed her filthy clothes and change for dinner, unsure what to wear. Deciding that cowboy high style would probably work, she dressed in leather pants, snakeskin boots, and a red silk shirt, set off with a simple turquoise necklace. Emerging from her room, she found Skip in the sitting area, already dressed. His idea of high style was jeans and a clean work shirt.

"What was Noam bending your ear about?" she asked him.

"Just this and that."

"That's rather coy," said Nora teasingly. "Like what?"

"You know, Bitan's a real genius," Skip replied. "He's got a library of air force videos and radar images of UAPs, interviews with people, all kinds of interesting stuff. I spent a few hours early in the day going through it. A lot of the people in the interviews are obviously nuts, but some are not. And the declassified air force footage is wild—high-speed objects maneuvering in ways far beyond any technology we have today. Not to mention interviews with people who'd been abducted."

"Abducted?"

"You've heard the stories. For experiments or possibly even breeding."

"I suppose you watched those videos, too. Alien sex porn."

Skip laughed. "You should take a look. I know you're a skeptic—and that's good. But it's also good to keep an open mind."

Nora looked at him. He was so sincere, his face glowing with enthusiasm.

"I promise," she said with an affectionate smile.

When Nora followed Skip into the "dining car" ten minutes later, she couldn't help but be impressed. A thirty-foot Airstream had been cleared out except for a kitchen in one end, with a table running the length of it. A white tablecloth was draped over the table, on which were arrayed silver candelabras, crystal glasses, snowy linen napkins rolled up in round holders, and ceramic chargers decorated in a retro thirties cowboy motif, with livestock brands around the rim and a picture in the middle of horses, cowboys, and other Western themes.

"Welcome!" said Tappan, gliding over, holding a silver tray on which half a dozen champagne flutes were balanced. "You're the first to arrive."

Nora and Skip each took one. Tappan was dressed in crocodile boots, jeans, and a brown cowboy shirt with pearl buttons and fancy stitching. A silk bandanna around his neck was held in place by a silver slide with an old pawn turquoise cluster. It was clearly not his usual attire, but with his curly black hair and dimples he managed to pull it off.

He put aside the tray, raised his martini, and they clinked glasses.

"To the dig," he said. "May it be out of this world."

"Hear, hear," said Skip.

Bitan arrived, wearing an ill-fitting suit with a poorly tied cravat. "Champagne!" he cried, coming over and lifting a glass off the tray. He glanced around. "It looks like the O.K. Corral around here. Am I the only one trying to uphold a sartorial standard?"

"Not with that suit," said Tappan with a chuckle.

"What's wrong with my suit?"

Tappan fingered the lapel. "A little too much polyester."

"This is the desert," Bitan said defensively. "Clothes need to breathe. I know. I grew up in the Negev."

Vigil and Riordan arrived and, over the next few minutes, the rest of the scientific crew, including the Three Engineers, who always seemed to travel in a group. Kuznetsov was carrying a case holding some sort of oddly shaped musical instrument, which he stowed in a corner.

They mingled for a while, drinking champagne and munching on hors d'oeuvres—smoked salmon, caviar blinis, chilled shrimp, and prosciutto-wrapped melon.

Kuznetsov scarfed down a blini and looked surprised. "I believe this is real Russian caviar!" he cried, helping himself to another.

"It is indeed," said Tappan. "Ossetra from the Caspian Sea, but aqua-farmed, not wild-caught, so it's *responsible* caviar."

Hearing this, Skip pushed his way to the blinis, eating one while snagging two more. Nora noted that he'd quickly polished off two glasses of champagne and was turning to reach for a third. She sidled up to him and gave him a gentle nudge in the ribs. "Take a breather, okay?"

"Right, sis." He withdrew his hand.

Tappan rang a glass and everyone fell silent. He glanced around with twinkling eyes. "I want to tell a little story before we sit down, a story some of you know already."

He paused. His face was flushed, and he radiated excitement and joy. Nora felt she had rarely seen a happier human being.

"The story tells of an incident that happened up at Los Alamos National Laboratory in the summer of 1950, when it was still a secret city. This was during the development of the H-bomb. Enrico Fermi, the famous Italian physicist, went out to lunch with Emil Konopinski, Herbert York, and Edward Teller. All four of them were working on the 'Super,' the original name for the H-bomb. As they were strolling to lunch, they began talking about the many recent reports of UFO sightings, including the Roswell Incident itself. The discussion centered on the probability of the existence of intelligent life elsewhere in space. They all agreed that advanced alien civilizations simply had to exist in the galaxy, given its billions of planets and the billions of years in which intelligent life could develop."

He paused.

"So they sat down to lunch and the conversation drifted on to other things: the usual stuff physicists discuss, like the possibility of faster-than-light travel and so forth. But then, during a lull in the conversation, Fermi suddenly burst out: *But where is everybody?*'

"After a stunned silence, the other physicists began laughing, because they understood Fermi was referring to their earlier conversation. If intelligent life was so prevalent in the galaxy, Fermi wanted to know, then where *were* they? Why hadn't we been visited, and many times?

"When Fermi returned to his office, he scribbled down some rough calculations. Given the vast number of stars in the galaxy like our sun; given the high probability that many of these had Earth-like planets with liquid water; given that many of these stars were billions of years older than the sun—it stood to reason some of those planets had developed intelligent life long ago. And those intelligent beings surely had conquered interstellar travel. Hence, Fermi's puzzlement: Where were they? They should have been here ages ago!

"And that, my friends, was the origin of the famous conundrum known as the Fermi paradox. The solution to that paradox is at the heart of what we're trying to achieve here. All evidence points to aliens having *already* visited Earth. And here, in this remote desert, is where we will finally find the proof. Suffice to say, it will be the greatest discovery science has ever made: to learn that we are not alone, that there are others in the universe like us, intelligent and self-aware, with knowledge and wisdom far beyond what we possess." He raised his martini. "So here's to our project—and the solution to the Fermi paradox."

He tossed down his drink. Nora and the rest did likewise.

"And now, let's take our seats."

Nora found herself seated with Bitan on her left, Kuznetsov on her right, and Tappan across from her. The conversation rose as Max, the sous-chef-cum-server, began bringing out salads and filling glasses with wine.

Skip, sitting on the other side of Kuznetsov, turned to him. "I'm Skip, in case you forgot," he said, proffering his hand.

"Vitaly, in case you forgot."

"Are you Russian?"

"As a matter of fact, I am. I'm here on an H-1B visa."

"What's that?"

As Kuznetsov explained, Nora tuned out the conversation and turned her attention to Tappan. "That was an interesting story you told about the Fermi paradox."

"Yes," Tappan said. "I feel a special affinity for Fermi, in a way. We're both of Italian descent—

my mother's name was Mazzei. Fermi was re-
cruited for the Manhattan Project and traveled
to Los Alamos in disguise under the name Henry
Farmer. But he had such a heavy Italian accent
that everybody knew it was a fake name as soon
as he opened his mouth. Previously, he'd built
the world's first atomic reactor, in a basement at
the University of Chicago."

"So what do *you* think is the answer to the
Fermi paradox?" Nora asked. "Why haven't we
heard from aliens?"

Tappan gave her a dazzling smile. "That *is* the
question, isn't it? Dozens of answers have been
advanced. I favor the zoo hypothesis."

"You mean, we're in a monkey house and
don't know it?"

Tappan laughed. "That's not far off. It's similar
to what Noam was telling your brother the other
day. The galaxy, the idea goes, is governed by
an alliance of highly advanced civilizations, but
we're not yet ready to join them. We're either
too primitive or too dangerous, or perhaps too
dumb. Contact would disrupt or even destroy
us. So we're kept in a sort of nature preserve,
where we're being observed but contact isn't
allowed."

"But by that chain of reasoning," Nora said, "don't you think that, if you do succeed and discover evidence of an alien visitation, people will be upset? I mean, we'll know we're in a zoo."

Tappan laughed. "I think we can handle it. That's the kind of knowledge that might transcend our petty squabbles and unite us, free us from war and conflict once and for all."

At this, Bitan raised his finger and leaned toward Nora. "I would take that one step further."

"How so?" Nora asked.

Bitan wagged the finger. "They're about to open the zoo doors. We're about to be set free. We're about to be given the secrets of the universe. And it will happen in our lifetimes—possibly within years or even months."

"What makes you so sure?" Nora asked.

"These UAP sightings, the Roswell thing, the abductions. We're being probed. Tested to see how we might react. And so far, so good. I expect at any moment they will draw back the curtain."

"Sort of like the Second Coming?" Skip asked.

"Well, in a way. Peace will reign. Poverty and hunger and strife will disappear." Bitan spread his arms like Moses on the mount, and his voice deepened.

"From what I've been reading," Skip said, "some think we have it all wrong. They say the aliens are the bad guys, set on conquest and pillaging."

"Doesn't it make sense," Bitan said, "that the more intelligent a being is, the more capacity it has for compassion and ethics—and the less logic there is in violence?"

"Makes sense to me," said Skip.

"I left SETI," Bitan went on, "because I realized they were only going to *listen* to the universe. I felt we needed to take the initiative, show that we're interested and willing to join the galaxy-wide civilization out there. When they shot down my proposal to create CE-TIP, the Contacting Extraterrestrial Intelligence Project—that is, to beam messages to nearby stars—I had to resign."

"So you're part of this project," Nora said, "because you feel it's important to discover intelligent life visited Earth—in hopes of hastening the day of revelation?"

Bitan beamed. "While at this point it's all still speculation, the answer is...yes."

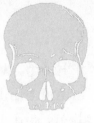

15

Corrie Swanson gazed at the two sets of human remains, carefully arranged on two gurneys in the middle of the forensic lab, under bright lights, in the basement of the Albuquerque Field Office. They had completed the autopsies—such as they were. Most of the flesh was gone, leaving only a few desiccated bits of muscle and internal organs. The meager haul of physical evidence lay spread out on a third gurney: two .45 shells, the object from HiChem Industries, some loose change recovered from the pocket of the male victim, and a key. Also on the gurney stood an array of evidence containers with samples and histology slides, ready for further testing and analysis.

"Are we all ready, then?" said Nigel Lathrop, the forensic laboratory manager, who had run the lab seemingly forever. He had a brisk British accent and was a sort of retrograde personality, even for the FBI. "Everything tip-top?"

"It would seem so," said Corrie carefully. In Lathrop's heyday, a single forensic pathologist was expected to do everything. The problem was, he hadn't kept up with the field since he left graduate school, but he still carried around a superior attitude and he had a tendency to pooh-pooh, in his condescending British way, Corrie's own experience and training. Not to put too fine a point on it, but he was a jerk. Morwood had warned Corrie to get along with him, and "getting along" was what she'd been doing for the past seven months. This was a perfect case in point: she had done 90 percent of the work while Lathrop fussed and fiddled with inconsequential stuff and tried to look busy.

Morwood arrived right on the dot of one, with Special Agent in Charge Julio Garcia, head of the Albuquerque FO. Garcia was a big, beefy, soft-spoken agent with a circle beard shot through with gray, impeccably dressed in blue. She'd only seen him in the path lab once before, and his surprise presence made her nervous.

"Agent Swanson," said Garcia, extending his

hand. "I hope you don't mind. Agent Morwood was telling me about your case, and I couldn't help but take an interest—as a bystander, of course."

"Thank you, sir." She liked that phrase, *your case*. Garcia seemed like a pretty good guy, even if a bit remote.

"That's right," said Lathrop, "the results of our work are quite striking, quite striking indeed. We've been working day and night on these two poor souls."

In the past few days, since the bodies had come in, Corrie had been working almost round-the-clock; Lathrop had gone home at six and returned at nine in the morning. But she said nothing.

Morwood turned. "Good lord, look at those faces."

"Let's start with that," said Corrie quickly. "The histology sections of the skin suggested a strong acid had come in contact with it, and a chemical analysis confirmed it: HCl, hydrochloric acid. It looks like both individuals had highly concentrated hydrochloric acid splashed or sprayed into their faces—repeatedly, in fact, as evidenced by the microscopic layering of damage I saw in the samples."

"Torture, in other words?" asked Morwood.

"They were tortured, yes. But not with acid. I believe the acid was applied postmortem to erase their facial features, make identification harder. The same acid was applied to the fingers—most likely to dissolve the fingerprints."

"Extraordinary. Does it mean we can't do facial reconstructions?"

"The acid penetrated to the bone in places, but no more than surface etching. We should be able to do reconstructions."

"And the cause of death?"

"Execution-style shots to the left temple of each victim, with powder burns and flakes. We recovered both shell casings. The muzzle of the gun, a .45, was pressed to the skin."

"I see," said Morwood. "What about the torture?"

"Fingernails were removed from the thumb and pinkie of the right hand of the man, and from the index and middle fingers of the woman's hands."

Morwood bent over the bodies. He pulled on a pair of gloves and gently lifted one of the hands, examining the fingers. "Crushed as well."

"Yes, sir. Several fingers on both victims were

fractured. Pliers or a similar tool, used to crush and twist."

Lathrop, impatient to break in, now interrupted. "It was torture most foul. We've removed the remains of internal organs to test for toxins and so forth. We'll ship out those evidence containers tomorrow."

"Excellent," murmured Morwood. "ID?"

Lathrop again spoke over Corrie. "ID, yes, very important. Extremely important. Both victims had dental work, and we've got X-rays and are looking for a match in the databases. Unfortunately the acid erased any chance of fingerprint identification. The male is about forty to fifty, the female thirty-five to forty-five. I might note both sported wedding bands, and she had a modest diamond engagement ring—deformed, no doubt during the torture."

This all came out in a rush.

"Wedding rings?" Morwood asked sharply. "They were married?"

"Certainly, and probably to each other," Lathrop said. "In 1947, a woman wouldn't normally go around with a man not her husband."

"And the date?"

"Based on the coins found in the pocket,"

Lathrop went on, "1947 seems like a probable date, since there was an uncirculated penny of that year, several coins predating that, but nothing later. So 1947 is the *terminus post quem*. The manufacturing date of the shell casings is 1947 as well."

Corrie was annoyed to hear that Latin phrase, which Lathrop loved to employ and had once mocked her for not knowing.

"Any trace of radiation?" Morwood asked.

"First thing we checked," said Lathrop. "None."

Morwood said, "You probably know of the two bomb scientists who went missing up at Los Alamos in 1947—vanished into thin air. They were later shown to be spies, and it was presumed they had defected to the Soviet Union. When these two bodies were discovered, I thought we might have found them...until one turned out to be female. Still, I wonder if there might be a connection. Corrie, what do you think?" he added as Lathrop started to open his mouth again.

"I think that's a lead worth looking into, sir," said Corrie. This, she realized, was why Morwood had been so interested in the two bodies— and why he'd looked disappointed when one turned out to be female.

"Any success in figuring out what the device is?" Morwood asked.

"Not yet," said Corrie. "HiChem Industries no longer exists. They did classified defense research, aeronautical engineering, missile and weapons design, that sort of thing. We've got pictures of it out to several engineers."

"I'd like to check it out of evidence," said Morwood, "and bring it to Los Alamos. There's a fellow I know up there, a scientist, now semi-retired. Dr. Angus Eastchester. He might be able to identify it."

"Of course," said Corrie. "If you want, you can take it now. We'll do the checkout paperwork after you leave." She picked it up and put it back in its evidence box, then sealed it and made a note on the label.

"Much obliged," said Morwood. "I'll sign it back in directly after showing it to Eastchester."

Garcia, who had said nothing, nodded approvingly.

Morwood looked at Corrie. "You're doing a fine job, Agent Swanson. And thank you, Dr. Lathrop, for your invaluable contribution. This is a most peculiar case." He shook his head. "I wonder what Dr. Eastchester will have to say about it."

16

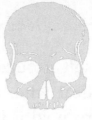

THE DAY HAD dawned, as usual, without a cloud in the sky. But what had started out fine had quickly been spoiled by a wind that kicked up early, and as the day wore on, it increased. Nora found working unpleasant, the wind scouring up billows of dust and blowing it across the excavation site. There were no trees to slow it down. The dust accumulated in her hair and face and clothes and got into her eyes, and she could feel it crunch between her teeth.

Mitty, who normally spent the day next to Skip, finally got so irritated that he abandoned the dig and retreated under one of the trailers.

Despite the dust, the dig was progressing apace. It was, as Vigil had said, some of the easiest excavation terrain she'd worked in—flat, soft ground, with no roots and few stones to deal with, and just enough caliche in the soil to hold it in place. She and Vigil methodically worked the quads, going down layer by layer, while Skip ran the screening operation, putting the sand first through a coarse screen, then a fine one. Kuznetsov and Cecilia Toth had used ground-penetrating radar to provide high-resolution charts of each quad, showing what might lie under the surface. But the shadows that appeared on the GPR, once they uncovered them, turned out to be of little interest.

Tappan had spent the morning watching the excavation, undeterred by wind or boredom. He was always about, asking questions, offering suggestions, and otherwise making his presence felt—but not, Nora thought, in a bad way. She wondered how he was running his other businesses remotely.

Nora carefully took the dirt samples from each quad Banks had asked for, one hundred grams at a time, sealing them in glass containers, labeled and set into a tray. When the tray was full, Skip carried them to the Three Engineers' lab in Quonset 1.

Nora was relieved beyond measure when

lunchtime rolled around. They all retreated to the shelter of Quonset 1, where a lunch had been laid out, with a variety of sandwiches, salads, tea, and coffee.

Nora helped herself to a cup of coffee and a sandwich as everyone sat down, tired and dusty. Nobody said much. They had now uncovered the beginning of the long groove in the sand, and she was curious to follow that to its endpoint, which went too deep for GPR or the magnetometer to reach. There might still be something there, she thought; fragments or pieces of whatever had plowed into the ground.

Just as she was finishing her sandwich and starting to dread going back out—she could hear the wind buffeting the Quonset hut roof—Greg Banks came into the room. He had been absent at lunch. He paused and held up his hands, a broad smile on his face. "Everybody," he said, "I have a little surprise."

He tried to sound casual, but his voice was tense with excitement.

"What is it?" Tappan asked.

Banks smiled mysteriously. "You shall see. Please follow me."

Everyone followed Banks into the next hut,

where Skip was already waiting. There, the few artifacts they had recovered that morning lay spread out on a large table, each one tagged and labeled. Nora had seen most of it already, except for the stuff recovered in the screening, and it was a pretty miserable collection of mid-century garbage: old cigarette butts, bottle caps, some pieces of glass, a broken whiskey pint flask, a withered pencil stub, a frozen penknife, several buttons, and a rivet from a pair of jeans. They had also found several pennies, a nickel, and a quarter—all dating to 1947 or prior—and a couple of prehistoric Indian flint chips, along with the base of a broken arrowhead. All very terrestrial. At the far end of the table lay a row of Banks's glass dishes full of dirt, next to a stereo zoom microscope.

"Now, there's an impressive collection of alien artifacts!" Tappan said with a laugh, scanning the table.

"If so, then aliens are as prone to littering as human beings," Banks said. "But that's not what I brought you to see." He led them to the stereo microscope. "I've spread some grains of dirt on the glass slide that's currently on the stage plate. I want you each to take a look, saying nothing.

And then we will go around the group and you'll each tell me what you saw."

For a seemingly quiet guy, Banks had a flair for drama. Nora's curiosity was aroused.

They each looked through the binocular eyepieces, examining the grains under high magnification. Nobody said anything, and it was soon Nora's turn. At first, all she could see were the giant grains of sand, bits of fluffy dirt, and fragments of plants and roots. But mingled among them were some round spheres of a greenish, transparent glassy material.

Nora stepped back. She wasn't entirely sure what it meant, exactly—but the implications were not lost on her.

"All right," said Banks. "What did you see? Let's start with you, boss."

"Well, I saw a lot of dirt and sand." Tappan laughed. "I'm not sure I know what to look for, frankly. Some of that sand came in interesting shapes, like crystals."

At this, Banks's eyebrows went up. He exchanged glances with Skip, who seemed to be in the know. "Anyone else see anything?" He went around the room, but nobody had noted anything unusual beyond the crystals in the sand, some of which, when magnified, looked rather like diamonds.

Banks began to grow impatient. "Crystals! My friends, all sand under magnification looks like crystals. It's mostly silicon dioxide, after all. Forget the bloody crystals! What about the microspheres?"

A silence settled.

"How did those grains become perfectly spherical?" He paused, looking around.

"Because they're molten droplets?" Nora asked.

"Finally!" Banks broke into a grin. "They're molten droplets that cooled in the air. Perhaps some of you also noted the greenish color? That's a typical color of sand that's been melted or vaporized. If you look closely, you'll see faint swirling lines on some of the droplets. Those are called Schlieren flow lines. They're typical of sand that's been vaporized and then condenses in the atmosphere and falls back to Earth while cooling from a molten state."

Tappan raised his head. "What does it mean?"

"Such droplets have a name: microtektites. Up until now, they have only been associated with powerful meteorite strikes. Yet I've found microtektites in every sample of dirt we've looked at so far. They're everywhere—millions of them." He looked around, the drama building. "So I wondered: Is there any evidence of a meteorite strike in this vicinity? I looked into that, and the answer is no."

Another dramatic pause.

"The conclusion is inescapable: something struck the ground here with such violence that it vaporized a mass of sand. Such an impact could not come from a terrestrial crash of any kind— a missile or plane. There's not enough energy in such situations to melt sand. It therefore had to have come from outer space. Something that entered Earth's atmosphere at very high speed and struck the ground here."

"Could it have been a satellite?" asked Nora.

"Yes, a satellite falling out of high orbit would be fast enough to melt sand on impact. The problem, Nora, is that in 1947, which is evidently when this impact occurred—judging by these artifacts you've found—there were no satellites. Sputnik wasn't launched until 1957."

A silence filled the room as the implications sank in.

"Well," said Tappan, "that's pretty stunning, Greg. I'd say we've just found the smoking gun, or something close to it. Proof that this was extraterrestrial."

"Could it have been," Nora asked weakly, "an *unknown* meteorite impact?"

"It's possible," said Banks. "But these microtektites seem to be associated with the groove you're excavating, and it's highly unlikely a meteorite made that trench. We would have found fragments. I've looked at numerous dirt samples, I've raked them with magnets, I've done chemical tests. There isn't a trace of meteoritic debris, neither nickel-iron nor chondritic. No—whatever plowed that groove did not break up into fragments. It may have left subtle chemical traces, however. I'm having that tested now—I should have the results in a few days."

Nora swallowed. This was pretty stunning evidence in favor of an extraterrestrial UFO. She glanced around the room and noticed an unusual expression on Bitan's face. It was almost beatific with excitement. The others, in varying degrees, also expressed elation. These were by and large true believers, and they'd just been handed the proof they so fervently desired.

Tappan stepped over and gave Banks's hand a vigorous shake, clapped him on the back, and turned to the group. "This is a big moment. This proves we're on the right track." He lowered his voice. "We need to keep this discovery under wraps. *Absolutely under wraps.* Do you all understand? You've signed NDAs, but I want to emphasize that we say nothing to no one. Because if word leaks that we've found proof this is a UFO crash site, the press will be all over this, the government might intervene—and our work will be disrupted, at the very least."

Everyone nodded their silent understanding.

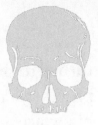

17

Corrie painstakingly attached the last flesh-depth marker on a cast of the first skull, glanced at the clock—precisely 5:00 PM—then stood back to admire her handiwork. At John Jay College of Criminal Justice, she'd graduated with a simultaneous BS/MA with a specialty in forensic anthropology and facial reconstruction. Usually, it took a team of two to reconstruct a face from a skull—a forensic anthropologist and an artist—but she had studied both disciplines and was qualified to do an entire facial reconstruction by herself. It was a painstaking process involving both craft and art. Computer simulations, despite what was shown on TV, were just not as good as what could be accomplished by careful reconstruction working by hand.

Of course, Lathrop knew nothing about this, having graduated a million years ago and never making any attempt to keep up with the field. She couldn't wait for him to retire. But here he was, busying himself with nothing while she warmed up a block of Plasticine in a bowl of water over a Bunsen burner, getting ready to sculpt the muscles on the skull cast.

"Knock, knock," said Morwood, leaning in the doorway.

"Come in!" cried Lathrop, rushing over to shift some boxes away from the entry. "We're making brilliant progress, Agent Morwood."

Corrie waited, saying nothing, while Lathrop led Morwood over to the worktable. Corrie decided to let Lathrop go ahead and talk all he wanted. She was tired of trying to compete with him, and besides, she felt confident that Morwood would see through it.

"As you can see," Lathrop said, "we've made a cast of the male skull, and now we're about to lay on the muscles and flesh—and give this poor victim a face and, hopefully, a name."

"Very nice," said Morwood, bending over the skull with a sidelong glance at Corrie that spoke volumes. "Nice work indeed. Any chance you'll get that ID soon?"

Morwood had looked at Corrie while asking the question, but Lathrop forged ahead anyway. "Without doubt. We also have dental records. Some rather odd dentistry, actually: the male had four crowns made not of gold, or even the silver amalgam typical of the time, but rather stainless steel."

The composition of the crown material was something else Corrie had discovered on her own.

Morwood raised his eyebrows. "How unusual is that?"

"Most unusual," said Lathrop quickly.

"That should help pinpoint where the dental work was done, shouldn't it?" Morwood asked Corrie directly.

"Quite possibly, sir," she said quietly.

Abruptly, Morwood was taken by a brief fit of coughing. Then he cleared his throat. "May I make a suggestion? Why not send those four crowns to the main lab in Quantico? They have world-class specialists in dental forensics."

"An excellent idea," said Lathrop. "Although unfortunately no prints remained for us to match against the databases, we've sent off DNA for sequencing. I'm quite confident, Agent Morwood, that we'll soon be able to identify both individuals."

"I'd like you both to present this at our weekly meeting next Tuesday. Think you'll have an ID by then?"

"Yes," said Lathrop, even as Corrie said, "No."

Morwood looked at each of them in turn. "Which is it?"

"The DNA sequencing," said Corrie, "won't be done by then. The dental work might lead somewhere, but I doubt we'll know by Tuesday. That only leaves the facial reconstructions, but they date back over seventy years, so it's unlikely anyone's alive to recognize them. It'll take some time to match them with existing photographs, if we can do it at all."

"Agent Morwood," said Lathrop in an ingratiating tone, "I'm rather more sanguine than our resident Cassandra here. On the contrary, I believe we *will* have an ID for you by Tuesday, or at least something close."

Morwood nodded and, as his eyes flickered again to Corrie, she thought she caught a veiled warning. He knew how offended she must be, and he was cautioning her not to react. She swallowed hard. *Our resident Cassandra here.* Was she really going to let that one go?

"You're both doing a fine job," Morwood said. "Corrie, as you're the agent in charge, I'll expect you to give the main presentation. I hope you won't mind, Dr. Lathrop."

He nodded curtly. "Of course not."

"Very good." Morwood looked at his watch. "I have to go—the good Dr. Eastchester has granted me a seven o'clock audience at his home in Los Alamos." And he left.

A long silence ensued. Corrie made a decision— she turned to Lathrop and said in a low, even voice: "I did not appreciate your Cassandra comment. If you make another remark like that, I'll file a complaint."

"Oh, what rubbish!" he said. "There was nothing wrong with my comment. Cassandra, as you apparently *don't* know, was the ancient prophetess who spoke the truth and was never believed. So you see, my dear, it wasn't an insult—it was a compliment."

This little speech confounded Corrie, but she nevertheless felt sure she had been insulted. The "my dear" didn't help.

"It isn't just the Cassandra comment. It's everything since I first arrived." She tried to speak in a measured tone, choosing her words carefully. "You've minimized and belittled my contributions. You've taken credit for things you didn't do. And you've treated me in a condescending and, frankly, sexist manner."

"Well, well," huffed Lathrop, "I didn't realize you were such a tender creature. This is the FBI, my dear, not the DAR."

That did it. Corrie lanced him with narrowed eyes. "Here's something you seem to forget: not only do I *outrank* you as a special agent, but I am far more educated in forensic science than you. I doubt you've cracked a book on the subject in twenty years."

All the color drained from Lathrop's face and Corrie realized she had scored a direct hit. Her feelings of triumph, however, quickly gave way to apprehension as she saw just how hurt he was. She suddenly wished she could take back what she had just said.

His face as white as a slab of suet, Lathrop stiffly walked away and exited via the lab door, closing it ever so fussily behind him.

18

THE GPS ON Special Agent Morwood's phone informed him to go left at the intersection of Trinity and Oppenheimer. He made the turn, marveling at the street names in this once-secret town that had launched the Atomic Age. He soon arrived at 122 Oppenheimer Drive, a modest condo painted gray with white trim, and parked the car in a designated spot in front, next to an antique pickup truck. He fetched the large evidence container by its handles out of the back seat and carried it to the entrance, but before he could even ring the bell, Angus Eastchester had opened the door. Years had passed since Morwood had first met him as a rookie agent, but the scientist had aged gracefully, sporting a shock of white Einsteinian hair, a ruddy face, horn-rimmed glasses, and an appropriately rumpled tweed jacket with leather patches. He was leaning on a beautiful old Malacca cane with a gold head.

"Please come in!" Eastchester said. "Come in!"

Morwood followed him into a modest living room. Eastchester offered him a seat in a wing chair that had seen better days. Morwood was surprised a Nobel laureate lived in such simple, even spartan, surroundings. Didn't a couple of million dollars come with the prize? Some people just didn't care about money or possessions.

"Thank you for agreeing to see me, Dr. Eastchester," Morwood said.

"Let's get one thing straight," Eastchester said. "I'm Angus and you're Hale. No need for formalities here."

"Of course," said Morwood. Eastchester was still as warm and unpretentious as he'd been twenty-three years ago, before he'd won his Nobel. It didn't seem to have changed him.

"Before we begin, can I offer you anything? Coffee? Tea? Water?"

"I'd love some coffee." It had been a long drive from Albuquerque to Los Alamos, and Morwood needed refreshing.

"Me too." Eastchester called: "Annie?"

A matronly woman came out of the kitchen.

"Coffee, please."

"Coming right up." She vanished again.

"When I hit eighty," said Eastchester, nodding toward the kitchen, "my children imposed someone upon me. To help out during the day. I broke a hip last year and it hasn't been easy."

"I'm sorry to hear that."

"Bah! The infirmities of age. What a bore. We gain honors, age, and wealth, and then just when we're ready to enjoy them, Father Time comes swooping down and screws up our bodies. *Pulvis et umbra sumus* and all that."

"I know what you mean. I've got this damn lung situation, which slows me down."

"I hear you're a supervisory agent these days. You've come a long way, Hale, from the nervous rookie I recall working his first case with that senior agent, what was his name?"

"Mickey Starr. A case that's still open, unfortunately. It rankles."

"I can imagine it would."

The coffee arrived in an elegant silver coffee set and Morwood took his cup gratefully, adding cream and two lumps of sugar. He stirred and took a long, satisfying pull.

"Now that we're fortified," said Eastchester, "let's have a look at this mysterious thing you brought."

"Of course." Morwood slipped on a pair of latex gloves, placed the box on the coffee table, and unlatched it. He took the object out with his gloved hands and laid it on the table.

A look of complete astonishment bloomed on Eastchester's face, and he exhaled abruptly. "My, my," he said. "Where did you get *that*?"

"You know what it is?"

"Would you mind turning it over, please?"

Morwood complied.

Eastchester looked at it carefully, then sat back, shaking his head. "If I'm not mistaken, it's a highly classified component of the early H-bombs. Known as a 'dial-a-yield.'"

"Which is?"

"That will take a little explaining. As you may know, a hydrogen bomb gets most of its energy from the fusing of hydrogen into helium. That reaction requires so much heat and pressure it must be initiated by an atomic explosion. The H-bomb is essentially a fission bomb that employs plutonium, which *then* triggers a fusion reaction in a mass of hydrogen right next to it."

Morwood wasn't sure he understood, but he let Eastchester go on without interruption.

"H-bombs don't use normal hydrogen," Eastchester continued. "They use an isotope called tritium, also written as ^{3}H. You see that symbol, printed on the side? It's a form of hydrogen that has two extra neutrons in its nucleus."

"Right."

"This device stores the tritium inside the bomb. You can change the yield of the bomb, in this case from one to twenty megatons, just by turning that dial. That device feeds either more or less tritium into the reaction chamber ahead of detonation. The more tritium, the bigger the explosion. Hence the name dial-a-yield. If you want to bomb Moscow, say, you might want to crank it up to twenty megatons to take out the entire city. If, on the other hand, you're bombing an airfield or a factory, a measly one megaton would suffice."

"Ghastly calculations," said Morwood.

"Without doubt the Russians have had similar devices in their H-bombs."

"It's still classified?"

"Very." He leaned forward. "Can I ask where the heck you got this?"

"It's a rather strange story. And it has to remain confidential."

"Of course."

"There's an eccentric billionaire, fellow named Lucas Tappan—"

"The satellite and green-energy fellow."

"Right. He's also into UFOs, and he's leading an archaeological investigation of the Roswell site, where that UFO was supposed to have crashed in 1947."

Eastchester's bushy eyebrows shot up. "Digging up the Roswell site? How perverse."

"During the initial survey, the archaeologist doing the fieldwork found a grave a few hundred yards from the site. Two bodies were buried in it—along with that device. They were a man and a woman, both homicide victims, bearing signs of torture—followed by execution."

"Good lord! Have you identified them?"

"Not yet. For a moment, however, I thought they might be the two scientists who vanished from Los Alamos in 1947. Those spies, Headley and Warshinski, who some say defected to the Soviet Union. Others, including me, think they might have been murdered. Except one of these bodies belonged to a woman—so it clearly wasn't them."

"Los Alamos was a secret city back then," Eastchester said. "Everyone leaving was thoroughly searched. I wonder how this device got smuggled out. That would be no easy thing. But, Hale, it makes me think: Could it be connected with that unsolved case you worked on as a rookie, the murder of our nuclear scientist in 1999?"

"Not possible. Those two bodies recently found at Roswell long predate the 1999 case."

"Of course." Eastchester frowned, his brow creasing in thought, lips pursed. A silence gathered in the room. He then said, "May I?" gesturing at the device.

"If you don't mind slipping these on." Morwood took a spare pair of gloves from his pocket and handed them over. Eastchester pulled them on, then picked up the device and examined it closely, turning it this way and that. "This is definitely of LANL making. Rather early one, I would think. What do you intend to do with it?"

"We have a secure storage area for classified

evidence. Now that you've explained what it is, it'll go in there when we've finished examining it."

He nodded. "Good." He turned it over. "It looks almost brand-new."

"There's not much rain out there in the desert, and it was buried three feet down."

Eastchester gingerly placed the device back on the table and peeled off his gloves. "You've certainly got a mystery on your hands, my government friend! UFOs, spies, torture, murder, H-bombs. Hell, when you retire, you can write a novel about it!"

19

Nora peeked in the lab door of Quonset 1. It was seven in the evening, the sun was setting, and the lab was dim and quiet. Everyone had gone back to their quarters to get ready for their dinner shift—except for one. She could see Tappan in the back of the lab, in a pool of light, bending over one of the tables.

When he heard her enter, he straightened up. "Nora!" His voice echoed in the empty space. "Thanks for agreeing to see me at this late hour. Lock the door, please."

Nora shut the door and turned the bolt. She was curious what he wanted to show her. He'd been closeted in the lab with Greg Banks most of the afternoon, and when Banks emerged, the man had been completely silent and gone straight off to his trailer.

"Come around the table, I want to show you something." He was dressed in a black collarless shirt, open-necked, and jeans, and she was immediately struck by the suppressed energy radiating from him.

She walked around the table, on which a number of charts were spread out.

"You've seen these before, right, Nora?"

"Of course. They're mass spectrometry charts."

"Good. I've got a little problem for you." He pulled a sheet from the top of the pile and slid it in front of her. "Take a look at this one."

Nora examined the vertical bar graph. It showed the "fingerprint" of some chemical compound she didn't recognize, quite complicated, displaying dozens of vertical bars of different heights across various elemental masses.

"See anything unusual?"

She looked closer and then noticed that to the far right of the graph was a vertical bar way out on the atomic scale.

"You've got an error here," she said, pointing to the bar.

"An error?"

"Well, it shows an atomic mass that's impossibly high."

"Impossible? What if I told you that Banks ran these mass spectra no less than five times with five different samples...and got the same reading every time?"

Nora shook her head. "I'm not a chemist, so maybe I'm missing something, but that mass is too high for any known element."

"*Known* element. Greg Banks thinks it's a super-heavy element that no one has seen before."

She looked at him quizzically.

"I spent the afternoon with Greg trying to figure out the molecular structure from these spectra. He tells me they appear to be similar to an oxide of the rare metals yttrium and palladium, with hydrogen cations. Except that the palladium has been replaced by this unknown superheavy element."

"I'm afraid my physics is a little rusty," Nora said.

He swiped his hand through his hair and went on. "The atomic number of uranium is ninety-two. That means it has ninety-two protons in its nucleus. Hydrogen has one, helium has two, and so forth. But every element *beyond* uranium can only be created in the lab—not in nature. As you go up the scale of atomic numbers beyond uranium, the elements get heavier and heavier, and they become increasingly unstable and short-lived. The atoms just fly apart. They have names like americium, berkelium, einsteinium, moscovium, all the way up to number 118, oganesson. That element was only confirmed in 2002, and it lasts for just one five-hundredth of a second before decaying into something else."

As he spoke, Tappan began pacing, his long legs taking big strides, then pivoting and walking, and pivoting again.

"But here's the weird thing: physicists believe that a little farther up the periodic table, around element 120 or so, there's an 'island of stability'—a cluster of elements that don't decay right away. They last a long time, possibly millions of years."

He stopped in front of Nora, and she could feel his excitement. "That bar you thought was an error? It's not. It's a superheavy element. It's element 126, in fact, because it has 126 protons in its nucleus. It also has 184 neutrons. Both of those numbers, 184 neutrons and 126 protons, are called 'magic numbers' by physicists because they exactly fill electron shells. That is what gives this element 126 its remarkable stability."

Nora listened, becoming increasingly spell-bound.

"The bottom line is this: Even though we know element 126 can theoretically exist, we can't make it. It's too difficult. We don't have an accelerator with enough energy, and we don't have the right ingredients. It is technologically beyond human science."

He paused. "But here it is. It looks like *someone* was able to make it. My question to you, Nora, is: *Who?*"

Nora hesitated. "Aliens," she said, half-jokingly.

He gazed at her a long time, and then smiled, his dimples appearing. "You said it, not me."

Nora tried to absorb this. In combination with the microtektites they'd discovered, this appeared to leave little room for doubt: this was indeed the crash site of an advanced, ex-traterrestrial ship.

She found herself breathing hard, her heart accelerating. Little room for doubt—and yet she realized she was clinging to that doubt with something like desperation. A part of her, she now understood, was simply not ready to accept a conclusion—however obvious—that would alter her perception of the world so significantly.

Her storm of confusion wasn't due to this discovery alone: it was, in part, because of the closeness of Tappan's physical presence. The intensification of her heartbeat, the tingling feeling in her limbs, the scent of his excitement—these were things she hadn't felt in a long time.

But Tappan seemed oblivious—he was too intoxicated with the discovery, it seemed, to think of anything else.

She took a deep breath and stepped back.

"And there's something else," Tappan said. "Even more important. That yttrium-palladium-hydron compound I mentioned earlier? It's almost a room-temperature superconductor."

"That's not possible."

"Then you know what I'm getting at! Something that conducts electricity at room temperature without resistance: we've been trying to make such a material for fifty years. It would revolutionize everything from computing to energy transmission. But in *this* compound, element 126 is substituted for palladium, and it appears to be a room-temperature superconductor: the holy grail of materials science."

He stepped forward and gripped her shoulders. "Nora, this nails it. This is the proof we've been looking for. This is an alloy that could only have been engineered by a technology far more advanced than ours. *Alien* technology."

As his hands gently held her, she tried to keep focus. Extraordinary conclusions, she tried to tell herself, required extraordinary evidence—and there was always a danger when people wanted very badly to believe something.

He embraced her shoulders for a while as silence fell. Then he dropped his hands. "Nora, you're not saying anything. What do you think?"

"I'm..." She halted.

His glowing face and shining gray eyes, so close to hers, were becoming increasingly distracting. "I'm impressed," she finally said weakly.

He laughed. "Impressed? That's all?"

"Give me a chance to process it."

"Of course, of course! God, I must sound like a fanatic." He waved it all away with a sweep of his hand. "But you *do* realize what this means, right?"

She fell silent.

"You're a natural skeptic. I get it. But as I said, we ran five independent tests on five samples. All came up with that same superheavy elemental line, way out there alone on the m/z axis."

"Which layers did the samples come from?" Nora finally asked.

"The beginning of the trench, where the object first struck the ground at high velocity. Whatever plowed into the sand shed that substance."

A silence fell as Tappan began gathering up the charts. "I'm going to lock these in my safe. I'd like to keep this under wraps for now."

"Wait. You're not going to tell the group?" Nora asked.

His smile went away. "Not yet."

"Why?"

Now the smile returned. "Because, Nora, I hope to win you over first! You're the skeptic I want to convert." Suddenly, he looked at his watch. "Good God, it's long past my martini hour. Would you care to join me? This calls for a celebration."

Nora felt herself blush at the invitation—even if it was harmless—because the thoughts that unexpectedly came into her own head were not quite so innocent. She hoped it wasn't obvious. "No thanks, it's been a long day."

"Of course, of course. A 'maybe' is fine for now. But I'm going to get you to *yes* before long—I promise."

20

Skip, in the process of giving Mitty his evening walk, watched Nora go off to Quonset 1. As he turned to take the dog back to the trailer, he was approached by Bitan. Twilight gathered over the immense landscape and the first star had appeared in the west—actually, Skip thought, not a star but a planet: Venus, setting just behind the sun.

"Got a minute?" Bitan said. His voice was hushed, confidential.

"Sure."

"Let's take a walk."

Bitan led Skip away from the encampment, walking quickly on his short, stubby legs. A fragrant spring breeze swept across the mesa, carrying with it the scent of dust and some mysterious blooming desert flower. Mitty followed them eagerly.

They walked perhaps a quarter of a mile; then Bitan abruptly stopped and turned back toward the encampment, nodding in its direction. "What do you see?"

Skip wondered if this was a trick question. "Nothing, really, just some lights."

"Precisely," Bitan said. "We've been walking for just five minutes, and covered—what, maybe several hundred meters? But already that dig is little more than a few gleams against the horizon."

Skip nodded.

"People are funny creatures," Bitan said. "Even the most intelligent of them—of us—are so easily swayed by self-deception. Here we are, talking about the Fermi paradox, the billions of planets teeming with potential life. But do you know something? This kind of talk is done mostly to reassure ourselves."

"I'm not sure I follow," Skip replied.

"We've walked such a short way, yet we can't see the dig site. How many molecules of earth lie between it and us, do you think? Even *this* landscape, on a scale we basically understand, is staggeringly large. Can we truly comprehend the vastness of the cosmos? No. So scientists talk about parsecs and astronomical units and light-years because labels and measurements are comforting. We invent labels because, when we use them, it makes us believe we understand what's really out there."

"I see what you mean," Skip said. "That's what humans do. We label, categorize, measure, and dissect because it gives us the illusion of control."

Bitan's eyes gleamed in the dying light. "I had a feeling you'd understand, Skip. What are your thoughts…"

Bitan hesitated and Skip had the strong sense he was about to be confided in.

"…about alien abductions?"

This wasn't the confidence Skip had expected. He paused a moment, then chose his words carefully. "I think some of them probably happened. Of course, some are just crazy people looking for attention. But some of the stories the abductees tell are just too grounded, too credible."

Now a long silence ensued, and then Bitan said: "Those are my thoughts exactly."

Another, still longer silence.

"Skip, may I speak to you in absolute confidence? About something never to be repeated to anyone?"

"Of course." Skip could hardly believe a world-famous scientist was speaking to him like this. He felt a flush of warmth.

"You remind me of my own son, Azriel, who was killed in the 2014 Gaza War. So very curious, so full of theories. Half of the questions you ask, you answer even before they're out of your mouth." He went silent a moment. "Are you familiar with the Golan Heights?"

"Isn't it the plateau that separates Israel from Syria?"

"That's correct. It was occupied by Israel during the '67 war. Israel retained it as protection, because Syria was shelling Israel from those heights. It is high and rugged and gets snow in the winter. It's barely inhabited."

Skip listened to Bitan's low voice in the growing darkness, inflected with a pleasing Hebrew accent.

"As you probably know, most Israelis have to do a year of mandatory military service. I was no exception. Back in 1998, part of my national service was patrolling the Heights. I was a member of a small patrol. Our platoon leader divided us up for an exercise, and I got separated from the others in a place called Einot Si'on. A very remote ridge in the foothills of Mount Hermon."

He paused to take a deep breath. Skip listened intensely.

"Toward midnight, I realized I was completely lost, so I settled down to spend the night on a ridgetop, where I had a view all around— keeping on the lookout for the lights of my patrol. I fell asleep. A few hours later, I suddenly woke to find myself in a bright, warm beam of light. I jumped up, thinking it was a search helicopter, but lost my footing and fell *upward*— yes, I know that sounds strange. A moment later I was inside a glowing, circular room, lying on a slab of iridescent material. Emerging from the glow came five alien creatures, humanoid in form, slender and gentle in their movements. They surrounded me. At the same time, I felt an incredible sense of peace, belonging, and one-ness with these beings."

Skip, hardly breathing, could tell this was no perverse joke: Bitan was telling the truth, or at least his recollection of it.

"My memory becomes hazy after this point. I was examined, and they communicated with me. What they said had a profound and life-changing effect."

Again he paused. Night had fallen, and a limitless dome of stars had begun to appear over their heads like so much glowing dust.

"What they told me was this: that they belonged to a galaxy-wide civilization of immense technological advancement, peace, prosperity, compassion, and happiness. The problems we face here, they had all solved. And one day, we would be invited to join them—*if* we could cure ourselves of war, racism, inequality, and the other social ills of our time.

"I asked them: Why me? And they answered, *You will eventually understand. You are part of the plan.* And then I felt like I was falling again and found myself on the Einot Si'on ridge. Dawn was creeping up in the eastern sky. A few hours later, my patrol came into view, coming up the ridge looking for me.

"I then did a foolish thing. As soon as I had the opportunity, I took the patrol leader aside—he was a lieutenant in the IDF—and told him what had happened. He was aghast.

He immediately assumed I was psychotic and said he was obliged to report me for my own safety and the safety of my fellow soldiers. It was only with extreme difficulty that I was able to quickly backpedal, retract it all, claim it was a dream, and talk him out of reporting it. If he had, I would have been cashiered. It would have gone on my record that I was mentally unfit, and my life would have been ruined. It was a lesson learned. For those reasons I never spoke of it again—save to my son."

His voice had fallen to a hush. Skip had to lean close to hear him.

"It did, however, encourage me to pursue a path in life, the one you're familiar with from my books and research. But I kept that encounter to myself, because if it ever got out, it would all be over for me. Even here and now, perhaps even among these open-minded scientists, I would be thought a crank."

"Yes, of course. I understand."

"You must tell no one, not even your sister. This is between you and me." Then he smiled and glanced at the dog. "And Mitty."

"I promise."

"For me, this project is more than just a

scientific effort. It has spiritual significance. This discovery will draw us closer to the day when humanity can cast aside its evil ways and eventually join *the galactic civilization*."

Skip felt a shiver of exultation. This was an incredible revelation, and Bitan, the famous scientist, had chosen to make it to him—and him alone.

"Thank you," Skip said, into a long silence. "Thank you for your trust and confidence in me."

"I had a purpose in telling you."

"What is that?" Skip said eagerly.

Bitan laughed out loud, grabbed Skip by the shoulder, and gave him a friendly squeeze. "All in good time. And now, let's go find out what our friend Antonetti has on this evening's menu."

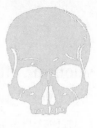

21

Hale Morwood pulled himself out of the driver's seat of his black Cadillac XT6, waited for a moment to catch his breath in the night air, took out the box with the dial-a-yield, then locked the SUV's door with his key fob. He began walking from the employee lot toward the entrance to the FBI building. It was a few minutes before midnight, and the night was dark and moonless, reducing the buildings in the nearby business park to low rectangles of light.

He wasn't a big fan of Cadillacs, or American-made cars in general, but he'd chosen the Caddy for the same reasons he'd picked an obnoxious decaled pickup for his work vehicle. It didn't look 5-O; it offered good protection in the case of a collision; and—perhaps most important—it took little effort to slip in and out of.

Morwood approached the front of the three-story central structure and went in through the main entrance. He signed in, exchanged brief pleasantries with the night guard, then walked with measured cadence to the elevator bank. The doors opened, he stepped in, and—instead of heading up to his second-floor office—he pushed the button marked *B* and waited for the lift to take its usual sweet time.

At least the slow ride to the basement restored his normal respiration—such as it was. It was quiet down here—no surprise, given the hour. He turned left down the hallway, dimly lit since half the overhead lights automatically shut off after ten, and started for the lab. Twenty paces—the distance, long memorized, rose to his mind whether he wanted it to or not.

The only advantage to an enforced sedentary lifestyle was that it gave him all the time he wanted, and then some, to indulge in his private passion: history. Specifically, American military history. In recent years he had read avidly and deeply. He could specify—down to the regiment, or squadron, or sometimes even the company—what turned the tide of battle at places as diverse as Bunker Hill, Gettysburg, or Midway…although, reserved by nature, he rarely put such erudition on display. In particular, he was fascinated by the technical aspects of war, and how developments such as the rifled barrel and Norden bombsight could play as much of a role in victory as courage or strategy did.

He reached the door to the lab and—alone and unobserved—paused to take a few breaths. His armchair avocation had occasionally helped in his investigative work. More than once, lying in bed and unable to sleep, his mind drifting over some detail of Thermopylae or World War I, he would find—among the litter of chaos and death—some insight into an elusive case he'd been tasked with. He would jot his thoughts down on a pad, and then check on them when he went in to work the next day. Normally they didn't pan out; now and then, however, they started a chain of mental dominoes falling.

Such a thought had occurred to him this evening, and he'd jotted down the particulars, as usual. But he hadn't gone to bed: he believed this particular revelation couldn't wait for the morning.

He pressed the keypad, and the lab door unlocked with a hiss of escaping air. It was almost pitch black inside, of course, with only the red exit signs for light. He stepped in, felt around with his hand for the bank of switches, flicked them on. Ahead lay the usual rat's nest of unopened shipping boxes Lathrop allowed to pile up, lining both walls and obscuring the view of the main lab around a corner and to the left. The place stank, too. All forensic labs stank, to various degrees, of chemicals and fluids and de-caying things, but this was worse than the others of Morwood's acquaintance: there was a vague aroma of food, reminiscent of liverwurst, that in this context was revolting. He understood why Corrie didn't like working with Lathrop: not only was he an old fussbudget, but he kept his lab in vile condition. He reminded himself to send out a gentle memo to that effect in the morning.

He stepped forward, past the stacks of boxes, toward the bend in the passage. Ahead, he could make out the shadowy set of light switches that would illuminate the lab itself. He found himself smiling at the thought of Corrie. She had a special kind of moxie: not studied or forced, but a natural instinct to lower her head and charge, that—

There was a blur of motion, gray upon black, in his peripheral vision: it was so rapid that, secure location or not, all Morwood's instincts shouted danger. He began to turn, but fast as lightning a hand slipped up beneath his arm, then seized the back of his head in a half nelson as solid as iron. Morwood opened his mouth to yell, dropping the box while at the same time raising his elbow to strike back at his attacker, but this move was anticipated and he felt himself shoved violently forward against a metal packing shelf. As he choked, the wind knocked out of him, Morwood felt the burning sensation of a needle being driven into his neck, at the scalp line. Abruptly, the viselike grip slid away, freeing him. Regaining his breath, Morwood turned, preparing to launch himself at the intruder. But even as he did, he felt a peculiar weakness shiver down his spine, and then out to his limbs. His muscles grew slack, then—with horrible rapidity—unresponsive. His legs gave out and he crumpled to the floor, unable even to stop his head from slamming against the concrete.

He was paralyzed: unable to move, unable to

work his jaw or even blink his eyes. As he lay there, dazed by the blow to his head and the suddenness of his attack, he noticed the rest of the lights coming on. A moment later, a figure came into view, looking down at him: a man in his thirties or forties with chestnut-colored hair. He was wearing a dark, conservative suit of the kind favored by the FBI. Morwood, frozen, saw an expression of both curiosity and concern on the man's face. He knelt and placed two fingers briefly against Morwood's neck. Then the man raised a latex-gloved hand and, very gently, closed Morwood's eyes.

As he lay—immobilized yet fully aware of his surroundings—Morwood heard the man's footsteps recede into the deeper spaces of the lab. But the man, and his sudden attack, were already less critical to him than they'd been a minute before: the paralysis had now spread to Morwood's pleural cavity, and his breathing—a burden at the best of times—turned into shallow gasps.

Having satisfied himself that Agent Morwood was no longer a threat, Lime glanced around the laboratory. The compound he'd injected Morwood with—similar to vecuronium bromide in its paralyzing effects, but undetectable in an autopsy—would do its work in fifteen to twenty minutes; perhaps less, given the man's already labored breathing. His preparations were almost complete; timing should not be a problem. If he hurried.

He moved toward a black bag of ballistic nylon, lying unzipped atop one of the metal examination tables; rummaged inside; and removed a few small tools and a sealed baggie containing what looked like brown, oversize grains of rice—rat shit, to be specific. Then he walked over to a far corner of the lab, used a stepstool to reach and unscrew a grille near the ceiling, and—balancing a penlight on the cavity within—began working quickly but efficiently. Within eight minutes he was done, the grille and step stool back in their places and the latter wiped clean of any footprints.

Lime glanced at his watch. He was on time, and the preparations were almost complete. Just one more thing.

A small screwdriver appeared in his hand, and he went to a battered round machine sitting in a dusty corner—the lab's autoclave. Working with speed and efficiency, he knelt and unscrewed a metal plate in the side of the machine. Setting the plate aside, he reached in with a penknife and worked for all of twenty seconds; then he placed the plate back on and screwed it into place.

Finally, he double-checked everything: a mental checklist exercise he had been conditioned to perform. He walked over to the door through which Morwood had entered, made sure it was securely closed and that its automatic lock re-engaged. Then he returned to Morwood, motionless on the floor. Kneeling once again, he determined the agent was now fully unconscious, his body still struggling to breathe but well on its way to death. That, at least, was a mercy: although the drug was Lime's preferred method for such business, suffocation by paralysis was an unpleasant way to go. Still, smoke had to be found in the man's lungs.

It was a shame, really: everything he knew about Morwood, based on the man's official dossier, would have made him a good candidate. Certainly, his character, beliefs, and outlook were in line with the Atropos creed. It was his unfortunate medical condition that had disqualified him from being approached.

More quickly now, Lime went through Morwood's pockets. He riffled through his wallet, checked his keys, then replaced both. There was a folded piece of notepaper with his wallet that he checked, glanced at its contents, then replaced it as well. *Rule 7: Whenever possible, take nothing, leave nothing.*

A muffled popping sound from the autoclave signaled that his operation was now underway. A moment later, this was confirmed by an acrid smell of smoke. Rising, Lime returned to the examination table that held his bag. He dropped his tools into it, made one more quick but thorough check of the lab. And then—with a rapidity born of familiarity—Lime removed his jacket and trousers and turned them inside out, revealing linings of black felt. He put them on again, then pulled a balaclava from the bag and rolled it down over his head. Smoke was now quickly filling the room, but there was no alarm, no drop-and-turn dance of the ceiling sprinkler heads.

Satisfied, Lime zipped up the bag, slung it over his shoulder, and walked back to the shuttered loading dock and the small service door that stood beside it. The door was slightly ajar, just as he had left it. He paused at the jamb for one last moment, then slipped out into the night, closing the door to the lab behind him. Then he turned and—moving away from the scattered lights of the business park—disappeared quickly into the dark.

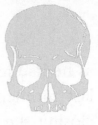

22

T HE CELL PHONE rang so loud and abruptly that Corrie jerked awake beneath the covers. Even in bed, she was still on edge. She'd felt restless and uneasy all evening—without knowing why—and tossed in bed for ages before finally drifting into a fitful doze.

Sitting up on one elbow, she plucked the phone from her nightstand. It was half past two. Shit, that meant she'd been asleep less than an hour. The caller ID came through as private: probably some robocall. Unbelievable. As she answered, she made a private promise to track down the bastard who owned the company responsible and drape his ballsack over her bathroom door.

"Yes?" she said, hearing the sleepy croak of her own voice.

"Agent Swanson?" came a male voice: urgent, abrupt.

Something in the authoritative tone made her flash back for a second to a night a decade earlier, when a Kansas sheriff was beating on the door of the trailer she'd shared with her mother.

"Agent Swanson?" the voice came again. Pushing the old memory from her head, she sat up and cleared her throat. "Yes?"

"SAC Garcia here."

Garcia, head honcho of the Albuquerque Field Office. It was true Corrie didn't see him very often, but nevertheless she knew his voice. The man on the other end of the line didn't sound like him. "Yes, sir?"

"I'm, ah, sorry to disturb you at this hour."

"That's all right, sir."

"I need to ask you a few questions, if you don't mind. Can you please tell me when you last saw Agent Morwood?"

Corrie's half-asleep daze made this question harder to answer than it should have been. "This afternoon, sir. Yesterday afternoon, that is. He came by the forensics lab."

She heard a shuffling of paper. "You were working on some facial reconstructions." Garcia might not sound like his usual self, but he seemed remarkably awake and alert, given the hour.

"I was preparing to, yes."

"Do you happen to recall what time this was?"

Corrie thought a moment. She was fully awake now, too, and increasingly alarmed by the direction these questions were taking. "It would have been about five o'clock, sir."

"And did he give you any indication of what he had planned for the rest of the day?"

"He said...ah, he said he was going to see an old acquaintance, ask him about the device found at the Roswell site."

More shuffling of paper. "That would be the scientist he mentioned—what was his name?"

"Eastchester."

"Very well," Garcia said. "Any idea why he'd be in the forensic lab a few hours ago?"

"A few hours ago?" Corrie paused. There was a low babble of voices in the background. Where was he calling from? "He might have been returning the device he checked out to show Eastchester."

"Yes, of course."

"Sir, would you please tell me what these questions are about?"

It was several moments before Garcia continued. "There was a fire in the lab tonight. A serious fire."

"What—?" Corrie began. Her mind raced. *In the lab?*

"I'm very sorry to inform you that Agent Morwood perished in that fire."

"*What?*" Corrie blurted again, not even trying to restrain the sudden spike in her voice.

"The investigation has just started. I'll know more tomorrow."

Corrie, stunned into silence, did not reply. The babble of voices on the other end of the call grew louder.

"I need to hang up now. I'm very sorry, Corrie. I know how much you respected him. This is a shock to you—to all of us. We'll talk again in the morning."

"*Wait!*" Corrie shouted abruptly, but Garcia had already terminated the call and she found herself crying into a dead phone.

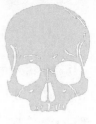

23

Skip was a little put out about a Saturday workday: he was tired of cataloging Bitan's books, or shoveling and screening dirt and finding nothing, and was looking forward to sleeping late and lounging in the RV. But Nora and the crew had wanted to keep working, as they were close to uncovering what Nora believed would be the terminus of the trench. At eleven o'clock that morning, the group assembled for the prelunch meeting around a table set up in a tent shade next to the dig.

This meeting, Skip sensed as he looked around the group, was going to be different from the usual. Emilio Vigil took a seat next to Nora, his normally black beard covered with dust. The other postdoc, Scott Riordan, sat on the other side, even more dusty.

Noam had joined them unexpectedly, and so had Greg Banks and the other two engineers. Tappan occupied the far end of the table. It seemed the perfunctory midmorning meeting had turned into a big deal.

Skip took a swig of coffee and waited.

"Well," said Nora, opening the meeting, "Emilio, could you tell everyone about the morning's progress?"

"Sure thing." He looked around. "As you all know, we've been excavating the outline of the groove left by the object in the ground. Dr. Bitan spent quite a lot of time taking measurements of the furrow."

Bitan had asked multiple times for them to halt work while he got down in their trenches and took precise measurements with a laser theodolite. Skip wasn't sure what he was doing, and Bitan had been vague when Nora asked.

"Perhaps Dr. Bitan would share with us the scope and purpose of his work?" asked Nora rather crisply. Skip could tell she was a little irritated—and he was equally sure Noam had his reasons for not revealing exactly what he was up to.

"Not yet, not yet! Soon. I'm working on a little theory of mine; that's all."

Little theory, Skip thought. He was sure not to make eye contact with the man.

"Very well," said Nora. "Go on, Emilio."

"Thanks. We had a major surprise this morning. We reached the end of the furrow, as far as we can tell... and found nothing. Whatever created that furrow seems to have vanished."

"Vanished?" Tappan asked, suddenly interested. "How so?"

"It's a bit mysterious, actually," said Nora. "The object came in at a shallow angle. The trench, of course, was backfilled in 1947, but we could still follow its outline. I, we, expected to find a terminus where the object came to rest. But instead, the trench just seemed to spread out and vanish, leaving nothing behind but a welter of sand and fused glass. Skip has been saving quantities of the glassy sand for further analysis by Dr. Banks."

Banks nodded.

"Our plan going forward," Nora went on, "is to excavate beyond where the furrow disappears to see what else we might find. We also plan to cut several transverse test trenches to see if the object might have scattered pieces to either side. Any questions or thoughts?"

She fielded a number of questions and a discussion ensued, coming to no conclusions. Tappan wrapped it up by thanking Nora and saying: "We seem to have a real mystery on our hands." He tried to sound chipper, but Skip could tell this news was a disappointment to him.

As the meeting broke up, Noam signaled Skip to join him. They walked back to Quonset 2, where Noam ushered Skip into his office and quietly locked the door behind him.

"Please take a seat."

Skip sat in the chair opposite the desk, thrilled with a sense of anticipation, sure that the man had more to say to him from their talk the evening before.

"You may have noticed me fussing around in the trenches this morning," said Noam, his eyes sparkling.

"I did. Some idea you were checking out?"

"Exactly. And my idea bore fruit. Last night I mentioned there was a reason why I shared my story with you. It's because I need your help."

"I'm ready to help in any way," Skip said.

"I know that. Your sister and everyone else are

puzzled about the shape of the furrow plowed by the object and the mystery of its vanishing. But it's no mystery to me. After taking careful measurements, I believe I know exactly what happened." He leaned back in his chair with a smile, tenting his fingers, letting a silence build.

"What?" Skip finally asked.

"Let me start by saying: I now know we're digging in the wrong place."

"But...the groove in the sand, the glass, the radar surveys—are you saying nothing happened here?"

"Something *did* happen. The object struck the ground. But my calculations show that the object came in at such a low angle it essentially bounced, like a flat stone skipped on the water— and became airborne again and landed somewhere else."

Skip stared. "Holy shit."

Bitan chuckled. "This of course explains why the groove just ended in a spray of sand and glass. The object simply rebounded back out and flew farther."

"And so the real crash site is somewhere else," Skip said.

"Precisely. Somewhere in the direction the

trench is pointing. And this is where you come in. You're going to be my confidential searcher. Together, we're going to find where the UAP *really* came to rest."

He unlocked a drawer and pulled out a large sheet of paper. He slid it onto the desk and turned it around so Skip could look. It was full of penciled mathematical equations, and a crude map was hand-drawn in the middle, decorated with arrows and vectors. At the top was an oval, drawn in heavy red pencil.

"Our camp is here." Bitan tapped the paper. "And here's the furrow, pointing northwest at a heading of 321 degrees. If you follow that direction, it goes across the dry lake bed and into these hills and buttes. I drew this oval where my preliminary calculations show the object probably came back down to earth. Of course, a lot depends on its velocity and mass, plus its shape and the amount of drag it produced. And when it hit the ground again, it might have rolled or bounced. We don't know—yet."

Skip stared at the map. "That oval covers how much area?"

"About a thousand acres."

"That's a lot."

"I know. Tomorrow is Sunday, our day off. I imagine some people are going to go into town, do some shopping or whatever. You and I are going to pack a picnic lunch and tell everyone we're heading off to find the old Spanish watchtower."

Skip hesitated. This was not directly relevant to Bitan's abduction story. "Is there a reason why you don't want to share this with everyone?"

"Yes. I *need* to be the one to discover it. This is my destiny. This is what I was chosen to do by the revelation on Mount Hermon. And when I do find it, naturally I'll share that discovery with the team—but not until then. Are you with me?"

"Yes," said Skip. "I absolutely am."

"Good! We'll meet here tomorrow morning early, at five thirty. Bring your day pack, water, and lunch."

"You bet!" In his excitement, Skip forgot to be taken aback by the ungodly hour.

Bitan leaned forward. "Here's the thing. If it did come down somewhere else, it's just possible the government never found it. Which means it's still there."

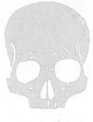

24

CORRIE ENTERED THE lobby of the Albuquerque Field Office at ten minutes to noon on Saturday. She passed through the security barrier, went to the elevator bank, and made her way up to the third floor, going through the motions without much conscious thought, like a zombie. She hadn't slept in the nine hours since the initial call, but it was shock more than weariness that made everything seem unreal.

After hanging up with Garcia, she'd spent a few minutes silently weeping. Then she just lay on her bed, staring at the ceiling, trying to convince herself that none of this was actually happening. It couldn't be. She'd go in to work and see Morwood at his desk, looking out through the glass at her, one skeptical eyebrow arched. But of course, it wasn't like that, and one way or another she had to pull herself together.

She'd never spent much time on the top floor of the FBI building on weekends, but she sensed an odd, church-like atmosphere the moment she stepped out of the elevator. As she walked through the cube farm, then along the row of offices set against the far wall, this stillness only added to her feeling of unreality. In the distance, barely audible, she could hear a woman sobbing. Funny how she forgot that Morwood had ghosted other agents besides herself.

As she approached the corner office, she began to see more people. The death of an FBI agent, even accidental, was not only a tragedy but a big deal that needed to be investigated. That it happened on the premises made it doubly serious. No doubt that was why Garcia had called her in today. Corrie had no illusions she'd been brought in for a grief therapy session.

There was no administrative assistant outside Garcia's office, and Corrie was still a few minutes early, so she sat down in one of the chairs outside the SAC's door. She closed her eyes and took slow, deep breaths. The sense of disbelief was, in a way, a protective carapace: if she could get through this meeting with that shell intact, maybe it could last the rest of the weekend.

The door opened and three or four senior agents in suits filed out. None of them looked at her. Silence for a moment, then she heard: "Swanson? Come in, please."

Corrie stood up and walked into the office. She'd been here only a couple of times, but it had always looked the same: American flag in one corner, FBI flag in another, framed photo of the president between them. Two windows on adjacent walls, offering views of the freeway. Neat files on the desk beside a few family pictures. Conference table; chairs; desert landscapes on the walls. She recalled that Morwood had brought her up for an initial meeting after—in his words—deciding she stood a fair chance of sticking around.

"Good morning," Garcia said in his soft voice. "Close the door and take a seat, please."

Garcia's alert brown eyes took her in quickly; he rose to shake her hand as she chose a chair, then sat down again and placed his beefy arms on the desk, hands clasped and fingers interlaced. His mouth was a straight line, neither smiling nor frowning; but then, she'd never seen Garcia either laugh or shout in anger.

"Thank you for coming in, Agent Swanson."

"Yes, sir," Corrie replied.

"Hale—Agent Morwood—was well liked here. He was a dedicated agent, respected for his loyalty to the Bureau. This is a tragedy for the entire office, Swanson: we share a common loss. I'm sorry if I seemed short with you on the phone last night."

"Not to worry, sir."

Now Garcia hesitated uncharacteristically. Through her haze of shock and sorrow, Corrie had noted there was no folder open in front of the SAC; no recording device visible. This, too, seemed unusual for what she expected to be a debrief.

Garcia took a deep breath. "I think it best to mention something up front, Agent Swanson, so that there's complete transparency— and so you'll better understand my line of questioning."

"Very well, sir," Corrie said. *Transparency about what?*

"As part of the preliminary investigation into the fire, I met with Dr. Lathrop earlier this morning. It is his, ah, recollection that—" another hesitation, this one briefer— "when you and he were together in the forensics lab yesterday, you did not observe proper safety protocols."

Corrie was still concentrating on keeping the protective shell in place, and it took a moment for these words to sink in. "Excuse me. I did what?"

"As part of your work yesterday, you were warming Plasticine. Correct?"

Corrie nodded.

Now at last the folder came out. Garcia opened it, glanced over a page or two. "Dr. Lathrop has stated, for the record, that you were not following guidelines for use of a Bunsen burner." Another glance at the page. "He said there was combustible material in the vicinity of the flame. He also stated that you had not inspected the hose for defects such as pinch points. Finally, he said this was a behavior he'd seen in you before— leaving a burner unattended, leaving the primary gas valve on after you were done, and the like."

As Garcia spoke, Corrie felt the protective bubble melt away and a combination of disbelief, hurt, and anger take its place. "Sir, are you saying Lathrop is accusing me of leaving a burner on... and being responsible for that fire? The fire that *killed my boss*?"

Garcia put his hands up in a calming gesture;

unconsciously, Corrie had begun to rise out of her chair. "Agent Swanson, please. I'm telling you all this now, at the start, as a courtesy, so you'll have the full picture. Lathrop made no specific accusations. You are not suspected of anything. You know better than anyone we have teams of professionals who are expert in reconstructing events precisely like this one. They've already sealed off the lab and begun work. It's their findings on the source of the fire that will determine what happened. Not a lone accusation. The recollections of Lathrop or other eyewitnesses—including yourself—are also important, but supplementary."

The SAC let a silence fall. Once again, his bright eyes looked intently at Corrie. She had sunk back into her chair, once again in shock— but now of an entirely different kind.

Garcia cleared his throat, and when he spoke again, it was in a quieter, almost confidential tone. "What I just told you was by the book. Off the book, I'm truly sorry this has happened. In a fairer world, you'd be given time to mourn, rather than feel a need to defend yourself. Dr. Lathrop is—well, I think you'd agree he has a certain reputation. But the fact remains he's been here many years and it's our job to investigate his claims. I hope you'll understand the necessity to ask you a few questions. Believe me: it's much better this way."

"Yes, sir." Corrie drew in a shuddering breath. "Thank you, sir."

Another clearing of the throat, and Garcia was once more his formal, commanding self. "This shouldn't take long." He plucked a pen from his pocket. "You told me last night that Morwood came by the forensics lab late in the afternoon. At that time, you and Lathrop were working?"

"*I* was working. Lathrop was watching." She'd be goddamned if she ever gave that son of a bitch another break.

Garcia made a notation. "What were you engaged in at the time?"

"I was warming Plasticine in a container of water over...over a burner. For the facial reconstruction. It was necessary in order to apply musculature to the cast of the skull."

"What did the three of you talk about?"

"Mostly about the chance of obtaining a usable ID from the reconstruction. Lathrop thought it likely; I thought it unlikely."

"And what did Morwood think?"

"He seemed pleased with my progress. He specifically asked me to make the presentation at next Tuesday's meeting."

"And then Agent Morwood left."

Corrie nodded.

"What happened next?"

"I— We had an argument. Lathrop and I."

"About what?"

Corrie sighed. "Sir, he has a habit of belittling me. Making snide, sexist, demeaning comments that—when I point them out—he passes off as jokes. He's been doing it as long as I've been here. He referred to me as a Cassandra in front of Morwood, which I felt was disrespectful. I said if he made another comment along those lines, I'd report him."

"Understood." Garcia was writing again.

"The fact is, I have a degree in forensic anthropology from John Jay, but he acts like—"

"Understood, Agent Swanson," Garcia said with a little more iron in his voice.

Corrie went silent as he continued to make notes. Finally, he looked up again. "You understand I must ask this next set of questions. Dr. Lathrop left the lab before you did?"

"Yes. It's what ended our argument."

"And you continued working?"

Corrie nodded.

"How much longer?"

"Another hour. Perhaps an hour and a quarter."

"So what time was it when you left?"

"Close to six thirty."

"And Dr. Lathrop did not return during that period?"

"No, sir."

"Was the Bunsen burner on when he left?"

"Yes."

"How much longer did you make use of it?"

"Maybe fifteen minutes. When the Plasticine was soft enough for use, I took it out and turned off the burner, as well as the gas at the main. At no time was gas or flame near any combustible materials."

"And can you go over with me, briefly, the steps you took to secure the lab?"

"When I'd made all the progress I could with the reconstruction, I put the model in a cabinet for safekeeping. I put away my tools, took off my gloves, cleared the work area. I'd already set the Bunsen's collar into the closed position and turned off the gas valve at the worktable, and by that time, the burner was cool. I put it away with the other equipment; checked that the main valve was off, made a final survey of the area, then shut off the lights and waited for the security pad to turn green before leaving."

As Corrie spoke, she expected Garcia to take more notes or record what she said. But instead, he just listened, stroking his beard and watching her. Then he asked a final question.

"And you think the reason Morwood went back to the lab that night was to return the object to the evidence locker—correct?"

Corrie hesitated. At midnight? "I'm not sure."

"Do you know any other reason related to what Agent Morwood was working on, or what he was thinking, that might have taken him to the lab that late at night?"

"No, sir. He sometimes worked late into the evening. Perhaps he wanted to check on the progress of my reconstruction."

Garcia took this in with no change of expression. Then, at last, he put the pen back in his pocket and closed the folder. "Thank you, Corrie."

Corrie felt as disoriented as a pinball on its table. "Sir, I want to help—"

"I know you do. But we have to let the investigation take its course. Since this allegation has been made, you can't be directly involved. You understand?"

"And my investigation into the identity of the two bodies...?"

"They were badly damaged in the fire. I'm afraid any more work on that will have to wait until the fire investigation is complete." This sounded dismissive, and Garcia grimaced slightly as he became aware of it. "Don't worry about Lathrop, okay? The best thing you can do is let yourself grieve. Get some distance from all this. In fact, I recommend you take next week off."

"But, sir—"

"Agent Swanson, please: a week off. All right?"

"Yes, sir."

"Here's my direct number, in case you need to talk or anything else occurs to you about why Morwood went into the lab late at night." He reached into a jacket pocket, pulled out a card, and handed it to her. "Now go home, Swanson. And thank you."

Corrie began to speak again, only to realize there was nothing more to say. She stood up, mumbled her thanks in return, and then exited the office, feeling even more numb than she had on her way in.

25

CARRYING HER LAPTOP and feeling oddly nervous, Nora knocked on the door of Tappan's giant RV. A moment later, he flung it open.

"Right on time! Come in."

She stepped into the elegant interior while he shut the door behind her. The table in the middle of the room was covered with various excavation charts and soil profiles.

"Have a seat," he said, sweeping aside the charts. "I asked you here because I'm flummoxed about what was found today—or, more exactly, not found—and was hoping we could brainstorm a solution. I'm not an archaeologist, so you'll have to be patient." He punctuated this with a dimpled smile and slipped into a seat on the opposite side.

"Of course. I do have some thoughts about it."

"So explain to me, archaeologically, just what it means that this furrow or groove seems to have just faded into nothingness."

Nora opened her laptop. "It's easier to show you a three-dimensional reconstruction of the site." She tapped away and the overall 3-D image came up. "You'll have to come around to see it."

Tappan sat on the couch next to her.

"This," she said, "is a 3-D rendering of the excavation so far. All we've really found of large-scale significance is the groove. You can see that here." She rotated the image with the press of a button.

"Understood."

"It shows that a fairly small object, less that ten feet in diameter, hit the ground at an angle of about twenty degrees from the horizontal."

"Ten feet in size? Really?"

"That's the width of the trench at its narrowest point. If it was round, it was ten feet in diameter. Of course, it might have been longer—say, cigar- or rocket-shaped—and struck point-first."

"Okay."

"It made a large, shallow crater where it first struck, here. The impact sent out a broad spray of sand, which is where a lot of those microtektites Greg found were created. As you know, it must have been moving really fast to do that. The groove gets narrower and deeper as it plowed into the ground, while the angle gets shallower. At a depth of twelve feet, the groove becomes almost horizontal. And then here, it just seems to dissolve into a big mess."

She rotated and magnified the image.

"It's like the UAP just vanished," he said. "Is that possible?"

"Whatever impacted wouldn't just vanish. I think what we're seeing is where the government bulldozers came through and dug around. They obviously removed whatever was there—and destroyed the archaeological integrity of the site in doing so. What's left is all confused: no layering, no structure, just churned-up sand and dirt." She paused. "So it isn't really the mystery it seemed at first. At least, that's one idea. More excavation and test trenches on either side should clarify things."

"I see," said Tappan. "So whatever made the trench is now sitting in one of those sealed hangars in Area Fifty-One."

Nora didn't reply.

He glanced at his watch and stood up. "Stay for a drink?"

Nora hesitated. Her immediate instinct was that this might be a bad idea—yet she had a hard time putting a finger on what made her, a woman in her midthirties, think so.

"Sure," she said.

"What's your poison?"

"A glass of white wine would be nice."

"Coming up."

He went over to the bar, pulled a bottle out of the fridge, opened it, and poured a glass. He set it down in front of her and quickly shook up a martini for himself, pouring it into a cocktail glass.

"Cheers." He tapped her glass and smiled. He took a sip and leaned a little toward her. "I'm wondering if you've gotten to 'yes' yet."

Nora was momentarily confounded by the question until she realized he was referring to their earlier conversation. She sipped her wine, then set down her glass. "Well, I was awake half the night, thinking about that superheavy element discovery and the microtektites. I guess you might say I'm still a skeptic."

"Really?"

"Extraordinary claims require extraordinary evidence."

"You don't think this evidence is extraordinary enough?"

"There still could be a mistake. Something we haven't thought of. The problem is, you're all true believers. You have to admit, that can distort results."

He held up his martini. "I salute, and respect, your skepticism—even if I think it's going a little overboard." Then he paused. "What is it?"

"What is what?"

"That look on your face."

"I don't have a look on my face."

"Yes, you do."

Nora sighed. *What the hell.* "All right. It's about you, actually."

"Me?" Tappan reared back in mock surprise.

"Well . . . it's just that you seem to shroud yourself in a veil of ignorance. I mean," she added hastily, "about technical stuff. You have a grand vision, you've certainly got the passion and the imagination—but when it comes to the details, you let the scientists speak for you."

"And rightly so. That's what I'm paying them for."

"I know. But when you get excited about something…" Nora was already sorry she'd brought it up, but she soldiered on anyway. "You forget about that protective shroud. It drops away."

"I don't follow," Tappan said.

"Like after you'd spent all that time in Quonset One with Greg. You started explaining super-heavy elements and the island of stability with almost as much familiarity as if you were a physicist yourself." She paused. "What I mean is, you seem to know a lot more about physics than you let on."

Tappan digested this. "I do?"

"Yes."

"Oh." He took a sip of his martini. "Busted."

Nora waited until, finally, it was Tappan's turn to sigh. "It's true—I'm a physics geek. Astro-physics, actually."

"I figured you didn't become a billionaire in-ventor out of ignorance. But why the act?"

"It's not an act," Tappan replied quickly, and for a moment Nora thought she'd gone too far. But he simply drained his martini and chuckled. "There are two reasons, really. The first is I've learned from experience to hire the best people, give them a nudge or reorient them from time to time, but let them do the talking...and the heavy thinking. If I strut my own knowledge, it just hinders them, intimidates them."

Nora nodded. This made sense. "And the second?"

"That's more complicated." Tappan looked at her glass, hesitated, then rose and made himself another martini—one more, she recalled, than he usually allowed himself. When he sat down again, his face had grown introspective. "You know the old story of the poor working-class parent who toils night and day so their kid can become a doctor or a lawyer...but all the kid wants to do is paint or write sonnets?"

"Of course. Sounds like the life story of most Victorian novelists."

"Well, that's my story, too...except in reverse. My father taught English at a community college in South Dakota. He lived and breathed literature and had dreams of being a writer. He'd struggled all his adolescent life to escape the family farm so he could write and teach. His leaving the farm enraged *his* father, but he did it anyway. But here's the tragedy: writing eluded him." Tappan paused, expression still introspective. "He always wanted to write that perfect, jewel-like novel. Like the fellow in *Breakfast at Tiffany's*: a book full of 'sensitive, intensely felt' prose. But he just didn't have it in him. So the mantle of famous family novelist fell upon me, his firstborn. The problem was, I was much happier fixing a tractor, or lying in the barnyard at night watching for shooting stars or learning the constellations or figuring out how a windmill worked. I had little interest in books."

He chuckled again, but this time rather mirthlessly. "My dad—when he wasn't busy teaching class or tearing up drafts of his novel—did everything he could to make me fall in love with literature. He tossed me books by Robert Louis Stevenson and H. G. Wells. Even offered me candy bars to finish them." He shifted on the couch. "It was around that time my mom left home, moved in with her in-laws on what was left of the farm."

Nora thought it best not to overtly sympathize. "So, did you? Finish the books, I mean?"

"Sure. I read them. But after a while, the page-to-candy-bar ratio began to feel onerous. The irony was that I *did* like books: books with numbers in them, such as my algebra and geometry texts. I liked Jules Verne, too, but only for the science and imagination. I tried building a submarine out of two ancient canoes lashed thwart to thwart. Almost incinerated myself improvising a two-stage rocket. I built a radio dish and tried to pick up radio waves from distant star systems. My dad was aware of the irony, of course. Instead of writing short stories, I was tinkering with mechanical stuff. So he just kept writing and rewriting that novel, and he started drinking while doing it. In time, his own failed dreams became...well, my fault. That's when his frustrations started getting physical."

"Jesus," Nora murmured.

Tappan shrugged this away. "So I followed my mom back to my grandparents' farm. With me there to help, the farm started to come back. And my juvenile studies went from algebra to electrodynamics, and mechanical engineering to radio telescopes, black holes, and cosmology. But I never lost my curiosity about the farm's windmill. Over time, I was able to make it generate more than five kilowatts of power. This was in the early nineties, after the government passed the PTC measure."

"The what?"

"A corporate tax credit for renewable electrical sources. It made wind turbines interesting. But they were big, and they were loud. All my tinkering with our old windmill, combined with what I'd learned about mechanical engineering, had given me ideas for a new kind of direct-drive generator. It could shrink a gearbox, allow for slower rotational speeds—and make the whole mechanism quieter. It was my grandfather who suggested I apply for a patent."

And he picked up his martini.

"And?" Nora asked.

"That little idea was the start of everything. At first it just provided seed money. Now sixty percent of the wind turbines out there use my patent, much improved, of course. And my childhood interest in rockets resulted in building an equally efficient vehicle for satellite launches." He took a sip. "But deep in my limbic brain, I feel guilty for not being a poet. My dad beat that much into me, at least. So keeping my scientific knowledge to myself became habitual."

"What happened to your father?" Nora asked.

"We never spoke again after I ran off to the farm."

"Is he still around?"

"In South Dakota, retired, frail, but still drinking and rewriting." He put down his glass with a little more force than necessary. "But enough about me. Let's hear your story. I know all the details of your CV, of course—very impressive: Grew up on a ranch outside of Santa Fe, worked at the Institute, then went east, got a position at the New York Museum of Natural History, came back to Santa Fe. But...I mean, the Institute's fine and all, but what induced you to leave New York and the museum? Was it...." He fell quiet, leaving the rest of the sentence dangling in midair. Nora was aware, of course, that he knew about her marriage and the death of her husband.

Now it was Nora's turn to finish her glass. "I loved the museum," she said. "And I loved New York. But, to answer your question, when Bill was murdered...well, I just couldn't look at the city the same way anymore. I wanted to be back and be with my brother, on home ground. Safer ground."

There was a silence.

"I'm sorry," Tappan said at last. "I shouldn't pry into such sensitive topics."

She shook her head. "No. It's not healthy to

shut it all up. It's just...well, it's a part of my past I'm still trying to put to rest."

Another silence followed.

"Anyway," said Nora before the silence became awkward, "when are you going to tell everyone the news? About the superheavy element?"

"Not quite yet." Tappan paused.

"Why?"

Another hesitation. "May I tell you something in total confidence?"

"Of course."

"I'm concerned we might have a mole on our team."

Nora waited for more explanation.

"It isn't anything definite," he said. "It's just that I know—*know*—there are people embedded in the government who have staked their careers on covering this up. They don't want us here, they are extremely concerned about what we're doing, and early on they tried to stop us. Very quietly. When that proved impossible, they seemed to melt away. But they're still there and they've got a lot riding on keeping the Roswell truth secret. And now we know; we have proof it was an alien spaceship. And I fear this might trigger...some sort of reaction."

"But are there any *specific* reasons to think there's a spy on the team?"

"It's just a feeling." He picked up his empty martini glass, twirled it between his fingers, set it down. "I know it sounds a little paranoid, but that's why I asked everyone to keep this discovery under wraps a while longer. Oh, and there's one other thing."

He leaned forward as if to impart a secret, but instead their lips touched, lingering gently.

Nora, surprised, drew back.

"I'm out of line," he said quickly.

Nora, breathing hard, her heart suddenly pounding, tried to compose herself. "This is a bad idea."

"Of course it is," said Tappan, leaning forward again, his breath playing on her face.

At that moment, Nora realized she didn't care whether or not it was right. She couldn't help bringing her lips in to meet his again. He slid his arms around her neck and they kissed ever more passionately, and then his warm hand slipped under her shirt and up her spine while he assisted her to a more reclining position on the plush leather banquette.

★ ★ ★

Nora walked back to her trailer in the dark, still reeling from what had just happened. It was crazy, it was wrong, it was exactly what should *not* happen on a project like this—and yet she felt a powerful glow, a whole-body tingle, that made her reservations seem trivial, if not irrelevant.

As she came in the door, a marvelous scent, underlaid by Mitty's welcoming bark, brought her back to the present.

"Where have you been?" Skip called from the galley. "A little longer, and you would have ruined dinner." He quickly poured her a glass of wine and gestured to the kitchen table, where he'd been making inroads into chips and guac. "Have some while I work this up."

"Thanks," she said, slipping into her chair. She was famished. She scooped a mass of guacamole onto a chip.

"I was getting worried," he said from the galley, "because someone said you'd gone into Tappan's RV. You were in there an *awfully. Long. Time...*" His voice trailed off suggestively.

"Tappan was just showing me some charts,"

she said briskly. She found herself flushing, to her great dismay.

"Charts...etchings...of course." Skip tipped a bit of red wine from his glass into the sauté pan with a great hiss of liquid. He stirred it gently, shook the pan, tasted the contents, and then spooned them onto plates, along with roasted potatoes and baby bok choy.

"Sauteed foie gras with red wine, balsamico, and mission fig reduction," he said with feigned nonchalance as he slid the plates onto the table.

"Wow, this is amazing, Skip."

"Least I could do." He sat down beside her and poured himself a fresh glass of wine. "You know, it wouldn't be so shabby having a billionaire brother-in-law..." His voice trailed off suggestively.

She hit him on the shoulder rather harder than she intended.

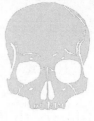

26

Bᴜᴛᴀɴ ᴀʀʀɪᴠᴇᴅ ᴋɪᴛᴛᴇᴅ out as if on safari, with a day pack, two water bottles strapped to his belt, a gigantic straw sun hat, sunglasses, and his nose coated with sunscreen. He carried an elaborate GPS unit.

Mitty spied him approaching in the dark and gave a bark, then rushed forward for a greeting. Bitan took a moment to rub his ears, murmuring affectionate words in Hebrew.

"We're going to walk in the direction the trench points us in," he said, immediately setting off, striding so fast Skip struggled to keep up, Mitty bounding ahead eagerly. "The oval I described is about five miles away, in the Atalaya plains, and it extends two miles into the hills."

"Right."

"I worked out a search pattern last night. I'll Bluetooth it to you. We're going to split up once we reach the valley to cover more ground."

The sun mounted over the horizon into a cloudless sky, casting golden shadows. It was still chilly in the early morning, but Skip knew it was going to warm up quickly. Hopefully it wouldn't get too hot.

For a man close to fifty, Bitan proved to be full of energy. As they walked, he told tales of growing up in Be'er Sheva in the Negev desert, which he mentioned was also the ancient Biblical town of Beersheba; and he talked about its history, the place where Abraham planted the tamarisk tree and the Lord spoke to Isaac and Jacob, and later where the Battle of Beersheba took place during World War I. He was a fount of knowledge and stories, and Skip hung on every word.

After about two miles, Skip saw they were coming to the edge of Diablo Mesa, the vast, low formation on which the camp was situated. A cliff abruptly dropped away to a huge, treeless valley with a dry lake bed in the middle.

They stood at the edge of the mesa in the

morning light while Bitan consulted his GPS. Skip took a moment to give Mitty some water.

"According to the map, that valley is called the Plains of Atalaya," Bitan said. "The white area is Dead Lake, and those hills on the other side are the Horse Heaven Hills. The buttes beyond are Los Gigantes, and the blue mountains, Los Fuertes."

"Picturesque names."

"It amazes me how much this landscape looks like the Negev. But now we have to find our way down into the valley."

Skip peered over the edge with a frown. It was only a few hundred feet, but the rimrock was sheer.

"From the topo map," said Bitan, examining his GPS, "it looks like there might be a way down the cliffs to the left."

They walked along the mesa edge as the sun climbed in the sky. The views were endless. There were no roads, no trails, no signs of human existence. It was a landscape that made Skip feel small, but in a good way. And the possibility of being part of a discovery that would change the world filled him with excitement and wonder.

From time to time Bitan halted and peered ahead with binoculars.

"I'll be damned," he said at one of these stops. "Take a look."

He handed the binoculars to Skip. In the distance, at the edge of the mesa, he could see a broken tower of stone.

"The watchtower," he said.

"Here we are, only pretending to look for it, and yet we found it! I take it as a sign we'll be lucky in what we *are* looking for." He hastened forward, Skip following.

The tower was circular, built of rough stone blocks mortared with adobe. Most of it had fallen down the cliffside, while other stones lay strewn about. Inside there was just enough shade for them to hunker down and have a drink of water. Mitty lapped his share furiously from a collapsible bowl.

Skip noticed some green-glazed potsherds and picked one up.

"What's that?"

Skip handed it to Bitan. "Spanish pottery, I would think."

Bitan turned it over. "Keep it. We'll show it to your sister. Maybe she can identify it."

Skip hunted around and found a few larger pieces, some with yellow designs, and slipped them in his pocket.

After a short rest, they walked past the tower and discovered the remains of an ancient trail going down into the valley. As they descended toward the base of the cliffs, the wind started picking up, carrying white dust from the dry lake bed. The temperature gradually rose. Bitan finally seemed to run out of conversation. When they had gotten back on course, they set off across the Plains of Atalaya toward the distant hills, Bitan periodically checking his GPS. After another two hours or so he halted. The hills were much closer now, and Skip could see they were covered with grass and dotted with low, twisted oak trees.

"We've reached the southern edge of the oval," Bitan said. "Time to split up and begin searching. We'll meet back here at five."

Five. That would give them three hours to get back to camp before nightfall. This was cutting it close, but Skip decided not to mention it.

Bitan went over the search pattern Skip was to follow: a downloaded Google Earth file that showed his location and suggested path. Even though they were out of cell range, the satellite coverage was good, and the GPS was working well. But as Skip looked ahead at the hot alkali flats where his search was to begin, his heart sank a little. Already, they'd hiked quite a distance in the growing heat. But it would get better, he told himself, when he reached those grassy hills. Mitty was still going strong, and Skip was glad to have him along.

Bitan, obviously in a hurry, went off with only a few more words, toward his half of the search pattern. Skip began tracing his own, hiking first one way, then the other. Bitan soon dwindled to a black dot on the plains, and then he vanished entirely.

After noon, the heat came up and at length Skip decided to take a rest and eat his lunch. He was starving and wolfed down the duck rillettes and Camembert sandwich he had prepared on French bread. Mitty got sardines in olive oil. Even though Skip was in good shape, he was starting to feel the trek in his legs.

He continued on, Mitty now following behind, long red tongue dangling. There was nothing to see, no indication of a UFO crash, just a flat white alkali crust that seemed to go on forever; but as he went back and forth, the inviting-looking hills got closer, and finally, around four o'clock, he entered them. At the first corkscrew oak, he took another rest in the shade, drinking the now-hot water from his canteen and sharing more with Mitty. He was starting to regret bringing the dog; it was so hot. Bitan was nowhere to be seen, but Skip wasn't worried: he knew exactly where he himself was, his position indicated by a little blue dot on the Google Earth image.

He went on. The hills were magical, covered with deep grasses that swayed and rippled in the wind, filling the air with the scent of verdure, the scattering of oak trees giving the landscape a park-like feel. And it was cooler, thank God. The buttes and mountains beyond formed a dramatic back-drop. He began to encounter faint trails winding this way and that, and quickly realized they were not human, but horse trails—wild horses. It excited him to think he might glimpse some. Horse Heaven Hills—the place lived up to the name.

The only problem was, as he tramped the hills, he could see no sign of an alien crash site. He checked his watch and, at four thirty, realized it was time to make a beeline back to their rendezvous point. He dropped a Google Earth pin to note where he was on the search pattern so he could resume later and headed back out of the hills.

He arrived at the rendezvous point at five sharp. There was no sign of Bitan. He checked his phone, but of course there was no cell reception.

The sun sank lower in the western sky, and the air cooled, the wind dying away. A pleasant evening commenced, golden light striping the hills and mountains beyond, the air as clear as a spring pool. He waited an hour. Still no Bitan. He thought about heading back, but then considered what would happen if he left and Bitan showed up to find him gone. The man would be furious—and might stop taking him into his confidence.

This was an annoying development, but perhaps not unexpected. Bitan was enthusiastic and easily carried away. On the flat plain, there was no hill Skip could climb to look for him. He felt a buzz in his phone, glanced down, and noted the battery was down to 20 percent. He quickly turned off the GPS and closed Google Earth, and for good measure put the phone in airplane mode to conserve its battery.

As dusk gathered, he settled in to wait.

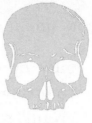

27

Corrie sat in the one truly comfortable chair in her apartment—a Peter Max–decorated beanbag relic from the previous tenant—trying to read a heavily abused paperback. The Sunday-evening light streamed through the windows that looked out onto the Jade Park neighborhood, throwing stripes across the floor that resembled prison bars.

At one point, she realized she wasn't actually reading anymore, her eyes merely scanning dumbly the printed words on yellowing paper. She mustered the willpower to try again:

Sometimes in the afternoon sky a white moon would creep up like a little cloud, furtive, similar to an actress who doesn't have to be onstage for a while, and so goes into the audience to watch the rest of the company a moment, keeping in the background so as not to distract. I liked to see her image reproduced in books and paintings, though they were quite different from the ones I enjoy today...

"Fuck!" she yelled, flinging the paperback across the room. It hit a small shelf holding a potted teddy-bear cholla, and the cactus, shelf, and book all crashed to the floor, scattering dirt and potsherds across the tiles.

In high school, back in Medicine Creek, Kansas, she had been an avid reader. She'd take her Gremlin and park under the power lines and read everything she could get her hands on—trashy science fiction, thrillers, horror novels, even the occasional classic. It was all good, as long as the book took her far away from Medicine Creek, her screeching alcoholic mother, and the bullies and "cool" kids at school. Out of principle, she hadn't paid much attention to her teachers, but one writer her English teacher had mentioned had stayed with her: Marcel Proust, a French author who, the teacher said, wrote books that rambled on endlessly about his experiences growing up. Somehow that odd idea, of a man who spent his entire life reliving his childhood, stuck with her—the sheer self-absorption of writing a million-word monologue about oneself. And so, one day she picked up *Remembrance of Things Past* and dipped into it. It was tough, tiresome going at times, especially since nothing ever seemed to happen, but slowly the sheer wistful dreaminess of it captivated her and became her go-to escape reading.

But not today.

Today, nothing helped her escape.

Corrie knew that spending more time grieving obsessively would be unhealthy. Her mentor's sudden death made her realize just how alone she was: in this new job, in this strange town, in this desert state. She'd thought of calling her father, or even—strangely enough—Nora Kelly, but neither of them was close enough to the situation to really understand. The only person she wanted to turn to would have been Hale Morwood himself...and of course, he was gone. Only too late she realized he'd been more than a boss. He'd been a stabilizing influence on her: not a father figure, but the solid, steadying person she needed at the start of her career.

She stared at the mess she'd just created, spread across the tiled floor on the far side of the room. Anger and anxiety began to replace her shock and grief. She could just imagine that pretentious old bastard Lathrop talking shit about her. He'd been against her ever since she arrived, a young woman who was a threat to him and his control of the lab. He blamed her for the fire, and probably thought it would be her word against his. But the fire investigation would surely clear her.

At this, she felt a fresh surge of anxiety. The thing was, despite what she'd told Garcia, she couldn't be one hundred, one *thousand*, percent sure she'd shut off the burner and the gas lines. She was pretty confident she had—it was something drilled into her during countless hours spent in the John Jay labs—but who remembered something like that? It was like locking the car door before you walked away.

This was bullshit. She'd be exonerated. She knew the fire wasn't her fault. There was no way she was responsible for killing her own mentor. Sitting in her apartment, she felt helpless, unable to do anything. A week off, the time hanging heavy, felt like anything but a period of healing.

"Fuck," she said again, but this time quietly, deliberately. She stood, swept up the broken pot and sad little cactus and dumped them into a trash can, and tossed the copy of Proust underhanded onto the beanbag chair. One thing was sure: wallowing in self-pity was the worst choice she could make.

Here's my private number.

She went into the bedroom, pulled Garcia's card from her bag, and—before she could reconsider—dialed his cell number. The phone rang twice.

"Garcia," came the voice.

"Mr. Garcia, sir?" she said. "It's Corinne Swanson."

"Yes?"

When he said nothing more, she plunged ahead. "Look, sir. I, ah, I really appreciate the offer of a week off. But I've given it some thought, and I'd rather be of use...one way or another," she ended lamely.

There was a brief pause. "Are you sure about that, Swanson?"

"Yes, sir. I am. I need to stay busy."

"Very well, then. It might be a good thing, after all. As it happens, we may have an interim mentor for you."

"Interim?" She hadn't known there was such a thing.

"Somebody willing to ghost you on a temporary basis until we can find a permanent replacement. He's been working in the D.C. area for a few years, but has just arrived in Albuquerque to gather evidence on a complicated fraud case. He'll be here for a while, and his background includes a little mentoring work. How about it?"

"Of course. Thank you, sir!"

"In that case, I'll reach out and see if he's interested."

And before Corrie could thank him again, the line went dead.

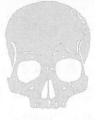

28

Skip waited at the rendezvous point, feeling increasingly alarmed. Noam was now more than two hours late, the sun was touching the horizon, and Skip could see no sign of him.

"Mitty, where the hell is he?"

Hearing his name, the dog perked up his ears and looked at Skip with searching eyes. Skip scratched him behind the ears, glad for the company.

Skip had spent the last hour searching for Bitan, following his footprints in the dry lake bed, which was easy enough, but they completely disappeared when Bitan had entered the grassy hills. Skip climbed a few hills to get a better view but could see no trace of him. He finally returned to the rendezvous in a rising panic.

A dozen scenarios ran through his mind: that Bitan had fallen and hurt himself; that Bitan had found the crash site and become so enthralled he'd lost track of the time; that Bitan's GPS had run out of juice and he'd gotten lost; that Bitan had been bitten by a rattlesnake.

He had turned off airplane mode on his phone to send Noam text messages, but reception was nonexistent, even on top of the hills. All it did was run down his battery, which was now at 5 percent. He'd finally turned off the phone entirely to preserve the last bit. It was at least six miles back to the camp, and without his cell phone's GPS, he wasn't sure he could find his way to the cliffs in the dark, where the old trail went up to the mesa top.

Moments later, the sun disappeared below the horizon in a boil of golden light, and twilight fell. Darkness, Skip knew, came quickly in the high desert, and now this had become an emergency. Something had happened to Bitan, and Skip needed to get back to camp and get a search launched. But he'd be returning in the dark—on a night with no moon.

He rose and swept his eyes across the dry lake bed one last time. Then he turned and looked back toward the distant rimrock of Diablo Mesa, a black line on the horizon. He couldn't see the watchtower ruins—they were too far away. He needed to figure out which direction to go, and for that he had to turn on his cell phone. He would get the heading and then turn it back off.

With trepidation, he switched it on and waited. The Apple logo appeared, much to his relief.

Still he waited as the phone booted up. The lock screen finally appeared, but the phone chimed and the battery monitor was red. He cursed as he hit the Google Earth app. Now he had to wait for his phone's GPS receiver to acquire satellites and load the app. The GPS in the phone worked even without data reception, of course, and the requisite images had been downloaded, but the program still needed to acquire his position. The GPS receiver used a whole lot of juice, and his battery symbol was just a sliver of red.

As if on cue, the screen went black.

"Son of a bitch!" he cried.

His heart began to pound. The sky in the west was deepening to purple. He had been stupid— very stupid. He should have started back to camp an hour ago. But he'd been too afraid Noam would return and not find him—and be angry.

He squinted back at the distant cliffs of Diablo Mesa. It was already too dark to follow his own faint footsteps. What he would do was walk in the direction they'd come as best he could estimate, and when he hit the cliffs he'd search for the trail. If he didn't find it in one direction, he'd go try the other. Once atop the mesa, he hoped he'd be able to get a visual bearing on the distant lights of camp. "Okay, pardner," he said to Mitty. "Let's go."

Having a plan reassured him, and he set off at a fast walk toward the distant line of cliffs. The stars began appearing over his head, first the brightest ones along with the planets, and then the vast panoply. The air was cooling nicely, and he still had a little water. He figured it was about eight o'clock. If all went well, he and Mitty would be back in camp by ten, and then he'd rally the group and return in the vehicles for a proper search. The mesa top could be easily crossed by jeep, and the trail down to the lake bed, next to the tower, was broad enough to be traversable—steep though it was.

This would be over soon. *Keep calm and carry on*, he kept murmuring, repeating the phrase that had gotten the British through the Blitz.

He continued toward the dark line of cliffs until night closed in for good. The stars, out here with no light pollution, were amazing, like vast clouds of glowing dust. The moon had not yet risen, and he could no longer see where he was going—the land ahead was just a sea of black. But he scanned the sky and quickly located the North Star, and from that adjusted his route to a southeast heading. If he kept the star at his back, behind his left shoulder, he should be able to maintain a steady course without getting turned around or going in circles.

An hour went by, and finally the alkali crust of the lake bed petered away. He felt the ground rising, and in another ten minutes he was standing at the foot of the cliffs—a black wall blotting out the night sky.

So far, so good. But where was the trail? He took a guess it would be to his left and began hiking along the base of the cliffs in that direction. It was so dark, and the cliffs so devoid of form, that he found himself having to stop and explore every ridgeline and slope for the trail—none of which panned out, the climb always ending in sheer rock.

A half mile brought him at last to a promising ridge. He wished for the thousandth time that he'd brought a headlamp—but who could have imagined they'd be out after dark?

He started up the ridgeline, his heart soaring with hope. It grew steeper—steeper than he remembered—but he kept going. Now it became steeper still. This wasn't the trail, he realized, but it still might be a route to the top.

He kept scrambling up, the rock face to the left and right falling away into sheer blackness, using his hands now as well as his feet. Mitty, with four legs, was doing better than he was, and he placed a hand on the dog's furry head, feeling reassured by the touch. The wind picked up and he abruptly felt wobbly, disoriented by vertigo, and quickly sat down to gather his nerves. He turned to look back over the Plains of Atalaya and suddenly caught his breath.

There were lights!

He peered at the tiny points, moving in the ocean of black. They were definitely lights, very distant, hard to resolve. As he stared, he became aware they were moving. One blinked out, then another, then both came back on again. It was impossible to tell exactly where they were in the dark landscape, but it seemed likely they were in the Horse Heaven Hills or possibly beyond.

Had Noam brought a flashlight or headlamp with him? He hadn't mentioned it. And he certainly wouldn't have taken more than one. Skip stared at the lights, growing thirsty as he did so, and took out his water bottle. *Damn.* He shook it, then took a swig, leaving the last bit. Skip and Nora had grown up on a ranch, and one of the unbreakable rules their father had taught them was never, ever drink the last bit of water in your canteen. Their father had tragically died of thirst in the desert, but when he was found, there was still water in his canteen.

After hesitating, he gave the last of the water to Mitty, who lapped it up in seconds.

He turned his attention back to the lights. They suggested Bitan might have encountered other people, by accident or design. Were they helping him? Were they just random people? Surely it wasn't a rescue party from camp—not yet. What the hell were they doing out there, with no roads for miles? The lights seemed to be moving around in strange, almost random patterns, but maybe that was an illusion caused by the blankness of the terrain. It was hard to tell with no fixed landmarks. On top of that, his eyes were dry and irritated from the dust and sun.

He tucked the empty water bottle back in his pack and continued up the ridge, which grew ever more terrifying. And then it dead-ended in a wall of rock.

Christ almighty, he would have to make his way back down that slope. Going down was always worse. He turned gingerly, knelt, and began scooting on his butt, little by little, but the slope was extreme and the ridge all loose gravel and sand, and he suddenly found himself sliding faster and faster. He raked the ground with his hands and dug in his heels, but it did nothing except scratch the hell out of his palms. He cried out, scrabbling desperately, Mitty suddenly barking, as he fell faster still, terror gripping his heart.

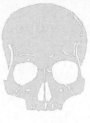

29

Nora woke with a start. She'd been waiting up for Skip on the sofa in their sitting room reading a thriller, and she hadn't intended to fall asleep, but the ridiculous story about the last living cyclops on earth hadn't held her attention. She was instantly wide awake. She checked the time: 5 AM. Had Skip come in quietly? But Mitty would have barked a greeting.

She sprang from the sofa. Skip's door was shut, and she knocked: no answer. She opened it to find Skip's room empty, bed made.

"Shit!" she said aloud, mind racing. Skip had told her he wouldn't be preparing dinner that evening because he and Bitan were going to spend the day trying to locate the watchtower. They had set off early. But Skip wasn't back.

What about Bitan?

She shrugged out of her pajamas and dressed in haste, then flung open the front door. Bitan's trailer was nearby, and she ran over and pounded on its door. No answer. Finding the door unlocked, she went inside. The place was a mess, bed unmade and no astronomer.

Now she went into full panic mode. Exiting Bitan's trailer, she made a beeline for Tappan's RV. Without even bothering to knock, she ran inside and pounded on Tappan's bedroom door. Within moments he opened it, dressed only in underwear and a T-shirt.

"Back for round two?" he asked, his smile disappearing as he saw the expression on her face.

"Skip and Noam are missing," she said breathlessly. "They went out on a hike yesterday and never came back."

"Just a moment." He pulled on some clothes and they went outside. Tappan cupped his hands and started crying loudly for everyone to get up, while Nora went around knocking on doors.

In five minutes, a bewildered, sleepy, and tousled group had assembled outside Tappan's RV. Abruptly, the camp lights snapped on, bathing them all in a bright yellow glow.

"We have two missing members," Tappan began—but suddenly stopped when a bark sounded from the darkness beyond. A moment later, Mitty flew into the light, barking loudly.

Nora called out: "Skip! Skip!"

An unintelligible cry came from the darkness.

"It's him!" someone cried as a figure staggered into the circle of light: clothes torn and dusty, hair askew, face scraped, nose bloody.

Nora rushed over and grabbed him. "Skip! Are you okay?"

"I'm fine!" he cried. "I just slid off a ridge. Listen: Noam—Bitan—is missing."

"You're bleeding!" Nora said as Skip tried to disentangle himself from her.

"I'm telling you, it's just a few scrapes. Please, let me talk!" His voice was hoarse.

Nora backed off.

"Could somebody bring me water?" he asked the group. "My throat's all dry."

As someone rushed off to fetch water, he continued. "We took a day trip to find the Spanish watchtower. And we found it. But we...we kept going down into the plains and the hills beyond. We separated and were supposed to meet back at a rendezvous point. He never showed. I waited for hours and then tried to come back here, but got lost, my phone went dead, I had a fall but I'm okay, just some scraped hands. Smacked my nose, too. I was hoping Mitty might go and get help, but he wouldn't leave me. We've got to go find Bitan."

All this came out in a breathless rush, and then Skip greedily took up a glass of water handed to him and drank it down. "More, please," he said, passing it back as a bowl was brought for Mitty.

Tappan spoke. "Skip? I'm a little confused here."

Skip glanced at him. Seeing the sudden guilty expression on her brother's face, Nora's heart sank.

"If your goal was the tower, why did you go so much farther? And why did you separate?" He paused. "I think there's something you're not telling us."

A silence descended. Skip glanced at Nora, who—temporarily forgetting her concern for his well-being—glared back.

"I was sworn to secrecy," Skip said at last.

"Now's not the time to hold back," Tappan said angrily. "For God's sake, Noam could be hurt—even dying. You've *got* to tell us what you were doing."

"Right. Okay." Yet Skip still hesitated, looking at the assembled group one after the other, gingerly. "Noam has this theory..." He stopped again.

"Go on," Tappan said.

Now Skip took a deep, shaky breath and let the words tumble out in a rush. "He'd decided this wasn't the crash site after all. He called it a 'skip site' instead, where the UAP bounced after impact and went airborne again, crashing farther away. He figured the location was out on the Plains of Atalaya or the hills beyond. That's what we were searching for—the real crash site."

"And where exactly does he think this site is?" Tappan asked, voice edged with exasperation.

Skip reached into his backpack and pulled out a rumpled piece of paper. "Here's a map he drew. The area we were searching is outlined in red pencil."

Tappan snatched it and stared. "What the hell were you two thinking, keeping this secret?"

"It was his secret. It wasn't mine to betray." Skip hung his head. "He said he wanted to find it himself. Then he would tell you."

Nora felt awful. Skip had managed to screw up—again. She could see Tappan was beside himself but controlling it well.

"Okay. All right. We'll address that later. Skip, can we reach this area by jeep?"

"Yes. You drive across the mesa top to the watchtower, and there's a way down. We marked the watchtower on the map with GPS coordinates." Skip paused. "There's something else, though. On my way back, once I'd given up waiting, I saw some lights in those hills. I don't know if it was Dr. Bitan or somebody else."

"Lights?" Tappan was silent a moment. Then he turned to the group. "Here's what we're going to do. We'll outfit three jeeps with water, food, and first aid, and head out at first light. That's only an hour from now. We're going to search the entire area marked on this map. Understood?"

He issued some more rapid, specific orders. Then he turned to Nora. "You stay here with Skip and get him cleaned up and bandaged. We're taking walkie-talkies, and we'll be in contact in case we have questions for him. Skip looks worse than he's letting on. And after you've taken care of your brother, I want you to get on the sat phone to that FBI contact of yours, report a missing person, and ask her how we should proceed."

"Right."

He laid a gentle hand on her shoulder. "Thank you, Nora." He turned. "Okay, everyone, let's get these jeeps loaded, gassed, and ready to roll."

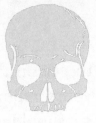

30

I'M FINE," SKIP said irritably as Nora tried to wipe his bloody nose with a damp cloth. It didn't look broken, but it was pretty scraped up. His palms were also skinned, a fingernail torn, and there was a bad abrasion on one knee. Mitty lay on his bed, utterly wiped out.

"Does that hurt?" she asked, moving Skip's fingers to see if any were broken.

"No," he said, wincing.

"What happened?"

"Like I said, I slid down a steep slope. What I really need is a shower."

"All right." Nora stood. "After you do that, I'm going to put some antibiotic ointment on those scrapes and bandage you up."

"Fine." Skip groaned as he eased himself

from the sofa and limped into the bathroom. A moment later she heard the water come on.

The time was six o'clock. Was it too early to call Corrie on a Monday morning? Probably not—she had a sense Corrie was an early riser. She went to the sat phone and dialed.

After several rings, she heard Corrie's voice. "Hello?"

Instantly, Nora could tell something was wrong. "Corrie? Are you okay?"

After a long silence, Corrie spoke. "Not really."

"What's happening?"

Another long pause. "Agent Morwood died in a fire."

"*What?*"

Another unsteady silence. "There was a fire in the forensics lab late Friday night. He was there for some reason. Killed by smoke inhalation."

"Oh, Corrie, I'm so sorry."

"I'm still processing it."

"What a shock. He was a good man. Do they know how the fire started?"

"They've launched an investigation. Everything seems to have gone wrong—the fire alarm didn't work, the sprinkler system failed…It's totally fucked up…" Her voice trailed off.

"Are you ... going in to work today?"

Another long silence. "They tried to give me the week off, but I'm going in anyway." She paused, then said: "I imagine there's a reason you called at six in the morning. I don't mean to burden you with my problems. What's up?"

"It's no burden. I had huge respect for Morwood." Nora hesitated, but decided to go ahead. "It's true: we've got a little problem out at the dig site, and I was hoping to get your advice. But this obviously isn't a good time."

"A good time?" Corrie laughed hollowly. "It's the perfect time. I could use the distraction. The only way I'm going to get through this is if I bury myself in work."

"Understood." Nora swallowed. "One of our scientists, Noam Bitan, went missing. He might be lost. He was way out in the middle of nowhere, wandering around in some hills, and he didn't return. We sent out search parties this morning and maybe he'll turn up. But Tappan asked me to check with you to find out what to do if he doesn't."

"Whereabouts did he disappear?"

"We think in an area called the Horse Heaven Hills. Northwest of Dead Lake."

"I have no idea where that is. Is it still in Chaves County?"

"I think so. Is this something the FBI would handle?"

"Only if it connects to the double homicide I'm working on, which seems unlikely. Because it's outside of a town jurisdiction, it would be handled by the county sheriff."

"Who's that?"

"I've no idea. I can call Sheriff Watts and find out. It would probably be smart to loop him in, anyway. He's in Socorro, a few counties to the west."

"You want to report it right away, or wait until we're sure Bitan's missing?"

"Best to report it ASAP," Corrie said. "If he turns up in a few hours, no harm done. Just to reassure you, the vast majority of missing-persons cases get resolved within twenty-four hours when the person reappears. Let me contact Sheriff Watts and find out who you should deal with. I'll call you back."

"Thank you, Corrie. And again, I'm sorry to hear about Morwood."

"Now I have something to do. Talk to you soon." She hung up.

The bathroom door opened and Skip appeared in a bathrobe, combing his hair.

"Now you don't look like a dirty, skinned cat," Nora said. "Sit down and let me at those injuries."

He sat down and she examined his nose again. He was going to have a black eye. The cuts and scrapes on his hands were, as he'd said, superficial. She smeared on antibiotic ointment and bandaged everything up.

"Good as new."

"Thanks, sis." He paused. "Guess I kind of messed up, didn't I?"

"What do you think?"

"Tappan is pissed."

"Probably."

"He might fire me."

"Maybe."

"I shouldn't have gone along with Bitan and his secrecy. He was so sure of himself. Christ, I always manage to fuck things up." He dropped his head into his hands.

Nora suddenly felt sorry for him. Poor Skip: he was so impressionable, so easily led astray. "It sounds like Bitan suckered you in. Maybe Tappan will see that." If necessary, she could talk

Tappan out of any really dire punishment. At this thought, her mind flashed back to the brief but wild interlude in his RV. She didn't ever want to use that as leverage.

"Tappan's going to fire me for sure," he said, too preoccupied to notice the flush that came over her face.

"Look, Skip, they're going to find Bitan, he'll apologize, and everything will go back to normal. What you said he figured out, that this is just a skip site—it actually makes perfect sense. I wish I'd thought of it. I'll bet Tappan will forgive him for going a little rogue. We'll have to find the real crash site now and start digging there."

"I can't stop thinking about those lights I saw. I think they were in the area we'd been searching."

"Maybe it was just a rancher looking for some lost horses. Maybe they were spies. Maybe Bitan was a spy, and he'd arranged to be picked up. In fact, I think that's probably the most likely."

Skip raised his head. "Bitan, a spy?"

"It's possible."

"Spying for who?"

"I don't know." She hesitated. "Between you and me, Tappan suspects there's a spy on the team. Maybe it was Bitan."

"I don't think so..." Skip hesitated, then continued. "Bitan told me a story. About something that happened during his national service in the Israeli Defense Forces. I promised not to tell anyone."

Nora waited. She wasn't sure she wanted to hear it, whatever it was. God knows, it might get Skip in deeper trouble. But after a moment he went on anyway.

"Bitan was abducted by aliens."

"You're joking."

"No. I'm not. On Mount Hermon in Israel. The aliens communicated with him, gave him a mission, a destiny."

"What kind of mission?"

"To prove intelligent extraterrestrials are watching us and waiting, that they have our best interests at heart, and that they have a plan for us—a *good* plan."

Nora stared at Skip. He was totally sincere.

"Okay," she said slowly. "You really think... what he said actually happened? Or is he maybe a little screwy?" She was sure it was the latter but wanted to know what Skip believed.

"I know *he* believes it. That's beyond doubt. Look, he's one of the most distinguished astronomers in the world. The Weizmann Institute, Caltech, SETI. I mean, this guy is as solid as they come. He's no fantasist. If he says it really happened to him..." He let this observation hang in the air between them.

Nora pondered this. Of course, the idea was absurd. If aliens wanted to announce their existence and reveal some plan for humanity, abducting a young man in Israel to deliver the news made no sense. But Skip was so serious, so earnest, she realized it was pointless to argue with him. She wondered if she should report this to Tappan. It didn't seem pertinent to Bitan's disappearance and might create problems later—especially if Bitan reappeared and found out Skip had divulged his secret.

"I think," she said slowly, "it would be best if you kept that story to yourself."

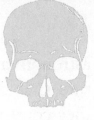

31

CORRIE SAT AT her desk, going over files she'd looked at half a dozen times already. Even though her meeting wasn't scheduled until eleven, she'd come in at eight, determined that—if she wasn't going to take time off—she would put in full days, whether there were fires for her to put out or not.

Fires. She winced, mentally kicking herself. Here she was, feeling annoyed that her progress was interrupted because the forensic lab was inaccessible...ignoring the fact this was because of a fire that killed her boss.

After speaking to Garcia the day before, she'd done a reasonably good job of not dwelling on either Morwood's death or Lathrop's accusation. The early call she'd gotten this morning from

Nora Kelly had helped in its own way: it gave her an excuse to phone Homer Watts, sheriff of Socorro County, to get his advice on the possible missing person. *Excuse* wasn't quite the right word, though: despite being attracted to Watts, with his brown eyes, black hair, movie-star looks, and Western rig—right down to the matching Peacemakers—she'd hardly given the sheriff a thought over the last few months. He'd certainly been happy to get her call, though, and his dismay over Morwood's death was obviously sincere. When she explained why she was calling, he groaned: the sheriff of Chaves County was a good old boy named Buford—the name said it all, he'd told her—more adept at striding around in a uniform with jingling cuffs on his belt than he was at solving cases. Nevertheless, Watts had promised to call his fellow sheriff and give him the details if Corrie agreed to meet him for breakfast tomorrow to catch up—professionally, of course. Though she hadn't seen any need to catch up on anything, she'd agreed, secretly pleased by the invitation.

"Hey, Corrie." The mail guy came by. There was a fat manila envelope in the stack, an FBI interagency-delivered package. She grabbed it and tore it open. It was what she'd hoped: the report on the crowns. She read through it with interest. The crowns, the report noted, were made of an alloy called AISI 321, with stainless steel, nickel, and chromium, cast and machined with great precision. There was only one place where such fine dental work was done with this alloy: the Soviet Union. And in only one time period: 1939 to 1954.

Corrie sat back and pondered this unexpected finding. So the man with the crowns was Soviet. Or, at the very least, he'd spent quite some time in the USSR. What was he doing in New Mexico in 1947? The answer to that wasn't exactly obscure.

She glanced at her watch. Shit: eleven on the dot. She jumped up and raced out of her cubicle. If this senior agent was really willing to ghost her, even temporarily, the last thing she wanted to do was be late for their initial meeting.

The door to Morwood's office—former office—was open, and she knocked on its metal frame. "Come in," a baritone voice sounded.

Corrie stepped inside.

She was surprised to find the office looked

about the same. Morwood's bric-a-brac was missing from the desk, and a few framed commendations had been removed from the walls, but all the furniture was in the same position, and neither the landscape paintings nor the shelves of books had been touched. This, along with her eagerness to meet Morwood's replacement, sent a stab of both guilt and grief through Corrie's heart. She wasn't sure if this lack of change was due to the senior agent's recent arrival, out of respect for Morwood, or maybe both. But it drove home the fact that her mentor had been a very private person—and had never put much of himself on display.

The new inhabitant of the office rose as she came in. She was struck by how young he looked in comparison to Morwood, then realized he had a kind of face that made it difficult to guess his age: he could have been thirty-five, or a decade older. His suit, clean shave, and haircut were all FBI issue, but there was something about him— maybe his friendly, unguarded smile, or the way that half a dozen open files were spread across his desk without false pretense of order—that reminded her of Agent Pendergast's insouciant disregard for red tape.

"You must be Agent Corinne Swanson," he said. "Very glad to meet you. Please, have a seat."

"Thank you, sir," she said. Unconsciously, she made for the chair she usually chose, then decided on the one next to it instead. "I wanted to thank you for agreeing—"

He stopped her rush of words by raising his hands, imitating surrender. "Please don't," he said. "For one thing, I'm not sure how long my case will keep me here, although it might be longer than expected. For another, you might find I'm an insufferable tyrant."

He smiled again, and she nodded, chancing a brief smile of her own. The relief she'd first felt at being given an interim mentor grew. Not only did this mean she was going to stay on track, career-wise, but her new mentor clearly understood the situation and seemed to be going out of his way to put her at ease.

"I'll tell you what," he continued, running a hand through his chestnut hair. "This being our first meeting, I'll do most of the talking. Maybe let you relax a little. I can imagine you've had plenty on your mind this weekend."

"Thank you," she repeated, then quickly added: "Sir."

"First, though, I wanted to tell you how badly I feel about Hale Morwood's death. I know it must have hit you hard. I never met him personally, but he was well respected among his peers, and he survived a couple of escapades early in his career that old-timers still like to recount. Maybe I can share one or two of them with you sometime."

"I would welcome that, sir."

"Probably the biggest favor I can do is to catch you up on the investigation of the fire. It's still in the early stages, of course. No accelerants were found—but then, it could hardly be arson in the FBI's own basement. Whatever caused it, the fire was fierce—I'm afraid there's not much left." He paused. "As for Agent Morwood, the initial findings are death by asphyxiation. The M.E. will have a more complete report in a day or two, after the autopsy is complete. You're welcome to join me for his review…if that's something you'd care to do, of course."

"Yes, sir. I would."

"Maybe by then we'll have some sense of what he was doing in the building so late—although I understand he was a night owl by habit." He raised his eyebrows, turning the statement into a question.

"Yes, he was."

"Good. Now, let's talk about what's been occupying your time. The—" he lifted a couple of folders from his desk, moving them around until he found what he was searching for—"the two unidentified bodies, shot and buried in the vicinity of Roswell. I've taken a glance over the file, but I'd rather get the details directly from you. After all, it's *your* case." He smiled again, and his eyes twinkled just a little mischievously.

Corrie took a deep breath. Briefly, she laid out the facts of the case—they could be summed up in depressingly few sentences.

"Thank you," he said when she finished. "And your next steps?"

"Well, just this morning, I got the report back on the four stainless steel crowns."

At this his eyebrows rose. "You'll have to forgive me—as I implied, I'm not yet up to speed on all the details."

"They were from the male victim. Given their unusual nature, I had them sent off to Quantico for analysis. It turns out they were Soviet made.

The man was probably Russian—and, given the time and place, very likely a spy."

At this, he nodded slowly. "And?"

"If he was a mole, he was undoubtably interested in the nuclear weapons program in the secret city of Los Alamos, which the Soviets knew all about in 1947. Most of those Soviet agents, I've been told, were based in Santa Fe."

"Very interesting."

"While it's a long shot, it might just be that dental records are still sitting in some dusty archive in Santa Fe that would help me ID the person. I plan to go to Santa Fe—if only because this is one of the very few bits of evidence we do have."

"A good plan," he said.

"Thank you, sir."

He put the file aside and leaned toward her slightly. "I would, of course, like to be kept in the loop. In fact, the best way to get me up to speed would be for you to assemble all the leads and evidence you've accumulated to date. Then we can decide together where we stand, and how you should best move forward—given what's happened."

Corrie, reminded again of the fire and Morwood's death, felt a stab of pain.

Her new mentor must have guessed what she was thinking, because he lowered his voice. "Listen to me, Agent Swanson. I've heard the imputation made against you, and I've also heard quite a bit about this guy Lathrop. You aren't accused of anything; you're not under investigation. For what it's worth, I think the fire investigation will clear you one hundred percent. So I would suggest—I'll even make it an order— that you do not beat yourself up about all this." He paused. "I've read Agent Morwood's reports about you, and—although he didn't say it in so many words—I got the sense he thought you the best rookie he ever ghosted."

This was so unexpected that it shattered all of Corrie's defenses. Something inside her crumpled; it was all she could do to keep back the tears.

"Thank you, sir," she said, fighting to maintain her composure.

"Okay, so here's my second, and last, order for this meeting." A faint smile now returned to his face. "Please don't call me 'sir.' 'Agent Lime' will do just fine. And I'll call you 'Swanson.' Deal?"

"Deal," Corrie replied once she was confident she could keep the tremor from her voice.

"Deal, *what?*"

"Deal, Agent Lime."

"That's better. Thank you, Swanson. Now, go see what you can assemble for us to review." And with that, he nodded his dismissal. Corrie rose, left the office, and headed back to her desk.

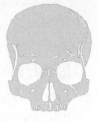

32

G REG BANKS, AT the wheel of a jeep, pulled up beside Tappan and the third jeep, driven by Cecilia Toth. A cloud of white dust settled around them as they got out and stood looking across the flat white landscape to a range of hills beyond. It was frightening in its emptiness, Banks thought, but beautiful in spite of that. He had seen nothing like this before, outside the science fiction films he'd devoured as a kid.

"This was Bitan's rendezvous point," Tappan said, consulting his GPS. "We'll start the search here."

The sun was well above the horizon and the heat was coming up. A distant dust devil twisted across their field of view like a pale vertical snake.

"Note the footprints," said Tappan.

It wasn't hard to see them in the light raking the soft alkali crust of the lake bed. One set went off to the left, the other to the right. As Banks scanned the vast empty lake bed, he could see no sign of Bitan.

"Greg," said Tappan, "you follow the left-hand tracks, and we'll follow the right. Cecilia, you go up the middle. We'll head to those hills."

They all climbed back into their respective vehicles. Banks eased the jeep into drive and slowly cruised along the dry flats, the trail of prints he was following doubling back and forth in what was evidently a search pattern before it entered the first of the hills. He stopped the jeep where the foothills rose—it was too rough to continue by vehicle. He got out to inspect the ground on foot, but it was impossible to see any tracks on the grassy slopes.

His radio crackled. "Banks?"

It was Tappan. "Let's proceed through the hills on foot, keeping a half-mile distance between us."

"Got it."

"Keep your GPS tracker on at all times."

Banks shrugged into his day pack, which

contained water and lunch. As he trudged up the hill, his mind drifted to Bitan and his eccentricities. He'd been suspicious of the bugger from the start. He wasn't sure why, but he always had the feeling Bitan had some sort of hidden agenda. Also, there was a certain aloofness, or possibly a feeling of arrogance, about the astronomer that put him off.

He arrived at the top of the first hill and scanned the landscape ahead with binoculars. A thousand yards to his right, he could see somebody else doing the same. Somehow it felt even more like an alien landscape here: all these little hills crowded together, carpeted with tall grass waving in the wind, dotted with oaks as twisted as bonsai. The hills were separated by small ravines. This was the kind of a place where, if you had an accident and your body was lying at the bottom of one of those ravines, you might never be found.

He caught movement out of the corner of his eye and quickly trained his binocs in that direction. A small herd of horses was cresting a hill and disappearing down the other side, moving fast, disturbed by the invasion of their domain. Horse Heaven Hills—an apt name, he thought as he made his way down the far side and continued on.

He hiked northward, up and down the hills, sometimes following narrow horse trails. But he saw nothing except occasional horses, shy as deer, fleeing as soon as they spied him. After a few miles, the hills petered out into a broad valley dotted with red sandstone buttes. This, he thought, must be Los Gigantes: the giant ones. Beyond that stood a range of foothills rising into mountains, purple in the late-morning light.

Banks took a break in the shade of an oak to drink water and eat a granola bar. It was a little crazy, he mused, the way he'd ended up in this place. It was all very sudden. He'd gotten the call just three weeks before, in his South Kensington flat—some woman on the phone saying that Lucas Tappan was on the line. At first he thought it was a joke, one of his friends taking the piss, but when Tappan got on the phone he quickly realized it was real. And then came the offer, the unbelievable compensation, and the demand that he drop everything. A week later he was here, at the ends of the earth, preparing to excavate an alleged UAP crash site.

Although he had long believed UAPs were real, he had serious doubts about the Roswell site. All those doubts, however, vanished when the mass spectra had come in, revealing an unknown superheavy element present in trace amounts. That floored him like nothing else had in his life. He'd gone over it a hundred times and there was no way of getting around the evidence. It was a smoking gun, proof that an intelligently engineered, extraterrestrial object made of exotic compounds had indeed crashed at the site. The full significance was still sinking in. Clearly, this discovery was going to change his life—but exactly how, he couldn't yet predict.

Other implications, too, were inescapable: that the U.S. government had indeed found a UAP at Roswell and covered it up. What had happened in the seventy years since? Had the bloody government been reverse engineering the technology? Had they been in contact with the ETs? How would they react to having their long deception uncovered? He felt himself sailing into uncharted waters.

And then there was Tappan, who insisted they keep the superheavy-element discovery under wraps. He wondered why.

His radio crackled, Tappan again. "Greg, any signs?"

"Nothing."

"Let's continue into the valley with the buttes and reconnoiter there." Tappan sent a GPS coordinate specifying where they should meet.

"Got it."

He finished the granola bar, took another gulp of water, and continued hiking into the valley. He wondered again what could have happened to Bitan. The man had grown up in the Negev, so it wasn't as if he was ignorant of a desert environment. It would be hard to get lost. Even if his GPS had died, all he'd had to do was climb a hill and look around to determine which direction to go. While he might have had a fall or been bitten by a snake, Banks thought it more likely Bitan had engineered his own disappearance. The lights Skip had seen hinted that someone might have met him out here and picked him up. Although if that was the case, why hadn't they seen any tire tracks?

The valley he was hiking in was a dramatic place, with the great buttes of sandstone rising hundreds of feet. There was no shade anywhere.

★ ★ ★

Three hours later, they were back at their jeeps, having found no trace of Bitan beyond the lake bed—no footprints or other evidence of human presence. At 1 PM, after seven hours of fruitless searching, to Banks's relief Tappan called it a day and they headed back to camp.

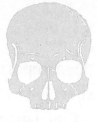

33

AT FIVE O'CLOCK, Nora entered Quonset 1, her brother reluctantly in tow, for a meeting called by Tappan. Skip hadn't wanted to come—he was embarrassed and afraid he'd be fired—but Nora had persuaded him it would be worse if he stayed away. All the scientific staff was there. They took seats around a large conference table at the back of the building. Tappan was the last to arrive, striding in at five minutes past, heading directly to the head of the table. Instead of sitting, he placed his hands upon the back of the chair and passed his gaze over the troubled group.

"Well," he finally said. "As you all know, we weren't able to find Noam Bitan. We aren't sure if the disappearance was intentional or accidental. Naturally, we're concerned, and it's been reported to both the FBI and the county sheriff."

He glanced around again.

"It turns out, as most of you now know, that Dr. Bitan had discovered something of great significance to our project—a discovery that may explain his disappearance." Yet again, his gaze swept the room, this time coming to rest on Skip. "He took his assistant, Skip Kelly, into his confidence. I'm going to ask Skip to now share that confidence with us."

Nora glanced over and saw pure panic on Skip's face.

"M-me?" he stammered.

"Yes, you." Tappan drilled him with his eyes. "I can understand why you felt compelled to keep that information from the rest of the team—but now the time has come for you to share it with everyone. We need to hear it from your own lips."

"Yes, sir," said Skip. "I'm really sorry. I realize I've let down the team."

Tappan waved his hand. "Please stand up so everyone can see you."

Skip got to his feet, nervously smoothing down his hair. "Well, as I mentioned earlier to some of you, Bitan decided—I mean, his observations and calculations indicated—that this site, the traditional Roswell site... was not where the UAP crashed. He believed the spaceship came in at such a shallow angle that it basically skipped off the ground, went airborne again, and crashed somewhere else. His calculations indicated where it might have landed. We were looking for that place when... when he disappeared."

"I assume you didn't find it?" asked Tappan.

"No."

"Thank you, Skip. Is there anything more?"

Nora saw Skip hesitate. "No, that's all." He sat down, his face covered in a sheen of perspiration. She was glad he hadn't gone on to share Bitan's story of alien abduction.

"The Three Engineers have gone over Bitan's calculations," Tappan said. "They've confirmed he was right: the UAP did indeed skip off the ground and keep going. What's more, the idea that this is a skip site is consistent with Nora's excavation of the groove, or trough, and its lack of substantial evidence. And this afternoon, Greg Banks did refined calculations of the UAP's possible trajectory. Greg?"

Banks rose, holding a sheaf of papers.

"We reran Bitan's calculations using computer modeling of the presumed shape, speed, and angle of the object, along with its mass, air resistance, and so forth. Obviously, we're lacking quite a few data points. But the model indicates Bitan was somewhat off in his calculations of where the thing might have landed. We believe its trajectory would have taken it farther, beyond the hills. It probably would have landed somewhere in the vicinity of the Los Gigantes buttes or in the foothills of the mountains beyond."

"How certain are you?" Tappan asked.

"About eighty percent, within the elliptical area we've outlined on our map. That's the area being overflown with the lidar plane as we speak."

"Thank you. And now Vitaly will cover that. Vitaly?"

Kuznetsov rose, smoothing down his hair. "Once we had Greg's calculations, we called in a lidar survey of the area. Fortunately, both aircraft and pilot were available at the last minute— for a price, of course. The plane flew up from Albuquerque around four and, as Greg just mentioned, should be on-site around now. It'll take about three hours to scan the five-square-mile target area. We should have the data processed by tomorrow morning. There is a little bit of a twist, however."

"What's that?" Tappan asked.

"There's an area in the eastern part of the Los Fuertes Mountains where the airspace is closed. It's quite a ways outside the projected landing area, so I don't think it will impede our discovery of the true crash site. But our pilot is having to fly a rather circuitous route to avoid that airspace."

"Closed?" Tappan asked sharply. "Why?"

"It's not as significant as you might think. About thirty percent of the airspace over New Mexico is closed to civilian overflights, for many reasons. Holloman AFB, White Sands Missile Range, large areas over Los Alamos and the Sandia Mountains, where nuclear weapons are designed and stored. It's basically a patchwork."

Tappan eased back. "I see. Thank you, Vitaly. Excellent and efficient work, all of you. If this lidar survey pans out, tomorrow we'll move our base of operations to the new crash site. Not the entire camp, of course—that's too complicated—but the excavation team. I've already spoken to Nora about this, and she's on board. We have the heavy equipment necessary to grade a road, so we can essentially commute back and forth from what will become a base camp—here—to the new dig site. It's all government land, so it's still covered by our permits."

Another sweeping gaze over the room. "Any questions?"

There was a general murmur, and Nora could sense the undercurrent of fresh enthusiasm and excitement.

"Do you think it might still be there?" Toth asked. "That maybe the government didn't find it, after all?"

"It's a possibility," Tappan said slowly.

"What about Bitan?" Emilio Vigil asked. "What are we supposed to do about his disappearance?"

"We've done all we can and reported it to the relevant authorities. The problem is now in the hands of the professionals. We'll cooperate with them. But in the meantime, we need to move forward full speed with our own project and leave the search to them." He paused, and said, his voice lower: "Earlier, I said it wasn't clear whether or not this development was an accident. But it's my opinion Bitan may have disappeared as part of a premeditated plan."

"Why?" Vigil asked.

"Who knows? He was keeping secrets, he suborned a member of our staff—I don't take kindly to that." His gaze turned to Skip, who turned red. "Skip, however, is contrite; he's leveled with us; and up to this point he's proven a valuable member of the team. So I've decided to keep him on the project. But I won't tolerate any more secrets. I hope that's understood." He checked his watch. "Six o'clock! That's happy hour for me. If there are no further questions, see you all tomorrow."

As everyone was filing out, he paused to touch Nora on the shoulder. "Nora, could I see you for a moment in my RV? I want to review plans for moving the excavation."

She tamped down on the acceleration of her heart. "Fine."

As they walked to his trailer, she said: "About Skip. I just want to thank you for understanding—"

He again placed a hand on her shoulder. "No worries about Skip. I told you my suspicions about a mole, and this abrupt disappearance seems like damning evidence to me. Skip fell under Bitan's spell, and that's forgivable. Besides, he's your brother, and..."

His voice trailed off. He opened the door for her, ushered her in, closed it behind them, then—his breath husky—pressed her against it, raised her thighs with surprisingly strong arms, and wrapped them tightly around his waist.

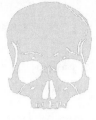

34

At the safe house he'd been assigned—a well-furnished condominium in the quiet Quaker Heights neighborhood of Albuquerque—Agent Lime looked out the living room windows, gazing with apparent disinterest at the dark, sleepy street. After a moment he closed the curtains, then lowered an inner set of blinds specially fabricated to give off a false heat signature, as well as to block "Havana syndrome" microwaves or signals from StingRay IMSI-catching devices. He walked over to a spare wood-topped desk, sat down, and unlocked the bottom drawer via a hidden thumbprint analyzer. The drawer—lined with a nitrocellulose accelerant that would destroy the contents if any tampering was detected—popped open. Among other things, it revealed five identical phones—arranged in a careful row—and a small lead-lined box. Taking out the box, Lime opened it and removed a one-time SIM card. He slid the card into the flank of the leftmost phone, put the box back in the drawer, and closed it.

The phone was small and without any identifying features. In many ways it was "dumb," lacking onboard GPS and other features common in recent years. This was by design. In one way, however, it was highly specialized: it used classified technology to bounce an encrypted signal off a network of spy satellites rather than relying on cell towers.

He looked at his watch, waiting for the seconds to tick off until it was exactly seven-oh-five. Then he entered some numbers; waited; tapped in his authentication; then entered another, shorter set of numbers. After a series of clicks, the familiar voice came on the line. *"Servandae vitae mendacium."*

"Nemini dixeris," said Lime, giving the counter-sign.

"I'll take your report now," Colonel Rush said.

Per his training, Lime wasted no words. "My insertion was timely. Agent Swanson has made more progress than expected on Hostile Interdiction Three. Despite the fire, she has aggressively followed up on the remaining evidence."

"Could this lead to further progress?"

"That remains to be seen."

"Don't you think termination would be a wise precaution?"

"With all respect, sir, it might be a little early for that. Swanson is the suspicious type and may be salting her evidentiary trail. We don't want to skin the rabbit unless we're sure no scat's been left behind."

"A colorful expression. Did you pick it up out there?"

"This morning, sir."

"I'll remember it. And you're confident leaving her in place is the right way to proceed?"

"Yes. I've eliminated the biggest, most immediate threat. If something happens to Swanson directly on the heels of that, it will raise questions. In my opinion, sir, the ongoing dig is far most dangerous." He paused. "May I ask how the debriefing is proceeding?"

"It reached its termination. No further information of use was extracted. He hadn't identified the location of Alpha, although he did discover that Beta was merely the ricochet location. Their team is currently searching for Alpha."

"If the group discovers... Well, sir, you know my concerns about the initial extraction being insufficiently thorough."

"It's not our place to question the actions of those who came before us."

"I'd never do that," said Lime.

"And you do understand the reasons why no further extraction or exploration was undertaken, or can be undertaken in the foreseeable future, at Alpha?"

"Yes, but that doesn't negate the possibility of..."

Lime's voice trailed off, and his superior completed the sentence. "Contact."

"Yes, sir."

"Duly noted."

"I want to assure you that I will keep my foot on the throat of Swanson's inquiries—and, if it becomes necessary, escalate with prejudice."

"Very good. If that's all, we'll talk again tomorrow at the scheduled time—unless an alert arises before that."

"Thank you, sir," Lime replied. Two additional clicks, then the line went dead.

Lime sat for a moment, mentally reviewing the conversation and whether it called for any restructuring of his plans. Deciding it did not, he took the SIM card from the phone, then turned toward an unusual device resembling a small oil drum, topped with a cylindrical steel cap tethered to the drum by a flexible pipe of metal mesh. Swinging open the cap, he dropped the chip of silicon in, then closed it again. The faintest *whump* sounded within as the barrel cyclone incinerated the SIM card. Next, Lime looked at the phone, mentally counting the number of times it had been used. Five. Despite its resistance to high-tech infiltration, tradecraft nevertheless dictated it was time to switch it out for another.

The *whump* the phone made as it was flash-incinerated was louder, but still nothing above a footfall, and in no way disturbed the somnolence of the evening.

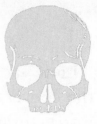

35

Corrie looked up from her desk, eyes fastening on the Pyramid clock hung above the exit to the elevator banks. Seven forty-five? It didn't seem possible. She'd been at her desk since meeting with Lime, putting together a timeline of the investigation all the way from Nora's initial call to her conversation with Sheriff Watts that morning. Wherever she could, she cross-referenced the details with database links to photographs, digital DNA samples, measurements for the facial reconstructions, ballistic tests, and all the other flotsam and jetsam that attached themselves to an investigation like iron filings to a magnet. She'd felt oddly satisfied upon completion: despite what was almost certainly lost in the fire, and no matter where the case led from here, she felt she'd outlined a solid foundation for Lime of the investigation to date.

Equally satisfying—and unexpected—was the number of people who had come up to her over the course of the afternoon to express their sympathy and support. Most were junior agents—including, surprisingly, a couple of the macho types who'd been standoffish when she first arrived. A few senior agents, who wouldn't normally have given her the time of day, had also paused at her cubicle to casually nod or greet her. Although no specifics were mentioned, Corrie understood: word of Lathrop's accusation had gotten around, and the consensus seemed to be that the man was full of shit. Corrie knew the forensic pathologist wasn't popular; perhaps that was influencing people's opinions. One thing, however, she wouldn't forget: Lime, her new mentor, had been the first to voice uncompromising support for her.

She began tidying up her cubicle in preparation for leaving. Despite the lingering shock and grief, she found herself curious about Agent Lime. She'd listened in on some of the water-cooler gossip earlier that afternoon, and it seemed his background was almost as mysterious as Morwood's had been. Only one agent on the floor had worked with him before, quite a while back, and had not gotten to know him well. That in itself was no big surprise: she knew that some agents liked to keep their CVs to themselves, especially if they didn't have all that stellar a history. And she'd overheard one person sniggering about Lime's luck: two years riding a desk in D.C. and here he was, being rewarded by ghosting recruits. The schadenfreudian tone of this observation had surprised her. Perhaps Lime felt like an outsider in Albuquerque.

That made two of them.

Cubicle in order, she turned to power down her computer. On the screen was a memo she'd received about the DNA results. There were no hits in any database, not even in the giant commercial genetic testing databases the FBI had access to. That was true of both autosomal and mitochondrial DNA—which was truly odd. These two people had to be related to some-body, somewhere. She made a mental note to have that rechecked.

She stood up, threaded her way out of the cube maze, and, bypassing the elevators, took the stairs down one level to the main entrance. By now it was nearly quarter past eight, but she was glad of the late hour: the less time alone with her thoughts, the better. As she approached the security barrier, she saw Shady the guard settling in behind his command station, preparing for the night shift. Shady was a rotund, affable ex-cop with a pale moonlike face and a head as bald as a cue ball, who insisted that everyone call him by the mysterious nickname nobody seemed to know the origin of. He was one of the friendliest people in the place, and Corrie always felt a rush of affection when she saw him.

"Hi, Shady," Corrie said as she came up to the barrier.

"Well, hello there, Ms. Swanson." Shady never called anybody *Agent*—it was either Mr., Ms., sir, or ma'am.

She smiled and, taking a pen from her purse, started filling out the pass required of all agents exiting or entering outside normal hours: *Swanson, C.; SA, GS-11/1; Section 2G.*

"Hey, Ms. Swanson," Shady said in an uncharacteristically serious tone. "I wanted to say that I was very sorry. About Mr. Morwood."

"Thank you," Corrie said as she added her signature.

"He was a straight-up guy. A lot of people rush in and out of here like their behinds were afire— excuse the expression. But Mr. Morwood, he'd stop to talk, ask how you were. Hell, he'd even listen to my stories from time to time." Shady chuckled.

Corrie looked up at Shady. He was an old-time beat cop, all right: even down to his sidearm, a well-worn Colt Detective Special. She wondered who he had at home, if anyone. It probably got lonely here, too: long nights with precious little to break the monotony. Maybe he was just a natural nighthawk.

"See you later," she said, pushing the off-hours pass through the security screen.

"Have a nice evening," Shady replied, taking the pass. Then he frowned.

Corrie was not letting go of the pass. She was thinking.

"Ms. Swanson?" Shady asked.

Corrie lifted her fingers from the counter, releasing the pass. "Sorry, I was distracted." She hesitated. "Shady, I wonder if you could help me with a question."

"Be glad to."

"When did Agent Morwood usually leave in

the evenings?" She knew he often worked late, but she'd never kept close track.

"Well, you know, there was no rhyme or reason to that. Not as far as I can tell, anyway. Here, I'll give you an example." Shady turned to his screen and began tapping the keyboard with his index fingers. "This last week, for instance. Monday, he clocked out at six thirty PM. Tuesday, eight twenty. Wednesday, nine oh-five. Thursday, five forty-five. Friday, five o'clock. See what I mean?"

"Yes, I do." No rhyme or reason, indeed. Corrie wasn't even sure why she'd asked the question; something was prompting her to pick up every crumb, turn over every leaf, of his final days on earth. Somehow, she'd begun to sense that Morwood was holding something back in those last days; but what it might be, or if it was only her imagination, she couldn't begin to fathom.

"Thanks a lot, Shady," she said as she turned away.

"My privilege, miss. Enjoy the rest of the evening."

Corrie passed through the barrier, then started down the steps, rooting in her bag for her keys. It was only when she reached the bottom step that she abruptly stopped.

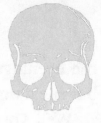

36

For a moment Corrie remained frozen, dimly conscious of the evening breeze on her face, the hum of traffic on I-25. Then she turned, ran back up the stairs, re-entered the building, and passed through the barrier.

Shady had just finished scanning her exit slip and was filing it away. He looked at her in concern. "Is there a problem?"

Corrie made an effort to seem nonchalant. "No problem. I was just curious about something you said. On Friday, Agent Morwood left the office at five PM?"

"Let me clear this screen." A few more finger taps, then Shady peered closely at the monitor. "Yup. Five-oh-one exactly."

"Then how was he found in the lab after the fire? That didn't take place until after midnight."

"He came back."

This was not unexpected. "What time was that?"

"Late. Shoot, it was only three days ago, you'd think I'd recall." A brief pause while he looked up the details. "Checked in at eleven fifty."

"And he went straight back to his office?"

"No, miss. He signed in for the lab."

"The lab?"

"Got it right up here on the screen."

"Was he carrying anything?"

"A blue evidence box, with a tag."

"Did he often come back to work late at night?"

"Not usually. He stayed late plenty of times— now and then, *real* late—but once he left, he was gone until morning."

Corrie did her best to look mildly curious, but her mind was racing. "You were on duty that night, weren't you?"

"I'm like a Swiss watch. Monday to Friday, eight PM until four in the AM."

"So were you—" she wasn't quite sure how to put this tactfully— "the first to learn of the fire?"

"That was Harold Lamson."

"Harold Lamson? Who's he?"

"Night maintenance. He was working down by the far end of the main building when the alarm went off."

"When was this?"

"Must have been shortly before one. He called me; I called the fire department, Mr. Garcia, then Emergency Response. In that order."

"You said the far end of the main building?"

Shady nodded. "Seems strange, doesn't it? An alarm going off that far from the fire, I mean. Of course, they tell me that lab's pretty airtight. I didn't smell any smoke up here, that's for certain."

"And once you called for help—?"

"That's all she wrote. Way I heard it, the fire had more or less burned itself out by then." He shrugged.

"Thanks so much."

Corrie made a show of heading once again for the exit, then paused one more time. "Damn," she said, turning. "You know, I left some files I wanted to review in my desk. Just locked them away and walked out."

"It's been that kind of a day, I'll bet."

"I suppose I have to fill out another pass?" she asked meekly.

Shady hesitated. "Guess so, miss. Especially now." He handed one through the barrier screen. "Sorry."

"It's my own fault." She filled in every detail, including her destination: section 2G. Then she signed at the bottom and passed it back. "Thanks."

"No problem at all."

She began to walk back toward the stairs, then stopped. "Oh, Shady: don't be surprised if I'm a couple of minutes. I also have a little work to finish up."

"Very good, Ms. Swanson."

She walked away from the security barrier and across the lobby, to the stairwell, then turned the corner, hearing the echo of her low heels in the empty space. Once out of sight of the guard station, she slipped off her shoes. Instead of turning left, up the stairs, she took another look around, listened to make sure all was silent, then made for the stairway leading down to the basement. The lab wasn't far from the foot of the stairs. Investigators had taped a large security tarp at one side of the stair-well; she slipped behind that, crouched, then descended as quickly and silently as she could.

There was a security camera at the bottom of the stairs, but she was banking on being concealed by the tarp and other debris she could see piled below, wrapped in evidence bags.

At the bottom of the stairs, she slunk around the corner, then paused. There were no warning shouts from above, no footfalls of Shady coming to investigate. Keeping behind the investigative tarp that lined one side of the hall, she headed for the door to the lab.

The tarp ended in a taped seal just beyond the lab entrance. The door itself was closed and covered with crime scene tape. Corrie was able to duck beneath it with ease. The security keypad was dark, disabled. She turned the safety handle carefully—unlocked—and then, as quietly as she could, fearing at any moment some maintenance person or late worker would come around the corner, pushed the door open just enough to slip inside.

Beyond was nothing but blackness—even the exit signs were off—and she was almost overwhelmed by an acrid odor of smoke, melted plastic, burnt electronics, and something else she didn't care to identify. She raised herself to full height, pushing the door closed behind her. Then, reaching into her bag, she located her SureFire Defender, pulled it out, and snapped it on.

The 1,000-lumen LED bulb illuminated a damp, hellish landscape. She directed the beam toward her feet, but not before noticing that the lab's lone security camera was partly burnt, covered by more security tape, and half-disassembled. At least she didn't have to worry about being seen inside.

She switched off the flashlight and stood motionless in the dark, catching her breath. What the hell was she doing here, anyway?

But she knew the answer even before she'd asked herself the question. On Saturday and again today, her eyes had darted more than once toward the basement stairs. Both Garcia and Agent Lime had told her she had nothing to worry about. But that was just talk. She couldn't leave it alone; she couldn't wait for however long the investigation might take to release a report: she had to know if she was responsible for Morwood's death. She had to know *now*. But even beyond that, she wondered why Morwood had come back to the lab at midnight on a Friday.

What was so pressing that he couldn't wait until morning?

She had to hurry. This had been an impulsive decision on her part—and if she was caught, she would be in deep shit, especially since she was a potential suspect. Christ, she had to finish and get out before she lost her nerve.

She turned her light on once again and shined it around. She was used to seeing a long, narrow hallway, made narrower by the rows of boxes and packing materials Lathrop never seemed to clear away. Now, however, only ruin lay ahead of her—charred piles of ash and half-burnt, unidentifiable things, sodden and sunken in on themselves and coated with foam retardant. Above them, soot streaks curled up the walls and across the ceiling, bizarre and clutching, like silhouettes from a German Expressionist film. All around her were little numbered flags—some red, some yellow, some blue. And on the floor directly before her was a particularly heavy swarm of flags that—she realized in sudden horror—formed the outline of a human being.

Stifling a gasp and looking away, she passed by this quickly, staying close to the ashen boxes that lined the wall, their contents now exposed. The Bunsen burner was her objective: she had to examine it and get out.

She turned the corner, placing her feet with care, and the beam of her light fell across the main lab. She quickly aimed it toward the soapstone table on which the burner sat, and there it was, scorched but intact... and turned off.

Thank God.

The rubber hose was unhitched and her light played on the valve, which was also turned off. Of course, one of the investigators might have turned it off, but that seemed unlikely: they would have shut down the gas farther back and left everything inside the lab as undisturbed as possible until their work was complete.

Embarrassed at her overwhelming and selfish sense of relief, she let her light drift over the rest of the lab. A platoon of flamethrowers couldn't have done a more thorough job. Storage cabinets hung loose from the walls, glass fronts melted; cabinets that had been full of papers and evidence were now just shapeless lumps of steel and carbon; the lockers that held the two sets of human remains had burst open under the heat, ghastly as crematoria, the evidence inside thoroughly burnt. And the table where she'd worked so hard on her facial reconstructions no longer existed; it was just a low pile of broken metal, covered—like everything else—with tiny evidence flags. It was as Agent Lime had told her. All the evidence—everything she'd been working on—was gone. And Lathrop was as full of shit as she'd expected—the fire wasn't her fault.

She'd better get the hell out. This was crazy. She couldn't afford to spend any more time here—not even a minute.

As she turned to leave, her light passed over something lying on the floor, in a melted evidence box, that gleamed dully. It was the device Morwood had brought back to the lab from his visit to Eastchester. Was that why he was there? If so, why wait until midnight? He would have been back from Los Alamos no later than nine thirty or ten.

She peered at it more closely. It was heavily blackened by smoke but otherwise intact. On impulse, she took her phone from her pocket and—leaning forward so as not to leave footprints in a layer of sodden ash and rivers of plastic—took pictures of the device: top, sides, and bottom, where the legend and some numbers had been stamped.

Walking gingerly, she reached the door, opened it slightly, made sure nobody was in the hall beyond, and slipped out.

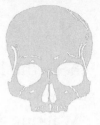

37

Nora woke to the smell of bacon and eggs and the sound of Skip's usual morning conversation with Mitty, who listened with great attention and zero comprehension.

As she came out of her bedroom, Skip, without turning around, said: "Bet you slept soundly."

"Now, why would you say that?" Nora asked, sitting down while Skip placed a latte in front of her.

"Well," he said cheerily, "when you came in rather late last evening you looked like you'd just run a marathon—all pink-cheeked and glowing."

"Please shut up," Nora said, and buried her lips in the warm foam, taking a deep draw of coffee.

"I figured you worked up quite an appetite, too."

She was, in fact, starving, but said nothing, her annoyance rising. A moment later Skip placed a plate of bacon and eggs in front of her. She tucked in right away, hoping she could finish and get out of there before he said more.

"You know, sis, I really like Lucas. He's a good guy. He could have raked me over the coals for holding out on him about Bitan, but he didn't."

"You're lucky, that's all I can say."

"I'd like to think it's because I've proven to be an important member of the team," Skip said with a note of injured pride.

"That's true," said Nora. And it was: Skip had risen to the occasion. Not only had he grown surprisingly knowledgeable about UAPs and become able to carry on deep conversations with the scientists, but he was curating the collection of artifacts well and keeping the library and archives in good shape. He had learned a lot in his time analyzing potsherds at the Institute.

Skip placed another plate down for himself. "Can I ask how serious this thing is with Tappan?"

"Is it really that obvious that we're, you know...having a relationship?"

"Are you kidding? You go in there, supposedly for some quick meeting, and come back out two hours later, blooming. Yeah, it's kind of obvious."

Nora felt a wave of dismay. Of course, Skip was right, and in an ant farm like this, everybody would notice.

"Are people talking?"

"Not to me. But I'm sure they're yakking it up among themselves."

Oh God. It was a stupid thing they were doing—both for her and for Tappan—yet, once again, a part of her just didn't care. It had been several years since Bill had died. She felt like something inside her was coming back to life—roaring back, in fact. At the same time, it was improper, inappropriate, and just plain reckless. Even more important, she had to be careful not to let her feelings cloud her professional judgment...and her objectivity. For example, she couldn't let Lucas's zealous belief in UFOs influence her own opinions.

On the other hand, life was short. And it was so much fun.

Skip laid a hand on her hand, suddenly serious. "Nora, you're not going to let yourself get hurt, are you? I mean, Tappan must have a million girls chasing him: those dimples and gray eyes and all that money. I think it's great you're having a little amuse-bouche—you certainly deserve it— but I don't want to see it go wrong."

"It won't." Even as she said it, she had to admit to herself she'd fallen into the deep end of the pool. Where it was going, she had no idea—and she figured the best thing was to avoid thinking about it. It had only been two days, after all. They were both adults and knew what they were doing. Or so she told herself.

"Okay. Enough said." Skip glanced at his watch. "Almost eight. Time for yet another meeting."

They arrived at Quonset 1 a few minutes later. Banks had set up a digital projector and screen, and they all took seats. Tappan was already there, and as soon as everyone was seated, he rose.

"The lidar survey came in around five this morning," he said. "Vitaly? Put it up."

The lights darkened and an image flashed onto the screen, a grayscale map of the landscape in incredible detail. Tappan said nothing further, and the image hung there silently in the darkness.

Nora leaned forward, staring. She saw it almost immediately—an old disturbance in the Gigantes valley, the faint ghost of a road that went into the valley and ended in a circle. A large area, strangely blurred from this height, with nearly invisible tracks crisscrossing each other in the middle of the circle. It sure looked like an old crash site, covered up and undisturbed for decades.

An excited babble of voices rose in the room as everyone else saw it.

"A picture's worth a thousand words," Tappan finally said. "And this one represents good news and bad. The good news is this must be the real crash site. They covered it up as best they could, and time has done its work—but nothing is invisible to lidar. You can clearly see the scars even after all these years. The bad news is that all those old tracks and disturbances indicate the government found it long ago." He looked around. "Any questions?"

"What's that mark going through the upper corner of the image?" Banks asked. "Is that a road?"

Kuznetsov answered. "Yes. It's not on our

maps, but then there are a lot of old ranch roads that were never put on maps. I don't think it has any relevance."

"Could that be where Bitan got picked up?" Banks continued.

"It's possible," said Kuznetsov. "But at first glance, the track doesn't look like it's seen any fresh traffic. We haven't examined it in detail."

"Thank you," said Tappan. "Nora? Your turn."

Nora stood up. She looked around the table but didn't detect any knowing smirks. "As soon as we grade a road to the site, we'll transfer our equipment and proceed with immediate excavation. All indications are that this is where the, ah, object landed after the skip site—and was then, perhaps, retrieved by the government."

"How long will it take to build the road?" Banks asked.

"We can almost drive there now, cross country. There are just a few small sections that need equipment to grade a safe passage for the jeeps. We'll have to skirt those grassy hills, but that's not a big deal. We should be able to complete a rough road in less than a day."

"How far is it from here?" Vigil asked.

"About eight miles."

"And how long will the excavation take?" Kuznetsov asked.

"We don't know how deep we need to go," said Nora, "but it looks like ground similar to here. I would guess a week or even less. It's a more compact site. By the way, just to be safe, I've reviewed our permits. We're clear to proceed. All we have to do is report the change of venue to the Department of the Interior."

As she sat down again, she was aware of a strange dynamic in the room. Everyone was clearly excited by this discovery. On the other hand, there was every reason to believe the government had gotten there first. But gotten there and done what? She just wasn't willing to accept it was some alien UFO. She even felt— ironically enough—her skepticism reasserting it- self, as if in reaction to her feelings for Tappan. After all, it could have been an advanced missile, or an unusual meteorite, or an experimental aircraft—any one of which could have been retrieved by the government, and the site then covered up.

But she didn't mention any of this. And when there were no further questions, Tappan adjourned the meeting.

38

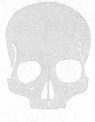

Watts eased his sheriff's vehicle down the road through the cottonwood trees until the view suddenly opened up to reveal a broad sandy beach—and beyond, the braided ribbon of the Rio Grande. The sun was just rising over the river, turning it into molten gold.

He brought the Explorer to a halt, powering down the windows and turning off the engine. He reached into the back and removed a coffee carrier. He handed Corrie a giant lidded cup and a foil-wrapped burrito. "Coffee and breakfast. As promised."

Sitting in the passenger seat, Corrie gingerly accepted them, spread some napkins in her lap, and took a grateful slug of coffee, noting the extra cream and sugar.

As if reading her thoughts, Watts said: "I remembered how you like it, sweet and thick."

Corrie had expected breakfast in a café, not this. This was, she thought, more like a... well, a breakfast *date*. She quickly pushed the thought out of her mind. FBI agents did not date county sheriffs. Especially over breakfast.

"When I was a kid, we used to ride our horses down here," Watts said. "It's one of my favorite places. We waded across the river and rode into the Bosque del Apache, that giant grove of cottonwoods on the other side. You being recent to New Mexico," he continued, "I thought you might like to see it."

He was talking fast, uncharacteristically nervous for such a laid-back guy.

"It's beautiful," Corrie said. "I'm glad you brought me here." And it really was beautiful, even magical, with the whispering sounds of the river; the sun shining through the cottonwoods; the distant purple mountains.

She looked over at him, seeing his relief that she wasn't bored. It would be easy to dismiss a man this young as a cliché, she knew, with the six-guns and holsters and expensive cowboy hat. But like an iceberg, Watts had a lot more to him than you could see at first glance.

She took another long sip of coffee and a bite of her burrito, listening to him talk.

"Bosque del Apache means Apache Grove. It's called that because the Warm Springs Apache used to camp there in the old days. Some of the biggest cottonwood trees you'll ever see can be found over there, trunks thirty feet in circumference. They go on for miles. And in those sand hills behind the forest is a lost Pueblo city called Senecú. The ruins were visible until the eighteenth century, when it was totally covered with windblown sand. Now its location is forgotten."

Corrie couldn't help but be impressed by his deep affection for the land and its history.

They continued their breakfast in silence for a while as the sun climbed higher in the sky.

"I guess we'd better talk shop," said Watts. "Since that's why you came down."

"Right," said Corrie, vaguely disappointed.

"I spoke to Buford about the case. It seems pretty straightforward. He thinks Bitan walked off the job and will eventually turn up. I tend to agree—especially considering those lights that were seen in the area where he disappeared. Buford speculated Bitan might have had some hidden agenda."

Corrie hesitated. She wasn't so sure about that, but she didn't have evidence either way. And, as Morwood had drilled into her, FBI agents never voiced hunches.

But Watts sensed her doubt. "You don't agree?"

Corrie shrugged. "I agree the evidence points to him taking off. But it seems a strange way to do it, in the middle of the desert, leaving Nora's brother alone like that. Anyway, it's not my case."

"Speaking of your case, this digging up the Roswell site sounds batshit crazy to me."

"It is."

"What can you tell me about it?"

Corrie wondered if it was kosher to share the details with him; she decided it was. She quickly sketched out the background, from Nora Kelly's involvement and the billionaire backing the project, to the double homicide they'd discovered—and, finally, to Morwood's death in the fire. When she was done, a brief silence settled over the vehicle.

"I read about Morwood's death in the *Journal*,"

Watts said at last. "That must've been pretty tough."

"It was." Corrie, to her horror, heard her voice cracking just a little.

"Hey," said Watts, placing a hand on her shoulder. "Wow, it really did hit you hard. I'm so sorry I didn't call you."

Corrie shook her head, mortified. "Why? We're colleagues. You don't owe me anything."

"You reached out to me...as a friend, I hope, not just a colleague," said Watts.

Corrie brushed away a tear. This was getting ridiculous. In another moment, she'd be bawling. "I suppose I did. That came out wrong just now."

"It's okay. I understand."

"I'm sorry for falling apart like this." She made a mighty effort to pull herself together. "I have to go over the autopsy results this afternoon, and that means having to view Morwood's body. I'm dreading it."

"Don't go, then. You can get all the information you need from the report."

"No," she said, "I have to. I *have* to do this."

His hand remained on her shoulder, and he gave her a reassuring squeeze. "You know, I'm

always here when you need me. As a colleague—
and a friend."

"Thank you. I appreciate it—I really do."

She finally managed to get herself under control. "It's more than Morwood's death. The fire
destroyed most of the crucial evidence in the
case. I'd done a reconstruction of the victims'
faces, and those were burned up along with the
remains. And..." She hesitated. "The pathology
technician accused me of leaving a burner on."

"What the— Like hell you did!"

"I didn't. And I know the fire investigation will
show that. But it's been stressful."

"I think it's remarkable you're handling it so
well. Do you have anyone you can lean on in the
FBI office?"

"I have a new mentor—Agent Lime. He's been
really supportive."

"I'm glad to hear that." He paused. "You'll get
through this, Corrie. You've got an inner tough-
ness, and I think you know that."

She nodded. She did know that. She was tough
and she would get through it. "We'd better
get going. Thanks for your help with Buford—I
really appreciate it."

Watts balled up their burrito foils, shoved

them in the empty coffee cups, put it all in the bag, and started the Explorer. "I'll let you know how the case develops, but as I said, it's probably as banal as it seems—the guy just disappeared himself."

Corrie nodded. "Thanks for showing me this special place."

"Maybe we can get together for dinner sometime?"

This had tumbled out abruptly. And the uncharacteristic nervousness had returned. "You mean, like...as in a date?"

"Well, you know, just to catch up. I'll fill you in on Buford's work."

Corrie felt, not for the first time, a strange mix of excitement and anxiety rising within her. "I'd like that," she said. "But let's make it lunch. Is that okay?"

He nodded, the relaxed smile returning. "No problem." And he eased the vehicle around and back down the sandy road.

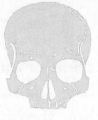

39

Corrie had seen many autopsies before, and this would be no different—or so she kept telling herself.

Lime had assured her several times it wasn't necessary for her to attend, that he could do it alone, and more than once she'd come close to canceling. But she felt it her duty to hear directly from the M.E. how Morwood had died.

Struggling to control her apprehension, she and Lime arrived at the door of the FBI medical examiner's lab and were welcomed by the M.E. himself, a short, portly doctor named Boyd Mason.

He led them into the brightly lit room, where a corpse lay on a gurney under a plastic sheet. His bustling, talkative manner was somehow reassuring. This was, she thought, the way to treat death: matter-of-factly, with a professional outlook. They were just dead bodies, nothing more, as inert as a tree trunk or a rock.

Mason reached out and grasped the corner of the sheet, then glanced up. "You've both…seen autopsied cadavers before, of course?"

They nodded, and he drew back the sheet.

Instantly, the sight froze Corrie with horror. Her gorge rose. She struggled mightily to control herself, but almost immediately realized it was going to be a losing fight.

"If I might—sorry—excuse myself—"

She stumbled into the adjacent restroom—thank God it was nearby—and violently threw up her breakfast. Then again. God, how she hated herself as she knelt over the toilet bowl, nose filling with snot, tears streaming down her face. Shame, self-disgust, and humiliation washed over her in waves as she kept right on retching. Finally she rose, staggered to the washbasin, washed and dried her face with paper towels, rinsed out her mouth, and hazarded a glance in the mirror.

She looked like shit.

Pull yourself together, get back out there, and finish what you have to do.

Adjusting her hair, straightening her jacket, and putting on a fresh coat of lipstick, she emerged from the bathroom and walked stiffly back into the examiner's suite.

"Agent Swanson," said Lime, coming forward with a concerned look, "this isn't necessary at all. In fact—"

"I apologize, sir," Corrie said as coolly as she could. Then she turned to the M.E. "Sorry. Please proceed."

"Of course," said Mason, looking as unperturbed as ever. Corrie had the impression this was nothing new to him—and it made her feel marginally better.

The body, more precisely the upper part that remained in decent condition, had been thoroughly autopsied, organs and brain removed, then stitched together in rough fashion, the cranium fastened back on sans brain, scalp wrinkling back from the bone and the eyes open—it was awful. But Corrie steadied herself. There was nothing more to come up. Even the dry heaves had exhausted themselves.

"As you can see, we did a complete medicolegal autopsy. In addition to examining all the organs, we did histological sections of the lungs, heart, brain, and liver, and a complete toxicological suite as well. The cause of death was clear: asphyxiation caused by lack of oxygen and carbon monoxide poisoning, both exacerbated by smoke inhalation. Agent Morwood had a chronic pre-existing condition: autoimmune lung disease, sometimes labeled interstitial lung disease. It's characterized by inflammation and scarring. He kept it under control with anti-inflammatories and corticosteroids, but his lungs were permanently damaged.

"The body was found in the front of the lab, and as you can see it is only burned on the lower half. That burning occurred after death—the victim succumbed well before the fire reached him."

His voice was professional and soothing.

"With his lung condition, even a small amount of carbon monoxide from the spreading fire would have incapacitated him. It might have happened even before he was aware there was a fire. His lungs simply had no reserves, no cushion to deal with a drop in the oxygen levels or rise in smoke."

He paused. "Are there any questions so far?"

Corrie mustered her voice. "You said you did histological sections of lung tissue?"

Dr. Mason nodded.

"May I see those?"

"Of course." He picked up a digital tablet, tapped it into life, brought up an image, then handed it to her. "You can clearly see the enlargement of the airspaces distal to the terminal bronchioles, accompanied by destruction of their walls. Along with fibrosis, of course."

She could indeed see it. Inside the bronchioles, there was a scattering of soot and smoke particles. But not all that many.

"That doesn't look like a lot of inhaled smoke," she said.

"True. As I mentioned, he was probably affected first by carbon monoxide as well as the rapid decrease in oxygen. The fire, after all, started in a rather small space. I would suggest he was unconscious by the time he actually began breathing smoke and succumbed not long after."

"Thank you." She handed back the tablet. "What did you find in the toxicology analysis?"

"Nothing. No sedatives, nothing that would incapacitate him, nothing that might indicate foul play. No alcohol or recreational drugs. He was clean."

"Forgive the question, but: Any chance you could have missed anything?"

"There's always the remote possibility of an exotic or unknown compound being present, but we did the full suite of tests. And believe me, that covers just about everything, including nerve agents, radionuclides, and the other suspects, usual or unusual."

Corrie forced herself to examine the body more closely. It smelled strongly of scorched hair and antiseptics. She felt another dry heave coming up but managed to suppress it.

"There's a scratch on his neck."

The M.E. bent over to look. "Yes, we noted that."

"And?"

"It's a superficial mark and could have been caused by anything. Bodies almost always bear signs of minor injuries—a scratch here, a bruise there. Especially active males."

"So it's not suspicious."

"In the absence of other signs of struggle, no, we wouldn't normally find it significant."

Corrie glanced at Lime, saw the look of sympathy in his eyes. He must be thinking she was grasping at straws. Maybe she was.

"Could I see his effects?" she asked.

"Certainly." He turned and wheeled over another gurney. Morwood's clothes had been laid out upon it. Pretty much everything below the waist had been badly burned. The jacket, shirt, and tie were mostly intact, as was Morwood's body from the waist up. Resting next to these were his glasses, some scorched keys, the spine of a burnt wallet, and a mass of credit cards melted around a piece of notepaper, its bottom half burned away. Centered on the remaining top half was a single word:

ITEM

"Any idea what this is?" she asked, pointing at the piece of notepaper.

Mason shook his head. "I assume it was the beginning of a list of some kind."

"And there's no way to retrieve the rest of the list—to read the writing remaining in the ashes?"

"Sometimes that's possible, but not when it's as thoroughly consumed as this was."

Corrie stared at the body, no longer horrified

but trying to extract some meaning, even some revelation. But there was nothing. What could have been on that list? Given the underlining, Morwood must have felt it highly significant. She wished to hell it hadn't burned.

"Any other questions?" Mason asked gently.

"So there's no indication whatsoever this is a homicide?"

"Whether the fire was accidentally or deliberately set is outside my purview. But as far as cause of death is concerned, I am one hundred percent sure this man died of suffocation due to a combination of carbon monoxide poisoning, lack of oxygen, and smoke inhalation. The fire started in the back of the lab, and he was near the front entrance, and by the time he realized what was happening he was either losing consciousness or already unconscious." He paused. "He didn't feel any pain."

"Thank you, Dr. Mason."

"You're welcome, Agent Swanson."

As they left the office, Corrie was relieved Lime didn't bring up her getting sick. Instead, she herself brought up Nora's call the previous morning about the missing scientist, Bitan. She'd intended to mention it during their initial meeting, but with everything else going on it had fallen between the cracks.

"Missing?" Lime said. "Did she mention the circumstances?"

"He was about five miles north of their camp, looking for an outlying site, and vanished into the desert."

"And they're concerned?"

"Not concerned so much as angry. From what I can tell, they suspect he was working for some other group or possibly Israeli intelligence—and once he had what he wanted, he'd arranged to be picked up far from camp."

"Anything else I should know?"

Corrie hesitated. "I spoke to Sheriff Homer Watts of Socorro County. I've worked with him before, and he seemed the right person to contact. He said he'd talk to the sheriff of Chaves County, where the dig's located—one Randall Buford." She didn't think Lime needed to know she'd had breakfast with Watts a few hours earlier—as it was, he already knew more than he probably wanted to about that meal.

"And how would you like to proceed?"

"I'd like to talk to Dr. Kelly again," Corrie said.

"Get more information. Maybe we need to go back out there ourselves."

She found Lime contemplating her with amused skepticism. "You sure that's the right course of action?"

Corrie looked back at him.

"Do you really think a recent disappearance could be connected to a homicide from the forties? If so, I'd like to hear your theory how."

She paused. "I see your point."

"And what is my point?"

"That not everything is connected to everything else. This disappearance probably has nothing to do with the double homicide."

He smiled. "I'll never be the mentor Agent Morwood was, but I'm trying. That's exactly right: since the disappearance of this Bitan is almost certainly not connected to your case, and because it's merely a missing-persons issue, it's been turned over to the rightful investigative body: the Chaves County Sheriff's Office. Turned over by *you*." He looked at her, still smiling. "Very good work, Agent Swanson."

"Thank you, sir." And as they waited for the elevator, she tried to remember if Morwood had ever smiled at her.

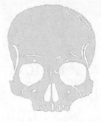

40

Corrie had never been to Los Alamos before, and she was curious to see the once-secret city that had built the first atomic bomb. But when she finally got there, she found it just another generic government town—albeit one wedged into a fabulous setting of mountain peaks, ponderosa forests, and deep canyons.

She stopped at a checkpoint and showed her credentials to the guard. She was given a special visitor's pass for one of the tech areas, where Dr. Eastchester had his office, along with directions on how to get there.

The area lay outside of town, occupying a long mesa extending from the Jemez Mountains, surrounded by two sets of chain-link fences topped with concertina wire. She pulled up at another security station and showed her pass to the guard, who told her where to park and how to find Eastchester's office.

The building had yet another guard at the entrance who checked her pass and ID again, then asked for her sidearm, which she surrendered. He escorted her down a long, cool hallway to an office at the end, door open.

"Dr. Eastchester?" the guard said. "Your visitor."

Corrie entered a spacious and rather austere office overlooking a stand of pines, with views to snowy mountains beyond. A large blackboard dominated one wall, covered with scribbled equations.

"You must be Special Agent Swanson," said an old man who rose somewhat creakily from a plush chair behind an old oaken desk piled with journals and papers.

"Please don't get up, Dr. Eastchester," Corrie said.

But he did anyway and took her hand. "Pleased to meet you. Have a seat."

The scientist eased himself back down and she took a seat before the desk. He looked at her, a grave expression on his face. "I'm so awfully sorry to hear about Hale's death. I suspect you must have been quite close to him. I, too, felt close to him. This is a terrible shock."

Corrie nodded, trying to keep her face from registering emotion at the man's sympathetic tone.

"I'd known Hale since he was in your position. He had recently joined the FBI and was being mentored by a senior agent, Mickey Starr. You have my condolences."

Corrie wanted to move the conversation as quickly as possible to firmer emotional ground. "Thank you for your sympathy. You have mine as well." She took the opportunity to consult her notes. "You mentioned Agent Starr. What was he like?"

"He was a tough guy. Square-jawed, buzz cut, blue suits. Clipped way of speaking. He was hard on Morwood, treated him roughly. To be honest, I didn't like him." He paused to cough. "Don't know what's happened to Starr. Is he still around?"

"He passed away a few years ago," Corrie said. She had established that from older agents in the office.

Eastchester nodded.

"I understand Agent Morwood brought a device to you for identification."

Hearing this, Eastchester hesitated.

"I know it's classified," said Corrie. "Don't be concerned—you can speak freely. I have clearance."

"Very well." Still, the man—obviously habituated to secrecy—waited a moment longer to answer. "As I explained to Hale, it's a device used to adjust the strength of a thermonuclear bomb by feeding more or less tritium fuel into the fusion chamber. Nicknamed the 'dial-a-yield.' At least one wag has joked the device set a bomb to either regular or extra crispy." He gave a quick, weak smile. "Are you familiar with the basic principles behind the hydrogen bomb?"

Corrie wasn't, but didn't want to admit it. "Somewhat."

"The fusion bomb is initiated by a fission bomb. That device determined the yield. I wasn't part of the development—it was years before my time, and in any case it's no longer in use."

Corrie jotted some notes. "Dr. Eastchester, what can you tell me about the case Agents Starr and Morwood were working on back then?"

"Quite a lot, actually. But doesn't the FBI have files on it?"

"We do. Some twenty feet of them. If you

don't mind, I'd like to hear about it in your own words—since you were Agent Morwood's direct contact within Los Alamos."

"I don't mind at all. It was strange. Have you ever read *The Hollow Man*, by John Dickson Carr?"

"No, I haven't."

"A chapter in the book deals with the many ways a person can commit the perfect murder in an apparently locked room. The case was like that—a locked-room mystery. But...if I may ask, what does this have to do with the current case?"

"Probably nothing. I'm just trying to create some context." Corrie actually had wondered if the two cases might be connected. After all, despite the time factor, there was some overlap. But she knew not to say anything until she had hard evidence.

"It's quite an easily described crime. That's one of the things that makes it so baffling—its simplicity."

Corrie waited while he took a deep breath, his eyes looking over her shoulder and into his own memory. "The victim was a senior scientist, a group leader. Name of Arvesen. Henrik Arvesen.

One morning, in January of 1999, his body was discovered in a high-security clean room within a secret area. The room was locked. It had a computerized device that recorded anyone who came in or out, not just by key code but also by photograph *and* right index fingerprint. Arvesen had been shot in the head at point-blank range. No one else was there. No gun was found in the room—so it could not have been suicide—and yet the computerized record of ingress and egress showed he had entered the room alone at nine the night before and never left—nobody else entered or left the room until the staff arrived the next morning."

"Could the security system have been hacked in some way?"

"That's what was initially supposed. But the most sophisticated analysis by computer security experts brought in from outside could find no trace of hacking. Believe me, the security of that room was—and still is, actually—considered unhackable."

"Who among the staff discovered the body?"

"Arvesen's lab director, who also had a very high-level clearance. He saw from the record that Arvesen had gone in at nine and never came out, which was odd, so he went in...and found the body."

"Could the lab director have killed him when he went in?"

Another faint smile crossed the old man's face. He seemed to admire her doggedness. "Even if he'd managed to evade the security camera, Arvesen's body temperature had declined too much. The M.E. placed the time of death around midnight."

"Could you please tell me what Arvesen did here?"

"He was group leader of the H-bomb nuclear chemistry department. The original H-bombs used pure tritium as a fuel, until it was discovered that tritium could be combined with lithium to make a compound called lithium-6 deuteride. When bombarded with neutrons by a triggering explosion, it creates a vast amount of tritium, which in turn becomes fuel for the second stage of the explosion. Lithium-7 proved even more effective under certain conditions." He paused. "That's probably as much detail as I should get into. Let's just say that Arvesen's team was always looking for better fuels for the H-bomb. This was extremely classified work.

Eventually, it rendered the dial-a-yield device Morwood showed me obsolete. That only worked with compressed tritium gas, dating from the 'Super' program of the Greenhouse tests in, let's see, 1951. The later H-bomb fuels were all solids."

"I see." Corrie hesitated, then asked: "Ah, can you think of any reason why someone might want to kill Agent Morwood?"

At this, Eastchester's eyebrows shot up. "There's a possibility he was *murdered*?"

"No, no," Corrie quickly backtracked. "It seems clear it was an accident. But it's a question we always ask, you know—routine." She hoped that would satisfy him.

"I can't think of any reason. A good FBI agent must have a lot of enemies—no? The people he's put away, their families and associates, that sort of thing. But I personally don't know of anyone who might have done him harm." He paused. "The problem with Arvesen's case was an almost complete lack of evidence. They recovered the bullet and its casing. And that was about it. The area showed no signs of unauthorized entry; Arvesen was very well liked, with no obvious enemies. The fact was, he appeared to be an unusually forthright, ethical, and straight-forward individual. Every single person who had access to the high-security room that night—and there weren't that many—had an alibi. A *good* alibi. Morwood and Starr came up against a brick wall almost right away and banged their heads against it for, oh, it must have been years—without success." The old scientist shook his head sadly.

As Corrie left the secure area and drove down the winding road from Los Alamos, her mind drifted back to the burned lab at her own office. The sight and smell of the soggy, acrid place—in the ghostly glow of her flashlight—would be etched into her mind forever. Her forensic drawings, dental X-rays, diagrams, and data were safely inside the computer network, where no fire could touch them. But they were incomplete. The dental records were also in the cloud, of course. But so far nothing had come from them. The homicide victims themselves were reduced almost to ash, and her reconstructions had been completely destroyed. Without intact skulls, she could not redo them. How was she going to identify the victims now?

Still, there was the dial-a-yield device. Now that she knew what it was, those numbers stamped on it might be serial numbers that could lead somewhere.

Exactly where, she had no idea.

41

Nora FELT A surge of excitement as she looked over the site. As soon as the road was finished, she had hopped in a jeep with Emilio and Skip, and they'd arrived at the Los Gigantes buttes a little past noon.

It was a far more evocative place than where they'd been excavating before, and as an added benefit, there was less wind here in the valley. The sandstone buttes stood here and there on the plain, glowing red in the noonday sun. As she looked over the area, Nora couldn't see any signs of the old 1947 disturbance. It was a tribute to the power of lidar that the site could be seen so plainly from the air.

She wondered again: Was it actually possible that an alien spaceship crashed here? She had to admit that the evidence continued to pile up. She had a feeling the excavation she was about to embark upon would decide the matter once and for all. The thought filled her with both excitement and anxiety.

"So what's the plan?" asked Skip, looking around, hands on hips.

"A ground survey," said Nora. "Then we'll grid out the area and start digging." She was pretty sure that before the end of the day, Tappan would show up. By the time he got there, she wanted him to see that she'd made good progress. "Let's get going."

The three of them walked the site slowly from one side to the other and back again, examining the ground for any surface artifacts. It took an hour, and they turned up almost nothing beyond a single rusted tin of chewing tobacco.

It was time to grid the site. Nora and Skip hauled out supplies from the jeep, including wooden stakes and Day-Glo twine. Vigil set up the theodolite while Skip held the stadia rod for him and Nora gave directions, and in another hour the area had been gridded in precise, GPS-delineated squares. At that moment, Nora saw a corkscrew of dust on the horizon. A few minutes later, Tappan arrived. He stepped out of the jeep with a big smile and looked over the gridded site.

"This is what I call progress," he said.

Despite herself, Nora felt a glow of pleasure. "You're just in time to watch us break ground."

"That was my hope."

Starting with the first square meter, Nora and Vigil gently dug out bunches of grass and set them aside, then began the serious work of removing the sandy soil, layer by layer. Tappan watched from a shade they had set up next to the excavation, from time to time speaking into the base camp radio.

It was quick, easy going—as Nora expected it would be in ground that had already been dug and backfilled before, even if many decades ago. She and Vigil worked the grids as Skip tossed the excavated sand through two sets of screens, for large and small items, respectively. As the hours went by, they encountered nothing but undifferentiated sand, nor did anything turn up in the screening. The site appeared to be clean—suspiciously clean. There weren't even the usual random stones.

As the afternoon lengthened, Tappan suddenly called out. "Nora, may I see you a moment?"

She climbed out of the hole and came over.

"I just spoke to Cecilia," Tappan said. "She and Kuznetsov have been going over the lidar point cloud using image enhancement, and they found something else. A disturbance that looks a lot more recent. I asked Cecilia to bring out the charts for us to look at."

Sure enough, twenty minutes later another cloud of dust appeared on the horizon. Soon, Toth pulled up in a jeep and retrieved a document tube from the passenger seat. She brought it over, red hair stirring in the light wind. They all retreated to chairs under the shade.

"Thanks for coming out," said Tappan.

"No problem." Toth slid a survey out of the tube and unrolled it on the table.

"We've been manipulating the point cloud data," she said. "Take a look at what we found. It's up in the corner, here."

About a mile and a half from where they were now working, Nora could see a blurry set of tire tracks entering from the west and winding through the foothills of the Los Fuertes

Mountains before heading out of the survey area to the north.

"Here's a closer view." Toth unrolled a second chart. The tracks came in from the left side of the survey, ran east through the Gigantes valley in the foothills, and stopped at a point near the far edge of the survey area. Here, they appeared to move around in a few erratic circles before turning and heading away in a different direction.

"These are fresh tracks," said Toth. "Very fresh. I think what we might be looking at is where Bitan got picked up."

Nora nodded.

"Not only are they recent," said Toth, "but what's more, it looks like an attempt was made to brush them out. They probably weren't anticipating a subcentimeter lidar survey." She whisked out a third chart. "This view has been further enhanced."

Nora peered closely and felt a chill travel up her spine. There was a vague confusion of tracks, both car and foot, evidently brushed out but still visible.

"Those tracks lead into the mountains to the north. But where, exactly?"

"We don't know. And it may be hard to find out."

"Why?"

"That's where the airspace is closed. The old Pershing Proving Range—a long-abandoned military base. Off-limits to ground entry, too."

Tappan gave a low whistle. "I'm not normally paranoid, but it's enough to make you wonder. Bitan vanishing...and those tracks going into an abandoned base. Supposedly. I mean, what's in there? Area Fifty-Two? Can we fly our drone over and take a look?"

"No," said Toth, "unless you want to lose your drone license."

"What about Google Earth?"

"I checked it out. Just shows some abandoned buildings. No sign of anything recent."

No one spoke for a moment.

Toth said, "Another thing. Two sheriffs showed up in base camp this afternoon, investigating Bitan's disappearance. They want to speak to you, Mr. Tappan, and Skip."

"Christ, just what we need," said Tappan. He turned to Nora. "Let's wrap up here and go see what they want. It's quitting time, anyway."

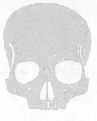

42

Lᴀᴛᴇ ɪɴ ᴛʜᴇ afternoon, as Corrie passed by the door of Morwood's old office—now occupied by Lime—the senior agent called out. "Agent Swanson?"

She backed up and paused. Lime was sitting behind his desk, the chief fire investigator in a chair opposite with a file open in front of him.

"Come in," said Lime. "Have you met Lawrence Feeney?"

"Yes," said Corrie as Feeney stood and extended his hand. He had questioned her early in the investigation. She felt a tightening in her chest.

"Please sit down."

They all sat, and Lime leaned forward on his

elbows, looking first at Corrie, then at Feeney. "Let's get straight to the point, shall we? I mean, as it concerns Agent Swanson."

"Right." Feeney turned to her. "We determined the source of the fire. It was a short circuit in the autoclave."

"In other words," said Lime, "*not* the Bunsen burner, as Lathrop suggested."

"We found the burner in the off position," Feeney added. "Disconnected, and the gas cock at the source turned off, as well."

Although none of this was a surprise to Corrie, she nevertheless felt a wave of relief wash over her.

"Furthermore," Feeney said, "our investigation showed that the autoclave had not been properly maintained. The lab's sprinkler and smoke detector system were inoperable because of chewed wires—a rodent infestation that went undetected. That fire-suppression system, of course, is supposed to be tested regularly. On two recent occasions, Lathrop asked the inspectors to come back another time when he was not busy, and as a result the system had not been tested within the prescribed schedule. Finally, the fire was accelerated by stacks of unopened packages, boxes, and deliveries that had been allowed to accumulate in the front hall of the lab."

"As chief of the lab," Lime added, "Lathrop had responsibility for all these issues."

Corrie was stunned by these last pieces of information. It took her a moment to process them—and then, suddenly, she felt a wave of anger at Lathrop's carelessness.

"What's going to be done?" Corrie asked. "I mean, Agent Morwood's death was Lathrop's fault!"

"He'll be given an engraved plaque—and retired."

"That's it?"

Lime looked at her. "I understand your anger. I feel it, too. But Lathrop didn't do anything criminal—these were a cascade of oversights that, taken together, combined to make an unlikely tragedy."

Corrie swallowed and said nothing further. It felt like manslaughter.

"The worst thing he did," Lime said, "was blame you. Your fellow agents feel that pretty keenly—a lab technician, casting blame on one of their own. The SAC has asked Lathrop to take his remaining vacation days starting tomorrow, then move directly into retirement. We won't see him around here again."

Corrie nodded. She still felt a burning sensation. It was so unfair. By all rights Lathrop should be locked up. On the other hand, she realized Lime had arranged this brief discussion to give her some closure, even if incomplete. And for that, she was grateful.

"Thank you, Agent Feeney," said Lime.

The fire investigator rose and left. Lime waited until he was gone before speaking again. "I know this is a lot for you to handle right now. But it's important to move forward, and I'm confident you agree. So: tell me how the case is going. I understand you interviewed Dr. Eastchester this morning?"

Corrie made a mental effort to get back into the groove of the case. She told Lime about the visit, and explained she'd be sending the serial number of the strange device to Quantico for tracing. She hadn't yet made further progress on the dental records but hoped to find time for that in the very near future—and she'd decided to conduct the search herself, rather than delegate it.

Lime listened intently, nodding, then congratulated her on the excellent work.

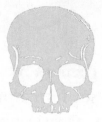

43

WHEN NORA ARRIVED back in the vehicle pool, she saw a pickup truck with a sheriff's decal emblazoned on the side. A big-bellied man in a cowboy hat stood nearby, notebook in hand, with a young sheriff she recognized immediately as Homer Watts.

Tappan got out of the jeep and strode over, Nora and Skip following. "I'm Lucas Tappan," he said, his hand extended with artificial cheer. "And these are my associates, Nora Kelly and Skip Kelly. Can I help you?"

"Nora, good to see you!" Watts said, coming over. She saw he was wearing his trademark rig: six-guns, fancy cowboy hat, and boots. The other man, who wasn't nearly so colorful, followed.

"Sheriff Randall Buford, Chaves County," said

the man, extending his hand and shaking theirs in turn. He was about sixty, clean-shaven, triple-chinned, wearing aviator sunglasses.

"Now, Mr. Tappan," Buford said. "Just the man I wanted to see. Sheriff Watts here has volunteered to assist me in investigating the disappearance of…" He consulted his notebook, flipped a few pages. "A Mr. Noam Bitan."

"Right," said Tappan.

"Great. And we'd like to speak with Mr. El-wyn Kelly, who was with the person who disappeared."

"That's me," said Skip.

"Why don't we do this in my trailer," said Tappan. "I'd also like to bring along Nora, who's our lead archaeologist."

"Sure thing."

Nora and the rest walked through camp to Tappan's trailer.

"A/C, now that's a welcome change!" said Buford after they'd gone inside, sitting down heavily on a sofa and laying his notebook on the table. "This is some kind of fancy ride you've got for yourself."

Watts took a seat near him, while Nora, Tappan, and Skip occupied chairs on the other side.

"Okay, let's start with Mr. Elwyn Kelly," Buford began, consulting his notes. "Tell me what happened, Elwyn. You were with the subject when he disappeared, correct?"

Skip ran through his story, clearly displeased to be called by his given name. Then Tappan told of their fruitless search, while Buford jotted a few notes.

"I understand this fellow was Israeli?" Buford asked.

Tappan nodded.

"What was he looking for out there?"

"An archaeological feature related to our current dig."

Tappan was being deliberately vague, but Buford didn't seem interested in detail. "So what kind of visa did this guy have? To be working here, I mean?"

"It was an H-1B, because of his specialty occupation."

"Which was?"

"An expert in SETI."

"I'm not familiar with that 'specialty occupation.'"

"The search for evidence or signals coming from extraterrestrial intelligence."

"And you couldn't find an American to do this?"

"Bitan was one of the experts in what is a quite rarefied field."

"Right. Searching for little green men." Buford gave a chuckle and glanced at Watts, whose face remained impassive.

"So what's *your* theory?" Buford asked Tappan. "About what happened to this guy?"

"As you heard, lights were seen in those foothills the night he vanished. I think he was picked up." Tappan hesitated, and then said: "A survey of the area revealed fresh tire tracks in the area where the lights were seen. They headed north toward the old Pershing range."

Buford nodded, scratching out notes. *"Lights seen in area at time of disappearance,"* he said out loud as he wrote it down. *"Fresh tire tracks."* He looked up. "Ninety-five percent of missing persons turn out to be missing by choice. It seems to me that's what we're dealing with here. Would you agree?"

Tappan nodded. "I would."

Buford slapped the notebook shut. "It's pretty clear he skipped out on you...for whatever reason. Maybe he was engaged in espionage for the Israeli government. Maybe there was a woman. Maybe a family emergency. Maybe he just wanted to go home."

He heaved himself up. "Well, Sheriff Watts, I think we're probably done here."

"Sheriff Buford," said Tappan, "before you go—what do you know about the Pershing range?"

"It's fenced. Closed for decades. Off-limits."

"Why?"

"There's unexploded ordnance in there, old ammo dumps and abandoned munitions. Rather than clean it up, the army just shut it down."

"So why would tire tracks be heading in there?"

At this, Buford looked puzzled. "Well, they shouldn't be. Tracks going right in there, you say. Through the gate?"

"We can't be sure if the tracks actually go *into* the base, but they head *toward* it. We aren't allowed to fly our lidar plane or drones near there, because the airspace around it is closed."

Buford grunted. "Half of Chaves County has closed airspace, on account of the military bases and testing ranges."

"Yes...but for a base that was shut down decades ago?" Tappan said. "That seems excessive."

Buford shrugged.

At this, Sheriff Watts finally spoke. "That seems awfully long to me, too."

Buford turned to him. "Good old government bureaucracy."

"And where do those tracks go? That might be worth investigating."

There was a silence during which everyone looked at one another. Then Buford chuckled. "Sheriff Watts, if you want to exercise your famous tracking skills, be my guest! Chaves County will thank you."

Watts seemed taken by surprise, but he laughed good-naturedly. "Well, if you've got no objection, Sheriff, I think I might just do that."

"None at all."

Watts turned to Tappan. "Do you have the scan to show where they are?"

It was quickly produced, and Watts examined it. "Interesting." He turned to Skip. "I'll need you to come with me, show me where the lights were. Can you do that?"

"Of course!" Skip said with enthusiasm. "Can I bring my dog?"

"No. We can't let anything disturb the tracks. We'll begin early tomorrow." He turned to Tappan. "May I keep this survey?"

"It's strictly confidential, but for your own use, yes."

"Good. Skip, I'll be here at five thirty AM sharp tomorrow."

"So early?" Skip groaned.

"We'll avoid the heat of the day. See you then, pardner!" He gave him a friendly clap on the back.

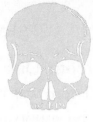

44

Corrie made a turn onto the dark residential street, cruised halfway down the block, then slid into a parking spot, engine idling. It was an older Albuquerque neighborhood, with Southwestern homes typical of the 1950s and '60s, but none of those overdone Pueblo Revival structures from which Fred Flintstone might emerge at any minute. She glanced around for a moment, making sure nobody was nearby. Then she examined the house opposite. It was of a type with the rest: single-story, split-level, with a yard of decorative lava rock instead of grass, punctuated by the occasional cactus or yucca. The house was painted beige, naturally, with low stone wall accents. The front light was on, as was a single interior lamp in what Corrie figured was the living room. On a timer, no doubt. Nobody was home. There was no Realtor's sign out front—but then, she supposed, it was too early for that.

She verified the house number with the contact list on her cell phone. This was it.

She pulled away from the curb and drove her twenty-year-old Camry around to the back of the block, where—as Google Maps had promised— there was a small park consisting of a turnout, swings, and a few picnic tables. It ran the length of the block and was too well lit to be a trysting spot or drug hangout. Across the street was an electrical substation, the kind that was never manned unless something broke down. This was a relief: no houses with security cameras or smart doorbells to worry about.

Glancing at her watch, she let two minutes go by as she listened to the night. Nothing but the sounds of ZZ Top coming faintly from one direction, and Nas just as faintly from the other. *Oil and water*, she thought.

She stepped out of her car, pulling a canvas duffel off the passenger seat, then leaned against the door, easing it closed. She made a leisurely tour of the parking lot, observing her surroundings casually but closely. As she began a second circuit, she stepped off the gravel at the spot with the least light, made her way past a row of box elders and through some undergrowth, crawled over an old split rail fence, and paused in the shadow of the back deck of the empty house.

After checking that everything was still clear, she ducked under the deck and, taking the hooded flashlight from her duffel, dialed it to the lowest level and examined the windows set near the basement ceiling. They were small but passable. Next, she ran the faint beam along the sills, then the interior itself, looking for any active security measures or alarm system. She saw nothing. Knowing Agent Morwood, he may well have acted as his own security.

In the beam of her light, she could make out a worktable with a long rack of power tools arranged carefully above it, along with several suitcases stacked neatly in a far corner. It seemed the house was untouched, exactly as Morwood left it five nights ago. As far as she knew, he had no close relatives; it would probably take a while for the wheels of probate or whatever to start turning.

Putting aside her flashlight, she reached into her duffel for a long, narrow shim, which she worked into the space between the window and its lower frame, using a technique she'd learned during extracurricular activities in high school. It was a tight fit—Morwood's house was, if not alarmed, secure from the elements—but after several minutes she felt a sudden loss of resistance as the casement latch slid free.

She paused again to look around. As she did so, she once again reviewed the reasons she was here. Technically speaking, she was engaged in breaking and entering; the fact that she was a federal agent didn't ameliorate that. If she was caught, the consequences would be severe.

So what again, exactly, made it worth the risk?

Her interview with Dr. Eastchester had, in retrospect, raised more questions than it answered. She also felt, rightly or wrongly, a sense of guilt that had nothing to do with the Bunsen burner—if she'd made more progress in the case, perhaps Morwood wouldn't have felt it necessary to take a midnight trip to the lab. She was more than ever convinced it wasn't just to return the device. The awful postautopsy meeting with the M.E., particularly the mysterious half-burned list of items, hung like a question mark over everything—as did the ruined lab that yielded so few clues. Then, of course, there was the biggest question mark: Why had Morwood left home in the middle of the night and gone directly to the lab? It seemed her best chance was to check whether her mentor had left anything behind at home that might shed light on the question. She felt sure any request she made to search his house would be turned down for lack of sufficient cause—and she knew it would betray her instincts that something was not right with Morwood's death, when it had been made quite clear to her that it was considered to be an accident.

Self-justifications aside, one thing she felt oddly sure of: Morwood would have wanted her to do this.

She eased the window open, pushed her duffel bag through, then followed it, dropping quietly to the floor. She paused to make sure she hadn't been wrong about the alarm. Of course, it might be silent: just in case, she'd leave the window open and keep an eye out for any cops arriving with their sirens deactivated.

The basement was unfinished, a concrete slab with the workbench she'd already noted. A staircase rose to the ground floor. Flashlight still hooded, pinhole light angled downward, she climbed the stairs and opened the door. She turned off the light, getting her bearings and confirming her intrusion had gone unremarked. The house smelled faintly of wood polish and—unexpectedly—Morwood's aftershave.

She composed herself as an involuntary sob rose in her throat. She was here for information gathering, not nostalgia. She'd quickly sweep the house, then focus on wherever Morwood had his home office. And she'd allow herself fifteen minutes—no more.

A brief recon revealed that the house had two bedrooms and two bathrooms. It also revealed Morwood's cologne: Creed Santal. She went quickly through the house, looking for the office she knew must be there, and found it. The walls were lined with shelves, and there was a desk with a computer, a pile of books, and papers strewn across its top.

If there was anything to be found, it would be here.

The room fronted the street. Setting down her duffel again, she moved quickly to close the wooden shutters. Even so, she could risk nothing brighter than her hooded light. A quick glance at her watch showed her self-imposed deadline was down to ten minutes.

She stood behind the desk, looking around. Trying the computer would be a waste: it would be password-protected. She looked at the shelves. There were no family photographs, no shadow boxes full of medals: just encyclopedias and reference books, along with back issues of *National Review*, *Aviation Week*, *Military History*, and a number of Janes periodicals covering various national security matters. There were no awards or certificates on the walls, either; just two photographs sitting on his desk. She let her light linger on them briefly. One was very old, perhaps from the turn of the twentieth century, showing a man and a woman in shabby clothes standing together on the front steps of a farmhouse. The other was a Polaroid from the 1980s, maybe: three teenagers standing on a baseball diamond, arms around one another's shoulders. The image was badly faded, but she had no doubt the boy in the middle was Morwood.

Taking a deep breath, she resumed her search. There was a standalone bookshelf beside the desk, which seemed to be where Morwood kept the volumes he referred to most often. Most were military history texts: *The Guns of August*; *The Two-Ocean War*; *Guns, Germs, and Steel*. There was also Herman Kahn's diabolic *On Thermonuclear War* and Rhodes's *Dark Sun*. All of the spines were rubbed from years of use. There was also a shelf, to her surprise, of early thriller novels: *The Riddle of the Sands*, *Watcher in the Shadows*, *Rogue Male*.

She turned to his desk. To one side was a stack of old issues of the *Bulletin of the Atomic Scientists*. Next to them was a pad of paper and a large book, lying open on the desk, pages down, its worn spine indicating it was a resident of the nearby bookcase.

But Corrie's eye went past it to the pad of paper. She picked it up. It was the same size and stock as the burnt sheet found in Morwood's jacket pocket.

Quickly, she took a seat at the desk and examined the pad more closely. Her flashlight revealed some faint grooves in the top piece of paper—the marks of something written on the sheet previously above it.

She took a pencil from a nearby receptacle, placed it parallel to the pad, and very carefully rubbed its point over the paper. Its uncoated surface quickly revealed what had been written on the now-missing sheet above:

ITEM

She frowned. This was strange. There was no list of written items following: the word apparently stood alone on the sheet. Was she missing something? She rubbed some more, but there was nothing else.

Tearing off the sheet, she examined it closely, turning it this way and that. Clearly, the sheet in Morwood's pocket contained this single word. He had never filled out the list. But why would he have torn it from the pad and taken it with him? It made no sense. She put it in her pocket.

Five minutes.

Her eye caught the garbage can sitting beside the desk. It held a few crumpled sheets that appeared to be from the same pad. She took them out and, one at a time, smoothed them on the desk.

These were equally mystifying. One said, in Morwood's hand, *E: boosting.* Another, *1947/51 DATE??* They made no more sense than the first had. Nevertheless, Corrie slipped them into her pocket as well.

With time running out, she turned her attention to the book that lay facedown on the desk. It was a fat volume entitled *Encyclopedia of the Atomic Age.* Carefully, she grasped it by the edges and turned it over.

It was open to a chapter entitled "Operation Greenhouse," and as she scanned it, she saw that it covered early nuclear tests, in particular the U.S. fission "shots" of 1951. The first test, the book went on to explain in vague terms, had apparently been devoted, at least in part, to testing the feasibility of the dial-a-yield device, the kind Nora had dug up with the two bodies.

The initial explosion, George, was undertaken to validate the theory behind the "classic Super" thermonuclear bomb, and paved the way for the full-scale Ivy Mike test that would take place the following year. The second Greenhouse explosion, code-named Item and conducted on May 25, 1951, was the first true boosted fission weapon, with tritium gas being injected—to a greater or lesser degree—into the fissile core of the initial detonation. This more than doubled the potential yield of...

Corrie looked up from the book. *Jesus Christ.* She recalled Eastchester's words: *This was extremely classified work...with compressed tritium gas, dating from the "Super" program of the Greenhouse tests in, let's see, 1951.*

The "Greenhouse" test, he'd said. But apparently, it should more properly be called the Greenhouse-Item test.

Item. This wasn't the start of a list, at all: Item was the name of a nuclear test. And this discovery must have been why Morwood laid the book facedown, left his house, and rushed to the lab.

But what the hell did he realize? And then the revelation came.

The two bodies Nora had dug out of the ground near Roswell—buried with the device— had been conclusively dated to 1947. But as the book clearly implied, *the dial-a-yield device was not ready for testing until 1951.*

1947/51 DATE??—Morwood had written it himself, before crumpling the sheet and tossing it away.

Her time was up. Rising, she made sure to arrange the desk precisely as she had found it. Moving to her duffel, she used her cell phone to take a dozen flashless photographs of the room and desk from various angles. Then she zipped the duffel closed, slung it over her shoulder, opened the shutters, and silently exited the house the way she had come.

Driving back to her apartment, she found her gaze straying, now and again, to the rearview mirror. But the roads were empty, and no one was following her.

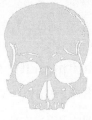

45

Skip Kelly was up at four, groaning and cursing. He took Mitty for his walk, fed him, then packed a day pack with water, snacks, a thermos of coffee, and several granola bars for lunch, doing his best not to disturb Nora. With the stars still glittering in the sky, he saw the lights of Watts's SUV approaching.

Watts pulled up and Skip hopped in, tossing his pack in the rear.

"Morning," said Watts, turning the vehicle around and heading down the new road toward the dry lake bed. "Coffee?" He indicated a cup sitting in a holder in the console. "That's for you. Might be a little cold."

"You're a mind reader." Even though he had his own, he didn't want to show a lack of appreciation, so Skip took the cup and sipped the lukewarm coffee. Watts was even younger than he was, but the sheriff projected self-reliance and had a calm, confident manner Skip admired. He looked more than a little like a Western movie star, with the silver-belly hat and those matching revolvers, currently hung by their belt on a rack in the back window. Somehow Skip felt the look was natural, and not a disguise or some kind of sheriff-y dress-up.

"I'd like to go first to the place where you saw the lights," Watts said. "You think we can find it?"

"I think so."

Watts headed cross country, bumping along the prairie. The broken tower soon loomed up on the edge of the mesa like a giant tooth. They drove past it and Watts edged the Explorer down the nearby ridge to the bottom of the cliffs.

He stopped. "Let's see if we can pick up your track. You're wearing the same shoes? And your dog was with you?"

"Yes to both."

They got out.

"Walk off about a dozen yards, then come back," Watts said.

Skip did as he was told, and Watts scrutinized his footprints. "Okay, thanks. Stay here for a moment while I cut for sign."

He went off, stooped and moving slowly, eyes on the ground, holding a flashlight at a raking angle. The eastern horizon was coloring a pale yellow.

Watts raised his hand. "Got it!" Skip came over and stared at the ground but couldn't see anything beyond a few blurry scuff marks.

"That's my track?"

"It is, and your dog's—both ways, coming and going. Now, would you say you were heading north or south of here?"

"North."

"Great. If you could walk behind me at, say, twenty paces? And follow my footprints, not your old ones. We want to keep those clear."

"Got it."

Watts set off at a brisk walk along the base of the cliffs. In fifteen minutes, he turned and began climbing a ridgeline, still following Skip's tracks.

"Is this the ridge where you saw the lights?" he asked.

"I think so."

They climbed higher as the ridgeline got steeper and narrower. The sun just peeked over the horizon.

"You came up here in the dark?" Watts asked. "Lucky you didn't fall...Oh. You did."

Skip stared. It didn't take a tracker to see all the scuff and claw marks in the loose sand where he'd taken a tumble.

"What happened was," said Skip, "I saw the lights as I climbed the ridgeline. I took a rest there. And then, on my way down, I fell."

"Okay." Watts looked around for a while and then climbed a little higher. "I can see here where you sat down to rest. Now if you could sit down and show me where in the landscape you saw the lights?"

"It was dark." Skip stared out at the white lake bed, which ended in the green hills of Horse Heaven, and beyond that the buttes of Los Gigantes. He squinted, trying to remember where in the ocean of night he had seen those lights moving.

"Concentrate, and try to think: How far below the night horizon were the lights? And in which direction?"

Skip visualized it, placing a mental overlay on

the landscape. "Right about…*there*. Beyond the last butte in the valley, in a flat area among the foothills."

Watts sighted down his arm. "Okay, I see it." He unrolled the lidar survey and examined it closely. "Very interesting. That's approximately the area where these fresh tracks are."

He looked at Skip and clapped him on the back. "Good work. Let's go."

They hiked back to the Explorer and Watts set off across the lake bed. Using the lidar survey as a map, he worked his way around the grassy hills and into Los Gigantes valley. He parked at the base of the foothills and they got out. Once again, Watts walked around in a wide circle, examining the ground.

"Aha!" he said. "Footprints. About three days old."

"I can't see anything," said Skip.

"Do you recall what sort of footwear Bitan was wearing?"

"These big old desert combat boots. They looked kind of silly."

"Perfect. This is him. Let's go."

Watts took off on foot again. He moved so fast that Skip struggled to keep up, catching him only when he stopped from time to time to consult the survey. The track they followed wound through the foothills of the mountains until it came to a dry wash. Here Watts paused, staring at the ground, his brow furrowed. First he walked in one direction, then another, and then a third.

"What do you see?" Skip asked.

"This was the rendezvous spot. There are tire tracks here, but they've been brushed out. It looks like a mat of chains was dragged behind a vehicle to cover their tracks. But it hasn't rained since then and everything is still clear enough. Mostly. You can't quite erase tracks in sand without the help of rain, wind, and time."

He wandered around some more, finally heading off toward an area of rocks. He began poking around, then gave a shout.

Skip came over.

"Down there. Take a look."

In between two stones, Skip could see the edge of what looked like a card, partially buried in the sand.

"Don't touch," said Watts. He photographed it with his cell phone, then removed a Ziploc bag. He pulled on a nitrile glove and picked up the card, slipping it into the bag and sealing it. He examined the find for a moment, then held it up for Skip to see.

"That's Bitan's employee ID card," Skip said. "We're all supposed to wear one. But what's that stuff smeared on it?"

"Blood. Almost certainly Bitan's." Watts slipped the bag into a pocket of his day pack. "It's becoming clear to me what happened here. Two vehicles—UTVs—cut Bitan off in this wash, one in front, the other behind. Bitan tried to run, but at least four men got out and chased him down. There was a struggle. Bitan must have been injured and bled. The bloody sand has been removed. At some point, it appears Bitan winged his ID card off into the darkness as a bread crumb of sorts. No other explanation: if his attackers saw him do it, they'd have searched until they found it."

"You can read all that from just this dirt?"

Watts shrugged.

"So he was kidnapped."

"Yes. And possibly killed, or badly injured, considering the bloody card and the fact he hasn't shown up in any hospital."

"These tracks they tried to cover. Where do they go?"

"North. Toward the Pershing Proving Range."

"How far away is that?"

"I'm not sure. Let's climb to the top of that hill. We're off the edge of the lidar survey here."

Watts headed up the back side of a rocky hill that rose above the wash, his wiry frame moving like a goat, Skip following. They were soon at the top, with a view looking north. Watts pulled out a pair of binoculars and glassed the landscape ahead, which consisted of gentle, rolling foothills and valleys leading up to a range of mountains.

He passed the binoculars to Skip. "Take a look at those far hills."

Skip looked and, after a moment, spied a chain-link fence crossing the landscape like a ribbon. He ran the binoculars along it and came to a closed gate. Signs that were too far away to read flanked the gate. Beyond, he saw some buildings, several skeletonized trucks, and an old wooden water tower with a staved-in tank.

"The proving range," said Watts.

"Looks abandoned."

"Yes." Watts paused. "Abandoned—except for the fresh tire tracks leading to it."

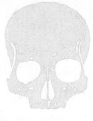

46

As CORRIE PULLED into the parking lot, what she saw was not encouraging. Consolidated Dental Partners occupied a brand-new building in fake adobe style off St. Michael's Drive. It didn't look like a place that would be storing ancient dental files.

She hung her FBI lanyard around her neck and walked in. She had tried to call ahead but got only an answering service and then, finally, a low-level employee who knew nothing about dental records and seemed disinclined to learn. Corrie had thought Lime might accompany her, but he'd made it politely clear he thought the trip was a waste of time and that no dental records going back seventy-five years would ever be found.

Corrie's research had come up with one large dental practice in Santa Fe, owned by a for-profit hospital chain that had bought up several dozen smaller practices over the years. She was clinging to the faint hope they might have preserved old medical records from those practices. The problem was, there were dozens of defunct dental offices going back decades in Santa Fe that hadn't been bought up. Lime was right: this really was a stab in the dark.

She entered a large, sterile reception area with three receptionists behind glass. She chose the most alert-looking one and walked over, raising her FBI badge. "Special Agent Corinne Swanson, Federal Bureau of Investigation, Albuquerque Field Office. How are you today, ma'am?"

The lady stared at her, clearly convinced Corrie was not a real FBI agent, and finally said: "Can I help you?"

Corrie maintained a pleasant disposition. "Yes. Could I speak to someone in authority, please?"

"Is this some kind of joke?"

"No, ma'am," said Corrie evenly. "I really hope there isn't going to be any difficulty here."

"All right." The woman got up and went into the back, and a moment later reappeared with a man in tow, wearing a shiny blue suit and knit tie. Not a dentist: he looked like some back-office drone. He introduced himself as Mr. Murphy.

"May I see your credentials?" he asked, a look of suspicion on his face.

Corrie raised the lanyard again. He stared at the ID for a long time. "How can I know this is real?"

"You're welcome to call the Albuquerque Field Office."

He continued to scrutinize the badge, lips pursed. "Do you have a warrant?"

This was not a promising beginning, but Corrie persevered. "This isn't an official search, Mr. Murphy. I'm trying to identify a homicide victim via dental records, and I was hoping to be given access to your files. Voluntarily, of course."

"Medical records are private. HIPAA rules."

"I realize that, but I'm interested in records at least seventy-five years old. And the patient is dead—did I mention homicide?"

"We don't have any records going back that far."

"Do you have files inherited from the practices you purchased?"

"Of course."

"Have you gone through them?"

"No reason to. Only if we needed to pull a file of a patient from before the consolidation."

"If you haven't gone through them, how do you know they don't go back that far?"

"I can't imagine they do."

"But you don't *know*."

The man frowned at her. "I'm sorry, Ms.—Agent—Swanson, but I'm going to have to decline this request. I'm not sure I have the authority to give you access, and in any case, I'd need more information."

Corrie took a deep breath, trying to maintain a pleasant face. "Let me lay out your choices, Mr. Murphy. One: You can say no to a voluntary search by me, which is your right. I will go back to my office, write up a warrant, take it to a judge, get it signed, and come back here with half a dozen agents. We'll have to clear the premises of patients and sequester the staff while we conduct our search—that's standard procedure. The search might take hours. Days, perhaps—I don't know just how extensive your records are. Two: You can give me permission—voluntarily, of course—to poke around informally, with a staff member present if you wish, while your business continues as usual. And let me worry about your authority in the matter."

She let this settle in for a moment, then flashed him a bright smile. "So what's it going to be: Door number one or door number two? The lady or the tiger?"

Murphy slowly turned red, wiped his lips with a handkerchief, and finally said: "I believe that, when you frame it in such a way, we can accommodate your request. Please come with me."

He led her into a warren of cubicles and called over an employee. "Darren, this is an FBI agent. Could you escort her to dead storage and help her find what she wants?"

Darren turned to Corrie, eyes widening in the way she'd grown accustomed to as he processed both her youth and her appearance. Corrie returned the look, stone-faced. She was done being pleasant. She held out her hand. "Special Agent Swanson."

"Um, Darren Schmitz."

She'd been exercising with grip strengtheners for months, and she took his clammy hand in hers and crushed it, establishing who was boss in the most elemental of ways.

"Follow me," he said, after retrieving his limp hand.

Schmitz led her to the back of the building and out the rear door. Behind, parked in a shipping and receiving area, was a shabby semitrailer on blocks. He walked over to it. A foot ladder was placed against its side, leading to a door. He climbed up, punched a code into a padlock, and the lock snapped open. He removed the pad-lock and opened the door, then went inside and turned on a light.

Corrie followed him up the stepladder. Her heart fell. Inside the trailer, old filing cabinets lined the walls from floor to ceiling, along with miscellaneous cardboard and metal storage boxes, in layers three or more deep.

"How is this organized?" she asked.

Schmitz stared. "What do you mean?"

"How do you find a patient's files in here? By last name?"

"Well, by practice, then by year, and then alphabetically by last name."

"Really? How can you locate anything in a mess like this?"

"I'm not sure."

"Does *anyone* know?"

"Nobody else comes in here. I'm the only one."

"Why do they even keep this trailer? Why not throw all this sh—stuff out?"

"We would have to go through the files before throwing them out. It's cheaper just to store them."

"So if you *die*, how will your replacement find anything in here?"

He stared at her.

Corrie realized she had gone too far. After all, if they'd thrown out the records, it would have made her visit academic. She looked at the nervous, sweating face of Darren Schmitz—it was like an oven inside the trailer—and suddenly felt sorry for him. She shook her head. "I apologize if I seem a little impatient. I appreciate that you're trying to help. Let me show you what I'm looking for, and maybe you'll have some ideas about where I might find it." She put down her briefcase, opened it, and slipped out a file. "Here are the X-rays we took at the FBI lab of a homicide victim's teeth. Those crowns are unusual—they're cast in a stainless steel alloy and then finely machined and polished. The work was almost certainly done in the Soviet Union in the forties, give or take."

The man stared at the X-rays. "Stainless steel?"

"Yes. We don't often employ that material for crowns in America, outside of pulpectomies in pediatric dentistry. You'd know that better than I. But the victim was an adult, murdered in 1947 . . . and here in New Mexico."

The man looked up. "Well, the only thing that comes to mind is a filing cabinet devoted to X-rays of dental oddities and pathologies. It was the hobby of a dentist in a practice we acquired years ago."

"Okay, let's start there."

Within five minutes, Corrie found herself staring at sepia-colored X-rays of the precise four crowns she was searching for. She was incredulous at her stroke of luck. They'd found them in the cabinet of oddities, in a section labeled UNCOMMON ALLOY DENTAL WORK. And right there, paper-clipped to the X-rays, was the name and Santa Fe address of the patient, as well as a date: August 3, 1945.

Corrie felt a flush of triumph. What a coup. Lime was going to be thrilled. She couldn't wait to get back to the office and tell him.

As she slipped into her car, her cell phone rang. Glancing at it, she saw it was Watts.

"I'm afraid we've got bad news," he said when she picked up.

"What's up?"

"Kidnapping and potential homicide."

Instantly, she forgot her triumph. "Who?"

"Noam Bitan."

47

As THE SUN crossed the meridian on its journey to the western horizon, the dig was progressing at its own swift pace. Nora couldn't have asked for a better site. The sand was clean, with no artifacts or rocks or anything to slow them down. The area was concentrated—only nine square meters. The work moved even faster when Tappan, with growing impatience, rolled up his sleeves and joined Nora and Emilio. Cecilia Toth came along with a magnetometer at Nora's request to see if they could image anything down below. Scott was back at base camp, organizing the equipment.

At seven in the evening, when they had reached two meters of depth—six feet—Nora halted work for the magnetometer survey.

The others climbed out as Toth booted up the ungainly looking machine and began adjusting dials. When it was ready, she trundled it down a ramp into the excavated area and began wheeling it like a lawn mower over the flat floor of the excavation.

"Whoa!" she said, halting in the middle of the very first pass. She leaned over the machine, fiddling with the dials.

"What is it?" Tappan asked.

"Just a glitch." She messed around for a while, then said: "I've got to reboot the thing."

She worked quickly, spidery fingers moving expertly over the controls. Nora and the rest waited.

"This is crazy," Cecilia said in irritation. "Let me try again."

More waiting. Finally, Cecilia looked up, brushed back her hair, and frowned. "Either there's a killer magnetic field here, or the machine is malfunctioning."

"Bring it out of the hole," Tappan said. "See if it works at a distance."

Toth wheeled it back up the slope.

"Farther," said Tappan.

She moved it fifty feet from the site and booted

it up again. "It seems to be working now. But the magnetic field is really distorted."

Tappan reached into his pocket and took out a compass. Nora watched as he walked in a circle around the dig. Then he came up to her and held out the compass. "Look."

"That's not north," said Nora.

"No, it's not. As I walked around the site, the needle remained pointing at the center of the dig. There's clearly some magnetic object down there."

A brief silence fell.

"How magnetic?" Nora asked.

"Follow me." Tappan walked down into the hole and held out the compass. The needle swung wildly around, spinning until it broke away from its spindle and battered against the plastic housing.

"Holy shit," said Nora.

Tappan turned to Toth. "Can you recalibrate that machine to measure stronger magnetic fields?"

"I can turn the sensitivity gain down to the lowest level and see what happens." She fiddled with the dials a moment. "Ready."

"Bring it back into the hole."

She wheeled it back down. "Okay, it's not acting crazy," she said as she began wheeling it across the excavation floor. She stopped. "Wait. I spoke too soon. It's just gone off the charts."

She reached down to adjust some dials, and there was a sudden popping sound from the machine as the screen shattered, scattering glass shards. Toth jumped back.

At the same time, Nora saw her own excavation trowel, sitting on the ground near the magnetometer, start wriggling—and then it swung around and sank into the sand with a twisting motion, quickly followed by two palette knives and a metal-handled brush. A shovel standing against the excavation wall fell over and began to drag itself across the sand, as if by an unseen force.

"What the fuck!" Emilio cried. "Are you guys seeing this?"

"Cecilia, get out of the hole," said Tappan. "*Now*. Everyone get back."

His warning was unnecessary, as everyone was already scrambling away as fast as they could, abandoning the expensive magnetometer along with the rest of the equipment. The magnetometer was now starting to vibrate, making a creaking noise, its wheels sinking into the sand as if being pulled down. Nora saw her tablet, which was sitting on the edge of the hole, jiggle and slide, before flipping into the hole and being sucked out of sight.

And then suddenly all was quiet.

"What the hell just happened?" Vigil said, venturing a step forward.

Tappan released his breath. He turned to Nora and the rest. "There's something down . . ."

He didn't finish the sentence. He didn't need to.

"What do we do now?" said Toth.

"What do we *do*?" Tappan's voice was incredulous. "We dig it up."

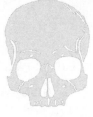

48

CORRIE HUNG UP the phone and sat, allowing herself to savor the moment. The FBI analyst she'd just spoken with confirmed it: she'd made a breakthrough in the case. Her "shot in the dark" trip to Santa Fe had paid off in spades. But self-congratulation could wait: she had to collect her thoughts and go see Lime. It was already quite late, almost seven. He sometimes worked late, and she hoped to hell he would still be in.

He was. Lime was sitting at the desk in Morwood's old office, door open. She knocked and he looked up, his face breaking into a smile. "Corrie! Come in and sit down. How did your trip to Santa Fe go?"

Corrie perched in the chair opposite his desk. "It went very well."

Lime raised his eyebrows. "Tell me about it."

"I discovered the identity of the homicide victims."

Now Lime looked genuinely surprised—and a little dubious. "Really?"

"Yes." She took a deep breath. "They were Soviet spies masquerading as French refugees. François and Marie Abadie. They arrived in Santa Fe in 1944, allegedly from France, at the beginning of the Manhattan Project, and continued spying on the nuclear program at Los Alamos as the hydrogen bomb began development. They disappeared in 1947. Word went out that they'd moved to L.A. But in fact, they were murdered at the Roswell site."

"That's very interesting," said Lime. "Remarkable, in fact. How can you be sure of these details?"

"I found the old dental X-rays I was searching for—in a storage unit in Santa Fe. I had an analyst look into the couple's history, such as it was. Nothing prior to 1944, and nothing after 1947. Their cover story was work as substitute teachers, husband and wife—but they had to have been spies, given their possession of that top-secret dial-a-yield device. It must have been an early prototype, the precursor to the one used in the first H-bomb test. Which was code-named 'Greenhouse Item,' detonated at Eniwetok Atoll—but not until 1951. Remember the piece of paper in Morwood's pocket? It said 'Item.' We all thought that was just the heading for some list or other, but I found out Morwood was *specifically* researching the Item nuclear test right before his death and had made a note of it. I'm pretty sure that's why he went into the lab— not just to return the dial-a-yield device, but for a much more important reason. " Here she hesitated. She didn't want to admit that some of her conclusions stemmed from breaking into Morwood's house.

"But what were these Soviet agents doing at the Roswell site? What does Roswell have to do with atomic espionage?"

"That's a harder question to answer. I've tried to put together the pieces of the puzzle, and there's only one scenario that fits the facts. I think the two scientists who disappeared at Los Alamos were passing nuclear secrets to the Soviet Union through the Abadies. The scientists were somehow discovered, unmasked— probably by the OSS. They were the precursors to the CIA—no doubt you know that. But those scientist spies would have needed Soviet handlers to pass along the secrets, and it seems the OSS couldn't figure out who those were. The Roswell UFO crash was front-page news when it happened, and such a thing would be of paramount interest to Soviet agents— Americans possibly getting their hands on advanced alien technology and all that. So it must have seemed a perfect place to stage a sting: the two scientists, now in the hands of American intelligence, would be brought out to Roswell to lure in the Soviet sleeper agents with the promise of vital information on the UFO crash—and, as a sweetener, to give them an early prototype of what Dr. Eastchester identified as a 'dial-a-yield.'"

"Wait," said Lime. "I'm not quite following you. Why not just force the scientists to identify the Soviet agents? Why lure them to Roswell at all?"

"They used a dead-drop system. The two rogue scientists didn't *know* who the Soviet agents were. For security reasons, they'd never met them. They would drop off information or items at some specified location that wouldn't raise alarm bells at Los Alamos—then leave. The Soviet agents would pick up the items later. That's how atomic espionage worked—from what I've read, it's standard tradecraft in the spy game. So American intelligence had to lure the phony husband-and-wife team to that location in order to discover who they were. Hence, Roswell. You can dead-drop a device, but you can't dead-drop a place."

"I see. Go on."

"So once the Soviet sleeper agents arrived, they were tortured for information, then killed and buried. Just in case they were ever discovered, their hands and faces were obliterated with acid. The two scientists may have been taken away for questioning or whatever, and then disappeared."

"Why not bring them to justice? Put them on trial?"

"Maybe because of the Klaus Fuchs case. He was a scientist at Los Alamos, passing secrets to the Soviets during the Manhattan Project. He was caught, confessed, and sentenced by the British to only fourteen years in prison. That infuriated the American counterintelligence community. I can imagine they, or some small group within them, decided to take matters into their own hands with these two scientists."

Corrie was gratified by the expression of amazement and approval on Lime's face. "It must be the latter," he said. "Our government wouldn't condone that kind of summary execution—not in cold blood."

"There's more," she said.

"Let's hear it."

"I spoke to Sheriff Watts a few hours ago. As you know, he's working with Sheriff Buford on the disappearance of Noam Bitan."

Lime hesitated. "Not our case, Corrie."

"Correct, sir. But maybe it will be. Watts learned that Bitan was kidnapped. His bloody ID card was found at the site where he disappeared. He was apparently ambushed by people in UTVs, there was a struggle in which he was injured, or worse—and then he was taken away."

"Taken where?"

"Watts noted the UTV tracks went northward toward a place called the Pershing Proving Range. He couldn't follow them all the way because it's off-limits, and so is the airspace. Pershing was apparently an artillery testing range dating to World War One, closed in the thirties. But maybe it's still being used by whoever kidnapped Bitan."

"This is extraordinary. Who could have kidnapped him?"

"I have no hard evidence, but if I might be allowed to speculate?"

"Please."

"Let's assume the Roswell UFO crash was real, and the government really did cover it up. Actually, 'the government' isn't correct. You agreed that only a group *within* the government, perhaps inside the CIA or Defense Intelligence Agency or whatever, would have murdered those spies and the sleeper agents who handled their case. Given that this took place near Roswell, and the secrecy that surrounded and still surrounds that place, doesn't it make sense the same splinter group would have taken possession of the UFO and its secrets?"

"If there *was* a UFO," Lime said. He tried to sound a little dubious, but Corrie could tell that was just for the sake of formality.

"Very well, sir: *if*. I know this is speculation. But everything fits. It explains much of the mystery: this group would have been guarding those secrets ever since, most likely, without the knowledge of the rest of the government. And here's what convinced me, at least: Bitan was the one member of the expedition most on the verge, it seems, of exposing Roswell's secrets. If there *was* no UFO, no cover-up beyond the execution of some spies back in the 1940s, then why kidnap him—unless they were afraid of those secrets being uncovered?"

She paused. It was obvious that Lime had followed her line of reasoning—but it was anything but clear what he thought of it. His face had gone strangely blank.

"Corrie, this is remarkable work," he said after a moment. "And I think you're onto something big. More than that: I *know* you are." He went silent. And then his blank look was suddenly replaced by what seemed to Corrie like grim determination. "We must act fast. And in secrecy: we can't yet know who precisely might be involved."

Corrie stared at him.

"Here's what I want you to do," Lime told her. "Go back to your cubicle, gather your notes and files on the case. If you're right, we may be up against some powerful operators— possibly within our own government. So our only option is to personally go to the Roswell camp, evaluate the situation, secure the site, warn that expedition—and, if necessary, take steps to protect them."

"Yes, sir," Corrie said, hearing the surprise in her own voice. She'd entered Lime's office pleased with just how much she'd pieced together...but she hadn't banked on how serious the next step would be—assuming she was right.

"We'll also need Sheriff Watts to show us these tracks," Lime said. He had mastered his surprise, and despite the gravity of the situation, Corrie couldn't help but be impressed by how quickly he'd put a plan together. "Is he out there with Buford?"

"Buford's not there—I heard he's laid up with a case of gout. But when I spoke to Watts by sat phone a few hours ago, he was still out in the desert with Nora Kelly's brother."

"You and I need to take a chopper out to the camp."

It was Corrie's turn to be surprised. "Right now?"

"Now. Even if we're proceeding on what you call speculation, surely you can see the situation is critical. Don't talk to anyone—just gather the information we need and meet me back here in ten minutes. We haven't a moment to lose."

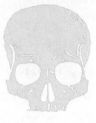

49

AT MANZANO BASE," Lime told Corrie as they left the field office and got into his vehicle, "there's a helicopter standing by to take us to the Roswell camp."

Corrie didn't know where Manzano Base was, but said nothing. New Mexico seemed to be dotted with military bases. Lime gunned the engine and peeled out of the FBI parking lot onto the Pan American Frontage Road, switching on his lights and siren.

"The reason I didn't requisition an FBI chopper directly," he said, "is because we don't know who might be involved."

He accelerated up the on-ramp to I-25, heading south.

"What makes you think the FBI could be

involved?" Corrie said. Her own speculations hadn't reached beyond the military, or perhaps the CIA and its predecessors.

"Corrie—I didn't want to say this before, but what you said back in my office jibes with certain anomalies that have been taking place within the DoD." He paused. "There's no reason to conceal it any longer: the real reason I was sent here was to investigate possible rogue elements within the FBI. Morwood knew that—and he may have been murdered because of it. I sense..." He gave her a significant look. "I sense you might share certain suspicions about his death."

Corrie nodded, feeling a flush at some confirmation—finally—of her instinctual doubts.

"Don't get me wrong," Lime said. "I don't have proof, nor does my immediate superior—yet. But what you've told me may well crack this thing wide open. Going outside standard FBI protocol is just a precaution, and I happen to have high-level contacts at Manzano. They're going to give us a chopper, a pilot, and a soldier—just in case."

Corrie nodded, surprised at Lime's high-level access and ability to scramble a chopper so quickly.

"And I'm especially concerned now that comms are down at the expedition."

Corrie's surprise jumped exponentially. "When did that happen?"

"I tried to call just after you left my office. They have multiple sat phones—why would they suddenly all go down at the same time? Something's wrong, perhaps very wrong, and we need to get there right away. I'm also concerned about Watts. Could you give him a call—see if his phone is still working? Tell him to stay where he is and we'll pick him up. On no account should he go back to the base—we've no idea what might be going on there."

Corrie dialed. To her relief, Watts answered.

"Homer? It's Corrie."

"Listen," said Watts, "we just got back to the jeep. We didn't dare approach Pershing, and we're about to head back to—"

"Hold on," Corrie interrupted. "We think the base camp might be in danger. Agent Lime and I are about to chopper out there ourselves. Their comms are down."

"I know—I just tried to reach them. Any idea what's going on?"

"None. But you need to stay where you

are, and we'll pick you up on the way." She glanced at Lime, who nodded. "What are your coordinates?"

Watts read them off his GPS.

"We'll be there in about an hour."

They left the freeway and headed south-east, through a checkpoint and onto Kirtland AFB, then down an access road behind the base that ran across empty desert toward the Manzano Mountains. They took a branching road to the base of the Manzanos. At a second, higher-security checkpoint, they passed through a gate in a chain-link fence, manned with guard towers, then into a complex that consisted of Quonset huts, hangars, and a low metal building. Bypassing these, they arrived at an airfield. A helicopter was on the tarmac. As she watched the rotors warm up, it began to dawn on her that Lime couldn't just be FBI: he must hold some classified rank in the military. She'd heard rumors of agents who also had high-level positions in the CIA, the DIA, or some other branch of U.S. intelligence.

Lime pulled up on the airstrip and stopped a hundred yards from the chopper. Two soldiers came over and helped them out, escorting them to the bird, one joining them on board. Corrie and Lime were given headsets and seated in the webbing. Even as Corrie was buckling in and adjusting her headset, the rotors spun up and the chopper lifted off. The sun was just touching the horizon as they rose into the clear desert air and accelerated southeast, over the Manzano Mountains toward the desert beyond. As Corrie watched the fir-clad slopes give way to desert, it occurred to her that everything had begun to move so fast, that the crush of urgency had swept her up so quickly, she'd had no time to think—only react. For reasons she couldn't quite identify, a sense of unease took possession of her. Something felt wrong—but she wasn't sure why.

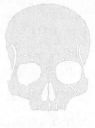

50

"Lᴇᴛ's ɴoᴛ ᴍᴇss this up at the last minute," Nora said as Tappan pushed the dead magnetometer aside and began shoveling sand willy-nilly into a wheelbarrow. "This is archaeology, not treasure hunting."

Tappan paused, leaning on the shovel, breathing hard. He nodded, wiping off the sweat. "Sorry. You're right."

"I believe the right thing to do," Nora said, "is to pause and take stock, figure out what's going on."

"Absolutely not," said Tappan. "We're almost there. I mean, Columbus didn't pause his voyage just before reaching the New World, did he?"

Nora felt conflicted. She looked around and could see, clearly on everyone's face, an eagerness to continue.

The strange magnetic activity that had wreaked havoc with their instruments and tools had vanished as quickly as it came—and not returned.

"All right. But let's please proceed by the book."

"Fair enough."

"We're going to need lights. Emilio, could you fire up the generator and get the floods in place? And let's get the magnetometer out of the hole so we can work."

Tappan leaned his shovel against the dig wall and helped Toth wheel the machine up the ramp and out. He came up next to Nora and watched as Vigil erected the lights around the sides of the hole. Tappan didn't say anything more, but Nora could feel the excitement radiating from him like an electrical aura. She felt a turmoil of emotions herself—intense curiosity, apprehension, anticipation. Rushing headlong to uncover what was in the hole went against her better judgment, but she understood that nothing would stop Tappan now...and she herself felt the tug of discovery.

"I believe we are on the verge," Tappan finally said in a quiet voice, "of the greatest archaeological find in history."

The sun at that moment dipped below the

horizon and a hush fell over the team. The silent sentinels of Los Gigantes glowed red in the final rays and then changed to a dusky purple as the light vanished.

"Ready," said Emilio.

The lights snapped on, bathing the hole in brilliant white light.

"Go slow," Nora told them. "Layer by layer. If you encounter anything, stop immediately. Emilio, you're in charge of wheelbarrowing the sand. We're going to focus on the four quads in the center—leave the outer squares for now."

They began work under the bright lights, in silence, the only sounds the scrape and tang of trowels, and Emilio's shoveling the sand into a wheelbarrow and wheeling it out to Cecilia Toth. The four quads deepened quickly as work progressed and darkness fell. A multitude of stars began to come out in the vast of night. Nora worked alongside Toth and Tappan, making sure things proceeded methodically, carefully, without haste, troweling down through the soft, damp sand with care, layer by layer.

"Hold it," Nora said abruptly. The others halted.

After years of dirt archaeology, she had developed a sixth sense for when she was about to expose an artifact, from the texture and firmness of the sand.

"I think we've got something," she said, laying the trowel aside and taking up a whisk.

Everyone crowded in to see. They were now about eight feet below the surface and Nora had an uncharacteristic feeling of claustrophobia. But the wet sand they were digging in had a lot of caliche in it, so the walls were firm and solid, and they had been hammering in braces as they went down. The lights above cast crazy shadows in the dark corners.

Tappan stood behind her as she hesitated. "Well? Are we going to see what it is?"

Nora took a few photographs, feeling impatience radiate from Tappan like heat.

"Can you give me a little more space, please?"

The group stepped back reluctantly. She swept the brush and uncovered another layer of sand... and then something happened: a strange green light could be seen filtering up through the grains of sand still lightly covering the object, dimly illuminating the surrounding faces with an unearthly glow.

Nora hesitated, then readied herself to make the final, uncovering whisk.

From above came a sudden throbbing: the unexpected sound of rapidly approaching helicopters. Nora looked toward the noise and saw, behind the perimeter of lights, two black helicopters coming in fast, doors open, bristling with mounted guns. The two birds swung around on either side of the dig for a landing as the backwash from their rotors whipped the sand into a blinding whirlwind that engulfed the hole and everyone in it.

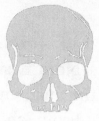

51

As Nora shielded herself from the hurricane, she heard commands barked from above. What seemed like a dozen soldiers leapt from the descending choppers. "Hands in sight!" somebody shouted. "Everyone out of the hole!"

"Who the hell are you?" Tappan cried.

There was sudden confusion amid the dust storm. Nora could barely open her eyes to see.

"*Out of that hole and back away!*" came the command. "*Hands in the air—or we shoot!*"

"Identify yourselves!" Tappan yelled. This was answered by a burst of automatic fire over their heads.

"*You won't be warned again!*"

As Nora and the others scrambled out of the hole, a soldier spun her around and pulled her arms behind her back. She felt zip ties, heard the zing as they were pulled tight—too tight. Meanwhile, six of the soldiers who had leapt from the choppers ran to the two jeeps, started them up, and immediately began heading off into the gloom, three men per jeep.

"Get your hands off me," Vigil shouted in the confusion.

Nora looked around, half-stunned. The helicopters, rotors still spinning, now had their spotlights on. She recognized them as Black Hawks—no numbers or insignia.

The four of them—Tappan, Vigil, Toth, and herself—were shoved into a line by the soldiers. A man with captain's bars on his uniform strode out in front.

"What the hell do you think you're doing?" Vigil shouted, wrenching free of a soldier and advancing on the captain.

"Halt!" the captain said, pulling out his sidearm.

"I did two tours in Afghanistan!" Vigil shouted, taking another step forward. "Don't you pull a gun on me, you bastard."

The captain fired two quick shots and Vigil pitched back. Toth, behind him, screamed and fell to her knees, grabbing her leg.

"Son of a bitch!" yelled Tappan. "You just shot Emilio!"

The captain spun around and whipped his gun across Tappan's face, then stepped back as two soldiers held the entrepreneur while he struggled. Vigil lay on the ground in a soaking pool of blood. Toth sobbed, on her knees, holding her calf, blood flowing through her fingers.

"Get them in the bird," the captain said, gesturing with his gun. "Now. Next person who talks gets a bullet."

Nora, numb with shock, was given a hard push toward the closest helicopter, with Tappan following, then Toth, two soldiers supporting her. In a moment they were shoved through the door and yanked over to the webbing frames.

The door slammed shut and the chopper rose into the night. Nora could see, on the dwindling landscape below, soldiers from the second chopper, cautiously approaching the fresh excavation.

She turned to Tappan, sitting next to her, blood streaming from a cut over his eye, and their eyes met. His were full of fury.

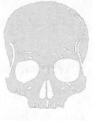

52

Greg Banks stepped out of the thirty-foot Airstream "dining car" and looked around, taking in the Quonset huts, helipad, motor pool, and small neighborhood of trailers and motor homes that made up base camp. He refused to call it "home," even temporarily: the landscape was simply too forbidding, too alien for someone raised in London. And, speaking of bloody aliens, the foul mood he'd been in all day hadn't lifted. Nor did he much want it to. Bloody Cecilia. Why had *she* been allowed to go out to the advance site today? It was likely to prove historic, or at least bloody interesting, and he'd had as much right to go as she had. Probably more.

With the sat phones and even the internet

down for some reason, he'd had little to do that afternoon. As a result, he'd had all the more time to brood.

He turned his gaze toward the new site. Or at least, in its general direction: everything was cloaked in the starlit mantle of night and there was little to see.

Tappan could be such a cipher. His easygoing manner was at least part façade, concealing the imperiousness Banks assumed was characteristic of all billionaires. Had Tappan been upset because he hadn't located Bitan? Banks had tried his best—they all had.

He decided it didn't merit further consideration: he'd never know for sure, and Tappan wouldn't tell him. One way or the other, the project would be over fairly soon, and then he could—money in his pocket—tell the billionaire to get stuffed.

As he'd relished this delightfully sour fantasy, Banks had stopped paying attention to his surroundings. But now, he realized that lights had appeared on the horizon. He peered at them closely through the dark. Two pairs of what were obviously headlights, bouncing up and down as the vehicles navigated the terrain of the alkali flats.

He glanced at his watch—eight twenty—then turned and hurried back into the dining car. The table was still mostly occupied by the first dinner shift: support staff, guards, flight-line workers. Everyone was taking their time, enjoying coffee and dessert, well aware that the forward team wasn't yet on the way back. Banks ducked through the door leading to the large, well-equipped galley, where Antonetti, the chef, was juggling four copper saucepans simmering with different ingredients. Despite being a two-star chef, Antonetti had once worked the line on an aircraft carrier, and he hadn't lost his obsession for running by the clock. If the second dinner shift—the scientists and bigwigs—wasn't on hand and hungry by eight thirty, he began to get agitated.

"Hey, Tony, it's cool," Banks said, using the chef's nickname. "They're on their way back—I can see their lights. Twenty minutes."

Antonetti's reply was to mutter under his breath, bang a few pots, and tell Max, the skinny youth next to him—sous chef, saucier, and kitchen dogsbody all rolled into one—to hold off on the beurre noisette.

Banks went back out into the dining room.

"Twenty!" he yelled at the diners, letting them know how soon they'd have to get the hell out. This bit of thoughtfulness was rewarded by groans, derisory hoots, and a variety of rude gestures.

He stepped back out into the evening. As he did so, Kuznetsov and one of the postdocs, Scott, wandered up. So did Mitty, Skip Kelly's big dog. Apparently he was hungry, too.

"Chow's going to be a little late, boys," Banks informed them. "I told Tony to hold off a little while."

"Why the hell did you do that?" asked Kuznetsov, aggrieved. On occasion, Antonetti had gone full prima donna and promptly served "second seating," regardless of whether all his clientele was back in camp or not.

"Because I saw the jeeps below the mesa," Banks said. "Maybe a quarter of an hour out."

"They look a lot closer than that," said Scott.

Banks turned back toward the distant landscape. Sure enough, the headlights were now closer—and up on the mesa. For whatever reason, Tappan was really putting a wiggle on. At this rate, the jeeps would be in camp in less than ten minutes.

The three stood in the reflected light of the dining car, watching. Something else about the vehicles seemed unusual in addition to their speed. Banks squinted to see beyond the flare of the headlights. The occupants appeared to be strangers—strangers in uniforms.

The short, dark Kuznetsov, also increasingly perplexed, said something in Russian.

And then, almost before he knew what had happened, the two jeeps roared around the last turn and into the complex, slowing abruptly, swerving and throwing up dust. They came to a stop on either side of Banks. Four headlights now framed the little group. Soldiers jumped out of each jeep. They were moving fast, all armed with submachine guns and a variety of tactical gear, including night-vision goggles that hung loosely around their necks.

Banks blinked at the jeeps. There was no mistake: these were the vehicles Tappan and the rest had taken out that morning. A prick of anxiety thrust itself into his confusion. He turned toward the dining car, but it was too late: he was surrounded by soldiers in camo with their weapons unshipped, pointed at the ground but ready for immediate use.

The soldier in charge—a major, apparently, oak leaves being the only recognizable element of his uniform—spoke rapidly to his men, issuing orders in a low tone. They saluted, then three of them ran off into the darkness of the camp, separating, while the other two trotted into the dining car.

The major looked at the three of them in turn. "On your way to dinner, sport?" he asked, his gaze settling on Banks. "Whatever's cooking in there smells good."

Nobody answered. Banks continued to struggle with confusion. The major spoke with an American accent. These troops had to be United States Army—nothing else made sense. But why were they here, heavily armed, driving jeeps belonging to Tappan's excavation? Something told him to stay quiet and let the major do the talking.

The major glanced through the windows of the Airstream. "Looks like a full house. Why haven't you joined them?"

"That's the first shift, finishing dinner." It was Scott, the postdoc, who spoke.

"Shut your cake hole," Banks snapped at him.

Hearing this, the major snorted a laugh. Banks

could hear the two soldiers inside, speaking loudly.

"Where's Lucas and the rest?" Kuznetsov asked.

"He and the rest of your team uncovered something extremely dangerous."

"What?" Scott asked immediately.

"Apparently, some kind of virus not native to Earth."

This information loosened Banks's tongue. "So where's Tappan?"

"He and the others are at a military compound northwest of here. They're not in great shape, I'm afraid. A large mobilization is underway." The major nodded toward the dining hall. "Let's head inside. What I have to tell you concerns everyone."

They hustled in. Banks noticed that all six new arrivals had been moving with great rapidity. *Terror is the best of guards.*

...Now, why had that, of all lines, just come to him? And where had he heard it before?

Once they'd filed in, one of the two soldiers already inside turned toward the major. "They're all accounted for except one man, down at the motor pool."

"Roger." Reaching for a radio attached to a

shoulder strap, the major repeated this information. Then he nodded to the two soldiers. One
ducked back toward the galley, while the other
stayed at the front of the mess. Banks noticed his
finger lay in the ready position directly above the
trigger guard.

The major took a moment to sweep the
room with his eyes. To Banks, he seemed oddly
pleased—as if, from an operational standpoint,
someone had already done his work for him.

The men and women at the table had pushed
aside their coffee and desserts and were looking
at the soldiers with a mixture of uncertainty and
increasing apprehension. One of the machinists,
a man named Wallensky, stood up. "Hey, Greg,"
he said to Banks. "What's up?"

"Something's gone wrong."

"Sit down, please," the major told Wallensky, talking over Banks. "We will brief you all
shortly."

At that moment, the second soldier returned,
leading the chef before him. "Another one in the
kitchen was working a gas range," the soldier
told the major. "He lit out a back door before I
could stop him."

"Gas range, huh?" The major spoke into his

radio again. Tony, the cook, was directed to stand in front with Banks, Kuznetsov, and Scott. The soldier who'd been in the kitchen now began going around the dining room, closing and locking the windows and drawing the cowboy-patterned curtains over them.

"Listen up," the major said in a harder voice. "Tappan and the others have been exposed to some unknown, apparently nonterrestrial virus. We're here to decontaminate this base, check all of you for possible infection, and then evac you to a safe location."

At that moment, the outside door opened and one of the three soldiers brought in the missing motor pool worker, along with Max. The young cook had dust on his T-shirt, and he was panting.

The soldier pushed the two inside with the barrel of his weapon. Looking over his shoulder, Banks could now make out one of the other two soldiers who'd been left outside, loading up the jeeps with laptops and scientific equipment. He was still moving fast, as if on a clock.

What the bloody hell was going on?

"Caught this one running," the soldier told the major, indicating Max.

Terror is the best of guards. Now Banks remembered: that was an expression Noam Bitan had used on occasion. But why?

"All accounted for," the soldier added.

"What the hell are you up to?" Wallensky demanded of the soldier who was closing and locking all the windows.

Something occurred to Banks. "If there's some kind of biological emergency," he asked the major, "why aren't you wearing protective gear?"

"Not necessary, sport," the major said with a friendly smile. Then he spoke quietly and quickly to the soldier who'd brought in the two strays. He nodded, disappearing out into the darkness once again. The soldier with the trigger finger took up position by the open door.

Now Banks heard crashing noises from outside. Looking past the soldier at the door, Banks could see two of the three others dumping all sorts of equipment from the Quonset huts—hard drives, notebooks, files, lockers for sample storage—into the empty space below the Airstream. Still at a dead run.

Wallensky, who was standing again, moved to block the soldier as he was locking a nearby window. "Answer my fucking question," he said.

The soldier turned, raised his weapon, and fired a short burst. Wallensky was kicked backward, falling onto the table and sliding across it, leaving a bloody smear in his wake. Dishes and silverware hit the floor, the crash of crockery mingling with screams and cries of surprise as a dozen more people jumped to their feet.

"Pity," the major said.

The soldier who'd run off into the darkness now returned. "You were right, sir," he said. "About the location."

"Stopcock open?" the major asked him as the other two soldiers covered the room.

"It is now, sir," the man panted. "Wide open." From outside, there was another crash as the two soldiers with armfuls of equipment returned, throwing more of the camp's expensive stuff under the Airstream.

"Everybody, stay where you are," the major said to the crowd in a warning tone.

"You shot him!" a woman cried.

"You're not army!" said the man from the motor pool.

"We could rush you, motherfucker!" said a third, a helicopter pilot.

All three had spoken simultaneously. But it was the pilot the major turned to answer.

"You'd never make it, sport." And he slipped his own automatic weapon off his shoulder as he spoke.

And now, Banks—having some trouble believing all this was not just a nightmare—recalled where Bitan's quote came from. Three of Bitan's grandparents had died in Nazi concentration camps. The fourth, who survived Buchenwald, passed on to a young Bitan a cruel motto the SS taught newly arrived recruits, explaining how so few could control and liquidate so many. Keep them moving, always moving. And afraid. *Terror is the best of guards…*

He wheeled around to grasp the major. But he was too late: the soldiers were already retreating out the door, machine guns held menacingly before them. The major glanced toward Banks, and their eyes met.

"Later, sport," he said.

Then he slammed and locked the door. At the same moment, Banks smelled gas.

Gas range, huh?

Looks like a full house.

It is now, sir. Wide open.

All this flashed through Banks's mind in a microsecond. And then he, like everyone else, was stumbling, clambering, clawing toward the locked door. Mindless screams deafened him. People began pounding on the windows with their fists. Through a gap in the curtains, he could see all six soldiers now back in the jeeps. The major was at the wheel of the lead vehicle. His automatic weapon was still out, and he was aiming it toward the back of the huge Airstream.

Where the auxiliary propane dump was located.

Banks opened his mouth to join in the shouting. But even as he did so, the major fired a short, measured burst...and Banks's world ended in a universe of flame.

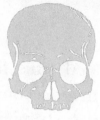

53

As THE HELICOPTER blades whipped overhead, cutting through the night, Nora sat against the webbing, Tappan to one side and Toth to the other. Toth was whimpering slightly, her shoulders heaving. One soldier had tied a rude tourniquet above her knee before pushing her into the chopper, but now she sat unaided as blood soaked through bandages that had been hastily wrapped around her calf.

Nora struggled against an overwhelming conviction that this had to be a dream: a terrible, nonsensical dream. Everything had happened so quickly. One minute they were on the threshold of a mind-blowing discovery...and then, seconds later, helicopters had descended like the chariots of malignant gods; Vigil was murdered in cold blood; and now she was a captive, flying through the dark to an unknown fate.

Nothing made sense…save the pain in her wrists from the zip ties, pulled cruelly tight, that kept insisting this was, in fact, no dream.

To her right, Tappan was silent. He was bleeding as well, from the gash in his forehead where he'd been pistol-whipped, but already the flow was ebbing. After exchanging glances with her when the chopper first rose into the air, he'd stared straight ahead, looking stonily at the figure across from them in the belly of the aircraft.

Nora stared, too. He was evidently a captain— the bars on his uniform indicated as much— but beyond that, she could discern nothing. He was dressed in combat uniform, but she didn't recognize the light gray color. There were small, unfamiliar badges where the breast bar would normally be.

The man stared back at them expressionlessly, forearms on his knees, SIG service pistol held loosely in his right hand—the same weapon with which he'd callously killed Vigil and wounded Cecilia.

Her brooding was interrupted by an unmistakable sensation: they were descending, and quickly. She looked out the chopper window: still nothing but the blackness of the high desert. But no: now she could make out something. Four lights, small and red, had come on, forming a square below them, winking slowly as they revolved. From inside the helicopter, it was impossible to determine how far below they were, or how large an area they circumscribed.

But as the chopper continued to descend—vertically now—it quickly became clear the lights were illuminating a landing pad.

A minute later, their wheels touched ground. It seemed to Nora they'd only been airborne five, perhaps ten minutes, but in her confusion she couldn't be sure. A door was opened from outside, and more soldiers with automatic weapons appeared. The captain leapt out, and then Nora and Tappan were led—none too gently—out of the craft and onto the pad. Another soldier helped the wounded Toth.

Nora looked around. In the darkness, she could make out very little. They appeared to be on a plain amid low dark hills, near a range of mountains, below a vast sea of stars. To her left was a large, low building that at one time perhaps served as a hangar, but the roof had partially fallen in, exposing metal struts like ribs. Beside it were the black silhouettes of additional buildings, equally decrepit, that resembled barracks. A broken water tower on the other side completed the picture of ruin. And that was all. Even the landing zone they were standing on seemed bare earth, its covering of sand stirred into strange whorls by the blades of the chopper.

The captain barked an order, and the soldiers, gesturing with the barrels of their weapons, lined the captives up again. Mute, still in shock, they complied, a soldier holding up Toth. Another barked order, unintelligible, cut through the night. For a moment of horror, Nora thought that they were about to be shot.

But no shot came. Instead, a green light appeared in the seemingly moribund water tower, winking on and off. Then she felt a sudden movement under her feet, and heard a deep, throbbing noise. Dreamlike unreality rose within her again. But then, to her shock, she realized they were descending. Chopper, soldiers, landing lights, and sandy desert floor were all on a platform, disappearing below the earth. They were standing on the equivalent of an aircraft carrier's giant elevator. They descended almost a hundred feet before coming to rest in a dark hangar bay, illuminated in reddish light.

Now, at a nod from the captain, another group of soldiers approached Nora and Tappan and—gesturing once again with their weapons—prodded them off the landing pad, the helicopter's blades still spinning down lazily. As they began to walk away, Nora saw out of the corner of her eye more workers approach, rearranging the soil and adding fresh sand, as the improvised pad and its chopper were made ready to rise once again to the surface.

Then a concealing door locked into place above and brilliant illumination snapped on, flooding the underground space with light. It was as busy as the desert above had been empty. Two other chopper bays sat vacant to one side, and beyond that a small motor pool of open-topped jeeps. In a far corner of the cavernous space, she saw a machine shop through a row of windows. A gowned worker came up, pushing a stretcher in front of him. Toth was placed upon it, and the sides were raised.

They were led down a wide corridor. Nora's hands were still bound painfully behind her back, one soldier leading the way and another bringing up the rear. She looked around, trying to get a sense of where they were, what exactly this place was—but the shock had not yet worn off and it was almost too strange to process. From the markings on the walls and the sterile, spartan appearance, it was obviously military, and much more recent than the ruins above. The walls and floor were made of poured concrete, painted light green. Now and then, they passed open doors or large windows, some dark, others affording views of soldiers hunched over workstations or, in one case, a larger server farm. Here and there, other corridors branched off. At the first of these, the gowned worker turned and wheeled the protesting Toth away. The main impressions Nora had were of immense size, comparative emptiness—and singular purpose. But what that purpose was, she couldn't begin to guess.

The soldier in front of them stopped at a door. A number had been stenciled on it in black paint, and nothing made it in any way distinguishable from dozens of similar doors they'd passed already. The soldier rapped twice with the butt of his weapon, then—with effort—slid the door open. It rolled into a pocket in the concrete wall.

Nora felt a rifle barrel in the small of her back prodding her forward. She and Tappan stepped into a large, bare, circular room. Long windows of dark glass, gently curved to conform with the walls, were set just beneath the high ceiling.

In the middle of the room was a table of bare wood, as spartan as the rest of the place, and three chairs. Behind was a single chair in which sat a man. Unlike the others, he was in uniform rather than fatigues, gold eagles on his epaulettes. As they came forward and were steered in front of the desk, the man remained seated. He was blade-thin, with pale eyes, gray-white hair cut short, and high cheekbones that could have been fashioned with a hatchet.

The soldiers each stepped to one side, taking up flanking positions, weapons at the ready. Once the guards were in place, the man nodded briskly at Nora and Tappan in turn.

"My name is Colonel Rush," he said. "I have some questions for you."

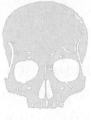

54

THE CHOPPER ROSE again as soon as Watts and Skip had been strapped into the webbing. Night had fallen. As they gained altitude, Corrie looked south and could see a bank of lights illuminating the dig at the crash site. Farther to the south, on Diablo Mesa, she could make out the much larger cluster of lights that signified the base camp. The rest of the landscape was a vast bowl of darkness.

The chopper reached altitude and then accelerated north. She waited for it to make a turn to the south, but it didn't. As she was about to ask Lime why they weren't heading to the camp, she saw a massive flash of light burst out from that direction. A moment later, a shock wave hit the chopper: a boom that caused the craft to sway in the air as a roiling ball of fire punched up into the sky amid a swiftly expanding cloud of dust, luridly illuminated by a sudden inferno below.

"What the hell was that?" Corrie cried in horror, staring out the window.

"Holy shit!" Skip said, face to the glass. "Was that the camp?"

The pilot stabilized the chopper from the wave of overpressure. When Corrie turned around to look back at the others, she was struck dumb: Lime had unbuckled himself and was standing, weapon out and pointed at her. The soldier, likewise, had his weapon covering them.

"Remove your sidearm," Lime said.

"What—?" Corrie couldn't process this rapid, unexpected series of events.

"You too, Sheriff. Slow and easy, with two fingers. Hold the weapons out and the soldier will take them."

Corrie stared, still flabbergasted.

"Do as you're told," said Lime, "or you'll be killed. This may be hard to understand, but trust me, it's your duty. As a patriot."

She still could not speak. Skip was staring at Lime, eyes practically bugging out of his head.

Watts recovered first. "Corrie said you were her boss," he told Lime, face dark. "Who are you really working for?"

"The United States," said Lime. "Just like you. Now do as I say—I won't ask again."

After a hesitation, Watts removed his two revolvers and held them out as instructed. They were taken away by the soldier.

"Corrie?" asked Lime.

Corrie finally found her voice. "'As a patriot'? What are you talking about?"

Lime slapped her across the face with an open palm—so hard she saw stars. "I'm sorry, Corrie. But you have to understand that I mean business. Better a slap across the face than a bullet in the brain pan. Now: your weapon, please. Two fingers."

The blow shook the confusion from her. Cheek aflame, she unsnapped the keeper in her holster and held up her 9mm with two fingers. The soldier took it.

"Are you some kind of Russian spy?" she asked.

"No. When we get to Pershing, you'll be debriefed. No more talk."

After securing the weapons, the soldier went around and unbuckled each one of them from their harnesses. Then he pulled Corrie's hands behind her back and zip-tied them together.

Skip suddenly spoke, his voice tight and high. "The camp. Was that an explosion?"

"Necessary but regrettable," Lime said.

"What the fuck? What about my sister?"

"She wasn't there. We have her at Pershing."

"And my—?"

"One more word and you'll get a bullet." His voice was calm—too calm—and Corrie knew he meant it. She prayed Skip would shut up.

Skip did. After zip-tying Corrie, the soldier bent over Skip, reaching out to grab his wrists. But, free of his harness, Skip abruptly lunged upward, ramming his head into the soldier's stomach and knocking him down. With a garbled scream, Skip leapt into the cockpit, whipping his forearm around the pilot's throat and wrenching back his head, twisting and choking him.

The chopper swerved abruptly, throwing everyone to one side. Still screaming like a madman, Skip throttled the pilot. The soldier jumped Skip from behind, trying to pull him off the pilot while yanking out a knife to cut his throat, but the helicopter spun so wildly, rotors screaming, that everyone was at the mercy of centrifugal forces. Everyone had been unbuckled except the pilot, and Corrie, still zip-tied, found herself tossed from one side of the fuselage to the other, helplessly tumbling with the others, hearing shots fired uselessly as the out-of-control bird went into a spiraling descent that swiftly ended in a massive, crunching impact—and then, darkness.

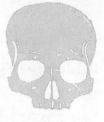

55

Standing in front of Rush, Tappan spoke first. To Nora, his voice seemed surprisingly calm. "What is this place?"

Rush looked at him steadily, hatchet-like cheekbones framing his pale eyes. A man in a lieutenant's uniform entered the room, came over, and bent toward Rush, whispering something in his ear. The colonel nodded and the man quickly left, feet echoing on the concrete floor, closing the heavy door behind him.

Rush turned back to Tappan. Although his uniform resembled that of an officer in the regular army, Nora noticed that—like the captain's—it bore badges, medals, and service ribbons that looked unusual. It was the same with this room, or for that matter the entire underground base:

while in her experience military quarters were never lavish, these surroundings seemed particularly spartan. In fact, other than the table, chairs, and smoked windows—which reminded her of the observation panels in a police interrogation room—there was only one piece of ornamentation: an emblem on the wall behind the colonel, showing an eagle hovering over Earth, its wings spread and talons out as if to protect its young. Beneath was a motto: SERVANDAE VITAE MENDACIUM.

"What is this place?" Tappan repeated.

This time, the colonel answered. "I presume that to be, at least in part, a rhetorical question. I suspect you have an inkling of who we are, why we're here, and what our mission is." He spoke in a clipped voice.

At that moment, the door opened again and two more soldiers entered, carrying between them a black box, about two feet on a side. They gingerly placed the box on Rush's desk. The colonel stood and took a step back.

"Evaluation complete?" he asked.

"Yes, sir," said one of the soldiers.

"And?"

"Full green."

"Very well." Rush nodded.

Nora watched as the other soldier unlatched the box and carefully opened the lid. The lid's interior, and the box itself, seemed to be lined with a thick grayish-black material resembling graphite. She could not see its contents beyond a jade-green glow that reflected off Rush's face as he stared down—a glow she remembered coming from beneath the sand of the dig site. The colonel appeared stunned, his face tense and his eyes glittering in the otherworldly light. An age seemed to pass before he stepped back again and nodded to the soldier, who shut the box.

"Take it to vault nineteen," he said tersely.

The soldiers left and he turned back to Tappan. For a moment he was silent, as if collecting himself. Then he spoke. "I suppose I should thank you for finding that. Now, as I said, I have a few questions."

"Go fuck yourself," said Tappan.

The soldier standing to Tappan's right stepped forward, slamming his fist into Tappan's face. He fell to the ground with a grunt.

"Sergeant!" Rush barked. "Help him up."

The man pulled Tappan to his feet, gasping and sputtering.

"As you were," Rush ordered. The soldier once again took up a position to Tappan's right.

"I don't wish to hurt you," said Rush.

"Tell that to our research assistant," Tappan said, spitting out a mouthful of blood. "The one your boys shot in the head."

"That's regrettable. But make no mistake: my troops are not 'boys.' And it wasn't a sandbox you were digging in, up there on the surface. Though you may not know it, you've infiltrated a war zone—and any resulting casualties are on your heads as much as they are on mine."

"What are you talking about?" Nora asked. "What war zone?"

Rush's eyes slid toward her. "I have two questions that are particularly pressing. I need to know, first, what you've found so far; and second, who else knows about it outside your team in the field."

"What we've found?" Nora said. "I don't know what you're talking about."

But even as she said this, she knew he could mean only one thing. Rush's lips twitched and she realized that—as he'd implied—he knew this as well as she did.

"Please don't insult my intelligence," he told

her. "As I said, I don't desire any more bloodshed than necessary. But you've put me in a difficult situation. If you don't provide me with the information I need, I'll have no choice but to assume the worst. And respond accordingly."

Something about the way he said this chilled Nora.

"Where were those men of yours heading in our jeeps?" Tappan asked.

Now it was the colonel's turn not to answer.

"You said you didn't want bloodshed," Tappan continued. "Guarantee the safety of my people—and I'll answer your questions."

Nora glanced at Tappan. He didn't look back.

Rush exhaled slowly.

"Nobody knows anything," Tappan burst out. "Just the four of us. Three, thanks to your trigger-happy captain. Okay? I don't know what you're after, exactly, but we don't have it. We don't know anything. But it's obvious you know who *we* are—and what we're doing. You probably even know the answers to these questions you're asking. Now: Will you guarantee the safety of my people?"

"I'll do my best," Rush said after a brief silence. "But as I said, this is a military facility, engaged in a war. That makes guarantees somewhat complicated."

Tappan scoffed in disbelief. "There's no war here."

"But that's where you're wrong. There most certainly is a war: a secret war. And it's been going on a long, long time."

Rush looked from one to the other for a moment. Then he appeared to come to a decision.

"Sit down," he said, indicating the chairs.

After a long pause, Nora took a seat. Tappan followed.

"As a gesture of goodwill, I'll answer your initial question. Because if my intel is accurate, you two—more than almost anybody—will understand."

He sat forward, lacing his slender fingers on the desk.

"We're a hybrid branch of both the United States armed forces and its intelligence community, established informally in 1946 as an offshoot of the OSS and, more formally, in the National Security Act of 1947. The name given us in classified civilian circles is Atropos. As a component of America's security network, we feel we need no name."

"Never heard of you," said Tappan.

Rush smiled mirthlessly. "It would be an intelligence failure if you had. Everything about us—from our history, to our appropriations, to our service members, to our installations—is black. Not for our safety, but for that of the countrymen we serve." He paused. "I can see the skepticism in your face, Mr. Tappan. But the fact is, we are almost certainly the most important element in keeping you alive—and safe."

"Funny, I don't feel very safe at the moment." And Tappan turned to spit another mouthful of blood.

"You may see things differently after a short explanation. In the simplest terms: we're the guardians of the Roswell Interaction."

"The Roswell Interaction," Nora said.

Rush nodded. "The custodians of the alien probe that crash-landed nearby in 1947. It was not a duty that we chose, or that we wished for. Rather, it fell upon us to form a new branch of service, dedicated to taking on this responsibility—in the aftermath of a discovery too monumental to be entrusted to an inept government, weak intelligence agencies, or a distracted military."

"Inept and weak?" Tappan asked in disbelief.

"In the confused aftermath of World War Two, with the rising Soviet menace—yes. We came together from many areas—army and navy special forces, X2 paramilitary personnel, the Strategic Services Unit—infuriated by the porousness of places like Los Alamos, Oak Ridge, and Richland. Supposedly, only a few hundred people knew what 'Little Boy' *really was* before Hiroshima...but within a year, almost all our atomic secrets had leaked to the Russians. Atropos was formed to put a stop to those leaks; to protect America from itself. Until we were suddenly given an even bigger mission."

"Roswell," Nora said.

Rush nodded. "In our early capacity of guarding secret sites and halting espionage interdictions, an Atropos team was sent out from Los Alamos to investigate what had taken place there. No doubt you can guess what they discovered."

"An alien vessel," said Tappan after a moment.

"Probe," Rush corrected. "Unmanned, if you can use such a term. But you left out a key word: hostile."

Tappan shook his head. "That's a paranoid Cold War assumption. There's no reason to think any extraterrestrial visitors capable of seeking us out would be anything but friendly."

Rush smiled mirthlessly. "Spoken with the ignorance only a wealthy dilettante could assume." He glanced at Nora. "You're an archaeologist, I understand. That makes you a scientist, at least marginally. What do you think? That alien beings are necessarily pacifistic, short and fat and so ugly they're adorable, with fingers that light up like a Christmas ornament?"

Nora didn't answer.

"You're wise not to speak. Because anyone with a little humility would realize we—despite what your friend here says—can't afford to make such assumptions. As Einstein said: most assumptions are wrong." He leaned forward, tented fingers pressed tightly together. "That 'friendly' probe killed over three dozen of our men. Had it not been damaged, it would undoubtedly have killed more. Most likely, a planet-full more."

He looked at Nora, then at Tappan. "Once initial extraction was complete and we had secured the probe, our analysis of the wreckage and its associated technology indicated the craft was sent by an alien civilization as a prelude to attack. A hostile scouting mission, as it were."

"How can you be sure they're hostile?" Tappan asked.

"You mean, in addition to killing two dozen soldiers during, ah, 'first contact'? In the decades since, we've run hundreds of tests and simulations. Perhaps you'll get to see the documentary evidence yourself. If you had only a little more objectivity, and a little less hubris, you wouldn't need to ask that question in the first place."

He paused for a moment. "Your resistance to the truth is understandable. We'd all like nothing better than to believe in a warm, hospitable universe. But those are pipe dreams, naive and utopian. Montezuma indulged in a similarly understandable fantasy when he welcomed Cortés as a god. We know how that ended: in the destruction of his civilization." He paused again, looking at the two in turn. "Go into the primeval forest at night. You'll find it teeming with life, from insects and spiders to salamanders, frogs, snakes, birds, and other animals small and large. And what are they all doing? They are *hunting*. Evolution produces a violent struggle for resources—nature 'red in tooth and claw.' *That* is the one universal, eternal constant. The galaxy is like that forest at night, roamed by hunters. They are hunting for resources. They are hunting for planets to plunder. They are hunting down emerging technological species to exterminate, lest they become competitors. The first commercial radio broadcast took place in 1920...and we've been shouting heedlessly into the universe ever since. Every planet within a hundred and two light-years can now hear us. And the result? The result was Roswell."

"Bullshit," said Tappan. "That's conjecture."

"I'd like to think you're an intelligent man. I mentioned Montezuma. Look at the centuries that followed and how our citizens—even more advanced—prospered by the enslavement of others. Or today, when we ravage our own planet far faster than it can restore itself." He shook his head. "Advancements in technology, evolution in intelligence, only serve to refine our cruelty. We'll fare very, very poorly at the hands of an alien race."

"This armed service of yours," Nora said. "What's its mission now?"

"It has evolved with time, of course. We remain a small, secret branch within the military intelligence community, our lives dedicated to just one thing: saving our planet. Part of that mission has been to keep Earth's threat profile as low as possible. Another part, naturally, has been to study the probe; try to understand its complexity—and, when the time is right, reveal its nature and help the world prepare for invasion."

"Keeping Earth's threat profile low," Tappan said. "I suppose that means you eliminate certain astronomers or physicists who might make breakthroughs you'd disapprove of? And sabotage satellites...or, perhaps, the optics of a space telescope? Destroy rockets on takeoff, shuttles on landing—with innocent people on board?"

Rush sat back, waved a hand. "We stop leaks. We kill traitors quietly—like those bodies you found in the desert—bypassing the weak criminal justice system when necessary. That has always been a part of our mission, and we have no doubts or hesitation about carrying it out. Indirect casualties, on the other hand, are regrettable—but sometimes necessary. Our operatives aren't trigger-happy, and any interdiction we sanction is chosen because it presents the greatest risk of exposure to our planet."

"I guess you don't approve of SETI, then,"

Tappan said. "Or more aggressive approaches: active rather than passive."

Rush said nothing.

"Speaking of that, what about Bitan? What did you do with him?"

"With one of the most dangerous people on the planet? The man behind the CE-TIP proposal itself? The man who wanted to shout out our presence to the entire galaxy? We did what we had to."

"Did you enjoy it?"

Rush sighed. "I've taken the time to share our mission with you. I've patiently endured your denials and objections, ignorant though they are. The truth is, you could both prove useful members of our organization, especially now. But time is short—and my patience has a limit." He rose. "I'll give you a brief period to discuss this between yourselves."

He nodded to the guards. They turned and led Nora and Tappan out of the room, down a long corridor, and then another, to a concrete cell within a small cell block. They were shown inside, their zip ties cut free. The solid metal door then boomed shut on them.

Nora looked around. The cell had a small cot with a blanket, a sink, and a metal toilet.

She sank onto the cot, numb, massaging her wrists. Slowly, Tappan eased down beside her, blood crusted on his face. He put his arms around her and they sat side by side, holding each other in silence.

56

CORRIE FOUGHT HER way back to consciousness. For a moment, the blackness that had swallowed her up during the helicopter impact remained—and, with a sense of panic, she feared she was blind. But then a deep breath of choking air—along with an intense heat—made it clear she was enveloped in thick, dark smoke.

Quickly, she crawled in the only direction she could think of: away from the heat. It was a slow process, her bound hands making it difficult to navigate the disorder that filled the cabin. Gradually the smoke cleared, and she felt dirt beneath her and staggered to her feet, stumbling away to a safe distance from the burning wreckage. Every part of her throbbed with pain as she looked around.

The chopper had crashed nose-first, leaving the pilot compartment a mangled ruin of crumpled, burning metal. Although killing the pilot, the impact had the effect of throwing Corrie free of the aircraft...and, judging by the missing doors of the cabin, the rest of the passengers as well.

Her eyes moved past the wreckage to the surrounding area. Her eyes fell first on the soldier who had been guarding them. He lay facedown in the flickering light, legs outstretched, the KA-BAR knife with which he'd planned to kill Skip protruding instead from the back of his own neck. Farther away in the darkness she could make out the form of Skip himself, also motionless, lying in a crumpled heap on the far side of the chopper.

"Corrie!"

She wheeled to see Homer Watts coming toward her. He'd retrieved one of his six-guns from the wreckage, and other than a slight limp seemed to be none the worse for wear. He pulled the knife from the dead soldier, wiped it off, and cut her bonds. "Are you all right?"

"I don't know," she said, still half stunned.

"Let me take a look." He patted her gently, head to toe, feeling her limbs, checking for injuries.

"No serious damage that I can see," Watts told her. "It's a miracle."

"I'm just shaken up, I think." She looked around for her own weapon and couldn't see it anywhere.

Lime. At this, she spun around, completing her 360-degree sweep. But even as she turned, she heard the sheriff shout: "Stop right there!"

A moment later, Lime came into her field of view. His clothes were torn and his chestnut hair streaked with dirt. In one hand he held the weapon that, just minutes before, had been leveled at her. At Watts's barked command, he stopped.

"Toss your weapon over here," Watts said.

Slowly, Lime lowered his hand, then tossed the gun underhand—but instead of pitching toward Watts, it landed away from the three of them.

"I said, *over here.*"

"Sorry," Lime replied. "I'm not in the best of shape at the moment." He leaned forward, lowering his head and putting his palms on his knees.

"Hands in the air!" said Watts.

"Give me a minute, will you? Let this dizzy spell pass."

They waited in the flickering light of the wreck. Corrie looked around again for her weapon. Maybe it was still on the chopper.

Slowly, Lime straightened. He wiped a sleeve across his forehead. "I guess your friend had a death wish," he said, nodding at the still form of Skip. "What a stupid thing to do."

"Hands in the air," Watts repeated.

Instead of obeying, Lime expelled a breath, then planted his hands on his hips, arms akimbo. "No."

"You want to get shot?"

"I doubt if you're going to shoot a federal agent."

Corrie saw Watts hesitate. Then the sheriff turned to her. "Who the fuck is this guy?"

"I don't know," Corrie said. "He's been acting as my supervisor since Morwood's death. He's a stranger to Albuquerque Field Office, but everyone thinks he's an agent, sent to us on temporary assignment."

"From where?"

"Washington," Lime answered. "Like I said: I work for the United States, too."

"Bullshit," Corrie said. "You're no patriot. You're some sort of spy." But even as she said this, doubts crept in. Every instinct drilled into her over the last year said obeying a senior agent should be as natural as breathing. And Lime— he'd helped her further the case, he'd believed in her when nobody else did...he'd defended her over Lathrop's accusations. *And* he'd scrambled the helicopter.

"Think about what you're doing," Lime said, looking from Corrie to Watts. "It's like I tried to explain on the chopper. All this goes a lot deeper than you realize." He looked back at Corrie. "You know how the system works. We operate by compartmentalization—by need to know. There are many, many layers of security clearance."

"Your point?" Watts asked, keeping the gun steady. "It doesn't seem to me a genuine FBI agent would disarm and zip-tie his own junior partner."

"That was for her own protection. My point is that Corrie knows only part of what's going on. She's accidentally become involved in an on-going military operation—one that's larger and more complex than you can imagine."

"Like what?"

Lime shook his head in frustration. "I told

you: everything would be explained at Pershing. Look, lower your gun. Please. You can see I'm unarmed."

After a moment, Watts lowered his weapon. "Explain it now. What's at Pershing? It's an abandoned ruin as far as I know."

"That's intentional. It's actually a classified military base doing vital national security work."

Watts licked his lips. Corrie could see he was growing uncertain, too. "And that huge explosion at the base camp?"

"Who told you the explosion was from the base camp?" Lime asked.

Watts and Corrie exchanged glances.

"Sheriff Watts, you seem like a good man. So I hope you won't take offense when I say you're even more marginalized here than Corrie is. Look: I don't expect you to believe something you don't understand. But again, I implore you: think about what you're doing. I have operational powers that include the FBI—and go beyond. You've got a choice. You can let me contact Pershing, get us a rescue chopper; we'll get you temporary clearance, and then...then you can help us. Frankly, we need your help." He paused. "Or you can shoot me. And you know what? After that, you'll remain in the system—but you'll find yourself on the other side of it. Prison is an ugly, brutal place. And it only leads in one direction."

There was a silence, broken only by the crack of flame, the groan of metal.

"It's not too late," Lime said. "Holster that weapon and let's work as a team."

Watts hesitated. Then he slipped his gun back in its holster.

Quick as an adder, Lime's right hand slid off his hip and darted toward the small of his back, re-emerging with a handgun that he aimed to fire. But Watts was quicker, whipping out his six-gun again and fanning two shots at Lime. Corrie heard the man cry out in surprise and pain, staggering back, as Watts grabbed her, pulling her behind a rock for cover. He waited a moment, then ventured a peek.

"He's disappeared," Watts said as he pulled her into a sitting position.

"You sure?"

"For now, I'm sure." He picked up Lime's weapon—the one he'd tossed aside—then showed her the small-caliber gun Lime had pulled out of his waistband, twisted grotesquely by one of Watts's bullets.

"You shot the weapon out of his hands?"

"Sure did. Took off a finger, too, I hope. That dirty little trick answered our question about his sincerity and patriotism—the bastard." He tossed the mangled gun aside and passed her the other one.

At that moment, another figure emerged from the gloom—Skip Kelly, walking toward them none too steadily, holding his head.

"What happened?" he asked stupidly. "What was all that noise?"

"The big noise was you crashing the chopper we were all riding in," Watts told him. "The little noise was a gunfight I just had with Lime."

"Corrie's boss? Get him?"

"Not as thoroughly as I would have liked. Hopefully he's somewhere, bleeding out."

As Watts was speaking, he seemed to notice something over Skip's shoulder. With a curse, he darted toward the still-burning chopper. For a moment, his form was obscured by smoke. Then he emerged again with something in his hand.

"My silver-belly Resistol!" he cried, brandishing his expensive cowboy hat—half of its brim scorched away and a burnt hole in its crown. "God *damn* it!" Watts turned the ruined hat over and over in his hands. Corrie had never seen him so upset. With another curse, he screwed it onto his head.

"I'm going to climb that little hill, see where we are," he announced.

As he walked off, Corrie ejected the magazine of Lime's weapon, checked it, reseated it, and snugged the gun into her holster. It was a Glock 19 identical to her own.

Watts returned from the rise.

"Where are we?" Skip asked.

"Pershing's about a mile north."

"We've got to get away from this crash site," Corrie said. "They're bound to send people here, to find out what happened."

"And drones," Skip said. "Listen."

Corrie could hear a distant sound, like a swarm of bees, getting louder by the second. There were no lights in the sky, and she could see nothing but stars.

"Flatten against the rocks," she said.

The others did as the sound grew louder still. A moment later, a pair of blacked-out drones appeared, circling the burning wreck several times before separating, the muffled sounds of their engines heading in opposite directions.

The three looked at each other.

"So what do we do?" Watts asked.

"We go to Pershing," said Skip. "My sister is there."

"That's suicide," Watts said.

"They've got my *sister*."

"We need to get the hell out of here and call in the cavalry," Watts said.

"How?" Skip asked fiercely. "We're forty miles from the nearest town. It'd take days to reach even a traveled road. We've got no water, no food. And they know we're out here—or *will* know, soon enough. They're going to find us for sure."

"I'm with Skip," Corrie said. "Going to Pershing is the last thing they'd expect."

A silence settled. Finally, Watts nodded. "If we're going to do that, we'll need a plan—and we'll need to execute it while we've still got the cover of darkness."

"First, let's get away from this crash site," said Corrie. "Before *their* cavalry arrives."

"They're already on the way," said Watts as the throbbing sound of rotors—much deeper this time—began to emerge out of the sky.

57

In the sterile, rudely furnished cell, it seemed to Nora that she sat next to Tappan for an age: in silence, her mind in turmoil, trying to make sense of everything, figure out what to do. In the wide corridors beyond their windowless door, it had been almost as silent, except for the rare tramping of feet.

"Lucas," she said at last. Her own voice sounded strange after long silence.

Tappan, on the bunk beside her, didn't answer.

"Lucas," she said again. "I've been thinking."

Then, turning to look at him, she stopped. The entrepreneur seemed frozen: staring ahead but not seeing, a faraway look in his eyes.

She reared back, cocked one fist, then hit him on the arm.

"Whoa!" he cried as he sat up, massaging his arm. "What was that for?"

"You were lost in thought. I needed to get your attention."

He glowered at her, one half of his visage crusted with dried blood, looking as two-faced as Janus. "Well, you didn't need to give me a hematoma in the process."

"You can fire me later. Tell me: What have you been thinking about?"

He paused, still massaging his arm. "That this is my fault. I've been so blinded by our progress, and by my success throwing money at a problem until it goes away, that I didn't see the warning signs."

"What warning signs?"

"The early pushback that suddenly went away. The disappearance of Bitan." Tappan shook his head. "The conspiracy theorists were right all along. There *was* a cover-up, even worse than anyone imagined. I should have expected a reaction like this."

"Well, since we're in the belly of the beast, we'd better figure out what we're going to do."

"Just what do you have in mind?"

"The colonel made us an offer. We need to

consider it." She then leaned over for a brief, affirming hug, then whispered ever so quietly in his ear: *"They're listening and watching, of course."*

Tappan nodded. He said, "I'm pretty sure he's going to kill us, no matter what we do."

"Maybe not."

"Explain."

"This organization operates way under the radar," Nora said. She wondered if Tappan was going to understand and follow her lead in pretending to cooperate, to buy them some time.

"Yeah. They probably killed Bitan 'under the radar,' too."

"The point is, they don't go around announcing their presence. They don't act hastily. We've been digging for, what, two weeks now? They must have been monitoring us the whole time. They only acted when their backs were against the wall, and we were about to make a shattering discovery. They're cautious, methodical."

Tappan shook his head vigorously. Nora persisted. "They're not going to suddenly break profile and wipe us all out."

"And you know this how?" Tappan waved a hand vaguely toward the cell door. "You've seen their reach. You've seen their resources. Sure—and once we've told Rush what we know, he'll kill us."

"I don't think so. In some ways they're as much in the dark as we are—about us, I mean, and how wide the circle of knowledge has grown. Remember that practically the colonel's first question to you was: Who else knows about this? But he also said we could be valuable to his organization."

"If he thinks I'm going to jump through hoops for him, after what he's done, he can go fuck himself."

Nora paused. She still wasn't sure where Tappan was coming from. But a further whispered confab would be disastrous. Without doubt, they were being watched as well as listened to.

"We're not going to jump through hoops. But we have to *consider* his offer."

"Why?"

"Why?" Nora laughed. "Because it just might save the lives of others, that's why! Think of it from Rush's point of view. You own Icarus Space Systems and half the wind turbines in North America. You've got plenty of resources—in certain areas, I'll bet more than they've got. That gives you leverage. And it gives Rush a huge incentive to recruit you."

"I don't sense any shortage of resources around here."

"Hasn't it struck you how huge this place is— yet how empty it seems?"

"Yeah. All their double-O agents are out, shooting everybody who knows or might know anything."

Nora shook this away. "No. They're clearly not the kind to go off half-cocked. Rush spoke of an organization at war. But where's his army? I'm betting they had a much easier time getting recruits in 1947 than they do now. Think about it: countless soldiers recently de- mobilized from World War Two; the Cold War and its attendant paranoia ramping up; patriotism at an all-time high. Do you think it surprising almost all the sci-fi movies from that period featured evil, destructive aliens?" She paused. "Things are different today. Our fears have changed. But *they* haven't."

"So do you buy what they say?" Tappan asked. "About these aliens preparing to attack the planet?"

Nora wished she could be sure Tappan

understood she was playing for time—a charade she was putting on for their eavesdroppers. "He mentioned documentary evidence, and he seemed willing to show it to us. He's sincere. We need to see this evidence."

"Okay," Tappan replied after a silence. "What you say makes sense. We owe it to ourselves to see just why he's so convinced Earth is in danger. We owe it to science." Suddenly, he took Nora's face in both hands. "And, now that I think about it, cooperation sure beats the alternative." He kissed her. "You're one hell of a woman, you know that? Just please don't ever hit me like that again."

"I promise," she said.

Footsteps in the hall...and with a turning of a lock, the two quickly separated. The door opened onto the same two heavily armed guards that had brought them to the cell. Silently, they gestured for Nora and Tappan to stand and step out into the cell block. Then, one in front and the other bringing up the rear, as before, they led Nora and Tappan back in the direction from which they'd come. But this time, they walked past the heavy door and farther along the wide corridor, to a set of doors larger than all the others. The label *019* was stenciled on them in large white digits. This time, the soldiers did not open the doors themselves; one covered the two prisoners while the other entered a number on a keypad. The huge doors whispered back to reveal an echoing hangar. Prodded by the soldiers, Nora stepped forward, began to look around—and then caught her breath in numb disbelief.

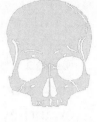

58

THE FENCE LOOMED out of the darkness, concertina wire at the top gleaming faintly against
the stars. They moved up to it silently, pausing to look around, Corrie scanning for signs
of security cameras. She could see none. The
fence itself looked decrepit and rusty, but on
closer inspection the dilapidation proved superficial. Battered NO TRESPASSING and DANGER: HIGH
VOLTAGE signs were attached to it at regular
intervals. Beyond, she could see the shadowy
outlines of ruined buildings.

"Check out those two heavy wires," Watts
murmured. "They're attached with insulators.
This baby's electrified."

Skip nodded. "I wouldn't be surprised if it was
alarmed, as well."

"How are we going to get in?" Corrie asked.

"Good question," Watts replied.

They stood for a while, just staring at the fence. Even if they could get over it without being electrocuted, which seemed impossible, Skip was right: it would surely set off an alarm. Once on the other side, they'd be hunted down quickly.

"Maybe we could short-circuit it," said Skip.

"That would set off the alarms even faster," said Watts.

While they were talking, Corrie heard the low hoot of an owl, and then a sudden crackling and flash of light appeared about twenty feet up the fence.

They ducked down and listened.

"What the hell was that?" Skip whispered. "Did an owl just get zapped?"

Watts gestured for them to move along the fence toward the flash. He knelt to inspect the ground, looking for a bird, but shook his head, unable to see what might have caused it.

"Let's walk a little farther," he whispered. "Just in case there's a weak spot in the fence."

They moved along in single file, scanning the perimeter, but nowhere did it look possible to breach. Watts stopped periodically to examine the ground.

"What are we going to do?" Skip finally asked.

Watts shook his head. "I'm stumped."

Another crackle split the night, with a flash of light a hundred yards farther up.

"You think it's a pack of animals?" Corrie asked.

"Maybe a short, if we're lucky," said Skip. "Let's go look."

They continued northward. Here, the fence ran through some steep outcroppings of rock, forcing them to walk in single file.

Watts crouched again. "I'll be damned." A stick lay on the ground, still smoking. "How did this happen?"

Skip bent over to look as well. Corrie, bringing up the rear, suddenly felt herself seized from behind. One arm wrapped around her throat while hard, cold steel was pressed against her temple, forcing her back behind the cover of an outcropping.

Watts jumped up and pulled his weapon—but didn't fire.

"You're right to think it through," came a voice. "Now drop it."

It was Lime. He must have taken the dead soldier's gun from the wreck of the chopper.

Watts didn't move.

"You have no shot, and you know it. Stretch out your hand and drop the weapon. *Now*. Or she dies."

Watts complied as Corrie felt Lime take back his weapon from her holster. Pushing her forward, he emerged from behind the rock. Lime kicked Watts's weapon away.

"We share a common problem," he said. "How to get through that fence. Right, Corrie?" He gave her a little shake.

"Fuck you."

"You were turning into a good agent. Unfortunately, in this particular situation, too good. I realized that when we watched you search Morwood's house and saw what even we had missed. I truly regret losing you. I can't say the same, however, about your friends." Lime gave a dry laugh. "Sheriff, they told me you were some sort of hotshot gunman. And you did outdraw me back there—that psychological trick of mine never failed me before. But it's a pretty sad commentary, how you let me get the drop on you. And given the way Mr. Kelly, here, crashed the chopper, I presume he suffers from suicidal mania."

He suddenly shoved Corrie to the ground.

Keeping the gun trained on them, he circled around to Skip.

"Move just once, and I'll indulge that death wish of yours." He took Skip's forearm and jerked it behind his back, forcing Skip to bend down. He shoved the gun in Skip's ear and said to Corrie, "You can get up. Keep your hands in sight."

Corrie rose cautiously, showing her hands.

Lime went on. "I've got a solution to our problem. A way for us to get in *and* alert the base in a hurry to your presence. Elwyn Kelly here is going to help. Right, *Elwyn?*" Lime propelled him toward the fence, keeping the gun pointed at his ear. "That fence carries six thousand volts at eleven amps—more than an electric chair. I saw a deer run into it once. That was some show."

He pushed Skip closer. Corrie could hear the wires humming and smell the electricity in the air—and she realized with sudden horror just what Lime planned to do. She braced herself as Lime spun Skip forward toward the fence, using himself as a pivot. But Skip twisted around just as Lime shoved him, and at that moment Corrie lunged forward, slamming into

Lime like a linebacker. The blow propelled the already off-balance Lime past Skip, turning his own momentum against him as Skip wrenched free of his grasp. The gun went off as it flew from his hands, while Lime windmilled, twisting backward and grunting in an effort to recover his balance. He succeeded only in striking the fence full-on with the back of his body, from head to thigh.

There was a great *flash-boom* of sound and light. Lime screamed briefly, once, as coruscating sparks rose like the embers of a disturbed campfire into the night sky. His skin began to fry with the sound of raw meat being seared in hot grease, first clothes, then hair bursting into flame. The wires popped and vaporized around him, whipping in sync with his writhing form. His eyes filled with crimson, swelled grotesquely, then popped, one after the other.

And then all was quiet, save for the crackle of smoldering weeds from a little ground fire triggered by the shower of sparks. The dead wires dangled, spitting ineffectually. Lime's smoking remains were stuck against the fence, now sagging inward, the concertina wire partially melted and falling away to one side.

For a moment, no one moved. Corrie stared in horrified fascination.

"Hey!" Skip said, breaking the spell. "The circuit's broken—we can get in. *Quick!*"

He scampered up and over the dead body, which, effectively glued to the sagging fence, bounced up and down like a spring under the impact of his feet. Skip eased aside the melted concertina wire, then ducked under and past. "Hurry up! They'll be here any minute!"

Corrie snatched up her gun from where it had fallen and then rushed across the improvised bridge—which had begun to smell like an over-done porterhouse—and under the fence. Watts followed suit.

"Into the ruins!" said Skip.

They sprinted into some sort of dormitory, with skeletons of cots arrayed in ghostly rows. They took cover in a small annex in the back, with a broken window facing northward.

"Jesus," said Watts, "did you two rehearse that martial arts move, or what?"

"Dumb luck," said Corrie. She turned to Skip. "Why did he call you Elwyn?"

"Forget it."

They waited, recovering their breath. Seconds

afterward, Corrie heard a low vibration. Peering through the window, they saw a rectangular shape rise from the side of—in fact, apparently *out* of—a nondescript hill.

"You see that?" Skip whispered. "It's a door. Embedded in the side of the hill."

Lights appeared in the portal, and then a jeep, then a second, emerged at high speed, headlights lancing through the darkness. They raced over the desert, heading toward the fence, where Lime's body was hung up amid the weedy ground fire.

The jeeps screeched to a halt while Corrie and the rest kept in the shadows of the ruined building. "Oh, Jesus," said a man in uniform as he leapt out, voice clear in the cool night air. The others all piled out, weapons in hand.

"The fucker tried to climb over," another voice said.

"What the hell was he doing out here?"

"Maybe from that crashed chopper?"

They clustered around the scorched corpse.

"See if he's got ID."

Corrie watched as they busied themselves with the body, prying it off the fence and shining the light in the face.

"Good God!" the commander cried. "It's Lime!"

"What the hell was he doing, trying to climb that fence?"

"Idiot."

"Stick a fork in him, he's done."

There was a burst of talk and radio chatter as they discussed what to do. Within minutes, they loaded the body into the back of one jeep, restrung the live wires, fixed the fence, and drove back to the portal in the hill, which then closed slowly and silently behind them.

All went quiet.

"It looks like we're in the clear," said Corrie. "What now?"

It was Skip who answered. "We go get my sister."

59

THE FACT THAT neither she nor Watts moved in response to Skip's statement drove home to Corrie that they had no plan. They were three people, up against some kind of military base.

"We can't defeat them all—can we agree on that?" Watts said.

"I'm not leaving without Nora," said Skip defiantly.

"Look," said Corrie, "for God's sake, think through the choices we're facing here. We can't stay where we are, we can't walk out to get help, and we've got neither truck nor radio equipment. Ergo, Skip's right. We go in."

"And do what?" Watts asked.

"Evaluate our options. We don't know what's

down there: how many people, how well guarded. But down there is where we've got to go. *Then* we figure out a plan."

"In other words, out of the frying pan and into the fire," said Watts. "Maybe that guy Lime was right about you, Skip. It's suicide."

"It's the only option," Corrie said firmly. "We're just wasting time talking about it. Let's check our ammo." She took out Lime's Glock 19 and ejected the magazine. "Fifteen." She racked the slide.

"I've got four," said Watts.

"It's obvious that whatever's here is underground," Skip said. "There have to be air vents or openings somewhere."

They cautiously moved out of the barracks into the landscape. Corrie hand-signaled for them to spread out. There was no moon, but the desert air was so clear that starlight gave them just enough illumination to see. Beyond the barracks were more ruins and a parade ground of concrete riddled with cracks, resembling a field of rubble. They kept to the darkest areas. It felt so desolate it was hard to believe there was anyone within miles, let alone a secret base under their feet.

"Over here," Skip suddenly said in a low voice.

Corrie and Watts came over to find Skip standing next to an old corrugated shaft sunk into the ground, covered with a corroded grille of wire mesh.

"Smell that air coming up."

Corrie leaned over. A clean, cool draft rose, redolent of warm electronics and, oddly, french fries.

"Here's our way in," Skip said.

"Are you kidding?" Watts said, staring into the black maw. "You have no idea where it goes. We don't even have a light. We might get stuck."

"I can shinny down," said Skip. "See where it goes."

"That requires chimney-climbing experience." Corrie paused. "You don't know the technique. I do."

"Oh, no," said Watts. "No one's going down there. We'll find another way in."

"We don't have time," said Corrie. "I'm going."

"No," Skip said. "*I* will. It's my sister."

"For fuck's sake, the person with climbing experience should go first." Without waiting for any more argument, Corrie yanked off the loose grille, then swung herself over the opening. She glanced around. Against the starlight, Watts's ruined Resistol looked utterly ridiculous: his silhouette was a cross between the Little Tramp and Chico Marx.

"Lose the hat," she said. "If we get killed down there, you'll want to leave a good-looking corpse."

"This hat isn't going anywhere until I can get another."

"Suit yourself." Then she lowered herself down, using the corrugated side of the shaft for footholds, back braced against the opposite side. Below her it was black as night, and there was absolutely no indication of how far the tube descended.

She inched her way down by a classic counterforce technique and was soon swallowed in darkness. Looking up, she could see a single star, which gave her comfort. But even that vanished as she went deeper, and despite herself, she felt a primitive terror begin to well up from within. It was so black that swirls and shapes began to cross her field of vision. Was Watts right, and the shaft was getting narrower? It felt like it...but, she told herself, that had to be her rising panic.

She stopped. How deep was she? It seemed like

she'd been lowering herself forever. Her muscles were trembling with the effort, her heart pounding. She wanted to call up, to hear a reassuring voice, but she didn't dare chance alerting whoever was below. If anybody *was* below. God, what if the shaft dead-ended and she didn't have the strength to ascend? What if it ended in a furnace? She tried to shut down her panic and focus on one movement at a time.

As she worked her way deeper, she became aware of a faint glow from below. Her sudden relief was quickly replaced by the uncertainty of what she might find—and who might be there.

She felt the tunnel branch into a horizontal T, and then her feet touched the bottom of the shaft. With vast relief she gingerly stood up to full height and recovered her breath. The dim light was coming in from the tunnel to her left.

She knelt and crawled along it. After a short distance, it ended in a flimsy louvered vent, set into a ceiling and overlooking a large, unlit room packed with blinking servers, the only sound the hum of air-conditioning. At the far door of the room was a man with a rifle, evidently standing guard. Eating french fries. Paying no attention to anything.

Corrie backed up, then climbed a few feet up the shaft. "Hey," she said in a low tone. "*Hey.*"

Watts's distant voice floated down softly. "Hey yourself."

"It's a way in. Come down. Brace yourself on opposite sides, feet on one, back and hands against the other. Keep up the tension or you'll fall. And for God's sake, be quiet."

"Copy. We're coming down."

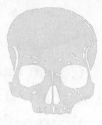

60

THE HANGAR WAS large—even by the standards of the sprawling underground complex. Along the reinforced walls, Nora saw a fantastic array of equipment: video cameras, computers, monitoring and recording devices, sensors, an array of large-diaphragm Neumann microphones. The ceiling was busy with cabling, studio spotlights, and dozens of small stainless steel devices that looked like industrial sprinklers.

But it was what lay directly before her, in the center of the huge space, that instantly caught and utterly dominated her attention.

A craft of some kind rested in a cradle made of a dull black material. The moment she set eyes on it she knew that the thing was not of this earth. Her lingering skepticism was instantly consumed in the face of this transfixing, irrefutable proof. The thing's surface shimmered like liquid mercury, seemingly in motion beneath the lights, as if so many coats of lacquer had been applied that it appeared more like the surface of a limpid pool than a hull. She could not say exactly what color it was—it seemed somehow like all colors to her, or perhaps even a color that was entirely new. It was not especially large: roughly the size of the *Apollo* lunar module. But it couldn't have looked more different from that ungainly craft. This had a sleek, flowing, organic shape, like a wingless bird hovering on a thermal. There were no sharp edges, no marks or insignia, no windows or portholes or projecting equipment except toward the nose, where an oval rent of some kind was visible, around which the metallic flow turned into something closer to a small whirlpool—she was reminded of Jupiter's Great Red Spot—roiling uneasily in a sickly green color. Placed around, at some remove, were several tall, monolithic barriers or blast walls of what again appeared to be graphite, arranged in an offset pattern like the sound baffles in a music studio. The spacecraft was surrounded by rings painted on the floor: the outermost yellow, the next one orange, and then the final, inner one red. Various warnings and numbers were stenciled between the nested circles.

Spacecraft. The word had come to her mind instinctively, unconsciously. But in just the last sixty seconds, all lingering uncertainty had drained from her. It was impossible for human science to build, even simulate, a hull like that. Despite the gravity of their situation—the armed soldiers, the hostile underground base—she felt an unexpected relief as she realized she could stop fighting now. She could let all her cynicism, doubt, and scientific skepticism simply melt away like an unwanted weight...to be replaced by wonder.

Without thinking, overcome with awe, she took a step toward it.

"I wouldn't do that," Rush said.

Nora stopped.

"It looks quiescent, I know. But the appearance is deceptive. During our initial reconnaissance in 1947, that thing killed two dozen soldiers. In the subsequent salvage operation, it took the lives of almost half again as many."

Nora listened, unable to take her eyes from the otherworldly ship.

"We only managed to get it back here to Pershing—as it turned out, the closest available site—by encasing it in graphite shields. As far as we've been able to determine, the neutron-reflecting properties of graphite offered protection. Partial protection, that is, and only temporary; it appears to have adapted its weaponry to compensate. As a result, we couldn't risk trying to move it elsewhere. However, Pershing ended up suiting our needs exactly: an abandoned base with tunnels that could easily be expanded, full of hazardous waste and unexploded ordnance, strictly off-limits."

But Nora was still staring. And then, she began to wonder if her eyes were playing tricks on her. When she'd first entered the hangar, she'd been sure the craft had a long, graceful neck, like a goose or swan in flight. But she blinked: what she thought had been a neck now looked more like a truncated collar. And yet no lighting or other optical effect of the room had been altered.

"Did it just change shape?" she asked.

Rush sighed, perhaps in exasperation. "We can

discuss such details later. It would be easiest if you just watched this. Follow me, please."

He led the way across the echoing hangar toward a small viewing area set near an equipment-festooned wall behind a plexiglass enclosure. As they walked, Nora saw the small black chest containing their recent discovery placed on a graphite table, with barriers being put up around it.

Rush motioned for them to sit down before the viewing area's large monitor, then took a seat beside them and reached for a remote control. "I'm going to show you a very brief overview of the last seventy-five years," he said. "It won't take long, but it's important to demonstrate the nature of the...device."

Now the monitor came to life, showing what appeared to be an old black-and-white filmstrip, full of scratches, warping, and jitter. Several anachronistic warning messages from the U.S. Army, the Department of Defense, and other entities appeared, asserting how sensitive the video was and offering a variety of maledictions against anyone who tried to duplicate it or otherwise make its contents known. Then the word ALPHA was displayed on a title card, and the scene shifted to a desert setting: a remote location with a high, cloudless sky of gray against a gray sun. Almost immediately, Nora recognized it as their forward dig site. The surrounding topography had changed, but it was nevertheless unmistakable. She could see a cordon of soldiers forming a secure perimeter, weapons at the ready. Various 1940s-era military jeeps, troop trucks, and ambulances were parked nearby. At the center was the same craft that now sat in this vault. It appeared to be half dug out of the earth—or perhaps that was where it had come to land—and the dirt and sand around it were dotted with large, dark stains.

"This was taken the day after we located the device," Rush said.

Now onscreen, two soldiers approached cautiously. The one in front held what looked like a minesweeper; the one slightly behind him had a carbine at the ready. They stepped closer, then still closer. Except for the carbine, their movements were not obviously threatening.

Suddenly, there was a bright light; so bright that the film lost all contrast, its emulsion fully exposed. Over several seconds, the light receded. Once the landscape came into view again, the soldiers were gone and there were two additional dark stains in the sand beside the craft.

"That is how we were greeted," Rush said. "Again and again."

"It probably thought they were armed," Tappan said. "And it wasn't wrong."

Rush laughed mirthlessly. "It was approached, has been approached, in every way you could imagine. The best minds have been tasked with solving how to communicate with it, to demonstrate our friendly intentions. We've been met only with sudden violence and death." He nodded toward the craft. "Like I said, it looks quiescent. But finding an environment to keep it that way has been the work of decades, at the price of countless millions of dollars and many, many lives."

Now the filmstrip changed. It was still black-and-white, but the orientation was different, and the position was farther away. Nora watched as two tanks approached the craft, which had now been removed from the earth and lay on its side—not unlike its current position here in the vault. Both tanks stopped some distance away, then fired a number of shells from their turrets directly at the craft, without discernible effect.

"Friendly intentions, huh?" Tappan said.

"This was 1947," Rush replied, as if that explained everything.

After a moment, one of the tanks drew closer. Again, there was a flash that blew out the film's exposure.

"Anyway," Rush added as the flash died away, "humans don't seem to have the technology to damage it. Or even look inside it. It has repulsed every effort. We've never been able to extract or derive any meaningful technology from it."

The film moved forward in time. The aspect ratio changed, and color was introduced. It had the faintly blurred look of videotape. The craft was in the hangar where they now sat, except the space was far barer, with less equipment and fewer monitoring devices. Scientists in white coats and support staff in street clothes—from which she guessed the era to be the 1970s—worked busily around the craft at a safe distance. As she watched, a rack with a DEC minicomputer cabled to measuring equipment was slowly lowered toward the object via overhead wires. The video now sported audio, and she could hear, in various languages, messages being piped toward the craft, telling it that no harm would come to it and that communication was the only goal. The minicomputer rack kept inching down, like a huge spider descending on its spinnerets. Moments later, the flashes began again. This time, filters had apparently been placed on the camera lens, and it was possible to differentiate three separate bursts of light—but beyond that, nothing more.

"We tried every possible means of signaling to it," Rush said. "Every means of studying it, reverse engineering it, even merely examining its technology. But every attempt, no matter how novel or advanced, ended in failure. Approaching too close inevitably triggers its weaponry."

"It's probably just a self-defense mechanism," Tappan said.

Rush glanced at him. "Indeed? If this device is so advanced, don't you think it would have learned by now, adapted, the same way its weapons have adapted to graphite? No. It's implacably hostile. It kills or destroys anything that gets close. We believe that if it weren't damaged—you saw that odd detent in its side—it would be far more lethal. The entire planet might be at risk."

Once again, the film jumped forward in time.

Now the hangar looked much closer to its current configuration. Nora watched for perhaps five minutes as a series of mobile robots approached the craft using a variety of tactics, followed by several small drones. Each met the usual end.

"We tried everything, even inert compounds," Rush said. "We understand from remote measurements how the weapon works, more or less—but we've made no progress at all on how to stop it."

"Those flashes," Tappan says. "Why can't you film them in slow motion and see what's going on?"

"We have. It appears the weapon analyzes the atomic makeup of what it perceives to be a hostile object, then inverts its atomic structure."

"Inverts? How?"

Again, Rush sighed in frustration. "Performs a logical OR on its natural state—that is, a logical disjunction applied to matter. The technology is far beyond our understanding." The monitor went blank as the film ended, and he turned to Nora and Tappan. "These questions you're asking—they're pitifully ignorant. We'd moved beyond them before you were even born. Maybe soon, you'll have the time to examine the thousands of pages of research papers, test results, theories, lab notes, and terabytes of data we've accumulated. Now, under the circumstances, I've been remarkably patient—especially given all the trouble you've caused us. The point you must understand is a simple one. All our painstaking lines of analysis have led to one conclusion: that craft is a weapon, from an alien civilization intent on destruction or conquest. At the very least, it's a recon vessel searching for targets. It's so dangerous that this base has an integrated self-destruct system so the probe, should it suddenly become mobile again, can't unleash itself upon humanity." Again he glanced from one to the other. "Look at you. You're so fascinated by the device, you've been blinded to the bigger picture. Who knows when the next one might come along, undamaged and perhaps even more advanced? That's why Atropos has made it our lifetime duty to thwart attempts to contact aliens or attract their attention. We can't do anything about the damned electromagnetic radiation streaming from Earth, at least not now, but there are other steps we have taken."

The colonel rose from his chair. "You've seen the evidence. I've shown you the history. I've kept nothing back. We can use people like you: your expertise, Dr. Kelly; and your money and reach, Mr. Tappan. We *need* you. We know of your relationship, of course—and there's no reason that can't continue. Now: Will you take up the cause?"

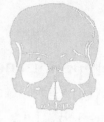

61

By virtue of her position, Corrie had to be the first out of the vent. There was no way to pass one another in the narrow space. That meant she had to be the one to take out the guard.

Watts held out a knife. "Cut his throat," he whispered. "Otherwise, he'll make noise."

Corrie felt sick. She'd never killed anyone—certainly not in a way as cold-blooded as this.

Watts sensed her hesitation. "It takes a lot more force than you might think. If you don't cut all the way through the cartilage on the first swipe, he could still manage to scream."

The guard in the doorway had finished his fries and was now just standing, slouched, marking time. He was surprisingly old, close to fifty, a sad sack of a soldier.

"I can't do this," Corrie whispered.

"We've got no choice. For all we know, they blew up everyone back at the camp."

Corrie swallowed. "I still can't."

After a moment, Watts sighed quietly. "I respect that."

Then she heard him tap loudly on the side of the pipe.

She waited, holding her breath. The soldier turned and glanced into the room, looking first one way and then the other. He took a step inside, hit a switch to turn on the lights. He peered around, then made a perfunctory tour; seeing nothing amiss, he returned to the door and turned off the lights.

Right behind her, Watts tapped again on the duct, twice, even more loudly. She could feel his breath on her neck.

The guard's head jerked upward. Now he was on high alert. He turned the lights back on and came slowly over to their area, looking around. He didn't look up. He walked past and stopped. And then he looked up.

Corrie didn't dare move. Her view was between narrow louvers. From below, the guard's eyes were fixated on the vent. He moved closer, squinting, and removed his rifle. The expression on his face was more suspicious than certain. He took another step, staring upward, scanning the ceiling beyond the vent.

She felt Watts touch her shoulder. "Plug your ears."

She did.

"Up here!" said Watts loudly. The soldier's face registered surprise and fear as he swung around, his eyes fixing again on the vent. He raised his weapon.

Watts fired through the louver. The soldier's head snapped back in a spray of blood and matter, the weapon clattering to the floor.

"*Go*," said Watts.

Corrie kicked open the vent and dropped down, followed immediately by Watts and Skip. The soldier lay sprawled grotesquely in a spreading pool of blood.

"We'll fight them from the cover of these computers," said Watts. "Nice knowing you."

They ran into the rows of servers and waited for the response. Seconds ticked by, then minutes.

"I'll be damned," said Watts. "I don't think anyone's coming."

They let another minute pass.

"I'll bet they're all busy with shit elsewhere," said Skip. "Looking for us outside, maybe."

They cautiously approached the door where the dead soldier lay. Skip hesitated a second, then reached down and took his sidearm, wiping it on the man's uniform. The gun was, she noted, identical to hers and Lime's: standard issue for military and law enforcement.

Beyond the door, a broad cinder-block hall, painted yellow and green, ran for a hundred feet. There were no signs of security cameras or guards and no doors.

Watts stepped out and led the way, walking silently, communicating with hand signals, while Corrie covered the rear. At the first corner Watts halted and peered around, then waved them forward.

The next corridor was lined with lettered doors. The corridors branched, then branched again: more lettered doors, more unknown rooms, but no people. The place was obviously huge—and although everything looked clean and well-kept, it was oddly deserted.

Watts stopped and touched his ear.

Listening, Corrie could hear sounds at the very edge of audibility. There were people ahead.

"Incredible there's no CCTV system in here," Skip whispered.

"They probably think it's so secure they don't need it," Watts replied.

The corridor ended at a T junction, and before them stood a set of steel doors, slightly ajar, with porthole windows. Cautiously, Corrie peered through the seam between the doors. It revealed a large room that had the look of a lobby in a hospital ward: brightly lit and sterile, with rooms on both sides, one apparently a kitchen. Now Corrie saw the first people since the guard: a woman in uniform beside a man carrying a tray of food. They crossed the lobby and approached a room. As the door opened and shut, Corrie briefly heard a woman's voice, loud and angry.

"God, that's Cecilia," said Skip. He glanced at Corrie. "Cecilia Toth, the engineer."

"She sounds hurt," said Corrie.

The two figures came back out, closed the door, and then disappeared around a bend in the hall. All went quiet.

"She'll have information," said Skip. "Information we need."

They passed through the doors, moving quietly, then opened the door to the room and ducked in. Cecilia was shackled to the bedframe, her leg bandaged. Watts motioned for silence as she rose, struggling against the shackles.

"Where's Nora?" Skip asked her in an urgent voice. "What is this place?"

"They took Nora away," Toth said. "Along with Tappan. Shortly after we left the motor pool."

"Where?"

"I don't know. Right, past those double doors you just came in."

"What happened to you?" Corrie asked.

"The bastards killed Emilio. I got hit with a stray round."

"We're going to get you out," said Corrie. "Can you walk?"

"I don't think so. They haven't given me any painkillers. Moving hurts like hell."

"Where's this motor pool?"

"Left, down the corridor beyond the doors. There's a helicopter bay next to it. Just keep going straight."

"Where is everyone?"

"I don't know."

"We're going to come back for you," Corrie said again. "Just stay cool."

As they moved back to the lobby and then

turned left beyond the doors, Corrie quickly sensed they were entering a more populated section of the facility. At several moments they had to duck into storerooms or abandoned labs to avoid soldiers. Another time, an electric vehicle—an armored, open-topped jeep—could be seen passing down the hallway.

"Let's commandeer one of those," said Skip. "Shoot the fuckers right out of the saddle and take it."

"You may not have noticed," said Corrie, "but they've got bulletproof glass and panels. You're not going to shoot out anyone driving one of those."

"Then we steal one from this motor pool."

They followed faint rubber tire tracks now visible on the cement floor, confident these would lead to the motor pool. As they crept farther down the endless hallway, Corrie heard voices and activity. Ahead, they could see the corridor open into a large space, a ramp leading up one side to a tall set of steel doors. As Corrie watched, they opened, folding fanlike back on themselves with a quiet rumble.

They ducked through the last door of the corridor, into what appeared to be a mothballed medical lab, but not before Corrie got a better glimpse of the cavernous room that lay ahead. There were a variety of parked vehicles, patrolled by guards who looked a lot more alert than the sad sack in the server room. There was also, as Toth had mentioned, a helicopter, sitting silent and dark on a steel pad. The ramp on the far side, she guessed, must lead up to the portal they'd seen hidden in the side of a small hill. Clearly it was a way out.

"I see only two guards," said Watts. "We can take those bastards."

"There could be more on the far side," Corrie said. "That's a big space."

"Shit," Watts muttered.

Skip hesitated. "You're a much better shot than me," he told Watts. "Maybe we should exchange weapons. This one's got a full sixteen rounds."

Watts frowned. "This Peacemaker was my granddad's." He took the revolver out and hefted it. "It kicks like a mule and it's hard to aim."

"Look, I can't shoot worth shit anyway. If it makes a big noise, that's all that matters. You've got five times the number of rounds in that Glock—and you're probably going to need them all."

Watts handed Skip the Peacemaker and accepted the Glock, which he tucked in his belt. "I wish to hell we could somehow shift the odds in our favor."

Corrie looked around. The medical lab they were in had obviously not been used in some time. Shelves of bottles and containers lined the walls. An old black soapstone table ran down the far wall, flanked by fume hoods. It was like the rest of the base: clean and orderly but fallen into disuse.

In the dim light, she crept over and began examining the bottles, squinting at the labels.

"What are you looking for?" Watts asked.

"This." She plucked a large bottle off a shelf. "What you find in every lab in the country. Ethanol."

Skip suddenly grinned. "That's what I'm talking about. Who's got a lighter?"

Watts removed one from his pocket and tossed it to Skip.

They quickly collected a half dozen smaller bottles with narrow mouths, emptied their contents, and refilled them with ethanol, stuffing wadded gauze into the necks. As they worked quickly and silently, the keen smell of pure grain alcohol filled the room.

"Skip, you'll be the Molotov cocktail guy," said Corrie. "Create maximum surprise and confusion. Hit the chopper if possible so it can't follow us once we escape. Shoot off that big old hogleg now and then to put the fear of God into everyone. The sheriff and I will go in blazing on either flank."

"Go in blazing," repeated Watts. "Still suicide. Only maybe not quite as certain."

62

Rush stepped out of the viewing alcove. "Come with me."

Nora and Tappan rose to follow.

He halted some distance from the craft, turned, and folded one arm over the other, clearly waiting for an answer.

There was a brief, awkward silence.

"Colonel," Tappan said, "you're a convincing recruiter. No doubt you've performed that little dog-and-pony show before. I could probably use you in the HR department of Icarus Space Systems. But how do I—" and at this, he stepped closer to Nora— "how do *we* know you aren't just milking us for information, to be shot and discarded when you've wrung us dry?"

Nora was glad Tappan had moved close to her.

The fact that Atropos knew of their relationship—not surprising, in retrospect—meant that to ensure the cooperation of one, Atropos would have to spare both. Even so, she wondered if Tappan was laying it on a little thick. It crossed her mind that she still didn't know what he was really thinking—if he was being sincere, or if he was going along with her scheme. Truth was, she didn't know him all that well, despite their connection.

"Colonel Rush," Nora said, "you tell us you've kept nothing back. Well, I'll be equally blunt. Did you blow up the camp?"

"No, we did not. We merely destroyed all your data and equipment. The people are fine."

"You've obviously killed other innocents, like Emilio Vigil."

"That was the unfortunate product of a soldier's overzealousness. However, you are right: we have killed. For a cause."

Rush waited.

"If the fate of Earth is at stake, maybe that could be justified. But the films you've shown us, the history you've cited…" She stopped and pointed toward the craft. "It all seems contradicted by *that*. It's done nothing in our presence. And the device we just excavated—it didn't zap anybody. How do we know those films weren't doctored? I'm not sure I buy your conclusion it's out to destroy us. Maybe it was intended to be benevolent."

"Benevolent!" Rush repeated, in a mixture of surprise and derision. With a gesture, he brought one of the guards over, then spoke to him briefly in a low voice. The man saluted, walked back toward the hangar entrance, then plucked a microphone off its wall cradle. After about ten seconds, he put it back.

Rush, meanwhile, strode back and forth, with the air of a man for whom both patience and time had run out. As Nora glanced from the colonel to Tappan and back, the hangar door opened and a soldier entered, holding a cage of some kind. She handed it to Rush, saluted, then turned and walked out. The guards remained in their positions by the hangar door, which stood open.

Rush turned toward his prisoners. "Come with me." Then he made a direct line toward the alien craft.

Nora and Tappan followed. The colonel walked so quickly that, despite herself, Nora soon felt herself slowing behind him.

Rush walked past the outermost, yellow ring of the concentric circles, then paused immediately before the orange ring and looked over his shoulder. He snorted when he saw that both Nora and Tappan were hanging back.

"What are you worried about?" he asked in an acid tone. "We've learned the hard way how close we can get." He put the cage on the floor, opened it, withdrew something, and straightened up again. Nora saw he was holding a lab rat. It had hooded markings, with a black head and white body. Like most such animals, it seemed naturally tame, unfazed by the strange surroundings. It looked around, beady black eyes glancing this way and that, whiskers bobbing as its little pink nose sniffed the air, disgusting bristly tail wrapped around the colonel's wrist for balance.

"Hurry!" he said sternly to Nora and Tappan. "Come up here." When they reluctantly joined him, he indicated the circles painted on the floor. "Over years of painful trial and error we've learned that, as long as we make no threatening moves, we're safe on this side of the orange line." He paused. "Or would you care to go farther, Dr. Kelly? Maybe touch it? Why not:

you, after all, were the one who used the term 'benevolent.'" He looked at her, one eyebrow raised quizzically. "No? Very well. I want you to remember: it was your own suspicious nature that made this necessary."

With his free hand, he stroked the big rat for a moment. "In my experience, these poor fellows live rather short lives—two years, maybe three. They always seem to develop tumors. I wonder sometimes if so many generations have been bred for experiments that cancer has become part of their genetic structure."

He continued stroking the rat for a moment, almost thoughtfully. He scratched behind its ears, thin almost as tissue paper, the tiny veins visible, like a young leaf's. Then he raised his arm and gently pitched the rat underhanded toward the craft.

Nora, taken by surprise, watched the equally surprised rodent arc through the air, front and back feet outstretched, tail whipping in a circular motion. It began to sail down toward the alien craft. And then the rat's fur suddenly glowed, flickering with unnatural colors. As the brightness became blinding, the animal's skin grew transparent and she could see the muscles and organs and skeletal structure. A sound like the shriek of violins cut the air. Instinctively, Nora turned away, shielding herself from the alien glare. And then, abruptly, both the light and the noise stopped, followed only by the faint sound of liquid hitting concrete.

She turned back. Everything was as it had been before—except now, there was a small splatter of indeterminate color on the floor just inside the dark red ring. Beside her, Tappan stared, thunderstruck. Rush took them both in, shaking his head almost sadly.

"You pressed me for an explanation of how the craft can invert molecular structure," he said. "That, of course, was before you mused about its benevolence. I've given you your example. The weapon scans an approaching form, determines its composition, then disassembles the atoms that compose its structure. In this case, it simply denatured the animal proteins of the lab rat— alas, now deceased. The creature essentially fell apart on the molecular level—as so many of our soldiers did, decades ago, leaving behind a soup of carbon, hydrogen, oxygen, water, amino acids, and salts."

Rush nodded at the guards, who stepped

forward, submachine guns held across their chests in readiness. "You've both been given a full explanation of the alien's malignancy. *And* a demonstration." He stepped back outside the ring of concentric circles. "I need your answer, and I need it now."

Tappan had an expression on his face Nora hadn't seen before, like someone who'd just been punched in the gut. After a long moment, he took a shuddering breath. He glanced at Nora, then back at Rush.

"All right," he said, voice low, chastened. "You've convinced me. I'm on board."

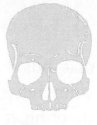

63

THEY MOVED BACK into the corridor, slipping around the corner that led to the motor pool, keeping out of sight. In front was a neat row of open-topped jeeps, along with the two guards she'd already noticed. Beyond the helicopter, resting on its elevator platform, she could make out two other guards, rifles slung over their shoulders. She could also see a couple of mechanics working behind one jeep, and a person in an officer's uniform speaking to one of the guards. They might not be on full alert, but they would wake up fast.

Corrie felt the sweat beading on her brow. Maybe Watts was right: this was suicide. Even though they had the advantage of surprise, they were up against trained professionals. Not only that, but they were outnumbered, with limited ammunition, and the moment they started shooting, it would be like ringing the dinner bell for the whole—

Her thoughts were interrupted by Watts, who had slipped up beside her and braced himself in a shooting stance. The time for thinking was over. She followed suit, then they raised their weapons simultaneously.

"On three," Watts whispered. "One, two, *three!*"

They both stood up and opened fire. Watts got off four shots in rapid succession, immediately dropping three guards. Corrie concentrated her fire on the officer, scoring a hit and sending him sprawling.

With a bloodcurdling yell, they charged in, Corrie and Watts flanking Skip. Corrie continued firing in the steady, measured way she'd been taught in countless live fire exercises at Quantico. Everyone in the motor pool who wasn't shot had immediately taken cover. In the brief moment before the soldiers returned fire, Corrie and Watts sprinted toward the closest vehicle while Skip tossed Molotov cocktails at the helicopter. There was the sound of shattering glass, followed by a *whoosh*: blue flames spread like spilled flambé across the floor around the chopper, flames licking up its sides, causing instant panic.

They reached the jeep and Corrie, being closest, leapt into the driver's seat, relieved beyond measure to see a key in the ignition. She turned it as Watts landed in the passenger seat. A burst of gunfire raked the vehicle, smacking the glass and hammering the armored sides, and they ducked, keeping their heads below the level of the glass. More soldiers were appearing from beyond the chopper, temporarily held back by the flames.

Head still down, Corrie threw the vehicle into reverse and pressed the accelerator. It shot backward with a squeal of tires. She angled toward Skip, who was lobbing his last Molotov, and jammed on the brakes, the gunfire deafening in the enclosed space, hammering the sides of the jeep. Skip vaulted into the back and Corrie floored it, tires screaming, the rear of the jeep fishtailing as more gunfire pounded the armored sides. She accelerated out of the motor pool toward the long hallway, back in the direction they'd come.

"Whoa, *shit!*" Watts yelled as they veered into

the corridor, Corrie braking hard, sliding into the wall with a heavy smack, the vehicle bouncing and swerving. Trying not to think of all the soldiers she'd seen boiling into the motor pool, Corrie concentrated on her time at the high-performance driving track at Quantico, turning into the skid and recovering.

Ahead of them, far down the corridor, soldiers were hastily assembling, blocking the way and aiming their weapons.

She had no choice but to go straight at them. Gunning the engine, Corrie shot down the hall as rounds struck the front windshield, turning it into a web of cracks, not penetrating but making it impossible to see through. Corrie was forced to raise her head, exposing herself. The gunfire was deafening in the enclosed hallway, and she could feel the snap of rounds passing her head— once heard, never forgotten. Some soldiers were firing low, but so far, the jeep's bulletproof tires were taking the punishment.

"*Aaaahhhh!*" Corrie screamed as the vehicle closed in, the shooters leaping to either side as it tore through, hitting one and flinging him up against the wall. She kept her foot pressed on the accelerator. A moment later, fire began pouring upon them from the rear, once again stopped by the glass.

"Toth is just ahead!" Skip shouted.

Corrie raced onward, glancing off one wall and almost losing control, then slowing, sliding over the slick concrete floor, bouncing once again off the wall before fishtailing back on track.

"*Here!*" Skip yelled.

They rammed through the double doors into the medical lobby, screeching to a halt at Toth's door. The corridor here was narrow, and Corrie could barely keep the jeep from sliding into an unrecoverable wedge between two walls. Watts jumped out and rushed into the room, cut the bedrail handcuffs with a few well-placed shots, and appeared a moment later carrying the engineer. He dumped her unceremoniously in the shotgun seat while she yelled in pain, then vaulted into the back himself.

"Now we get my sister!" Skip yelled. "Where were they taken?"

"Through the doors, then right," Toth gasped.

Corrie bashed back out the set of doors and roared down the wide corridor, following Toth's directions. But, as she sheered the vehicle around a dogleg, they came face-to-face with a near phalanx of soldiers. The squad lowered their weapons, and then—with the bark of an order—unleashed a withering barrage, so intense it finally penetrated the windscreen, shredding it and sending bits of glass like gravel everywhere.

This had to be the end.

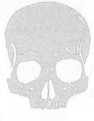

64

And you, Nora?" Rush asked, turning his gaze to her.

Nora returned it. She wondered if Tappan was sincere or just playing for time. She needed to know. "I'm not on board."

"That is truly unfortunate. Your partner seems to have grasped the situation; I'm surprised you haven't done the same." He turned to one of the soldiers. "Take her back to the cell."

"Wait," said Tappan. "Nora, look at that thing—think about what it just did."

"What about what *we* did?" She gestured toward the graphite box. "We found that thing. It didn't kill *us*."

"This is a waste of time," said Rush. "Either you're with us, Dr. Kelly, or you're not. And the longer you dither, the less inclined I am to trust you."

"She just needs more time," Tappan told him. "You're asking us to absorb all this too fast. If I'm going to join you, put my billions to work on this project—I can't make such a huge leap alone. I'm going to need her with me." He turned to her. "Nora, you've *got* to think this through."

"I want to see what's in the box," she replied, doing her best not to glance toward the soldiers' position. "What we found but never got a chance to see."

"What's in the box is irrelevant to your decision," said Rush.

"What's its purpose?"

"How can we possibly know that?" Rush asked, exasperated.

"Bring it to me," Nora said. "I...need to see it. I want to decide for myself if it's truly hostile."

"That's a distraction. A sideshow."

"Open the box," said Tappan. "Or I'm out, too."

After an agonizing silence, Rush gestured to the two soldiers to bring the box. They carried it over and placed it on the floor.

"Open it," Rush ordered.

One soldier bent down, unlocked the box, and raised the lid.

For a moment, Nora hesitated. Then she stepped forward and peered in.

Inside was a cube, about two inches on a side. It appeared to be floating just above the bottom of the box, with no obvious means of support. Then again, she wasn't sure: its edges were blurry. And now, inside the cube, she could make out a sphere from which greenish light ebbed and flowed like water, creating curlicues and eddies. As she watched, the sphere inside the cube began to rotate; slowly at first, then faster and faster as the glow brightened, its hue changing to chartreuse, then to an indescribable, otherworldly yellow.

She abruptly knelt and reached gently into the box.

"What are you doing?" Rush cried. "Are you insane? That thing might kill you at any second!"

But Nora—in an almost mystical, transcendent state—cupped her hands beneath the cube. Her years of disbelief and academic dismissiveness had—in the face of all she'd seen—given way to something else entirely; something almost completely the opposite. She tried to grasp the cube, but it rose along with her hands, always hovering a few inches above them.

"Shut the box!" Rush ordered the soldiers.

But as she lifted her hands, raising them and the alien artifact above the confines of the box, the cube abruptly flew upward, expelling a coruscation of colors like glittering chaff, and then shot toward the probe. As it did, the oval whirlpool in the hull—the damaged area, a tiny storm in an otherwise placid surface—abruptly opened wider, and the cube darted into it. Instantly, the hole irised shut, then vanished into a swirling pool of color.

"Son of a bitch!" Rush cried, backing up. "*What have you done?*"

Ducking below the dash again, Corrie stamped blindly on the pedal. The shouts and cries of her companions, the noise of automatic rounds pounding against the vehicle, were deafening. The last of the bulletproof glass shredded under the onslaught. She kept the pedal pressed down hard, unable to see where she was going but keeping the wheel as straight as she could, until she suddenly felt a sickening smack. A moment later, the body of a soldier bounced and rolled over their vehicle from front to back in a geyser of blood. Thinking fast, Watts grabbed the man's weapon, and Skip propelled the body off the rear. But the impact caused the jeep to stall, and the soldiers rushed them as Corrie frantically worked the starter. Watts popped up from the back seat and let fly a spray of automatic gunfire just as the engine again rumbled to life. Rising above the dashboard, Corrie jammed down the accelerator with a fresh squeal of rubber, the remaining soldiers running in hot pursuit.

They hit a T intersection, caroming off the far wall. At the end of this new corridor was another intersection, and at its center Corrie could see a metal door, rolled wide open. Beyond was a huge vault, its walls covered with electronics...and in the center lay a bizarre object. Standing in front were Tappan, Nora, and a man in uniform, flanked by two soldiers. As she accelerated down the corridor, she saw a flash of green, followed by a brilliant streak of light. The object lit up in an intense and crazy swirl of colors, followed by a deep bass note that rattled her teeth and shook the subterranean foundations of the base itself.

The jeep sped down the hall, closing in on the hangar.

Nora was transfixed by the sight. The deep note that sounded upon the closing of the iris was strangely pure and throbbing, almost human. As the probe lit up in dazzling colors, the note rose in pitch, climbing ever higher until it passed the range of audibility. The craft also appeared to be changing shape once again, only this time the change was far more evident: it was growing larger, rounder, with coruscating, jewel-like dimples appearing and disappearing on its surface.

"It's activating!" Rush cried, his voice breaking. "My God, it's become sentient!"

He looked hard at Nora and Tappan for a moment—and in that moment, Nora saw fear, desperation, and fury. Then he pivoted and dashed toward the entrance. For a moment, Nora thought he was running away. But then she saw he was headed toward something mounted on the hangar wall.

"Sir! Wait!"

Rush's abrupt move took the guards by surprise. They seemed suddenly alarmed—more by him, almost, than by the alien craft. "Sir!" one of them yelled. "Hold on!" He ran to intercept the colonel. "Not yet!"

Rush was headed for a red lever fastened to the wall inside a wire cage, a large orange warning sign above it. Reaching it, he flung the protective cage away, ripped off a striped piece of warning tape, placed a thumb briefly against a scanner, then yanked a cotter pin out from the lever's handle.

"No!" The closest soldier reached him and tried to grab his arm, but Rush yanked out his sidearm and fired point-blank into the man's face.

"Don't do it!" the other soldier cried, hesitating as his comrade fell. "We need to follow protocols!"

"No time!" Rush yelled back. As the second soldier began to raise his rifle, the colonel pulled the lever.

For a moment, all was silent, except for the squeal of tires and distant gunfire. Then a siren sounded, and red lights began flashing in the ceiling.

"*Five minutes to omega,*" a mechanical feminine voice boomed from everywhere and nowhere, echoing crazily in the confined space. *"Evacuate now."*

A small knot of soldiers ran into the vault. "He did it!" the one holding his weapon yelled at them. "He fucking pulled the lever!"

"He can't do that!" one yelled back. "Not without the checklist!"

"Don't you understand? He used the base commander's panel—with an abbreviated countdown!"

At this, the soldiers ran for their lives, many abandoning their weapons. Only Rush remained. The warring emotions on his face had cleared, leaving only resignation in their wake. He saw Nora and Tappan staring at him. In the background, Nora heard a sudden spike in the gunfire outside.

"Ironic, isn't it?" Rush said to them. "You had a purpose in coming here after all. I just didn't recognize what it was. All along, at some level, I've known there was ever only one course of action. I was just too blind—or too weak—to see it." Now, as he stood by the lever, he straightened his uniform, assumed an erect posture. "This thing was, *is*, too dangerous to remain intact. It must be destroyed. And now my mission is complete."

"*Four minutes and forty seconds to omega,*" the voice boomed. "*Evacuate now.*"

There was a beat as the three—Tappan, Nora, and the colonel—looked at each other. "Don't forget," Rush said, with the stoic expression of a captain going down with his ship. "*Servandae vitae mendacium.*"

More shooting in the hall, and a moment later a jeep, torn up and ragged with bullet holes, careened into the room and slewed to a stop. Corrie, at the wheel, stood up.

"Get in!" she cried. "*We're out of here!*"

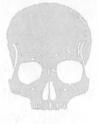

65

Nora grabbed Tappan and shoved him into the jeep, jumping in herself as he sprawled on the back seat atop Skip and Watts.

Corrie dumped the transmission into reverse and then, accelerating to full speed, she grabbed the hand brake and twisted the wheel simultaneously, spinning the jeep around and then flooring it, executing a perfect reverse 180 and sending them back the way they'd come. The gravitational forces of the J-turn whipped the burnt cowboy hat from Watts's head. He clutched for it wildly, but it went spinning off behind them. Red lights flashed along the corridor and the doomsday voice informed them in a measured cadence that there were four minutes to omega.

Numerous soldiers and staff were sprinting at

top speed, most fleeing in a panic but a few still firing at the jeep as it tore down the now-seething corridors.

"We're being chased!" Watts cried.

Glancing over her shoulder—the rearview mirror was long gone—Corrie could see another jeep accelerating behind them, two soldiers within. Skip raised his gun to fire, but Watts grabbed the barrel. "Not yet."

The jeep caught up and tried to ram them from behind. One of the soldiers stood up to fire his weapon, but Watts hit him with a short burst and sent him tumbling back onto the concrete.

"Three minutes to omega," came the voice, with a surreal calm.

The lone soldier driving the jeep came up on them from one side, then steered hard into the rear of their vehicle, the corridor just wide enough to allow for such a PIT maneuver. Corrie slowed briefly to allow her rear tires to maintain traction, then accelerated again, deftly working out of the skid. Now Watts rose, aimed, and fired down into the pursuing jeep, which veered off, hit a wall violently, then rolled in the corridor, tumbling and ricocheting like a pinball knocked from bumper to bumper.

They re-entered the motor pool and, without slowing, headed toward the ramp. The portal was already wide open, exposed to the night. Everywhere soldiers were scrambling into the assembled jeeps or running out on foot, desperate to flee. The entire far end of the hangar was ablaze, the chopper engulfed in flames.

The jeep hit the ramp at full speed, suspension bottoming out, then roared up and out through the door into the fresh night breeze, catching air briefly before slamming to the ground and skidding over gravel and sand. Corrie tried to put on the lights, realized—of course—they'd been shot out, but maintained full speed nevertheless, gunning it down the track and along the route they had followed so recently from the perimeter gate, weaving among the fleeing soldiers. Watts, braced, fired the automatic weapon he'd appropriated at any threatening soldiers, but most were paying them no attention in their panic to get out. Skip fired the Peacemaker with an ear-splitting roar, while Tappan, plucking the service piece from Corrie's holster, shot back at soldiers foolish enough to take potshots at them.

But now, as if to ensure complete destruction,

mounted weapons rose up from hidden silos in the ground, six-barrel rotary mini-guns that swiveled around, seeking motion, firing at everything.

Corrie swerved and swerved again as the guns fired across their path, spitting thousands of rounds a minute and tearing up fleeing soldiers indiscriminately. Now, beyond the mini-guns, additional munitions were appearing from hidden emplacements in the surrounding landscape, their long evil barrels lowering from a skyward elevation to a few degrees above the surface.

"Jesus!" said Tappan. "Are those 40-millimeters?"

"Old Bofors, from the look of them!" Watts yelled in return. "Probably antiaircraft defense, retrofitted for automatic deployment!"

"Think they still work?" Tappan shouted. But his question was answered by the roar of the autocannons as they began pumping out shells with a hellish muzzle velocity. All around, soldiers disappeared into reddish clouds of matter as the armored shells rammed into the ground. The shock waves and cavitations caused by the explosions almost made Corrie lose control.

Two jeeps were behind them and one was pulling alongside. As it did, mini-gun rounds tore through its armor like butter, throwing the vehicle sideways, where it flipped and rolled.

Corrie swerved again as yet another line of fire rippled past them, kicking up a twenty-foot curtain of dirt, missing them by inches.

And then, with the shriek of a harpy, a 40-millimeter round tore obliquely through the side of the jeep, throwing it over on two wheels. Corrie—temporarily blinded as well as deafened—robotically kept her hands on the wheel and her foot pressed to the floor. A second passed before the other two wheels crashed back to earth and her vision began to return. In the glow of the firefight, she noted with horror that the passenger seat beside her—and its occupant, Cecilia Toth—was missing. All that remained was a ragged circle of punctured metal where the door had been.

Instinctively, Corrie let up on the gas.

"Keep going!" Tappan said, leaning forward and yelling into her ear, his face covered with gore. "She's gone!"

The gate was up ahead and it was rolling closed. Corrie accelerated one more time, hit it as it was halfway shut, ripping the left section off its track and flinging it out into the dark. The front end of

DIABLO MESA 531

their vehicle sheered to one side, but with grim determination she quickly regained control.

Down the sandy arroyo the jeep sped, fishtailing in the sand, wheels spinning, until Corrie began gaining traction. The vehicle behind them hit the right half of gate just as it closed and electrified. There was a sound like a monstrous bug zapper, and then a fountain of sparks lit up the sky like lightning.

Corrie continued down the arroyo, possessed with the singular purpose of getting as far from the base as possible before the main explosion. And then it happened: the night sky behind her was illuminated by a burst as bright as the sunrise, followed by a rippling series of booms that accelerated into a single gigantic roar. Glancing once again over her shoulder, Corrie glimpsed a horrifying sight: the entire landscape was rising up, fragmented into a web of white and gold cracks. Brighter and brighter, a mountain of fire escalated into the night like an eruption from hell itself, and then a blast of overpressure slammed into them, knocking the vehicle sideways.

The flaming debris now began to fall like bombs all around as Corrie recovered and continued speeding down the arroyo, weaving and slaloming among the flaming meteors. A few terrifying minutes later, they were out of range.

She brought the jeep to a halt. Everyone, exhausted beyond speech, looked back at the boiling fire-mushroom in the sky, half a mile tall and climbing, shot through with purple and green, the atmosphere reverberating with the thunder of secondary explosions.

"Armageddon," murmured Skip at last.

But Corrie was most shocked by the expression on Tappan's face. Tears were streaming down his cheeks, glistening in the reflected light.

"We'll never know," he said. "Now we'll never know."

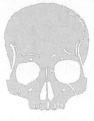

66

3 months later

THE SLEEK BOEING 737, its only marking a red cheatline running horizontally along the windows, banked over the desert and began its final approach. The jet's configuration was unusual: it was not divided into first and coach classes, but rather had twenty rows of seats, two on each side, positioned to face each other in groups of four, with an aisle down the center. There was a single flight attendant: a young man who wordlessly brought the passengers flavored seltzer shortly after takeoff from Alamogordo, then disappeared. Nora sat next to Skip, with Corrie by the window on the other side. Tappan sat across from Nora, beside a general who had identified himself only as Greyburn. He was dressed in field camo, two black stars embroidered on the front of his uniform.

Lying curled up on the carpeted floor at Skip's feet was Mitty, the hair of his tail still singed. Somehow, he had escaped the inferno at the camp, to be found later by first responders, cowering in a nearby arroyo. When the general had arrived at their house, with almost no advance notice, to take them on this mysterious outing, Skip had refused to leave Mitty, who he claimed was suffering from PTSD. He raised all kinds of arguments and crazy pleadings, finally getting the two-star to cave.

The general had told them nothing. Not even where they were going, or what was to take place. It had been made clear that no questions would be answered or explanations proffered until they arrived at their destination.

Nevertheless, Skip—with his vast knowledge of conspiracy theories and urban legends, recently enhanced by browsing through Noam Bitan's library—was smug.

"We're on Janet," he murmured sotto voce to his sister.

"Excuse me?"

"Janet airlines. A top-secret shuttle the air force

uses to ferry spooks from their local airports to classified locations and back again. Apparently, it stands for 'Just Another Non-Existent Terminal.'" He cackled. "The only airline where the flight attendants need SSBI clearances."

Nora didn't reply. If this was true, she wondered why he wasn't just a little more nervous.

A minute later, the wheels touched down on an endless runway laid out along a perfectly level salt flat. "Welcome to Groom Lake," said the general, nodding out the window.

"Otherwise known as Area Fifty-One," Skip said. "I *knew* it!"

The general merely smiled. In the seat beside her, she could almost feel Skip puff up with braggadocio.

The plane taxied and came to rest. Two jeeps were waiting for them on the edge of the tarmac. The late-July sun burned down from an empty sky as they climbed in and were whisked away, past row after row of hangars and giant Quonset huts, to a small, nondescript building without windows. The general, entirely silent, led them through several sets of guards and into the building, which proved to be no more than the housing for a giant freight elevator.

Mitty's leash was passed off to a soldier at the entrance, to await their return. "No canines allowed," was the only explanation given. Nora could hear the dog barking piteously as Skip vanished inside.

They got on the elevator, its massive doors boomed shut, and they descended for a disconcerting length of time before it halted. The doors opened to reveal a vast underground hangar. Nora, for whom all this had an unpleasant feeling of déjà vu, stared in shock. There, directly before them, was the alien probe, resting on a graphite cradle.

"We are now free to talk," said the general.

"What's this?" Tappan exclaimed. "Another one?"

The general gave a small, dry smile. "Do you really think an object that had spent ten million years crossing the galaxy would be so easily destroyed? We found it quite intact amid the smoking wreckage of Pershing."

Tappan almost staggered. "Thank God. I thought we'd lost it!" He took a step forward—then turned around, face shining. "Have you had a chance to study it?"

"We have," said the general. "That's why

you're here. I know you've already been warned about the highly classified nature of what you... experienced. I want to emphasize that warning—and to remind you it applies just as much, if not more, now."

"You know I disagree with that," said Tappan. "There's been far too much secrecy already. The world is ready to handle this information."

"That's not your decision to make. In any case, once you hear what we've found, I think you'll agree that the world is *not* ready."

"Can we get closer?" Nora asked.

"As close as you like. It's no longer dangerous."

Despite this assurance, the four approached warily. The air smelled faintly of electricity and ionization. Nora tried to remember what the probe had looked like before, because it was now clearly different, more a dumbbell shape with unequal weights on its ends. It still had the swirling, angry oval patch near the bow, but even that miniature storm seemed to have abated somewhat. The rest of its surface also looked quieter, less manic, almost as if at rest. It lazily cycled through various colors, some quite strange, before returning and beginning again.

"I'll start with Atropos," said the general.

"Good idea," said Tappan. "Who the hell were they? They murdered most of my team in cold blood—the bastards."

"Yes. And we're very sorry for the loss. Some of this you may have already heard—from the source—so forgive me if I cover any old ground. But much of it will be as new to you as it was— regrettably—to us. Atropos was a counteres- pionage organization that went awry. It had its roots in the OSS, founded by presidential order in 1942. The first OSS agents were primarily members of U.S. Army and Navy special forces, secretly trained in psychological warfare, sabo- tage, and assassination. They were billeted at the Special Training School Number One Oh-Three, 'Camp X,' set up by the British thirty miles over the Canadian border.

"The OSS was terminated in 1945, with several of its branches subsumed into the Strategic Ser- vices Unit, then the Central Intelligence Group, and finally the CIA in 1947. During this confused period of transition, we had an acute problem with Soviet espionage. Several scientists work- ing on the Manhattan Project, and later, on the H-bomb, were passing on secrets. In mid-1946, a certain zealous and patriotic officer convinced his superiors to spin off a tiny, top-secret intelligence branch, composed of hand-picked members from the old Camp X and paramilitary branches of the OSS. That, we now know, became Atropos. Its mission was simple: to protect U.S. assets against foreign espionage, with 'fire free' license to torture and kill spies and others as necessary. In other words, they could bypass the cumbersome and ineffective court system and take justice into their own hands. The secret Mossad execution team Kidon—the 'tip of the spear'—was later modeled on a similar philosophy.

"Beginning in early 1947, small detachments of Atropos were housed at high-value targets, especially Los Alamos. Soviet infiltration of the U.S. was by then well advanced, and the Atropos units were able not only to eliminate many traitorous scientists, but also to identify, monitor, and if need be kill Soviet sleeper agents embedded here."

"You almost sound as if you approve of this, General," said Tappan.

"I don't disapprove. The problem is, the unit apparently operated with unlimited funding and no accountability. That's a recipe for corruption—or, perhaps worse, hubris and radicalization.

"When the Roswell crash occurred, the Atropos team from Los Alamos was first at the site. Finding an alien ship with advanced technology was not only extremely interesting—but once it appeared to be hostile, that discovery ended up morphing into their raison d'être. At the cost of numerous casualties, they recovered the craft and moved it to the Pershing site. Eventually, rather than try to move it again, they built a secret base around it, dramatically expanding the underground bunker system."

"What about the two bodies we found?" Nora asked.

"Those, as Agent Swanson here determined, were two Soviet sleeper agents, killed by Atropos. The dial-a-yield device was used as bait, its guts removed—and it was a prototype anyway, which is why it was of no value and buried with the bodies."

"Why did Atropos just leave the bodies there?" Tappan asked.

The general gave a cynical smile. "Hubris, initially. That's an extremely remote location, and at the time they were in a hurry—and mightily distracted by having found an alien spaceship, as you can imagine. Later they seem to have decided the bodies were safe there, and that any attempt to remove them carried a higher risk than simply leaving them. As you know, they doused the faces and fingertips with acid to hinder identification. They didn't know, obviously, about the Soviet dental work. The two scientists who disappeared from Los Alamos in 1947 were, of course, the contacts of those murdered sleeper agents. Atropos also killed them, erased their features with acid, and buried their bodies elsewhere in the desert. We found them as well."

He went on. "As the years passed, it seems Atropos became almost a cult. They made very little progress in understanding the ship. Yet their appropriations from the government's black budget were vast, and they had spread their operatives through not only the CIA but the FBI, the military, and—unfortunately— NASA. They were extremely adept at scrubbing any obvious signs of their existence from government bureaucracy, hiding their movements behind veils of secrecy, and keeping a minimal profile, interfacing with authorized branches enough to ensure legitimacy. The fact that they had formed so early, in addition to the continual and inevitable turnovers in government, helped. Anyway, in the absence of hard information, a lot of paranoid ideas evolved. Guarding the thing became a sort of religion, in which they continued certain rituals passed on from the earlier generation. Anyone interested in contacting beings from other planets started to look like enemies to them...because getting the attention of the alien civilization that sent this probe was, in their view, akin to inviting extinction."

"*Servandae vitae mendacium,*" Tappan quoted.

"Lies in service of lives," the general said. "Precisely. In any case, new inductees, poached from the special forces, were sworn in at a secret ceremony, where they would be given a blood oath and then be shown the alien ship. While the rest of the world got over its 'Invaders from Mars' phobia, their secrecy and paranoia increased. They found fewer and fewer candidates worthy of recruitment, and their numbers dwindled. That only made them more insular and unaccountable. And then you came along, Mr. Tappan, and overturned their little world."

"But how did Lime infiltrate the FBI?" asked Corrie. "Everyone thought he was totally legit."

"And he was: at least on the outside. He was a patriot in his own way, like all Atropos members, and he contributed to the success of several important FBI operations. As I intimated, numerous Atropos agents led double lives in the three-letter agencies: lives that they could slip in and out of if and when necessary. They continued to kill espionage targets and sleeper agents, even after the two bodies at Roswell. That included the scientist so cleverly murdered at Los Alamos in the nineties—he was spying for the Chinese, actually."

"How did you find all this out?" Nora asked.

"We captured some low-level fugitives from the base and picked up others embedded in the various agencies. The core brain trust, people like Rush, who were at the site at that time, decided to go down with the ship, so to speak. The major general directing Atropos from Washington committed suicide. So did that Nobel scientist, Eastchester. Tragic. Clearly, there were skeletons in a great many closets. Additional information was gleaned from search warrants and extralegal intelligence gathering in the wake of the explosion...and your own earlier debriefs. Much of the last three months has been dedicated to piecing this history of Atropos together. The fact that it operated so long, in secrecy and with minimal interference... well, it's extremely distressing, to put it mildly."

"And what about the probe?" Tappan asked.

"We had a great deal more success than Atropos did—although we can't really take much of the credit."

"Why do you say that?"

"One simple reason: that little cube you unearthed was, it seems, the probe's central processor and ship's log—in effect, its artificial intelligence module. All Atropos had for seventy-five years was the ship, dumbly defending itself. You found the brain."

"But how did it become separated from the ship?" Skip asked.

"It seems the probe was severely damaged roughly ten million years ago, shortly after it was launched. When it crashed here, that cube either separated from the main craft and hid for evasive reasons, or perhaps it was ejected by the crash and became buried nearby. Atropos, as I alluded to, never went back to the site after its initial excavation: there was too much public curiosity by then. Their hope was that time would do their work for them, concealing any remaining traces of the crash...and for a great many decades, it did. But that's one reason your own dig caused them such anxiety—they couldn't be sure nothing remained behind from the 1947 extraction that might be found more easily today." The general paused. "In any case, you can see the scar on the ship from that earlier damage: the oval wound in its side. Now that the cube has been reunited with the probe, however, the ship has become docile. It's no longer dangerous, in protective mode."

"Wound?" said Skip. "You almost speak of it as if it's alive."

"It's not definable as living or dead. It's a part biological, part mechanical hybrid, so advanced we can't say where the biology ends and the machine begins. Anyway, under normal circumstances it would never have crashed—but it had been crippled in an attack. We've used a great deal of computing power the last few months, and enough electricity to power Phoenix in the process, to analyze it. We believe Earth was not its final destination. We were merely an accidental obstacle on its mission to carry a vital message across the galaxy—a message to others."

"'Vital'?" Tappan asked. "How so?"

"It was one of countless such probes, launched eons ago by a now-extinct civilization on the far side of the galaxy. They all carried the same message, and they wanted to spread it to as many sentient beings as possible."

"How can you know all of this?" Nora asked.

"From the cube. It's desperate to communicate with us. It doesn't know our language, but it can display some pretty nifty holographic, or more accurately volumetric, videos. You don't have to be a specialist to understand them. We in the intelligence community who've seen them are…well, I guess the right word would be 'alarmed'—if not 'frightened.'"

They looked at him with varying degrees of incredulity.

"There's no easy way to put it, I'm afraid. For all their cruelty and zealotry, Atropos was fundamentally right. There *is* an alien threat of unimaginable evil out there. Only it's not this probe—or the civilization that created it."

"Who, then?" Nora asked.

"Let's look at a video, shall we?"

Greyburn spoke to an aide, who briefly worked a nearby keyboard. A flickering of light shone from a small laser tube directed at the probe. As it did so, one of the lazy, swirling patterns on its hull seemed to come to attention.

"It communicates through the five-hundred-fifty-nanometer wavelength of electromagnetic radiation—in other words, green light."

Nora watched the peculiar interaction of terrestrial laser and alien technology for a moment. And then, everyone gasped as an exquisite three-dimensional movie materialized in the air in front of them: in vivid color, visible from all angles. It showed first a star map, the POV zeroing in on a green-and-blue planet much like Earth, undoubtedly the probe's home, orbiting a star. From the planet came a launching of thousands of probes, arcing out in all directions. This was followed by the materialization—or manifestation, it was too unfamiliar for Nora to fully comprehend—of something utterly bizarre. It looked at first like a cloud: a dark mist larger than the planet, a shape that was not a shape but rather the absence of light. But the way it moved gave an indication of sentience that, for no reason she could explain, chilled her to the core. Then it did *something*—something inexplicable— and the planet burst like a rotten tomato. The video went on to show a subsequent attack on the probe itself by a similar dark, cloudy entity, gigantic and hard to see. There was a cry of pain—was it really pain?—from the probe, but the holograph went on to show them its evasion from the thing, hiding on the dark side of a barren asteroid while it was hunted, and then finally escaping. Next, a pullback to the galaxy as a whole, showing the probe's long, drifting path over what must have been millions of years. The solar system came into view, Earth appeared, then the crash—and darkness.

Nora was awestruck. An entire history, many millions of years, had been compressed into five minutes and made simple enough for a child to understand.

The general let a shocked silence fall over the group. Then he turned to Tappan. "So tell me. Do you still think keeping this secret is a bad idea? Is the world truly ready to 'handle' this information?"

Tappan licked his lips. "No," he said at last. "No, it's not. In all honesty, I'm not sure *I* can handle it."

"We're counting on you to do so."

"Why do you say that?"

"Do you think I brought you all here just to

satisfy your curiosity? Mr. Tappan and Dr. Kelly, I need you both—and your resources—to help us with this. In time, we'll reach out to other important and influential people as well: some who can help...and others who could, if left ignorant, inadvertently endanger our planet. I refer, of course, to SETI and especially the more active attempts at extraterrestrial communication that are now gearing up to follow it. All that effort must be halted. And we must, as a species, find a way to shut down the vast quantity of electromagnetic radiation leaking into space from our activities."

He fell silent again.

It was Nora who spoke next. "You said earlier it was delivering a message. Did you decipher it?"

"We did. It was very short. The equivalent of one word, really."

"What was that word?"

The general smiled grimly. *"Hide."*

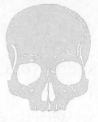

67

CONNOR DIGBY STOOD just outside the closed door for a moment, squaring his shoulders and slowing his respiration. He glanced at his watch: twelve noon exactly.

Ordinarily, a summons from Dr. Marcelle Weingrau, president of the Santa Fe Archaeological Institute, would not trouble him. He'd been her graduate assistant at Boston University, and felt he'd grown to know her rather well. In fact, normally he'd welcome a chance to ingratiate himself further with her.

But the last couple of months had been anything but normal. The department he'd headed for almost a year had begun to come apart. Two important projects—the excavation at Cornpollen Ridge and the preparatory work near Hottaktion

Ranch—had gone awry in different ways. In the first, it seemed permits had not been drawn up properly, and there was an embarrassing matter about an accumulated fine. In the second, the rancher who owned the property and had given his permission for the Institute to proceed had a change of mind. Apparently, one of the archaeological undergraduates working for the Institute on the ranch had hit and killed a calf with his jeep, quickly identified by its J-O brand. Digby had done his best: he'd gone before the appropriate board regarding the Cornpollen permit, and he'd compensated the ranch owner—but somehow, in both cases he'd only managed to make things worse. On top of that, he'd heard rumors that some of the postgrads in the department were circulating a petition about him. Digby had no idea about its details, and he felt sure it had no merit...still, he'd recently had some run-ins with lower-level staff over budgets and his efforts to weed out the tradition of slovenly attire that seemed pervasive in archaeology.

Weingrau's unexpected call ten minutes earlier had been more terse than usual. So he raised his hand to the wooden door and gave what he thought was a confident-sounding rap.

"Come in," said the familiar voice immediately.

Digby opened the door and stepped inside—and was surprised all over again. There was Dr. Weingrau, behind her large desk that seemed to exhibit fewer native artifacts by the day. But sitting in a large leather chair in front of that desk was Lucas Tappan. He looked more or less as he had when they'd first met—four months back?—but he was more tanned now, a little thinner, and he'd ditched the hipster-cowboy look for what was obviously an expensive bespoke suit.

"Connor!" said Weingrau in an unexpectedly bright voice. "Thank you for coming so quickly. You remember Mr. Tappan, I'm sure."

"Of course. What a pleasure to see you again." Digby began approaching Tappan in order to shake his hand, but the billionaire had already risen, smiled, nodded, and was taking his seat again, so instead Digby changed tack toward a vacant chair.

"Mr. Tappan has come to us with wonderful news," Weingrau informed him. "He's planning on making a contribution to the Institute. A *sizable* contribution, it would seem—to endow a research chair."

"I've spoken to the Executive Committee already," Tappan said with another smile, "and they're on board—forgive the pun."

"Perfectly wonderful," Digby said, nodding in an instinctual cadence. He was now thoroughly confused. As far as he knew, Tappan's ill-fated, ill-advised expedition—the one Dr. Kelly had been fired over—had ended in disaster: an accident with a propane tank that had killed a number of people. They had found nothing of value, naturally, proving once again that the whole Roswell thing was a hoax. If that was the case, then why was he back here now, bearing gifts?

Weingrau must no doubt be wondering the same thing. Nevertheless, she was beaming to the point where he feared the makeup on her cheeks might crack off. A contribution would be welcome right now, Digby knew. In fact, it was desperately needed. Several donors the president had been counting on had recently backed out of their pledges for vague reasons, and that—combined with some poor investment choices—had left the Institute's endowment in a fragile state.

Tappan intruded on his speculations. "But there's no reason to draw this out," he said. "I'm sure you both have a lot to do." He turned to the president. "As I mentioned, Dr. Weingrau, I've also chosen the person to occupy that endowed chair, someone with impeccable credentials and a distinguished career, with a long list of seminal publications. May I introduce you?"

"Of course!" Weingrau said, clasping her hands together. In his mind's eye, Digby imagined a bag of gold coins clenched tightly between them. He shook this away.

Tappan pulled out a phone, tapped it, and slipped it back into his jacket pocket. "It shouldn't be more than a moment. She's just down the hall."

"'She,'" Weingrau repeated.

At that moment, the door opened and Nora Kelly stepped in.

Digby rose to his feet in surprise. This was the last person he expected to see. It took him a moment to recognize her. Instead of the usual grubby jeans and work shirt, she was wearing a pleated midcalf dress of pale ivory, obviously expensive, and she'd ditched the Doc Martens for a pair of Gucci flats. Her glossy, layered hair fell to her shoulders with the kind of informality only good stylists could achieve, and her skin glowed with a radiance that had nothing to do with sitting for hours at an office desk.

"Oh," she said. "I'm sorry. I'm supposed to knock first, then enter. One forgets." She raised two knuckles, touched them to the door. "There!"

She came forward, shook hands with Tappan, nodded at Digby, and turned to Weingrau. "Hello, Marcelle. May I sit down?" This question was asked while she was already seating herself in the last empty chair.

"Please," said Weingrau.

"And now," said Tappan, "would you care to discuss the particulars, or should I?"

"It would be best coming from you, don't you think?" Nora told Tappan. "After all, it's your money."

"No, it's not. It's now, in a way, yours." The entrepreneur turned to Weingrau. "As you know, the endowed chair comes with excellent compensation, but even more important, it also includes a large sum to support research—spent at the sole discretion of the chair's occupant."

Digby had never dropped a tab of LSD, or smoked a crack pipe, or even blazed up a joint. But it was clear he must have ingested something hallucinogenic, because this simply could not be happening. He glanced toward Weingrau, but her own speechlessness did little to restore his composure.

Now Tappan was looking back at the president. "In other words, it's hers to spend. Care to tell them how much, Nora?"

"A hundred million."

This only prolonged the strangled silence.

"Dollars?" Weingrau finally asked.

The absurdity of this question took hold in the gathering silence. "I suppose we *could* make it pennies. If you'd rather."

A beat. Nora looked like she might laugh but quickly controlled herself.

"We're most grateful for your support," Weingrau said in a robotic voice.

Tappan added, "The sum isn't just for the chair. I understand from my meeting with the Executive Committee that the Institute is in some financial difficulties—a junk bond fund almost in default, an unwise land speculation, REITs that have declined in value. At the request of the Executive Committee, Nora and I have directed thirty million of our donation as unrestricted funds to shore up the general endowment. The capital improvement project, stalled for lack of funds, also needs financing. How much is that? I've forgotten."

"Eight and a half million," Digby heard himself say.

"Well, let's say ten. For the sake of round numbers." Tappan turned from him back to Weingrau. "And Nora thought—well, we *both* thought—that another ten million could be put toward increasing the salaries and research budgets of the academic staff. Again, round numbers." He paused a moment. "And the rest, fifty million, would endow the Tappan Chair. How does that sound?"

Weingrau and Digby both nodded weakly.

"Think about it," Tappan continued. "With the endowment saved, the capital improvement project back on track, the staff motivated, and Nora in the Tappan Chair, well...you could say the Institute will be transformed."

There was a pause of at least a minute while Tappan let this hang.

"You could indeed." Dr. Weingrau at last found her voice. "I expect you'll be asking for my resignation."

"Not at all!" Tappan said. "You're welcome to stay on as president. You know, it takes a certain je ne sais quoi to scrape funds together, tickle wealthy benefactors into opening their checkbooks—things like that. You're admirably suited to the presidency. Are you amenable to that? Retaining your position, I mean?"

After a moment, Weingrau said slowly: "Yes, of course. Thank you."

Tappan turned toward Digby. "There is one other matter—a slight reorganization of the hierarchy. It would involve a promotion for you."

Digby nodded obsequiously.

"My people did a cost-benefit analysis of the organization and suggested a new position be created: director of institutional development. Reporting directly to Dr. Weingrau. You'll be able to put your not-inconsiderable social skills to work getting the right word out—to the right people—about the Institute and its funding needs."

Digby thought quickly. The offer almost felt like being thrown a life preserver. With the endowment safe, and the capital improvement project back on track...The title sounded important, and he might never have to get his hands dirty again on a dig, or slap mosquitoes, or sleep in a tent.

He nodded vigorously.

"Nora, as occupant of the Tappan Chair, will assume leadership of the archaeological division in its entirety—as executive director. She will report directly to the board." Tappan looked around. "Any questions? Thoughts?"

There were none. Weingrau struggled to speak. "Again, Mr. Tappan, we're so very grateful for your generosity."

"Excellent!" Tappan cried. "In that case, I don't want to take up more of your valuable time. It's twelve thirty. Do you know, spending money always makes me hungry. With both of you at the helm, the Institute will be in great hands going forward."

"Thank you."

"And I know Nora must be excited about taking over as chief archaeologist—and figuring out what fabulous expeditions and projects might come next, given an unlimited budget and complete control."

"I confess I am, at that," Nora said.

Tappan and Nora rose together, said their goodbyes, and walked out of the building into the New Mexico sunshine. A minute later, they were in the parking lot, where Tappan's ice-blue Tesla was waiting.

"I remember this place," Tappan said, stopping abruptly on the gravel. "You called me an asshole here once."

"We ought to put up a plaque." Nora looked around, squinting against the sun. "But shouldn't we be going? You said spending money makes you hungry."

"Oh, I'm quite hungry. Ravenous, in fact. But...not for lunch."

Nora looked at him. "Why...you *naughty* man." And she slapped his face...but very gently, and with considerable affection.

ABOUT THE AUTHORS

The thrillers of **DOUGLAS PRESTON** and **LINCOLN CHILD** "stand head and shoulders above their rivals" (*Publishers Weekly*). Preston and Child's *Relic* and *The Cabinet of Curiosities* were chosen by readers in a National Public Radio poll as being among the one hundred greatest thrillers ever written, and *Relic* was made into a number-one box office hit movie. They are coauthors of the famed Pendergast series, and their recent novels include *Bloodless, The Scorpion's Tail, Crooked River, Old Bones,* and *Verses for the Dead.* In addition to his novels, Douglas Preston writes about archaeology for the *New Yorker* and *National Geographic* magazines. Lincoln Child is a Florida resident and former book editor who has published seven novels of his own, including such bestsellers as *Full Wolf Moon* and *Deep Storm.*

Readers can sign up for The Pendergast File, a monthly "strangely entertaining note" from the authors, at their website, PrestonChild.com. The authors welcome visitors to their alarmingly active Facebook page, where they post regularly.